SECOND SHOT

SECOND SHOT

CINDY DEES

KENSINGTON
PUBLISHING CORP.

www.kensingtonbooks.com

KENSINGTON BOOKS are published by

Kensington Publishing Corp.
119 West 40th Street
New York, NY 10018

Library of Congress Card Catalogue Number: 2023930886

ISBN-13: 978-1-4967-3975-9

First Kensington Hardcover Edition: June 2023

ISBN-13: 978-1-4967-3976-6 (ebook)

10 9 8 7 6 5 4 3 2 1

Printed in the United States of America

SECOND SHOT

CHAPTER 1

*H*ELEN WARWICK STARED AT THE GLOSSY BLACK DOOR WITH ITS period-accurate brass knocker and kickplate. It was as carefully understated as every other door in this upscale Georgetown neighborhood and screamed of wealth and privilege.

Since when did her middle child become all of this? For that matter, when did Peter grow up? One minute he'd been a bright, charming child with no talent for sports but a discerning eye for everything and everyone around him, and the next he was an upwardly mobile Gen Whatever-they-were up-to-now'er with a live-in boyfriend, an art collection, a prestigious address, and a puppy.

It was her fault, of course, that she'd missed so much of his childhood. She'd missed far too much of all her children's lives. But, at long last, this was her chance to make up for it in some small measure.

Retirement. Motherhood. She could do this.

She lifted the knocker and let it fall.

Liang—Li to the family—opened the door immediately. "Mrs. Warwick. So good of you to puppysit for us tonight."

She air-kissed him on both cheeks and held out a slightly singed apple pie balanced in her left hand. "Housewarming gift."

"Did you bake this?" he asked in genuine surprise, taking the pie as she set her purse down on the impeccable Louis XV credenza.

"I did. Eat it at your own peril."

He laughed warmly and led her into the kitchen where a small Renoir pastel casually filled a wall beside the refrigerator. It was the study for part of a more famous piece, but still a work of art in its own right. Where the boys got the money for such things, she didn't know and didn't ask. Of course, it didn't hurt that Peter was an art dealer in an auction house that sold antiques and fine art. But still. Renoir?

"Don't you look nice tonight, Mother," Peter said coolly, sweeping into the kitchen with all the style he usually did. He wore a crisply tailored black suit that was just shy of being a tuxedo.

She'd agonized in her own closet for longer than she cared to admit, pondering what to wear to a puppysitting date. What clothing struck a tone of apology, commitment to building a relationship, and motherly love without sacrificing the cool sophistication she knew Peter cherished in all things? She'd settled on black wool slacks, a simple cashmere sweater, and a pair of black, Italian leather, stiletto-heeled bootlets that had to have cost more than her car. Thank God the agency had footed the bill for them as part of a disguise she'd worn a few years back at an Italian opera house.

"You look dashing as always, darling," she murmured, air-kissing him as well. When did her children stop actually hugging her, anyway? Probably too many parental mistakes ago for her to remember.

"Your mother baked us a pie," Li announced to fill the silence already filling the chasm yawning between her and her offspring.

"You bake?" Peter asked blankly.

"Shocking. I know. Who'd have guessed I was capable of mastering the domestic arts?" When Peter pulled a skeptical face, she added, "Don't answer that."

The silence crept forward again.

"So, where's this new granddog of mine?" she asked with cheer she hoped didn't sound forced.

"He's having a time-out at the moment," Li supplied, gesturing toward a custom wood crate with sliding screen front doors that looked like a piece of furniture. A small Calder sculpture was displayed on top of the . . . puppy cabinet.

Peter added, in complete seriousness, "We got a little rambunctious earlier and refused to poop after our supper."

"Is that a group activity in your house?" she asked dryly.

Peter rolled his eyes as Li opened the large crate and scooped out a roly-poly blond furball that was possibly the cutest creature she'd ever seen.

She cooed in genuine adoration of the twelve-week-old golden retriever. "Have you boys settled on a name for your progeny?"

Li and Peter smiled at each other and said together, "Biscuit."

"Too cute." She reached out. "May I?"

Li passed her the squirming pup, who had a fat pink tummy, sharp little claws, huge, bright brown eyes, and a black button nose. She held him up to gaze into his eyes. The little scamp stuck out his tiny pink tongue and licked the tip of her nose.

"I'm officially in love," she declared.

"Gee. If that was all it took, I'd have licked your nose years ago," Peter muttered.

"Be nice," Li murmured.

She absorbed the jab without comment. After all, she hadn't raised any of her children to be weak souls afraid to express their opinions. In that, at least, she'd succeeded as a parent.

"What's the routine with young Master Biscuit?" she asked.

"He'll need to go out once an hour on the hour," Li answered briskly. "Carry him to the backyard and put him down in the grass. Whistle until he potties. You can whistle, can't you?"

"Yes, dear. I can whistle."

"Perfect. He goes to bed at ten. Put him in his crate and close the slats. He'll complain, but ignore him. He'll go to sleep in a few minutes."

"He has already had supper, and we're not feeding him people food," Peter added. "So no snacks."

She sensed a grandmotherly rebellion forthcoming. It was clearly her job to spoil her granddog, and she wasn't about to shirk her duty.

"Mother . . ." Peter said warningly.

"All right, already. I'll behave." *Not.*

Li took up reciting the puppy instruction manual to her. "We're staying for the fireworks but should be home by two a.m. After bedtime, Biscuit only needs to go out every two hours. If he gets hungry, at midnight you can feed him the snack I left in the fridge. It's in a bowl with his name on it."

"What's in it?"

"Ground lamb, fresh pumpkin puree, scrambled egg, and rice."

"This dog eats better than I do," she commented.

"Here is his gear drawer." Peter showed her, pulling a wide, shallow drawer in the puppy crate–cabinet-thing open. "There's a harness, leash, ThunderShirt, earmuffs for fireworks and other loud noises, teething ring, plush toys, and a spare blanket with his mother's scent on it. Emergency veterinarian's phone number is on this card, and text me if you have any questions."

"He's a puppy, Peter. He eats, poops, and sleeps. How hard can he be to take care of? I didn't kill you, did I?"

As if to make up for the dire look her son threw at her, Li kissed her on the cheek. "Hang in there," he whispered as he leaned close.

She smiled gratefully at him for the vote of support. But she knew full well how far she had to go to rebuild bridges with her family. If it was even possible.

She and the puppy walked Peter and Liang to the front door and locked it behind them. And then it was just she and Biscuit. He gave a little whimper, and she tucked him under her chin, nuzzling his silky soft fur fondly. "You don't hate me, do you, little nugget?"

The boys had purchased two town houses side by side and knocked out the walls between them, gutting and renovating them into a grand and gracious space. On the left side of the ground floor were a formal living room, dining room, kitchen, and breakfast nook. A long hall ran down the center of the house, and on the other side were two offices, a library, and a fully equipped home gym. A casual family room ran the entire width of the back of the house with floor-to-ceiling glass windows looking out on the newly landscaped formal garden and outdoor kitchen/living room.

The boys had only moved in a few weeks ago but had already done wonders with the place. In her wildest dreams, she could never pull together a space this eclectic, chic, and achingly sophisticated. Maybe she could hire them to redo the house she nominally shared with Grayson Warwick, her mostly absent husband.

She didn't want to think about that problematic relationship right now. Dealing with Peter's simmering resentment was enough for one evening.

She dutifully took Biscuit to the backyard and felt like an idiot standing there beside him in the dark, shivering and whistling until he squatted and peed. Shaking her head, she scooped him up and carried him inside.

"Congratulations on successfully training your humans to make complete fools of themselves in twelve short weeks, my friend."

Li had thoughtfully chilled a crisp, white wine and laid out a selection of old-world cheeses and sausages for her. Biscuit loved the cheese and sausage, and they reminded her of Berlin. Good times in that cosmopolitan city . . .

She noshed on the snacks and sat down to watch television in the family room, where the massive flat screen took up an entire wall. She cruised through the channels until she found a movie. *Ahh. Casablanca.* An oldie but a goodie, even if the spy tradecraft in the film was dreadful.

Biscuit curled up beside her on the overstuffed sofa and settled down to sleep. Ten o'clock came and went, along with a potty check, but the puppy didn't wake. Common sense told her not to disturb the little guy.

Rick told Louis he thought it was the beginning of a beautiful friendship, and the credits began to roll when she heard faint popping noises outside. She tensed sharply, and her gaze darted around the room. French doors to the backyard. Kitchen entrance to the left, library entrance to the right. Hallway in the middle. It had the best sight line to the backyard but no cover. Sofa would provide visual cover only. That poker table could be turned on its side in a pinch to defend against gunfire. Better to head for the kitchen with its stone counters and solid wood cabinets for protection from incoming rounds—

Oh, for the love of Mike, stand down, Helen.

It was New Year's Eve, and that was just some kids lighting off firecrackers in the alley.

Whether it was the *pop-pop-popping* or her sharp reaction to it she couldn't tell, but Biscuit jerked awake, lifting his head and listening alertly, his fuzzy, little ears perked.

"Past time for a pit stop for you, young man."

She carried him outside and set him down in the grass. The popping noises were louder out here. Amazing how much they sounded like gunfire. No wonder veterans had PTSD problems on nights like this.

Apparently, she, too, was going to have to learn not to reach for a weapon whenever she heard fireworks. Her nerves were too on edge to bring herself to whistle—one did not call attention to oneself when bullets were flying. The dog showed no interest in voiding his bladder, perhaps because she refused to mortify herself with the whistling routine.

Regardless, she picked him up and scuttled inside, eager to get under cover as yet another volley of loud pops erupted in the alley. This one was accompanied by raucous shouts and girlish screams. *Kids.* They had no idea how their commotion unsettled people like her.

It was almost midnight. She should cut herself a slice of pie and make a celebration out of her first New Year's as a retired person. That, and she would prove to the boys she hadn't poisoned their housewarming gift.

She opened drawers until she found one in the quartz waterfall island with a built-in knife rack and a dozen chef-quality knives. She pulled one out, sliced the pie, and used the blade to scoop a piece onto a plate.

A bright red glow flashed, and a second later, the distant thunder of the big New Year's Eve fireworks show on the Mall began.

Mindful of the puppy not being traumatized by the loud noises, she held him tucked under her left arm and dug around in the puppy drawer with her free hand. "Now where did your fathers put your earmuffs—"

The lights went out, plunging the house into darkness.

Adrenaline surged through her veins unbidden, and her body went light and fast, ready for violence.

What on earth?

The clock on the stove and the touch pad on the refrigerator had also gone dark. Starbursts outside sent neon strobes of green, blue, and red through the black house. Her instincts fired off a strident warning, so insistent she couldn't possibly ignore the alarms shouting in her skull.

Grabbing the pie knife, she dropped to a crouch beside the crate and listened tautly. All she heard was the steady, distant *boom-boom-boom.*

Sheesh. Overreacting, much? It was just a fireworks display. And she was a civilian, now. Out of the game—

Deafening automatic weapon fire erupted all at once. With an almighty crash, the entire glass-walled back of the house exploded inward. Glass flew *everywhere* as gunfire raked the family room.

Crap on a cracker.

Feathers filled the air as the sofa exploded. The glow of fireworks punctuated the attack, and wood and pieces of furniture flew every which way in the strobe-like flashes. Something hot and wickedly sharp sliced across her left arm with the neat precision of a scalpel. She knew that pain. She'd gotten winged by a bullet.

Instinctively, she folded over the puppy, protecting his little body with hers. Fast roll into the puppy crate. Breathe in. Hold. Breathe out.

A quiet crunch of a boot on glass. Another. A hostile was moving into the kitchen.

Quietly, carefully, she tugged the blanket inside the crate around the puppy, wrapping him like a burrito, praying it would keep him quiet and still. Gripping the knife tightly, she waited in an agony of suspense for what came next.

Legs came into her line of sight. Military-style boots, black cargo pants, leather thigh holster strapped down. A few more steps—

The gunman passed the crate.

She rolled out and stabbed with all her might, burying the sharp blade of her knife in the back of the man's knee. He screamed and went down as she jumped and landed with both knees in the middle of his back.

He was fast and strong and tried to roll over. He almost succeeded in throwing her off, but she hung on grimly as he rolled onto his side and then on top of her. He failed to trap her arms underneath him. She grabbed a handful of his hair, yanked his chin back, and slashed hard with the knife.

The assailant thrashed on top of her, knocking her head hard against the floor in his death throes. She shoved for all she was worth and managed to roll him off her. She scrambled to her feet, blinking away the spots dancing in front of her eyes, her high-heeled shoes slipping and sliding in the spreading puddle of blood.

In the flashes of fireworks, black blood welled from her attacker's mutilated throat. His hands fell away from clutching at the mortal wound, and she dived over him to snatch up his weapon, which had clattered to the floor.

It was an urban assault rifle. Russian ASh-12.7. She dropped it into place against her shoulder and rested her index finger on the trigger. Pausing to kick off her high heels, she advanced fast and silent, knees bent, on stockinged feet.

Odds were the other shooter was advancing through the far side of the ground floor. Crouching, she swung low into the hallway. Clear left. Clear right.

Using the tip of the weapon's barrel, she nudged open the half bath door under the stairs. Clear.

She heard a bump and a faint grunt in the library and raced

down the hall on the balls of her feet, ducking into the dining room, listening hard for any more shooters than just the two.

Then the front doorknob rattled slightly, and she swore under her breath. A third hostile outside. Bastards must've planned to herd her through the house and out the front door into an ambush. By her recommendation, Peter and Liang had installed a top-notch German lock in the front door. If the guy out front thought he was picking it fast and joining the fight, he was sadly mistaken.

Gliding into the formal living room, she cleared the space quickly and eased across the foyer into Peter's office. His desk was an antique, a massive wooden beast that would stop a small tank. Crouching behind it, she propped the barrel of the weapon on the writing surface and pointed it at the door to Liang's adjoining office. Exhaling slowly, she forcibly slowed her heart rate.

Now it was a waiting game.

Then she heard a sound that made her blood run cold. Little claws scrabbling on hardwood. She swore silently. Biscuit had wiggled free of his blanket restraint. Little scamp was running through the living room. Did she shift her aim to the foyer on the assumption that the shooter would be drawn to the sound of the puppy, or did she hold position, aiming at Li's office?

She had a split second to decide.

Instinct said to stay put.

In the very next breath, a black shadow spun fast through the doorway between the offices, crouching low, sweeping the office with his weapon.

She double tapped two shots at his center of mass, counting on the high-powered rounds to slam him backward against the wall and knock the breath out of him even if he had on a bullet-resistant vest.

The guy grunted and landed on the floor, leaning against the wall, but he was still functional enough to swing his weapon toward her.

Adjusting her aim a hair's breadth higher, she squeezed off two more fast shots. The hostile's throat exploded in a fountain of blood, but the weapon jammed on her second shot, the trigger balking and refusing to pull through. *Piece of crap Russian hardware.* Her target toppled over and lay still while she rapidly considered her options.

What she really wanted was her own trusty pistol, currently in her purse, sitting on the Louis XV credenza in the foyer. Laying down the Russian weapon, she eased out from behind the desk.

But then the downed man across the room moved, so she bolted forward, darting back out into the foyer and out of range of any dying-breath heroics.

The front doorknob was turning. She dived for her purse, snatching at it as she sprinted past the table, searching frantically for Biscuit ahead of her in the living room.

She missed the purse and only succeeded in knocking it on its side, the shoulder strap dangling just above the floor. But she couldn't go back. The door was opening. She lunged past it, scooped up the puppy, and dived for cover behind the sofa.

Landing hard on her shoulder—the one that had gotten hit in the initial attack—she lost her grip on the frantic, wriggly puppy, who rolled out of her arms.

Crap, crap, crap.

Peering under the couch, she saw the third hostile come in hot, charging into the foyer, aggressively swinging his weapon left and right. He raced down the hallway, his boots disappearing from her limited line of sight.

Biscuit raced after him, running into the middle of the foyer when a new barrage of fireworks, as loud and insistent as an artillery battle, peppered the night. Underneath the deafening thunder of noise, she whispered urgently, "*Biscuit! Come, Biscuit!*"

The puppy panicked and bolted straight ahead, ramming nose-first into the credenza, where he yelped and promptly got tangled in the dangling shoulder strap of her purse.

Frantic, he scrambled to free himself, to no avail.

Terrified, and completely overwhelmed, Biscuit squatted right there in the front hall and peed on the antique Aubusson rug.

The pantry and wine room doors slammed open in the kitchen.

Holding her hands out to the puppy, she tried again. "*Come to Granny. Come, Biscuit.*"

Perhaps her outstretched fingers still smelled like salami, or maybe he wanted a hug, but the pup, still tangled in her purse strap, stumbled toward her, dragging her purse off the credenza. As it thudded to the floor behind him he lurched forward, dragging the purse behind him through the puddle of pee and into the living room doorway.

He finally jerked free but not before the shoulder strap fell within reach of her outstretched hand.

She was out of time. With a shove, she pushed up off her belly, burst out of her hiding place, and leaped forward. Staying low, she scooped up the dog with her left hand and her purse with her right, and bolted for the stairs.

The shooter in the kitchen leaped out into the hall and fired wildly, sending a spray of lead into the wall below her feet. She ducked as splinters of wood pelted her and dived for the steps, fumbling frantically in her purse.

Her fist closed around the familiar grip of her EDC X9 Wilson Combat handgun. She didn't bother pulling it out of the bag. She rose to her knees and fired down at the shooter below through the leather of her purse—two fast shots, one through the top of his head, the second through the back of his neck as he pitched forward, facedown.

A cloud of mist hung in the air where his head had been, illuminated by the now continuous flash of fireworks. She pushed to her feet, picked up Biscuit, and raced upstairs, tearing into the master bedroom. She paused inside only long enough to lock the door.

Sprinting for the bathroom, she locked that door as well, stopping only when she'd jumped into the separate throne room, locked that door, and sat down on the floor beside the toilet, panting.

Finally freeing her weapon from her ruined purse, she set Biscuit on the tiled floor and dug around in her bag for her cell phone. She dialed 911 as reaction set in and her fingers began to tremble.

"Go ahead," the dispatcher's voice said cheerfully.

God. He sounded about twelve years old.

She took a deep breath and reminded herself to sound like a panicked civilian. "You have to send help! There's been a shooting at the following address." She rattled it off. "Do you have anything nearby with a siren? Maybe it would scare the bad guys away."

"Ma'am, those are fireworks you're hearing—"

"I've been shot. I think I saw three bad guys. Maybe more!"

"Where are you now, ma'am?"

"Locked in the master bathroom, upstairs."

"I've dispatched a police cruiser."

"Send *all* the police!"

"Ma'am, if you'll tell me what's going on—"

She interrupted impatiently. "I told you. A gang of armed bad guys broke into my son's house and shot the place up. And they shot me, too."

"Where are you shot, ma'am?"

"In the arm."

"I've dispatched an ambulance. You should lie down on the floor until medics arrive."

"It hurts like fire, but it's not bleeding a lot. I don't think it's serious . . . not that I know a blessed thing about gunshot wounds," she added.

Her left arm was, in fact, burning as if a hot poker lay across her biceps. *Dang it.* Her new sweater was ruined, too. She tore off a wad of toilet paper and used it to dab at her wound. The hot lead must have partially cauterized her wound, which would explain the lack of profuse bleeding.

"Umm, who is this?" the dispatcher asked warily.

She ignored the question, asking instead, "When are the police going to get here?" She dropped her voice to a whisper, as if it had just occurred to her the bad guys might still be running around the house. "What if the intruders find me up here?"

"The first police cruiser will be there any time, now."

Sure enough, a police siren became faintly audible. It rapidly grew louder until it was screaming outside the house. If that hadn't scared away any remaining intruders, nothing would. Thankfully, the police turned off the siren before long, and deep silence fell over the house. The distant rumble of the fireworks continued unabated, heedless of the death and destruction going on below their star-spangled roar.

She strained to hear any movement but heard only her own breath and the puppy's anxious panting. Li'l guy had been a champ, all things considered.

Outside, police would be stacking up beside the open front door, diving in guns first, clearing the ground floor room by room. She heard them shouting back and forth. Reaction started to crowd forward in her body, a stew of mostly rage and a little fear.

Who were the shooters? Why here? Was *she* the target? She was out of the game. Off the chessboard. Why this, then? Who had it in for her bad enough to break all norms of civilized spy behavior?

A male voice spoke up right outside the commode door. "Ma'am, are you in there? The house is secure."

"What's your badge number?" she demanded, pointing her pistol at the door. He was a hostile until he proved otherwise.

He rattled off his name, rank, and badge number without any hint of hesitation.

Her body went limp with relief. She stood up, her legs protesting as she unfolded her body from the cold, hard floor. Sharp needles of returning circulation made her wince as she picked up the dog, unlocked the door, and squinted into the beam of a high-intensity, military-grade flashlight.

"Three men are dead downstairs," the cop reported. "And it appears that a fourth one fled through the alley, perhaps on a motorcycle."

Four men? She should probably be complimented that such a big hit squad had been sent in to take her out. Still, this wasn't supposed to be happening. She was *retired.*

"Who else was in the house with you at the time of the incident, ma'am?"

"Nobody. It was just me and my granddog."

"*You* shot those men?" the cop blurted.

Crud, crud, crud. Speaking in a breathless soprano, she gasped, "I was so scared, Officer. I just closed my eyes and pulled the trigger. Did I hit anything?"

"You could say so," the cop said dryly. "Since you discharged a firearm that resulted in a death, we're going to need you to come down to the station, answer some questions, and make a written statement. After a medic takes a look at your arm."

"Of course." She added a nervous, fluttery wave with her hand for effect. Although, the pistol gripped in her fist probably ruined the helplessness of the wave. "You're sure it's safe out here?" she asked nervously as she stepped into the bedroom.

"Yes, ma'am. The scene is secured." The officer snagged her gun as she waved it past him, then checked the chamber and safety before saying, "This weapon will have to be entered into evidence."

With Biscuit still tucked under her left arm, she followed him downstairs to the foyer, picking her way cautiously through the splinters, broken glass, and puppy pee. "Is there any chance I could get my shoes? I must've run right out of them, I was so scared."

"Wait here, ma'am. This is an active crime scene."

Keen observation, Sherlock. Careful to keep her eyes wide and wondering, she looked around the destroyed ground floor. It looked like a freaking war zone. As the cop held out her designer bootlets, she wailed, "Look at this mess! My son is going to kill me."

CHAPTER 2

*H*ELEN FINALLY DROVE AWAY FROM THE POLICE PRECINCT AT NEARLY 3:00 a.m. The police were unsure of what to make of her. On the one hand, they had three dead bodies, shot with all the cold precision of the trained sniper that she was. But on the other, they had the flustered middle-aged woman sitting in a chair in front of them, wringing her hands, adamantly sticking to her story—she'd simply closed her eyes and pulled the trigger in self-defense. Poor coppers just couldn't seem to reconcile the two.

It had gotten a bit tricky to explain the knife in the back of Hostile Number One's knee, but she claimed that Biscuit had peed and the bad guy slipped in the puddle. As best she could tell, he'd grabbed at the counter as he went down, knocked the pie knife off the counter, and somehow landed on top of it, stabbing himself in the leg. Bad luck, that.

She readily admitted to using the knife to cut herself a piece of pie, of course, which explained her fingerprints on the weapon.

Her lawyer, whom she'd called from the foyer of Peter and Li's house, met her at the police station. He argued stridently that the hundreds of rounds the intruders had fired made her armed response an open-and-shut case of self-defense. Eventually, without any hard evidence to refute self-defense in response to a home invasion, the police had been forced to let her go. But they didn't like it. They smelled a rat, but they just couldn't spot it.

She made a mental note to avoid crossing paths with the Metropolitan Police of the District of Columbia—the Georgetown precinct in particular—any time soon.

She'd barely pulled out of the police parking lot when her cell phone rang. Who could be calling her at this hour? Peter had already made his opinion abundantly clear of his brand-new house being completely trashed on her watch. She doubted he would be speaking to her again this decade. At least she'd delivered Biscuit unharmed into Li's arms. That had to count for something.

The phone rang insistently. She transferred the call to her car's Bluetooth system, and it showed no name in the caller ID. Frowning, she pushed a button and took the call.

"Hello?" she said cautiously.

"Helen, Helen, Helen. What have you done?"

She sagged in relief. It was Yosef Mizrah, her longtime CIA handler. He must be calling from a burner phone. "Yossi. How did you hear about tonight's excitement? I don't work for you anymore."

"I thought I was finally rid of you, too, my dear."

She ground out, "What the heck was that? They shot up my son's house. They can come after *me* all they want. I'm fair game . . . arguably. But the bastards came after my *family*. I want names. I want *blood*."

"Metro police are saying it was a robbery gone bad. How about we figure out what happened before we jump to any conclus—"

She cut him off sharply. "You and I both know what that was. Four men armed with Russian assault weapons, who moved like a Spetsnaz team and shot out the entire back end of a house by way of entering the premises, were not trying to rob the place. They were after me. But they didn't even have the decency to wait until I was alone in my own home."

A long-suffering sigh in her ear. "I know—"

"I swear to God, if the FSB is behind this, I'll make them regret even thinking about knocking me off."

"I understand your feelings, Helen. But let's take a moment to find out who the shooters were. Collect intel on who sent them before you start a one-woman war with the Russian government."

"They started it. And I won't take this lying down."

"Let me find who 'they' are before you kill anyone else. Okay?"

She scowled fiercely. In her line of work, killing was an emotionless business transaction, but this was personal. And they'd involved her family. Still, a tiny voice of reason in the back of her head murmured that, like it or not, he wasn't wrong.

"Who's the puppy I heard about at the scene?" He was blatantly trying to distract her.

She let him, answering grumpily, "My granddog, Biscuit."

"Only you could go through a firefight badly outgunned, outnumbered four to one, with a puppy under one arm, and come out unscathed."

"I suppose you're going to need me to come into the office and make a report, aren't you?" she asked in resignation.

"'Fraid so. But Monday will be soon enough. Take the weekend to relax."

"I *was* relaxing! I was babysitting a puppy and having a piece of pie—that I made with my own hands, I'll have you know—when, poof. All hell broke loose."

Yosef was silent. The kind of silent that spoke loudly of him being as worried about this attack as she was. He, too, understood the unwritten rules that had been broken tonight.

"Promise me you won't kill anyone else before you come see me."

She rolled her eyes, even though he couldn't see them. He knew her well enough to hear them.

"Promise me, Helen."

"Fine. I promise. No murders before Monday. I'll take the rest of the weekend off."

"Nice shooting, by the way."

She snorted and hung up, without deigning to respond.

Helen turned into her driveway, and the motion-activated lights came on around the house. She waited while the steel garage door opened before driving inside. She waited for the door to fully shut, and only then climbed out of her car.

She unlocked the kitchen door and laid her hand on the biometric panel that deactivated the home alarm system. The network of red infrared sensor beams went off, and regular lights illuminated throughout the house.

She went over to the kitchen island and dumped everything out of her pee-stained, bullet-riddled purse. Lipstick, spare ammo mag, perfume roller, fountain pen filled with a fast-acting neuroparalytic, powder compact, a wire garrote carefully wrapped around its rubber handles, and crumpled dry cleaning and grocery receipts that went every which way.

Opening a kitchen drawer, she pulled out a 9mm Glock 43X she kept there in case of emergency. Chambering a round, she carried it and the ruined purse outside. A quick sweep around the yard over the end of her weapon's barrel, and she laid her purse tenderly in the covered trash can behind the garage.

"Rest in peace, you beautiful girl," she murmured over her purse's corpse.

The wooded hillside behind the house was silent and still tonight, but she gave it another long, hard look anyway.

The shooters had attacked her family. They'd had no way of knowing Peter and Li would be out tonight. Outrage literally stole her breath away. *How dare they?*

The quid pro quo was ironclad: *You don't mess with my loved ones, I don't mess with yours.*

She almost wished someone would move on that hillside. Give her a reason to go hunting and kill whoever'd wrecked her son's beautiful new home and almost offed her.

A puff of wind stirred the cold air, and the trees waved at her eerily as her hair lifted from her neck. She lurched into motion and headed back inside the rambling, two-story farmhouse where she and Grayson had raised their family. It reminded her of a well-worn sofa, overdue for new upholstery or a trip to the dump, but it was comfortable, and it was home.

Her knees felt weak all of a sudden, and her hands shook as the aftermath rolled over her, flattening her in its wake. She was too old for this crap. Moreover, she was supposed to be finished with all of it.

She was just starting to set aside the constant tension, the cautionary room searches, the roving gaze, the twitchy reflexes. But here it all was, roaring back, ripping away the gauze of normalcy with which she'd bandaged her tired soul, exposing the raw nerves of a killer once more.

One last double check of the twin deadbolts in the steel reinforced door with its impact-resistant glass, and she was safe. At least as safe as she could make this place without turning it into a straight-up fortress.

Good grief, she didn't want to play this game anymore.

She folded her arms on the cold granite counter and buried her face in them. For just an instant, she gave in to despair. It was a luxury she hadn't afforded herself these past twenty years and more. It felt good to let go of all the discipline, all the tension, all the constant vigilance. Maybe she should just hang it up. Let whatever might come her way, come.

As soon as she gave in, even for an instant, she knew the indulgence for the mistake it was. Right now, her focus had to be on surviving. Not just for herself, but for her family. She had to figure out who'd tried to have her killed and take them out. Only then would her family be safe. Maybe then she could finally rest.

Of course, she knew what Yosef would say. She could rest when she was dead.

Tonight had been a close call.

She allowed that knowledge to pass through her. Became one with it. She'd gotten separated from her firearm. She'd left curtains open, lights on—made a stupidly easy target of herself. Worst of all, she'd gotten complacent. Let herself be distracted by her family. Heck, she'd allowed emotions in.

Brick by brick, she rebuilt the emotional wall around herself that she'd been working so hard to tear down. She locked away the budding feelings, put away her hopes for restoring her marriage and relationships with her kids.

Maybe someday, she silently promised her husband and children. But not yet.

First, sleep. Then a serious conversation with her former CIA handler. He had better come up with the names of those assailants, and fast. She was not on the company payroll anymore, and she had no compunction about going on her own to mete out a little jungle justice.

She needed to know who'd ordered the attack on her. And why. What did he or she want? What would make them go away? Could a settlement be negotiated, or was this going down old-school—spy on spy, assassin on assassin, until there was only one man—or woman—left standing?

She shoved all the stuff from her purse into a plastic grocery bag. Plucking the spare ammo clip from the detritus of her attempt at normal life, she limped to the stairs. It felt as if the bottoms of her feet were cut up from running around barefoot on the shards of glass and splintered wood littering Peter and Li's house. Muscles all over her body were sore from the violent activity, and her upper arm was hurting again. A medic at the scene had insisted on taking a look at it, and even bandaged it, but she'd lied through her teeth when he'd asked her if it hurt.

She checked the security panel by the front door one last time—*Hello, paranoia, my old friend. I've come to talk with you again*—and trudged upstairs in her ruined stockings, bloody bootlets dangling from her left hand, pistol dangling from her right.

Into the master bedroom. Solid wood door locked. Steel painted to look like wood plantation shutters closed. She exhaled in relief as her cocoon of safety locked down around her. She wouldn't let down her guard tonight, not entirely, not scant hours after someone had tried to kill her in the most emphatic possible way. But she could breathe in here.

Stripping off the ruined sweater, she dropped it on the floor. Slacks, unzipped. She shimmied out of them and left them where they lay. Tomorrow was soon enough to throw out the bloody garments. The shredded stockings went in the trash with a certain satisfaction, and, standing in her underwear, she stared at herself in the mirror.

Her body showed the wear of bearing three children and fifty-five years of life, much of it lived on the edge of danger. Some sun damage around her throat and on her arms, a few wrinkles creeping in around her eyes and mouth. Gravity was having its due here and there in the form of loose skin, but she was still lean and hard underneath. And she wasn't dead—yet—by God.

Her bun had given up the ghost at her first dive for cover, and her hair straggled around her face. Once naturally blond, she'd faded to a dishwater color somewhere between blond, brown, and gray. Which meant she got peroxide help now from a hairdresser in northwest DC. She'd been looking forward to growing it out ever since she'd cut it all off twenty years ago. In her line of work, she couldn't afford to have it get in her eyes at exactly the wrong moment. A mistake like that could get her killed. But even growing out her hair would have to wait, apparently.

Craning her chin to the left, she peeled back the bandage from her arm.

The bloody stripe where the bullet had creased her was covered with a clear salve that had numbed the skin along with providing antibacterial coverage. The cut was more of a scoop than a slice, the length of her finger and shallow. Darn it, she'd been so looking forward to being a sissy in her old age and not having to deal with wounds like this.

She replaced the large, square bandage over the wound. It would scab over and heal soon enough. Probably would leave a scar, but it wasn't like she didn't have any of those. She took note of the thin one on her side where she'd nearly been gutted a decade back. Without seeing it, she knew there was a round bullet scar under her right shoulder blade, and various small nicks and marks from other close calls over the years.

She called them her teachable moments. Each scar held a valuable lesson for her. And so would this one: Never let down her guard. Ever.

As she headed for the bedroom, ominous little aches announced themselves in her hamstrings and back, and both shoulders already pained her. She wasn't cut out for tonight's gymnastics anymore and was definitely feeling her age. She winced in dread of tomorrow's stiffness.

She took one of Grayson's big T-shirts out of his drawer, pulled it over her head, and crawled into their cold, empty bed. She reached for his pillow and hugged it close. Almost all the smell of his aftershave had faded from it. Would it be weird to buy a bottle of it and dump it on his pillow?

He was somewhere in the Amazon jungle right now, crawling around on his hands and knees, looking for a new species of poison dart frog he'd gotten a lead on. Knowing him, he was as happy as a pig in mud. He loved his work as a naturalist fully as much as she'd loved hers. Past tense, damn it.

She lay in the dark, staring up at the ceiling, replaying the events of the evening in excruciating detail, analyzing and parsing her performance, which, on the whole, had been pitiful.

No doubt about it. She was out of practice.

At the end of the day, she faced a cold choice. She could roll over passively and wait for the next attack to finish her off. Or, she could pick her sorry derriere up off the ground and fight back.

As much as she hated what she had to do, it wasn't much of a choice. If nothing else, she needed to stay alive if she was ever going to make up to her family for the past two decades.

Her gaze narrowed in the dark. Somebody was going to pay for making Gray and the kids wait. That, and they'd scared her granddog half to death.

CHAPTER 3

*R*YAN GOETZ JERKED AWAKE IN THE PRE-DAWN DARKNESS, STAR-tled. *Shoot.* He'd dozed off. Urgently, he yanked his sleeve back to check his watch. If he'd blown his debut thrill kill by napping—

A little after 6:00 a.m. *Okay. Whew. Still a few minutes before go-time.*

He peered through the high-powered Zeiss telescopic sight he'd duct-taped to the top of the industrial-grade laser cutter, which was basically a laser pointer on steroids. It was larger and more powerful than the ones people carried around in their breast pockets, but it operated basically the same way. A concentrated beam of laser light would shoot out in a straight line, passing harmlessly through glass—while poking holes through plastic. Or a mylar balloon.

He glanced up at the half dozen large gas tanks he'd hauled up to the roof last night. They still lay neatly beside the chimney, which he'd covered with plastic and taped to seal. Only he knew that a small pump had emptied all the methane from those tanks and into the house overnight.

He panned across the back of the house and saw movement in the family room to the left of the kitchen. The family were early risers, were they? He hadn't planned for that.

He didn't dare risk someone opening a door. It would release the highly flammable methane he'd so carefully built up inside. *Drat.* He hated going off schedule.

No choice, though.

Picking up his makeshift laser gun once more, he shifted the Zeiss sight back to the kitchen. The woman of the house was moving around the space, making herself a cup of tea and pulling ingredients out of the refrigerator. If she was about to turn on the gas stove, she would do the job for him.

No! He got to make the kill. *Not her!*

He shifted his aim to the bouquet and balloon he'd had delivered to the house yesterday. The woman now moving around had put them, ever so conveniently for him, on the kitchen table.

The balloon was actually two balloons, one inside the other. The exterior balloon was filled with pure hydrogen; the interior balloon, pure chlorine.

Funny thing about hydrogen and chlorine. When they come into direct contact with each other, they spontaneously combust. And in a space saturated with methane and oxygen—well, he expected the results to be spectacular.

He turned on the video camera and double-checked to make sure it was recording.

Then he settled himself more comfortably and pressed the power button on the side of the laser. This particular cutter used infrared light, which was invisible to the human eye. A second, smaller laser light was mounted beside the primary laser that shot out a line of red light for aiming purposes.

Indeed, a red dot danced on the house's exterior siding just below the window. It was too dark to see the black burn the laser would be making on the side of the house. Moving the weapon gently, he raised the red sight-beam to the sill, then through the window. Laser beams were amplified light, and in general passed harmlessly through glass unless they were high-powered enough to vaporize the glass molecules, which this cutter was not.

He took a deep breath. His moment of greatness, so long planned for and anticipated, had arrived.

Slowly, carefully, he raised the red dot to the New Year's balloon.

The industrial laser instantly burned holes all the way through both balloons. As chlorine gas from the inner mylar balloon escaped into the surrounding hydrogen, it ignited with a bright flash. The entire kitchen window momentarily filled with light as the methane-saturated air around the balloon ignited.

Then the entire house exploded.

Kaboom!

The sound was deafening, and the brilliance of the blast was blinding. Heat seared his face, so he dropped flat, pressing his cheek against the damp, cold ground.

Oh, man. That was spectacular.

He panned the camera across the scene as pieces of the house and its contents began to rain down.

He had all the footage he needed to craft the greatest thrill kill video of all time. Grabbing the video camera and folding the tripod, he pushed up to his hands and knees and crawled backward the twenty yards or so beyond the ridge behind the houses. A great pillar of black smoke rose into the air, and the blackened skeleton of the chimney was all that was left intact of the house below.

Welp. That should keep the fire department busy for several hours. Long enough for the remains of his cheap plastic tanks to melt into nothing, assuming any parts of them had even survived the initial blast.

The methane had all been consumed in the initial explosion, and his innocent little mylar balloons had been vaporized. No fuss, no muss, no evidence.

CHAPTER 4

*H*ER DOORBELL RANG FAR TOO EARLY THE NEXT MORNING TO BE polite, and Helen looked up sharply, wincing as the muscles across the back of her neck screamed in protest. She glanced over at the iPad mounted on the kitchen wall and saw her eldest child, Mitchell, staring irritably at the video doorbell.

He always had been the most impatient of her three children, constantly demanding answers, insisting on understanding why everyone did everything. It made him a fine prosecuting attorney, but a bit of a pain in the butt as an offspring. She had no doubt Peter and her youngest, Jaynie, had elected him to come over here and find out what the hell had happened last night.

With a sigh, she put the pair of ice packs she'd been applying to various joints this morning in the sink and hoisted herself out of her chair, groaning as her protesting body creaked upright. She was fully as miserable today as she'd anticipated last night. Hobbling painfully to the foyer's wall-mounted tablet device, she brought up views from the cameras mounted on the corners of the house. The sides of the house were clear; no hostiles lurked out of sight waiting to rush the front door.

She pasted on a smile, straightened her aching bones, and threw open the door. "Good morning, darling. You're just in time for breakfast. Can I make you an omelet?"

"Really, Mom? Pete's place gets blasted to smithereens, and you want to pretend nothing happened and cook breakfast for me?"

"Why, I'm fine. Thank you for asking," she responded with light sarcasm. "I only have a minor flesh wound where a bullet creased me. And last time I checked, people still have to eat."

She made sure to walk behind Mitch as he barged into the kitchen. He was too observant to miss how creakily she was moving.

He sat down heavily on one of the barstools at the island. "You were *shot?* Why didn't anybody tell me that? Why didn't *you* tell me?"

"Because it would have involved me sharing that information with the police. It was only a flesh wound, anyway. I cleaned it off and slapped a bandage on it. Ham, cheese, and green pepper, right? Still no onions?"

"Right. No onions," he answered absently. Abruptly, like the cross-examining assistant district attorney he was, he demanded, "Who attacked you?"

"We don't know that last night was aimed at me. For all we know, it could've been an armed robbery, which I just happened to be there to foil. Your brother and his boyfriend do have a rather expensive art collection, and they don't exactly make a secret of it."

Mitchell threw her a skeptical glare. "Or it could've been someone trying to kill you."

She shrugged and busied herself whisking cream into the eggs and pouring them into a pan.

"Who wants you dead, Mom?"

"You mean besides your brother?"

"Be serious."

She turned, wielding her spatula like a pointer. "I am being serious. I don't have the slightest idea. What makes you think anyone wants to kill little old me?"

"I saw the police report. Four armed gunmen? Assault weapons? Entry from both the front and rear of the house? Nothing stolen? That sounds like a hit job, not a robbery."

He was undoubtedly right, but she wasn't about to concede the point. Her children had no idea what her real work had been, and if she had her way, she would go to her grave with them in ignorance of it. Her cover had always been that she was a foreign trade specialist at the State Department. Oh, she admitted to working for the CIA from time to time, on loan from State, but purely as an analyst. The secret black ops, the off books assignments, the blood in her ledger, none of that was ever spoken of.

She laughed lightly, all the while adding fillings and folding the omelet in the pan. "Honey, I'm retired. Who in their right mind would care about me enough to kill me? I analyzed trade deals and tariff legislation. Not exactly the most exciting stuff on earth. The day I retired, some poor schmuck took over my job exactly where I left off. I was a small cog in a very big machine."

Skepticism flashed in Mitch's gray gaze, so like her own. But then it was gone, so fast she wasn't even positive she'd seen it. Surely she was mistaken. He didn't know what she did. It wasn't possible. She'd never breathed a word of it to him.

"Still. You did work for the CIA, sometimes."

"Along with thousands of other paper pushers and desk jockeys. I'm sorry to disillusion you, but only a handful of CIA officers ever leave Langley, Virginia, and only a few of them ever do anything the least bit exciting, let alone dangerous. Television is not real, Mitchell."

"Yeah, I got that memo," he grumbled. "I'm an actual prosecuting attorney, remember?"

"How angry is Peter about the house?" she asked as she plated the omelet and set it down in front of him.

"He's incandescent with rage."

She winced. "I swear, I was babysitting the puppy and minding my own business. And I would like to point out that Biscuit didn't get a single scratch."

"Three men died in Pete and Li's house. What do you know about that?"

"They must've gotten into a shootout with the SWAT team." She added innocently, "Are there, I don't know, bloodstains? What a shame it would be if the new floors got ruined."

Mitch snorted. "The floors are the least of the damage. The ground floor is completely trashed." As she winced again, he tucked into his omelet. She sipped her tea in silence, trying and failing to think of an appropriate way to apologize to Peter and Liang for the carnage to their beautiful, brand-new home.

"Where did Peter and Liang stay last night?" she asked to fill the silence.

"Gran's house."

Helen groaned. She was never going to hear the end of this from her mother. The woman took her role as family harridan *very* seriously.

Mitch glanced up at her and shrugged. "She was going to find out one way or another. Nothing goes on in this town that Gran doesn't hear about."

"Truth." Her mother had been a fixture in the Washington political scene ever since her husband had come to her as a naïve, starry-eyed young congressman from Indiana. Constance Stapleton knew *everyone* in Washington, and her gossip network was legendary.

"Will you be seeing your brother in the next day or so?" she asked.

"I'm going over there in a bit to help him make a statement to the press."

"The press?" she exclaimed.

"You know the motto of the media: If it bleeds, it leads. It was quite the violent shootout, Mom."

"Yes, I got that memo," she retorted dryly. "I was there. Granted, I was locked in the toilet, hiding, but still. I heard it." Sometimes she really hated how easily she lied to her family.

Mitch rolled his eyes at her.

She said, quite seriously, "Please tell Peter and Liang they're always welcome here if they need somewhere to stay while their house is getting repaired." Although, as the invitation came out of her mouth, she privately hoped they didn't take her up on the offer. Not because she wouldn't love to have them stay here but because she wasn't sure they would be safe here. If those gunmen had been after her, it was entirely possible the next hit squad would be coming to this house.

Mitch was talking again. ". . . ground floor is going to have to be redone almost from scratch. It'll take months. Turns out they're going to be able to get the apartment back that they stayed in during the first renovation."

Guilt rolled through her. Even if she hadn't done anything to directly provoke last night's violence that she was aware of.

Silence fell between them, and she studied her eldest closely as he ate his breakfast. He was a good-looking man with dark, wavy hair and light brown skin from her husband's half-African heritage. Cameras loved him. He radiated poise, assurance, and most importantly to his political ambitions, honesty.

In truth, Mitch was arguably one of the most calculating men she'd ever known. Which was saying something, given her former employer. She knew he aspired to political office, and she had no doubt he would end up in Congress, or higher, if work ethic counted for anything.

She leaned a hip on the edge of the counter. "Did you only come here to ask me about last night, or was there something else you wanted?"

"How are you liking retirement?"

Ha. No denial he had an ulterior motive. Her mama radar still worked like a charm.

"I haven't been retired long enough to really know, I suppose. And with the holidays here, I've been too busy to slow down and enjoy it. Why do you ask?"

"I had a conversation with a defense attorney last night at a party, and it made me think of you."

"How's that?"

"She could use the services of a decent analyst."

"Why would a defense attorney be involved in a trade deal?"

"She's not. But you know how to read a complex report and translate it into a clear understanding of what happened."

"Isn't that what you lawyers do?"

"Look. I came here to throw you a bone. If you don't want to hear about this opportunity, I'll leave."

She exhaled hard. She and Mitch always had fought like cats and dogs. Gray said it was because they were so identical that they drove each other crazy. "I'm sorry. Tell me all about it."

"I don't know the details. But this lawyer—she's really sharp. One of the best we go up against. Over the past year, she's had several clients convicted of crimes they swear up, down, and sideways they didn't do."

How good a lawyer could she be if her clients still got convicted? She frowned and kept the thought to herself.

He continued, "She thinks she may have found a pattern to the crimes her clients were accused of."

"Why didn't she go directly to the district attorney?"

"Conflict of interest. She's sleeping with him." He continued, "She couldn't say much about it last night because we were at a big, loud party, but she said enough to convince me it's worth taking a look at what she's put together."

"Good for you for having an open mind. But why can't you do this yourself?"

He scowled. "I'm a lowly ADA. I can't run around casting doubt on cases my boss won, at least not without royally pissing him off. I need someone I can trust, someone discreet, to take a look at Angela's information and give me an honest opinion about it."

"Is that where I come in?"

"Correct."

"I'm not a private investigator, Mitchell—"

"No, but you are smart and analytical. And you can keep your mouth shut."

"Thank you, I think?"

"Think of yourself as a test jury. If Angela can convince you there's something fishy about the convictions, could she convince eleven other people, as well?"

Her inclination was to run screaming from dry, dusty legal files. There was a reason she hadn't actually worked at a desk all these years. But this was Mitchell. And it was the first and only time he'd ever asked her for help professionally. She couldn't possibly turn him down.

"Of course, I'll be delighted to take a look. But I am going to tell you honestly if I don't feel qualified to make a decision. Particularly when someone's entire future hangs in the balance."

"Fair enough. Can you see her today?"

"I've got lunch today with an old friend, but I can swing by and talk to this lawyer of yours tomorrow."

He stood up, speaking briskly over his shoulder as he strode toward the front door. "I'll text you her information. Name's Angela Vincent."

CHAPTER 5

*H*ELEN TUGGED AT HER WOOL JACKET IN DISTASTE. THE SUIT, HOSE, and heels were horribly uncomfortable after spending the past two months in yoga pants and tunics. Why did women allow themselves to be forced to dress like this, anyway? To quote her daughter the raging feminist, *F the patriarchy.*

Her cell phone rang. She pulled it out of her purse with the intent to decline the call. But then she saw the caller ID. *Ugh.*

"Hello, Mother," she said into the phone.

"What's this I hear about Peter's new house getting robbed and shot up?"

Helen answered lightly, "I'm so relieved to know you aren't worried about my safety or well-being. I would hate to have you fretting over how traumatic it might have been for me to be there when armed men invaded the boys' house."

"Don't take that tone with me, young lady."

Helen rolled her eyes. She was on the back side of her fifties and an accomplished assassin. She didn't need her mother treating her like a naughty twelve-year-old.

"I called to let you know the boys are going to be staying with me for a few days."

She'd called to rub Helen's nose in the fact that Peter liked her more than his own mother. But it wasn't worth rehashing that tired old argument with her mother.

She replied tiredly, "Thanks for putting up the boys on short notice." And then, because she couldn't resist getting in her own little dig, she gushed, "Isn't Biscuit adorable? You're going to love getting to know him. He's such a cuddle bug."

Her mother hated animals of all kinds and had never allowed any pets in her house.

Constance snorted. "I'm thinking of asking Peter to kennel that dog until they move back into their old place—"

"Sorry, Mom. I have to go. My appointment is starting."

She unceremoniously hung up on her mother and took secret pleasure in doing so. It wasn't often she got the last word on Constance Stapleton.

She dropped her phone into her purse and smoothed her damp palms down her tailored wool skirt. Today, her identity was that of a businesswoman—calm, cool, and professional. Why walking into CIA headquarters in Langley should inspire autonomic nervous reactions in her after all the times she'd walked into this place as an employee, she had no idea. She hadn't done anything wrong. Killing those men had been purely self-defense.

In truth, this wasn't a place she'd come to all that often. When she'd had to analyze the odd trade legislation for the sake of her cover, she'd generally worked from home. Now and then, she was called in here for a face-to-face meeting or for a particularly classified briefing, but that was the exception and not the rule.

Her real work took her overseas several times a year, always under the guise of attending some trade conference or a research trip for her job. A clean kill could take anywhere from a few days to many weeks to set up. She'd never known when she walked out of her house how long she would be gone.

She looked around the spacious, square-columned lobby with its giant seal of the CIA set into the terrazzo floor. This whole building was a mid-century modern take on an idealized future. The building was light and spacious in stark contrast to the dark secrets and grim work that lived within these walls.

Today, she felt more at odds than ever with the bureaucrats

hurrying past her in their uptight suits and intellectual self-righteousness. They didn't fool her. They made guesses for a living. Educated ones, but guesses, nonetheless.

As for her, she dealt in hard truths. Life and death. Win or lose. Boots on the ground, facing down the nation's enemies one at a time. These chair warmers had no idea what people like her, living at the sharp end of the spear, really did. No idea who they were. She didn't often feel like a wolf among sheep, but she felt that way strongly this morning.

She approached the visitor's desk just inside the front lobby of CIA headquarters. *Showtime.* She donned the identity that went with her suit and became one with it. Polite but distant, pleasant but professional.

Vividly aware of the irony of being an outsider now to an organization she'd been so very deep inside, she attached the visitor's badge that a guard passed her to her lapel.

The guard phoned up to Yosef's office to let him know she was here, and she was left loitering uncomfortably in the lobby.

"Helen! You're looking wonderful this morning," Yosef exclaimed as he came down the glass-walled hall to collect her.

"You mean for a woman who nearly got murdered mere days ago?" she said, low.

He must've heard the bitterness in her voice, since he glanced around quickly and murmured, "Walk with me."

He led her through the turnstiles, up a set of stairs, and down a long hall to his office, which was shockingly cramped for the power this man wielded. He ran one of the largest networks of spies in the world. Almost all of the undercover operatives and double agents in Europe, and more importantly, Russia, reported to him or one of his subordinates. As her main theater of operations was Europe, he'd been her primary handler for most of her career.

The CIA was all about who you knew, who you could horse-trade favors with, and who had your back when the politics got ugly. Which they seemed to do every other presidential adminis-

tration or so. During the inevitable shake-ups and house clean-
ings to follow, a girl had to have connections to survive. Yosef had
been her lifeline through it all.

Moreover, they were friends. Truth be told, she felt more comfortable with him than with her husband. Lord knew, she spent
more time talking with Yosef than with Gray these days.

He ushered her into his tiny office and closed the door. She sat
in the lone chair beside his desk while he fell into his desk chair
and passed the back of his wrist across his forehead. Poor man
looked utterly exhausted.

"You need to unchain yourself from your responsibilities now
and then. Take a walk. Get some fresh air."

"You're only my work wife, not my real one," he grumbled.

"Darling, if something happened to you, I would be desolate."

He snorted. "You're the one who retired and abandoned me."

"I was forced out, and you know it. Aged out, to be precise."

He shook his head. "Some of my best sources are a lot older
than you."

"Tell the Special Operations Group that. The new director is
gung-ho to fill his whole team with macho ex-soldiers. Which
leaves civilians like me out in the cold."

"I'll always have your back, Helen."

"Speaking of which, have you learned anything about the New
Year's Eve attack on me?"

"I've identified the three men you took down."

"Do tell."

Yosef opened a folder and pulled out three eight by ten glossy
photographs. He laid them side by side, facing her. The pictures
were postmortem and grisly. On top of those, he laid three more
photographs of each man alive. They were surveillance shots,
which meant the quality wasn't spectacular. But each guy was rec-
ognizable as the corresponding corpse.

"Mercenaries," Yosef murmured. "A Romanian, a Bulgarian,
and a Serb."

"That sounds like the first line of a bad joke," she commented.

He smiled a little. "These guys were no joke. They arrived in the

States separately several days before the hit. Stayed at the same hotel, where they presumably connected, received instructions, and planned the attack. Someone hired them to take you out."

"What about the fourth guy?" she asked.

"No idea who he might be."

"How did they know I would be at my son's house and not my own home?" she asked thoughtfully.

He shrugged. "They could've tapped your phone. Or perhaps they followed you to your son's place."

"While they coordinated reasonably well as a team, they didn't seem familiar with the layout of the house. Otherwise, I would be dead. They had me outgunned by a mile and caught me flat-footed. My guess is they followed me to my son's place and merely took the target of opportunity that I presented them with."

"Don't be too hard on yourself. Not too many operators would walk away from a four-on-one like that alive."

"I was ridiculously lucky," she replied flatly. "What else can you tell me about these guys?"

"Not much. No serious criminal records, no records of extensive international travel, no known government connections."

"So, whoever wanted me dead burned *four* clean killers to take me out? I'd be flattered if that didn't worry me so much."

Yosef leaned back in his chair. "I reached out to my FSB counterpart in the Russian embassy. We're due to meet in a few hours. I thought you might like to observe. Maybe provide a little overwatch. Unofficially, of course."

"Where's the meeting?"

"National Zoo."

"Outdoors? In this weather? You're killing me. You couldn't choose a nice warm restaurant somewhere? You're gonna freeze me half to death."

He shrugged. "Outdoor meetings at this time of year are less likely to be watched. And it's not as if Russians aren't used to the cold. He picked the location, anyway."

"Where in the zoo?" she asked in resignation.

"Where else? Outside the bear house."

She rolled her eyes. "Will you wear a microphone, or am I stuck using a parabolic mic to listen in?"

"For you, my dear, I will wear a wire."

"Text me the frequency. I'll have to hustle to get home, grab my gear, and get into position at the zoo before you meet."

"Be careful. Anatoly Tarmyenkin isn't the type to come alone."

She snorted. "Of course not. But neither are you."

Goetz leaned back in satisfaction, stretching painful kinks out of his back and cracking his neck. It had taken hours and hours of painstaking editing, capturing individual frames of his video and splicing them into a super-slow-motion sequence of exploding house and flying debris.

Because he hadn't been able to stick around long enough to get video of the body parts being recovered from the scene, he'd gone to the internet to copy images of dismembered body parts and chunks of pink human meat to finish out his composition.

And now it was ready. An homage to Kandinsky's final masterpiece, *Composition X.*

And more importantly, it was an homage to his hero, a thrill killer famous on the Dark Web for the past two decades, dubbed the DaVinci Killer by his fans.

The DaVinci Killer had not only filmed his murders and posted them on thrill kill sites, but he'd gone to great pains to pose the corpses of his victims to imitate great works of art depicting death. He'd taken murder and lifted it into the realm of classical art. The guy was a genius.

And he, too, was going to be remembered as a genius. For his plan was to elevate the DaVinci Killer's still photographs and grainy videos to full-on music videos with outstanding production values.

He'd chosen Wassily Kandinsky's painting as his subject for this, his first art kill because it was a challenging piece to duplicate, a collection of bright colors and geometric shapes flying outward from a single, central point on a perfectly black background.

He'd dubbed in a soundtrack to the video, Bach's Toccata and

Fugue in D Minor, a dark and violent organ piece that crescendoed in perfect time with his unfolding explosion. His finger hovered over the play button on his computer for a moment, and then he pressed it. The jarring organ notes blared as the house blew up in slow motion, then again in slower motion, and then a third time in a stop-frame format that highlighted every gory detail of the explosion.

Then the heart of the video took over, a black background upon which he superimposed images of the house blowing up in geometric arrangements that matched the Kandinsky painting.

Finally, when the entire composition was complete, he superimposed the Kandinsky piece over his re-creation of it, fading in and out of the painting and the exploded house and body parts.

He signed on to the Dark Web under his alias, RealDavinciKiller, and went to the most heavily trafficked thrill kill site on the illicit internet. He spent a few minutes watching other murders filmed in real time and snorted at their utter inelegance. Wait till they all got a load of his kill. With great relish, he uploaded his video and sat back to wait for the reaction.

It didn't take long. At first, he got a few likes and a couple of comments:

Mind-blowing, man.

Wowsers. Now that's art.

Best. Kill. Ever.

And then the frenzy was on. The likes tally clicked up fast, first by dozens, then by hundreds, then by thousands as his video went viral.

Exultant satisfaction rolled through him. They recognized his genius. They admired him. And best of all, they wanted more.

Before he was done, they would acknowledge him as the greatest killer of all time.

CHAPTER 6

*H*ELEN PUSHED THE HIDDEN LATCH ON THE SIDE OF HER PURSE rack, and the whole shelf unit swung open, revealing a hidden room she'd hoped never to have to enter again.

She pulled a hanging string attached to a light bulb, and a room tucked under the rafters was revealed. Along each wall, dozens of pistols and rifles hung from pegboard mounts. Metal crates of ammunition stood in a row on the floor beneath the wall of weapons. On the opposite-side wall were chest-high cabinets, tucked into the acute angle of the ceiling. They held her other tools of the trade: drawers containing binoculars, hidden cameras, bugs, parabolic microphones, throwing knives, satellite burner phones, and a host of other gadgets and gear. A closet in the corner stored the clothing of the craft: Kevlar vests, infrared blocking bodysuits, camouflage clothing, and more.

She pulled out a rucksack and assembled a quick surveillance kit. She disassembled a short-range sniper rifle and put it in the bag along with a white camouflage suit for crawling around in the snowy woods.

Backing out of the hidden room and closing it up, she donned a red raincoat out of her regular closet and headed out.

The zoo was deserted when she walked in. No crowds to provide cover. Not even any school field trips to pretend to chaperone. Only a few patrons huddled in their coats scuttled from heated animal house to heated animal house.

She would have to do this purely with stealth, and she was short on time for that. She hurried along the south side of the zoo. She veered onto the American trail, one exhibit shy of the bear house, and followed its winding course about halfway around a circular loop through a carefully constructed American meadow habitat.

With a casual look in both directions to ensure she was alone, she stepped off the trail. It had rained recently, and the low spot where she went off the trail was shin-deep in standing water. It was icy cold and made her suck in her breath sharply.

Moving through water was noisy if done too fast but had the advantage of hiding her footprints. She followed the gully for perhaps fifty excruciatingly cold feet before finally climbing up and out the other side. She crouched behind some brush and watched the trail for a couple of minutes. Nobody came along.

She changed out her red raincoat for the white-and-gray camouflage jacket, and pulled on matching camo trousers over her slacks. Last, she put on a beige slouch hat with a broad brim to break up the silhouette of her head, shadow her face, and retain a bit of warmth.

Staying low, she moved up the hill and into a stand of tall bamboo. The zoo grew a lot of its own food for its famous pandas, and this was part of that effort. The shoots were the thickness of her arm and stiff with cold. Her backpack promptly got hung up, and she had to slip it off and carry it in one hand to make any progress. She was leaving deep, black footprints in the spongy soil, but there was no help for it.

She stopped to catch her breath at the top of a steep hill. She was too old for this crap. Besides, her specialty was working as an urban sniper. She usually set up a hide in a convenient building and waited for her target to come to her. Then, after the shot, she walked away, no fuss, no muss. None of this tromping through the mud in freezing cold, outside in all the elements.

The bamboo ended at a tall iron fence that surrounded the zoo property, and she turned left, paralleling that until she estimated she was behind the bear house. The bench Yosef and his Russian counterpart would meet on was slightly east of the animal enclosure.

As she moved away from the fence and into an area of relatively open forest, she eased into the deep shadows below a bushy, soft-needled spruce and crouched down, utterly still. Her thighs were not impressed with the pose and burned in protest. She shifted uncomfortably.

Her wet feet were numb with cold and her hiking boots squished as she continued forward in a half crouch. But she'd had the foresight to wear wool socks, and even wet, they would retain enough heat to protect her toes from frostbite. She hoped.

The trees were mostly bare at this time of year, with bushy pines here and there breaking up the monotony of stark black trunks and bare branches. She scanned the forest, looking for motion or any shapes that might be human.

Her Russian sniper counterpart was surely out here. But where? She paused, sinking into another painful crouch to scan the area. Perhaps he'd set up shop on the other side of the bench at the far edge of the meadow section of the park. Cover wasn't great over that way, but that was the point. Who would look for an armed sniper in a field of dead grasses?

For long minutes, she held her position, waiting and watching. The Russian spymaster would definitely bring his own armed backup to a meeting with a high-level CIA agent. The Russian shooter was out here, somewhere. She could *feel* him. But he was good. She still hadn't spotted him.

Furtively, she checked her watch. Thirty minutes until the meet. Both Yosef and the Russian, Anatoly Tarmyenkin, would be punctual to the minute. Spies were like that.

It was time for her to move in on the bench, set up within line of sight, and settle into her shooter's zen. Except she still hadn't spotted the Russian sniper.

Five minutes ticked by. Ten. The woods around her were utterly still and silent except for the wind blowing through the trees, knocking branches together overhead. An elephant trumpeted somewhere nearby, and she smiled briefly at the incongruous sound in this Washington suburb.

Ten more minutes passed.

Yosef's voice came through her earpiece, just a mutter. "At the front gate." He would time his walk through the sprawling zoo to arrive at the bench exactly on time.

She made a low clicking noise in her mouth without moving her lips to acknowledge his report and to act as a radio check.

He murmured back low, "Check."

She estimated it would take her sixty seconds to top the ridge between her position and the path where the meeting was. Assuming she could walk there normally. If she had to low crawl for it, she was already going to miss the first minute or two of the conversation. Stay or go?

Practicality said to move now. But her gut shouted at her to hold her position.

She hated being out of practice like this. Normally, she would know whether or not to trust an intuition. She could usually tell when they were born of nerves or danger, but today she couldn't tell the difference. Surely, the sniper out here wouldn't take a pot shot at her. Not here, on US soil, in a tightly fenced park where the exits could be locked down in a matter of seconds, trapping the sniper inside like a fish in a barrel. This was a terrible place to stage a hit.

But, she also had a certain reputation after all these years. She was known to be wily and slippery, a nightmare target to pin down and kill. Maybe the Russians would be willing to sacrifice one more killer to take her out.

If the Russians were behind the New Year's Eve attack.

The nationalities of the would-be killers pointed at the Russians as the organizers of that little fiasco. Of course, some other player could've used Eastern European assassins precisely to point the finger at the Russians.

Three minutes till the meeting. The woods around her were as still and quiet as they'd been the whole time she'd been out here. She gathered her muscles to rise . . .

And a beige shape rose out of the dead leaves directly in front of her.

Sonofa—

Man. He was good. He'd been lying no more than fifty feet in front of her, right out in the open the whole time, with only his camouflage suit and some leaves to hide him. She should've brought heat-seeking gear with her. He'd have popped right out at her then. But she'd gone old-school and relied on her eyesight. And it had failed her.

Times were changing too much and too fast around her. She was too old for this game. New technology was coming along quickly, and she wasn't adapting rapidly enough to it.

Had he seen her?

She held her position in dismay as he scanned the forest in front of him in a hundred-eighty-degree arc, a rifle resting against his shoulder. She was just far enough behind him that he didn't turn to face her.

He moved out fast, knees bent, with the rolling, heel-to-toe stride of a Special Forces trained soldier. Although she was infinitely more comfortable in city settings than natural settings like this, she could play in the woods with the big boys. Moving more slowly, she trailed behind the Russian, keeping him in sight ahead of her.

The forest floor was damp enough that the leaves didn't crunch underfoot, and she was able to move in complete silence, as well. The best vantage point for the meeting was to the west of the bear house. The sight line was unbroken—thick underbrush went right to the front corner of the stucco structure, and the building itself would provide excellent cover from incoming fire in a pinch.

The shooter fanned out to the left, crossing her field of vision from right to left. *Darn it.* He was heading for the spot she'd chosen for herself.

She was forced to freeze behind him as he shifted direction. The only other decent spot to observe the meet was along the ridge well east of the bench. And she was out of time to get there.

"Delay," she breathed into her microphone.

The Russian sniper slipped once on his way down the hill, righted himself, and disappeared behind the bear house. Now was her chance. She broke into a run, heading away from the other shooter. She prayed the building between him and her would muffle any sounds of her movement.

She only had about sixty seconds left to get in position.

The wide, paved path came into view down the hill from her between the trees. She spotted the bench.

Still empty.

Was the Russian being coy? Didn't want to be the first to show up and sit down, apparently. And with Yosef slowing down his approach, the Russian must be doing the same.

She continued moving to her right, following the curve of the path toward the north. She hit another thick stand of bamboo, which worked to her advantage. She moved fast behind it, advancing another hundred yards past the bench. Down on her belly she went, wiggling through the thick poles of bamboo. Thankfully, the wind would disguise the swaying of the huge grass shoots as she shoved them aside.

There. The back of the bench came into sight. She tucked her rifle against her shoulder and put her eye to the rubber cup of the sight. Yosef was approaching slowly from the west, and a gray-haired man in a wool coat and fur hat was approaching from the east.

"I'm in position," she murmured.

She scanned the hill beyond the bear house.

Bingo. She spied the unnaturally straight shape of a rifle barrel first. *Sloppy.* Her weapon was wrapped in rags that broke up the man-made line of her weapon.

"I have the Russian sniper in sight. He's at the west corner of the bear house. Take the end of the bench away from him."

Yosef didn't say anything in acknowledgment, but he did take the end of the bench nearest to her.

Within ten seconds, the Russian spymaster closed in and sat down.

The two men sat in silence for a moment, contemplating nothing in particular. Yosef was the one to break the ice, asking gravely in Russian, "What is the Russian definition of a string quartet?"

Anatoly grinned. "A Russian symphony orchestra that has just returned from an overseas tour."

Yosef grinned back.

Anatoly demanded, "What did the Russian say to the donkey he saw in the zoo?"

"I don't know that one," Yosef replied.

"Poor, sweet, bunny. What have the Communists done to you?"

Yosef laughed aloud, and Anatoly grinned broadly.

"Thank you for meeting me, today," Yosef said formally.

"What is this about? You seemed upset on the phone."

Now that the two men were settled in and talking, she took a moment to pan her weapon across the path to where the other sniper was hidden.

Holy effing balls of manure. The bastard had his weapon trained on her. Trying to intimidate her, was he? Think again, grasshopper. She flicked her thumb along the side of her rifle, activating the laser function of her telescopic sight. To drive home the point, she put the laser designator on the ground about twelve inches in front of the asshole's nose, where he couldn't fail to see it.

Then, very calmly, she murmured into her microphone, "Darling, tell your Russian friend that if he doesn't order his overwatch to back down right now, I'm going to blow his sniper's head off."

Yosef said kindly to Anatoly, "You might want to have your sniper quit playing chicken with mine. The one I brought with me today is in no mood for games."

Anatoly muttered something in Russian about testosterone-induced stupidity and then, in quick Russian, told his man to stand down.

The other sniper turned his weapon away from her and pointedly aimed it down at Yosef. A small red dot illuminated on the side of Yosef's neck.

Jerk.

She shifted to her right and placed her own designator on Anatoly's left cheek.

The two men on the bench shook their heads, and Anatoly murmured in Russian to his man, "You've made your point. Stand down or go home."

The red dot disappeared from Yosef's neck. She reached up and thumbed her laser function to the off position as well.

"Children," Yosef muttered.

She took offense at being lumped in with the overeager sniper across the way. Unlike him, she'd been prepared to come out here, be patient, listen, and fade away with no one but Yosef the wiser that she'd ever been here. But Laser Tag Boy over there just had to make his presence known. *Amateur.*

Yosef said to his Russian counterpart, "One of my operatives retired a few months back after a long and distinguished career. She has settled into retirement and is enjoying spending time at home with her family."

"God willing, I shall do the same one day," Anatoly murmured.

"And when you do, my people will leave you to your old age in peace."

"Of course. That is how it goes, is it not? We spend our twilight years regretting the choices of our youth."

"Agreed," Yosef said tartly. "Which forces me to ask, why did you send a team of assassins to take out my *retired* operative?"

She zeroed in on the Russian's face as Yosef asked the question. She wanted to see Anatoly's reaction for herself.

"I would never do such a thing!" he exclaimed.

Huh. She lifted her eye away from her sight. His body language was clear. He wasn't lying. But his choice of words had been telling. *I* would never do such a thing. Not *we* would never do such a thing, or *my government* would never do such a thing.

She pressed her eye back to the sight.

The two men on the bench fell silent as a family with several children walked past them. Once they'd disappeared around a bend in the paved path, Anatoly spoke again. "I will let you know if I hear anything. And who was this operative that retired?"

"You know full well who it was," Yosef retorted.

"I will tell you this, Yosef Jakobovich. I was glad to hear she finally laid down her rifle. She was a thorn in my side for more years than I care to count."

She muttered into her microphone, "Aw. That was sweet of him to say." Coming from the Russian, it was high praise, indeed. She thought she detected a faint roll of Yosef's eyes in response.

The meeting paused again while a woman runner went past. *Ugh.* Helen couldn't imagine running at all, let alone in weather this cold. And up and down all the hills and valleys in the zoo? *No, thank you.*

Yosef's voice held a warning note when he said to his counterpart, "The balance of power is a delicate thing. We have a saying in America: Don't upset the apple cart." He added gently, "You may not like where the apples roll, Comrade."

"*Ponyatna*," Anatoly said briskly. *Understood.*

The two men stood up and turned their backs on each other. Yosef walked up the path toward her, while the Russian headed toward his sniper.

Into his coat collar, Yosef muttered, "Those Russian jackasses ordered the hit. Not him, but other Russians. And he knows who."

That was her read on it too. She uttered a single word in response. "Why?"

"That is the question, indeed. Meet me at my house, tonight. Nine o'clock?" he said low.

"If my feet are unfrozen by then," she groused.

She held her position for another ten minutes or so, until the Russian sniper faded back out of sight. She didn't know where he'd entered the park from, so she gave him a ten-minute head start at clearing the area before she finally stood up. Her feet were instantly stabbed with a thousand needles of agony, and only the sturdy bamboo cane that she grabbed kept her upright.

She disassembled her rifle and stowed it in her backpack, then limped down the hill to the path. She took a brightly striped wool hat out of her pocket and pulled it onto her head, swearing under her breath at how cold it was out here. As she approached the bear house, she pulled out the matching scarf. Mitch's wife, Nancy, had knit the set for her, and it felt weird having something personal on her when she was working like this.

The wind whipped around her as she cleared the corner of the bear enclosure, snatching the scarf out of her hands. She lunged forward to catch it, and a metallic *schwing* just behind her made her drop into a crouch and look back quickly. A chip of stone was missing from the corner of the building exactly at head height. It hadn't been missing a few seconds ago.

Sonofa—

She dropped and rolled until she lay against the side of the building, frantically reaching into her pack to pull out her rifle. She snapped the pieces together by feel and eased up to her feet, rifle pressed against her cheek. Laser Tag Boy thought he was going to take her out that easily, did he?

She reached up with one hand to pull off her brightly colored hat and stuff it in her coat pocket, shrugged into her backpack, then crept up the hillside. By the time she reached the top of the steep slope, she was breathing harder than she wanted to, and her thighs were just about done with all this foolishness. She took several deep breaths and scanned the trees for any sign of the Russian sniper.

Don't make me run. Don't make me run . . .

There. Racing left to right across her field of view, about one hundred fifty yards out. It was a difficult shot. But she was a world-class shooter. She led the movement, aimed for center of mass, held her breath, and squeezed the trigger.

Her target staggered hard to one side but kept running.

Being no amateur, she'd kept her weapon trained on him after the shot and led his movement again, this time compensating for his slower, stumbling pace. He was moving erratically now, the way he should have been before, and was impossible to target with any certainty. She would have to get closer to finish him off.

He's making me run.

He disappeared over the apex of the hill. Swearing under her breath, she lowered her weapon and took off running. Was this the fourth shooter from the New Year's Eve attack? She had a hard time believing Anatoly Tarmyenkin would have the gall to bring along the guy who'd try to kill her to a meeting with Yosef to discuss the attempt on her life. It would be too ironic.

She ran hard through the woods, thighs burning, hamstrings screaming. Her lungs were on fire, and she heaved in great gulps of frigid air. Lord, she hated running.

She topped a slight rise about where she'd first hit the sniper and spotted a line of blood spatter on a tree. She'd hit him, then. It had been possible he was faking being shot to lure her closer.

Rifle back by her cheek, she walk-ran forward, scanning the forest. When he'd gone behind this rise, he would've changed direction. Her money was on him heading for the zoo's perimeter. He would want to get out of this enclosed space as quickly as possible. She turned left and raced toward the nearest fence.

She spied a flash of beige camo clothing. He was almost to the fence. An employee parking lot stretched away beyond it. If he made it over the fence before she caught up enough to stop him, he would get away.

She ran hard, putting on a burst of speed. He reached the fence, and she was out of time. This was as good a shot as she was going to get. She estimated twenty-five yards. With all this tree cover, the wind correction would be negligible. It was basically a straight up shot.

He reached up to grab the iron fence bars and gathered himself to jump. She dropped to one knee and aimed high in the middle of his back. She pulled the trigger. He slammed forward into the fence and slid slowly down the iron grille toward the ground. Aiming carefully, she sent one more shot into the back of his head. She wanted there to be no chance of the sniper getting back up and taking a potshot at her.

His fists fell from the iron bars, and he slumped in a heap at the base of the fence. She had no need to move in to confirm the kill. She didn't miss stationary targets at this range.

Should she move in, however, and get a snapshot of his face for identification purposes? She eyed the parking lot beyond the fence warily. It was a public place, lots of people coming and going—no, she'd better not risk trying to get an ID on the Russian sniper. Besides, Yosef shouldn't have too much trouble finding out who the dead man was later, once local authorities found him.

She knelt quickly, doffing her pack and unscrewing the sound suppressor and barrel from the compact rifle. Her fingers were numb from the cold, so she fumbled as she folded the butt and stuffed all the parts into her pack. *Time to get out of here.* Sound suppressors minimized the boom of rifle shots but didn't entirely muffle them.

She stripped off her white camo outfit and reached into the backpack for the red raincoat. She shrugged into it and wrapped Nancy's scarf—the one that had saved her life—around her neck and over her lower face. Disguise wasn't about being invisible. It was about being expected. She raced back down the hillside, angling toward the American meadow she'd used when she first arrived at the meeting place.

A young couple was walking along the path. She crouched behind a tall clump of dead grass until they disappeared and she determined no one else was coming. Then, avoiding the low, swampy area, she raced down the hill to step onto the path.

She slowed immediately to a casual stroll and jammed her half-frozen hands into the pockets of her coat. The fabric was too thin for this cold, but at least it broke the wind.

It was a long walk to the front exit of the zoo, but she had come in that way wearing this red coat, and when police checked the surveillance footage later, they would match everyone leaving the zoo to whoever had come in. Schooling herself to patience, she hobbled toward the main exit with the gait of an elderly woman whose joints were feeling today's cold. It wasn't entirely an act.

The woman runner had finished her workout and was huddling in the lee of an information kiosk, stretching her legs. *Yep. Terrible idea to run in this kind of weather.* Muscles couldn't help but tighten up in this cold.

From behind her scarf, covering her face nearly to her eyes,

Helen watched alertly for any kind of raised alarm. Apparently, nobody had discovered Laser Tag Boy yet.

A pang of regret at killing the kid startled her. Normally, she didn't think twice about whomever she killed. They'd been deemed a threat to the United States and orders had come down from on high to eliminate the threat.

But the Russian behind her—he'd only been a threat to her. Still, he had taken a shot at her. He'd have killed her with a clean head shot had Nancy's scarf not chosen that moment to slip out of her grip.

It had been a kill-or-be-killed scenario. Operatives were allowed to go off script a bit when someone tried to take them out. Self-defense had always been authorized—

Of course, she wasn't an active operative, not anymore. Which she supposed technically made what she'd just done murder.

Funny, but she didn't feel any different about this killing than she did most of her other jobs. She should call them what they were. Killings. Her job had been to kill people. Bad people. And the kid behind her had made a very, very bad decision when he took that shot at her.

Unless, of course, someone had ordered him to take the shot.

Which opened a whole other can of worms.

Yosef was not going to be happy when she told him about this development.

She left the park but knew better than to let down her guard. Keeping to her hobbling gait, she saw that it was a long, cold walk to the nearest Metro stop, so she turned up her collar against the frigid air. Still, the bitter wind whooshed up the hem of her coat and crept up her sleeves. She didn't think she was ever going to be warm again.

About halfway to the Metro stop, she heard several police sirens in the distance. Had the dead man slumped inside the fence at the back of the National Zoo been spotted? She neither length-ened nor hurried her stride. There were closed-circuit cameras mounted on the light poles along this avenue, which, of course, she didn't look up at. She was just an old lady walking to the sub-way on a cold day.

She bought a one-way Metro pass with loose change and gratefully fell into a seat on the heated Metro train. She left on the hat
and scarf. If police asked anyone about her appearance, the loud
accessories would likely be all they remembered.

When she finally got home, she cleaned her weapon and stored
it with the rest of the tools of her trade in the small room hidden
at the back of the walk-in closet.

At long last, she stripped down and eased into a steaming hot
bath. She closed her eyes and let the water and blessed heat soak
away the terrible tension of the past few hours.

Odd, how, now that she considered herself retired, killing
someone bothered her this much. It was as if she'd set aside her
mental armor against the knowledge that she'd ended a human
being's life. She had no idea who he was, but Laser Tag Boy
would've had a family somewhere, or friends at least, who would
be devastated by his death.

Idiot shouldn't have taken that potshot at her.

She waved her hands back and forth slowly through the water,
concentrating on the flow of it over her skin. Would her family
miss her if she died? Or would they secretly be relieved that their
complicated and problematic relationships with her were ended?
She'd done her best over the years to make sure she was expend-
able in her children's lives, not because she didn't love them
fiercely, but precisely because she did. She'd needed to know they
would be okay and that their lives would carry on, largely unaf-
fected, if she died in the line of duty.

But now, it left her in the position of being more or less useless
to her family. One of the costs of her chosen profession. That and
the hard, ugly little knot of guilt low in her belly at killing the
Russian today. In her head she knew she'd had no choice, but apparently she'd grown a conscience since she retired. Or perhaps
she'd always had the conscience and it was simply choosing this
moment to reassert itself.

She laid her head back on the edge of the tub and closed her
eyes. Forcibly blanking out her mind, she soaked for long enough
to turn her entire body into a giant prune. She reheated the

water to as hot as she could stand, and eventually the warmth crept all the way to her bones.

Even then, after she got out and dressed in fleece-lined leggings and a thick sweater, she built a fire in the family room fireplace and huddled under a thick blanket while she pulled out a pad of paper and a pen.

She wrote down her last ten kills, which went back about two years. Surely, if someone was out to get revenge for her work, they'd have come after her within two years of the assassination.

She tried not to think about her targets as people. The US government had decided they needed to die, for whatever reason. If she didn't pull the trigger, someone else would. She was merely the sharp instrument of her country's foreign policy.

Contrary to popular belief, America didn't run around offing everyone who got in its way. It was actually pretty rare that kill orders were sent out. All of the names on her paper were bad, bad people who'd posed direct threats to the United States and/or to its citizens.

Six of the names were straight-up terrorists. She crossed them off because their terror cells were made up of zealots who would do their own revenge killing. They wouldn't have used the FSB or hired Eastern European assassins to take her down.

That left a Swedish neo-Nazi, a Chinese spy operating in Europe, and two Russians.

The Swede had been a young man, still in his early twenties. He'd been trying to get funding to come to America and kill outspoken liberal politicians. She highly doubted his buddies had the contacts or resources to hire four hitmen. She crossed him off her list.

The Chinese almost without exception used their own people for wet work. They were deeply distrustful of outsiders and rarely resorted to using contract killers. That name got crossed off as well.

Which left the two Russians. Anatoly's anemic denial of his government being the source of the hit added up to a high likelihood that one of these kills was the catalyst for the New Year's Eve attack. Had the sniper today also been under orders—or perhaps paid on the side—to kill her, or had he decided to exercise a little initiative and take her out after hearing she was retired and no longer protected by the agency?

She stared at the two remaining names.

Alexei Ibramov and Pyotr Sorkin.

Was one of them the source of a revenge assassination attempt? Or was something deeper afoot? When she took an assignment, she rarely got more than a photograph, a name, and a schedule of their known daily activities. It was not her job to know why an individual had been sanctioned.

In most cases, it became obvious to her in the course of scouting and eliminating her target. But not always. She actually knew very little about either man behind the two names staring up at her. Yosef would know more, however. Much more. He did most of the legwork of choosing where she would execute sanctions and how. Which meant he thoroughly researched all of her targets.

Executing sanctions. Such a civilized term for the messy, awful reality of killing another human being. She rarely stopped to think about her work for long. That way lay madness. Or at least a conscience-induced burnout. She was a tool of American foreign policy. A dangerous, sharp-edged tool. That was as far as she usually allowed herself to think.

Her job was to make the kill neatly, cleanly, efficiently, in a single swift stroke. Not to make her target suffer. Get in undiscovered, execute the mission, get out undiscovered. Period. She took professional pride in her work, took no joy in causing suffering, and moved on to the next assignment.

Oh, she'd had all the training and counseling over the years, heard all the warnings about sniper career flameouts and crises of morality. She'd taken all the tests looking for sociopathic or psychopathic tendencies and had passed them all with flying colors. She was a well-adjusted, reasonably normal human being with minimal psychological anomalies. She just happened to do an unusual job that few other people were capable of doing.

Did it come with a certain inherent mental toughness? Yes. Was she able to compartmentalize her emotions better than most? Of course. But did it make her a monster? She sincerely hoped not.

She tore off the top several pages of the notepad and tossed them into the fire, thoughtfully watching them burn.

CHAPTER 7

*R*EAL*D*A*V*INCI*K*ILLER*? S*ERIOUSLY*?*

The original DaVinci Killer glared at his computer screen in burgeoning rage. How dare this punk try to steal his glory—his name *and* his reputation—like some groveling sycophant? He was the greatest killer of all time, not this measly copycat. Re-creating great works of art in human flesh had been his invention. His signature. And now this wannabe had come along posting his crappy little Kandinsky killing as if he'd invented the freaking wheel?

He stabbed at his keyboard, hitting play, and watched the video again. Film editing technology had come a long way since he'd been actively killing in that style, of course. And the high-resolution images were better than what he'd been able to achieve with a handheld home movie camera back in the day. The soundtrack was a decent addition. Gave the video a more visceral impact—

But still. The jerk was a copycat.

And said jerk had chosen the wrong guy to copy.

Eyes narrowed in fury, he typed furiously at his computer. The first order of business was to ascertain the identity of this Real-DaVinciKiller. The guy would undoubtedly have covered his tracks. Even a moron would know to do that after posting videos of himself murdering a family of four. *Hmm.* US government channels could be risky to use to track down the copycat. But it would also be the fastest way to find out who this punk was.

He drummed his fingers on his desk as he considered options. Some of the top hackers in the world were in the Ukraine's Foreign Intelligence Service, the SZR. And they weren't likely to leave a trail if they went hunting for the copycat. What incentive to offer them though?

He thought through the intel briefings he'd seen over the past couple of months. About a month ago, he'd seen a piece of intel from a Russian double agent planted inside the SZR. If he burned the agent, the US would lose valuable intelligence on what the Ukrainians were up to. But he had to know the name of that cursed copycat. Not to mention, burning the mole would screw the Russians.

Opening the highly encrypted laptop he used for cruising the Dark Web, he initiated a VoIP—Voice over Internet Protocol— call to a contact within the SZR. It was early morning in Ukraine. He would undoubtedly wake up his contact, but tough.

A grumbling voice asked in Ukrainian, "What do you want?"

He answered in Russian. "It's your friend from Zurich." That was where they'd first met years ago.

The man at the other end was suddenly much more alert. "It has been a long time, my friend."

"Too long. I need a favor. And in return, I have a piece of information for you."

"What is this favor?"

"I need the identity of a killer. He posted a thrill kill video on the Dark Web a few hours ago. He staged it to look like a painting."

"Ah, yes. The Kandinsky killing. I was briefed on it last night. They're saying it's the return of the DaVinci Killer."

Rage roared through him, and it was all he could do not to scream in fury and swipe his arm across his desk, throwing everything off it in wrath. Fuming, he spoke between gritted teeth, "He is not the DaVinci Killer. He's a copycat."

"He's bound to have many layers of encrypted security between himself and his videos. He'll be tough to find. We might end up having to brute force his identity. That will take many resources. Much time and manpower . . . and money."

"I'm aware of this. And that is why I'm willing to offer you the identity of a Russian mole very high within your intelligence service." He left out the part where the mole was a double agent for the United States, of course.

"Indeed? How high?"

"High enough to know when your president takes a dump," he snapped. He added, coaxingly, "High enough that it'll make international news when you uncover this mole. It will embarrass and infuriate the Russians, not to mention cost them extremely valuable intelligence."

"Interesting. But if we know now that there's a mole, can we not find him or her ourselves?"

"Assuming the mole hasn't taken precautions to frame someone else for his or her leaks. Maybe you'll take down the right person, maybe not. It's your call." He dared not sound too eager to make the deal or his contact would squeeze him for even more than the name of the mole. It was what he would do in the same position.

"You have proof of this mole's existence?"

"Of course. We are both professionals. I know what proof is required to take out a mole, and I would not make this offer to you without it. I'll turn the proof over to you along with the mole's name when you give me the killer's name."

"Why are you coming to us? Surely, your own people can uncover the identity of this killer?"

"Undoubtedly. But let us be honest. We would like to stop this sick individual before he kills again, and your hackers are faster and more efficient than ours."

"True." The Ukrainian was silent, and he let the man think. "How will I contact you when my people have found your killer?"

He unwrapped a burner phone and gave his Ukrainian contact the number. They ended the call, and he put the burner phone in his shirt pocket. It would ring only once. But when it did, he would know the name of RealDaVinciKiller.

And then . . . then there would be a reckoning.

*   *   *

Helen stood on the narrow stoop and rang the doorbell. Everything about Yosef's Old Town Alexandria town house was narrow. The street it was on, the porch, the house itself. The tall town house had been his mother's, and he and his wife Ruth had moved in to care for her in her later years.

And then, of course, Ruth had gotten her devastating diagnosis of ALS, a degenerative nerve disease that had no cure and was always fatal. Helen knew that an elevator had been installed on the back of the house once Ruth became wheelchair bound. Near death now, she had a nurse with her during the day when Yosef was at work. At night, he insisted on caring for her himself.

It had been a terrible thing watching his wife gradually lose all control of her body as they waited for her to lose a vital life function and die. Helen pitied him the sad task. He rarely spoke of it though, and she honored his silence.

The front door opened and Yosef stood inside, swathed in shadow, well back from the door. Good operational security behavior.

As she ducked inside, the house held the musty funk of old age, and the medically antiseptic notes of a dying patient. Nothing had changed here since Helen could remember. Maybe the book shelves were more crowded, the flat surfaces more cluttered with old mail, political magazines waiting to be read, and piles of books. Always more books.

"How's Ruth?" she asked as he took her heavy wool coat from her and hung it on the overloaded coat stand just inside the front door.

"A little worse every day. Doctors say it won't be too much longer."

"I'm so sorry to hear that. Is she in pain?"

Yosef shrugged. "She's having trouble breathing. They've got her on oxygen full time now. I think that bothers her. But she hasn't had speech for a while, so she doesn't complain."

"That's cold humor."

"Ruth thinks it's funny."

"How are her spirits?"

"Hard to tell. She only communicates by blinking these days."

"How does she pass the time?"

"The nurse and I read to her a lot. And she likes to watch television. She sleeps a lot. She's asleep now."

She laid a hand on Yosef's arm, just for a moment. Touching was a boundary the two of them were generally very careful not to cross. They were both married, and nothing good could come of the attraction that had simmered between them for all these years. "I'm so sorry. For both of you."

He shrugged, mumbling, "God works in mysterious ways. And for some reason, he chose to deal Ruth a difficult hand of cards."

She wasn't sure she believed in God, but if doing so gave Yosef comfort, who was she to argue with him? And, for the record, she thought he'd been dealt a pretty difficult hand of cards, too.

"Thanks for inviting me over," she said in an effort to move to a happier topic. "Care to tell me why you wanted to meet here and not at your office?"

"There are ears everywhere at the campus."

"Are you saying the agency bugs your office?"

"They don't have to. There's listening technology so sensitive it can hear and record everything that goes on in a large building. They run the soundtrack through supercomputers to separate out the conversations, and voila, whole building surveillance without a single bug."

"What's to keep the government from recording entire neighborhoods of citizens?" she asked in dismay.

"Not a thing."

"Sometimes you scare me, Yossi."

He shrugged modestly. "Tea?"

"That would be lovely." She followed him into the tiny kitchen and they chatted about desultory things while he boiled water and steeped tea leaves in a blue, Tardis-shaped tea ball. He was such an adorable geek. They carried their mugs of tea back to the living room where Yosef was surrounded by his beloved books. He obviously felt most comfortable here.

Yosef sat in the armchair that matched hers, and she knew him well enough to read from his extreme stillness that he was both troubled and thinking hard. They sipped in silence for several minutes, both lost in their own thoughts. It was a tribute to the longevity of their friendship that they were comfortable in silence together like this.

Eventually, she set her half-finished mug of tea down and asked, "So, what couldn't you say to me at the office today about the attack at my son's house?"

"I may have a lead on the fourth attacker."

"Do tell." She leaned forward eagerly.

"A gentleman named Nikolai Ibramov was flagged on a CCTV feed outside a hotel in downtown DC the day before New Year's Eve. Your three corpses were all staying at that hotel. There's no footage of him going inside, and he wasn't registered at the hotel. But—"

She interrupted. "How is he related to Alexei Ibramov?"

He smiled ruefully. "You ruined my big reveal. Nikolai is Alexei's older brother. And the more dangerous of the two, I might add."

"Nikolai didn't happen to be the sniper at today's meeting at the zoo, did he?"

"I have no idea. Why?"

"Well, um, after you and Anatoly left, and I was egressing the zoo, the Russian sniper took a shot at me."

"He *what?*" Yosef set his tea mug down abruptly, sloshing tea on a book about foreign policy. He swiped absently at it with his palm. "Don't tell me you—"

"Afraid I did."

"Jeez, Helen. You're not an active officer for the company anymore. You can't just run around killing people like this!"

"He tried to kill me! A gust of wind yanked my scarf out of my hand and I lunged for it, which is the only reason he didn't kill me. I don't take attacks like that lying down. Never have, never will. You know I had to shoot back."

"Did you have to kill him, though?"

She huffed. "Do you seriously wish I'd missed? Gave him another shot to finish me off?"

Yosef sighed. He was silent a long time, and she let his formidable mind work on the problem. Finally, absently, he murmured, "I get that you had to kill him. But this complicates matters greatly."

"How?"

Another long-suffering sigh from him. "People at the office were not thrilled that you murdered three operatives who likely were working for the Russians, or at least for a faction within the Russian government. There was some talk of renditioning you."

"Renditioning me? For what? I defended myself from an attempted assassination! I don't deserve to be snatched up and tossed into some black site prison to rot for that!"

"We can't have former agents running around killing people."

"I don't run around killing people—" She broke off. "Well, okay. I ran around and killed that sniper in the zoo today. But I don't run around killing innocent civilians. Every person I've killed since I retired shot at me first."

"I know that. You know that. The senior brass knows that. But they don't like it when people who don't even work for them anymore cause them headaches."

"Then have the senior brass tell the Russians to freaking back off and let me live out my old age in peace."

"Helen, my dear. You were very good at your job. Our adversaries have greatly resented your successes over the years. You made enemies. A lot of them."

"I did my job. It was never personal. You know that."

"I do." He paused, then continued, "You were a consummate professional throughout your career. I need you to be that same professional, now."

As if, on the exact day she'd turned fifty-five, some switch had flipped inside her brain and she was suddenly a totally different person. "There's nothing magic about turning fifty-five, you know. The day before my birthday I was at the top of my field, and the day afterward, despite agency policy, I was not suddenly in my dotage."

"I wasn't suggesting otherwise. But I need you to work with me here."

"And do what?"

"Behave. Just a little."

"Who, me?" she retorted. "Since when?"

He sighed in resignation.

"You want me to take orders from an organization I no longer work for? An organization that is apparently willing to throw me to the wolves after my many years of exemplary service and may actually be trying to kill me?"

"Don't be bitter—"

"I am going to be bitter if the CIA's answer to two assassination attempts on me is to pat me on the head and say, 'There, there, Helen. You're being a hysterical female. Go home and crochet a doily.'"

Yosef winced, but thankfully he didn't argue with her. At length he said, "Fair enough. If you were a man who'd just retired from black ops, nobody would be telling you to take these attempts on your life lying down."

She did her best to win gracefully and merely asked, "What can you tell me about Nikolai Ibramov?"

"He ran with Chechen rebels as an infiltrator for the Russian government. Picked up some lethal tricks. His baby brother, Alexei, followed him into the Chechen brigades of his own volition. Alexei ran afoul of the Chechens—we don't know what he did. Best guess is he stole from them to fund a rather extravagant gambling habit.

"At any rate, Nikolai had to extract Alexei and blew his cover in the process. Alexei was a true believer, however, and went back to the Chechens. They wanted to kill him, but he volunteered to be a suicide bomber instead. He suggested targeting a major Western capital, and his boys were all over it. That's when you were sent in to eliminate him."

"Did we ever find out where he planned to target?"

"No. Best guess was a European capital."

"How did Nikolai end up here going after me then?"

"The FSB had to move him out of Russia after his cover with the Chechens was blown. They retrained him to work in North America, which I'm guessing he volunteered for after finding out who killed his baby brother. He arrived in New York a few months ago on a temporary work visa. He set up house in Brooklyn, got a job in a Russian import-export company, and was living the dream."

"Until he showed up in front of a hotel where the assassins from my son's house were staying."

"Correct."

As if Nikolai being at that hotel was the slightest coincidence at all. "Is he still in town?" she asked.

"Unknown."

"When will you know?" she demanded.

"The CIA is not all-seeing and all-knowing. These things take time."

"Have we got anyone inside the import-export company?"

Yosef answered, "It's a Russian mob outfit. They're tough to infiltrate."

She swore under her breath. "Is Nikolai full Bratva?" If he was a member of the Brotherhood and had its protection, killing him could have ugly implications. The Russian mob was known for taking messy revenge when its own were killed.

"Not to our knowledge. The Chechens wouldn't have let him get within a mile of them if he was. They only hate the Russian mob slightly less than they hate the Russian government."

"Well, yeah," she replied. "The Russian Brotherhood is full of old KGB types who got fired when Yeltsin emptied out the *Komityet* and put in his own loyalists whom he could control. Those old KGB types did a bang-up job of suppressing the Chechen cause when they were minding the shop."

"Exactly."

She leaned back in the wingback chair, thinking. "So, if Nikolai is still in DC, he's likely in touch with the Russian spy network in town. Any funny movements out of them recently?"

"Not my desk. I run Europe."

"Well, can you ask the North America desk for me?"

He sighed. "I can, but I'll have to be careful. The agency is not supposed to provide real-time intelligence to former operatives with itchy trigger fingers."

"I don't have an itch—"

"I know, I know," he interrupted gently. "But that's how my boss and his boss see you."

"How are Richard and Lester holding up, anyway?" Richard Bell was Yosef's direct boss, the deputy director of operations, and Lester Reinhold was the Director of Operations.

"Richard is his usual cold-as-ice self."

She snorted. "I don't think I've ever seen that man smile. In fact, now that I think about it, I'm not sure I've ever seen him blink. Are we sure he's not a lizard? Or a robot?"

Yosef smiled a bit. "Not entirely. As for Lester Reinhold, he's jockeying hard to be considered for DCI when the current Director of Central Intelligence retires."

"And when is that supposed to happen?"

"Rumor has it the director will bail out as we head into the first primary elections."

"Maybe Reinhold will have a little more spine than the current DCI," she commented.

"Not likely. Lester's a political creature. So's Richard Bell, for that matter."

"Bell?" she blurted, surprised. "He strikes me as a numbers twink. Just the facts, ma'am."

"Nah. There's more to him than meets the eye. Gives me the creeps sometimes."

That made her stare. Under his mild exterior, Yosef had nerves of tempered steel. She'd never seen anything or anyone who could rattle the man. "Bell creeps you out? How? Why?"

"I dunno. There's something . . . off . . . about him. He's too cold. Too calculating."

She picked up her tea and took a sip of the now tepid brew. "It's not as if the agency doesn't hire a lot of cold, calculating people. A little sociopathy is a good thing in our profession, is it not?"

Yosef shrugged. "Personally, I prefer to think a little humanity is a good thing in our line of work."

"Ah, you were ever the starry-eyed idealist. And that's why I love you," she said lightly.

He smiled warmly at her. She met his gaze for just an instant of shared understanding, and then looked away.

"Yosef, I need to ask you a favor. And you're going to tell me you can't do it, but I need you to find a way."

He released a pained sigh. He clearly knew as well as she did that he would find a way to do whatever she asked of him. He asked, defeated once more, "What's the favor?"

"I need you to protect my family."

"There's no way! Not only are you retired, but you have three children, a husband, a mother, and significant others for your kids."

"And a puppy," she added.

He rolled his eyes and went silent, thinking. She didn't disturb him.

"What I might—*might*, mind you—be able to pull off is some security surveillance on your house. Since the attack on you was possibly retaliation for an agency-sanctioned operation, we could plausibly owe you protection from the fallout."

She huffed. "They came into my son's home, guns blazing!"

"I know. But I can only swing protection for you. Invite your kids to your house so they'll fall under the umbrella of the protection I set up for you."

"As if they'd come stay with me. I'm Satan's handmaiden to my kids, remember?"

"Give them time. Now that you're retired and can spend quality time with them, they'll come around."

If only. "I get that a team on my house may be all you can pull off. I'll take it. But can you at least arrange for someone to drive by Mitch and Nancy's house, and the condo where Peter and Liang will be staying until their house is fixed?"

"That's easy. I'll make a call to the local police. I can probably arrange for cruisers to park out on a daily basis, too."

It wasn't full-out bodyguard-style protection, but it was a far sight better than nothing. "Thank you, Yosef."

He nodded. "I know how important your family is to you."

"Well, it's getting late. Thank you for the tea," she murmured. She moved to the front hallway to collect her coat and said, "Give Ruth my love. And take care of yourself, my old friend."

"You do the same."

She reached for the front door, but something stopped her. Call it instinct or maybe old habits kicking in again.

"What's wrong?" Yosef asked quickly from behind her.

"I don't know. Stay back from the door and windows."

She eased into the living room and slipped close to the long drapes to peer outside.

"Do you see anything?" Yosef asked in a hush.

"No. But I wouldn't expect to. The Russians are not slouches at surveillance."

"You're sure it's Russians?"

She shrugged. "Unless it's Americans, the Russians have the best tradecraft of the possible candidates for who's out there. Always assume the worst. Isn't that what you preach to me?"

"It is." A pause. "Do you need me to call the agency for support?"

"I don't work for the agency anymore, remember?"

"I do. And my wife is upstairs."

She appreciated the fact that he believed her intuition, no questions asked. She murmured, "Make the call. I'm going to slip out the back way. Maybe I can lead them away from here."

"Whoever them is," Yosef muttered as he pulled out his cell phone and made a quick, quiet call.

When he finished, she murmured, "If you could go into the kitchen, darling, and try to act natural as you turn off the lights, that would be immensely helpful."

"You think they'll have someone out back, too? Shouldn't you wait to slip away until help arrives?"

She smiled tightly at him. "Oh, I'm not slipping away. I'm going hunting."

"Helen. You're not an active operator anymore."

"They attacked me in my son's house. They're outside your house, now, Yosef, where your invalid wife is asleep. Whoever is out there has made this very, very personal to me."

Yosef stared at her a moment longer. Then, "Do you have a weapon?"

She glared at him from under her eyebrows. "Is the pope Catholic?"

"I'm a good Jewish boy. I wouldn't know."

Smiling a little, she moved away from the window and headed quickly down the hallway into the kitchen with Yosef in trail. As soon as he'd turned off the lights, she slipped into the kitchen beside him and handed over her car's key fob to him. "If you wouldn't mind driving my car to your Metro stop tomorrow, I'll ride over and pick it up."

He pocketed the fob without comment.

"Lock the door behind me, and you might want to fetch whatever firearm you have in the house. Just in case."

With that, she slipped outside into the tiny backyard. She was still achy from running around in the zoo, so she moved slowly, skirting along the high fence in the shadows. She eased open the back gate and slipped into the cobblestone alley.

Once away from Yosef's house, she moved quickly, racing down the block in a half crouch, pistol at the ready in front of her. Her back complained at the bent-over posture, but there was no help for it. She reached the end of the alley and scanned the street before her. It was quiet, but her gut jumped and twisted.

It would be of no use to disguise herself. On a street this deserted, any half-competent Russian operative would assume that whatever woman walked away from Yosef's home was her. She would have to rely on stealth and speed. Neither of which came so easily to her anymore.

She straightened and slipped around the corner, keeping her back plastered against a brick wall as she eased toward the next street. She paused, crouching beside a line of hedges, to check for movement. All was quiet. She raced across the street, running lightly on the balls of her feet. Her shoes had soft rubber soles and made no noise as she ran hard for several more blocks. The cold air made her lungs tight, and she gulped in great gasping breaths, cursing herself for not keeping up her regimen of jogging daily since she'd retired.

She turned the corner and paused by a delivery truck, ducking between its bumper and a car to catch her breath and check for followers. She waited while a car drove past, its headlights not revealing any potential followers.

She looked around, got her bearings, and headed for a commercial district of Alexandria, checking over her shoulder continuously. Either she was clear or her followers were better than she was.

Although Old Town's streets were mostly deserted on this cold night, the restaurants and bars were open and busy. She slipped into an Irish pub with a live band that was raucously loud and faded into a dark corner. She phoned for a ride share, and when it arrived, slipped outside as unobtrusively as she'd entered.

In an abundance of caution, she didn't have the driver take her directly home. Rather, she had him drop her off near the L'Enfant Plaza Metro stop where four Metro lines came together. She zigzagged all over inside the underground station and in the relatively well-lit space decided she definitely wasn't being followed.

Finally, she took the red line north toward her house. Once in Rockville, she had to wait a while for a ride share to pick her up, but at nearly midnight, she finally made it home.

She *would* get her normal life back. Even if it meant hunting down Nikolai Ibramov and taking him out herself.

CHAPTER 8

*H*ELEN STARED AT THE SHABBY BRICK BUILDING IN FRONT OF HER. It looked straight out of the Industrial Revolution, complete with a thick layer of soot over its tired reddish façade. The left half of the ground floor was occupied by a pizzeria, closed at the moment. The right side was occupied by a Chinese restaurant that was already open, even though it was barely 9:00 a.m. The two were separated by a stairwell that led upward into the bowels of the three-story structure.

She looked down at the address in her phone that Mitch had texted to her. This was definitely the place. Surely the attorney he'd sent her to see didn't work out of the back of a takeout joint.

She stepped inside the Chinese restaurant and called out over the blaring Asian pop music, "Excuse me, I'm looking for Angela Vincent!"

"Upstairs," a male voice shouted from the kitchen.

"Thanks!" At the top of the first flight of stairs was a small landing with a single door. The frosted glass pane was painted with plain black letters: ANGELA VINCENT, ATTORNEY-AT-LAW.

She pushed open the door and had to smile. It was as if she'd walked into a time warp or onto the set of *The Maltese Falcon*. The floors were linoleum, the desks oak and oversized. Metal filing cabinets filled one wall, and a no-kidding radiator clanked and hissed under the far window, which would look out on the street below.

The Black woman who looked up from the desk by the radiator could be forty years old or sixty. Her eyes were sharp, and Helen felt thoroughly scrutinized as she made her way to the desk. Only when she reached it did the woman stand and hold out her hand.

"I'm Angela Vincent. How can I help you?"

No nonsense, this woman.

"My name is Helen Warwick. My son, Mitchell Warwick, asked me to come speak with you."

"Are you in legal trouble?"

"No, ma'am. My son wanted me to speak with you about a pattern you've seen in certain cases over the past year or two—"

"The ADA sent his mommy to talk with me?"

Helen was taken aback, but she saw the woman's point. "I'm recently retired from the State Department. An analyst. Mitchell thought I could visit with you. Hear you out. Give him my impressions. He's in a rather delicate position, working for the DA and reviewing his boss's cases behind his back."

The attorney snorted. "Office politics. The reason I refuse to join a large law firm."

"Mitch says you're one of the toughest defense attorneys in DC. Which is high praise coming from my son."

"Your son isn't half bad himself, in a courtroom."

Helen smiled. It wasn't often she got to be a proud mama, and it felt good. She looked forward to doing more of it once the mess with the Russians was sorted out.

She gazed around the retro-throwback office with curiosity. It was plain. Utilitarian. Ugly, even. It stood at complete odds with Mitch's assessment and her own impression of this woman as an exceedingly sharp person. "Why does a lawyer of your caliber choose to work in a place like this?"

"Call it remembering where I came from. I started out in this office twenty-five years ago. Only difference is now I own the building and I installed decent air-conditioning."

A woman of character, too. Impressive.

"Also, my clients tend to feel more comfortable in a space like this than a plush corner suite belonging to a partner in a bougie law firm."

"What's upstairs?" Helen asked.

"An apartment. I stay there sometimes if I'm working late on a case."

"Do you mind if I sit?" Helen asked.

"Please." Angela also took her seat in a high-end ergonomic chair.

"My son is concerned about what you've found. Enough to risk his career to look into it, which is no small thing."

Angela rolled her eyes. "Your boy's an ambitious one, all right. He's gonna go places if he can keep his nose clean."

"Hence me sitting here as his surrogate. So. What's this pattern you've found in your cases?"

Angela leaned back, studying her hard for several seconds, and Helen waited her out. Either the woman chose to trust her or she didn't.

Abruptly, the lawyer began talking. "I've represented four murder cases over the past sixteen months where my client was found guilty of a crime they swore on their mother's grave they didn't commit. Thing is, the evidence was so neatly sewn up there was no way I could get them acquitted."

"And you're certain your clients weren't lying?"

Angela planted her forearms on her desk and stared Helen down with disconcerting intensity. "I'm an excellent judge of character. And I routinely represent clients who are lying through their teeth. I make no apology for that. It's how our justice system works. Even the guilty ones should get the best representation available."

Sensing a test, Helen said evenly, "I agree."

"Not one of my four clients in question was a saint. But I'm convinced—*convinced*—they were all framed for murders they didn't commit."

"Were there similarities in how the murders were committed?" Helen asked, interested in spite of herself. The woman's passion for her clients' innocence was tangible. She could see why Angela was great in a courtroom in front of a jury.

"The killings were all ADWs—assaults with deadly weapons. All at night, all without witnesses. My clients were lured to a location, heard a gunshot, and saw someone fall in front of them. When they ran to the victim to see if they could help, cops arrived with shocking speed to arrest them."

"How do the police explain your clients not having the murder weapon on them?"

"Funny thing. The murder weapons all magically appeared close to where my clients were standing when they heard the shots."

"You think the police planted them?"

"Whoever framed my clients planted them. Whether that was the police or not, I can't comment." Her gaze was hard. Suspicious.

"Okay. So I need to look into how the weapons appeared." Helen thought for a second. "Were any of your clients able to tell what direction the gunshots came from?"

"One thought the shot came from behind him. The others were too startled by the shot itself to register where the sound came from."

In her experience, if a gunshot went off directly behind a person, they knew where the sound had come from no matter how startled they were. It was darned hard to miss the direction of an explosion of that magnitude. If three of the clients couldn't tell where the shot had come from, the shooter had probably done something to obfuscate the direction of the shot.

Thinking out loud, Helen said, "If I were setting up someone, I would let them walk almost directly into the line of fire between myself and the victim. Then, I would shoot past your client— around them, or over their head or shoulder, depending on my elevation. My target drops. Your client races forward. I race in behind your client to where he or she was standing when I took the shot, and I drop the weapon nearby. Toss it in a trash can or mailbox or down a drain. Make it hard enough for the police to find that they don't suspect a plant."

Angela tilted her head, studying her intently. "Continue."

"Range from your client would have to be carefully calculated. I would want to be close enough behind your client that I wouldn't have a long run to plant the weapon. I would want to get to the spot where I dumped the gun and also leave the area before your client reached the victim, figured out they were dead, and looked up from the body in search of the shooter or to shout for help."

"So you're saying the real killer was close behind my clients."

"How loud did your clients say the shots were?"

"One—the guy who said the shot came from behind him—said it was very loud."

It was Helen's turn to lean back thoughtfully. "I'll bet that was the first murder."

"That's correct." A hint of surprise was audible in the lawyer's voice.

Helen nodded. "The killer learned from his mistake in giving away his location. Were the last three murder weapons outfitted to accept sound suppressors?"

Angela's eyebrows sailed up. "I have no idea."

"Can you find out?"

Angela stood up and went over to one of a half dozen filing cabinets lining one wall. She opened a drawer and pulled out a thick stack of files.

"Paper? Really?" Helen murmured.

"I'm old-school."

"I'll say." She was intrigued that Angela didn't hand over any of the files to her but instead set aside the top one and opened the second one herself. The lawyer didn't trust her, did she? Or was she just being careful about attorney-client privilege?

"Murder weapon in this case was an HK-45," Angela announced.

"Regular or tactical version?"

"How the heck would I know?" the lawyer snapped.

"Is there a picture of it in there?"

The attorney thumbed through the papers and eventually passed over a picture. The photograph was almost life-sized and showed a stocky, square pistol. A distinctive threaded barrel extension jutted out from the blunt nose of the weapon.

Helen picked up the photo and tilted it toward the window. "This little threaded extension, here," she said, pointing to it, "means it's a tactical version of this particular weapon. You screw a sound suppressor onto the threads." She pointed again. "See here, where a little silver shows through the black finish? The threads are worn. A sound suppressor was used on that weapon at some point. Maybe not in your shooting, but it could've been."

"Meaning what?"

"Meaning the killer could've been standing within a few dozen yards of your client, and he or she wouldn't get any accurate sense of how close the weapon actually was."

"He," Angela supplied. "All four of my clients are men."

Helen nodded. "Some sound suppressors can actually throw the sound of the shot off to one side by a dozen yards or more, as well."

"And how do you know that, Mrs. Warwick?"

How, indeed. Because she had such a sound suppressor, custom-made for her short-range sniper rifle. "Retired government analyst, Ms. Vincent."

"Call me Angela," the lawyer said absently, staring at the picture of the weapon she passed back across the desk.

"And I'm Helen."

The lawyer asked, "How long does it take to detach one of these sound suppressors?"

"Three seconds if you're in a hurry and you're wearing gloves."

"Gloves?"

"The barrels of weapons and sound suppressors get hot when bullets pass through them at high speed. It typically takes multiple shots in fast succession to heat up a pistol, but a sound suppressor heats up noticeably after a single shot. You need gloves to grasp one immediately after shooting through it."

"Ah."

"Shooter would probably be gloved, anyway. I'm assuming no prints were found on the murder weapons?"

"None."

"How did the prosecutors explain that at trial?"

"They claimed my clients wiped off the weapons before tossing them."

"That's pretty calculating for a random crime in the middle of a street," Helen commented.

"I argued that but couldn't get traction with juries on the point."

"Did any of your clients feel the shot go past them? A whiff of air on their faces or ears, maybe?"

"Not that they told me."

"Hmm."

"What are you thinking, Helen?"

"Streets in urban areas are fairly narrow, confined spaces. If I put a shooter at one end of a street, the victim at the other end, and your client in the middle, the angle at which the shooter would have to shoot around your client to still hit the victim is pretty difficult. And given that these were one-shot kills—which are tough under the best of conditions—the shot was even harder to make."

"Meaning what?"

"Were there two-story or taller buildings near where your clients stood during the shootings?"

"You think the shooter was in a building, shooting down?"

"It would solve the problem of shooting around your clients."

"Then how does the shooter get downstairs, out the door, plant the weapon, and hide or run away before my client looks up from the body?"

"I don't know. But answering that question may be the key to explaining how the real shooter got away with the crime and framed your clients. Assuming, of course, that the same shooter perpetrated all of these crimes."

"You think that four killings happened in the exact same way, and it was random chance?" Angela blurted, sounding surprised.

"I'll keep an open mind until I know more about each crime scene. Speaking of which, do you have photographs of the crime scenes in your files?"

Angela pulled out a half dozen photos of the crime scene that went along with the HK-45, and Helen examined them while Angela dug out the types of murder weapons from the last two case files.

Helen put down the pictures in disappointment. "I can't see enough of the surrounding terrain to tell if there was a decent spot for the shooter to have set up shop and work out of."

She caught Angela's quizzical glance. *Oops.* Mustn't sound like too much of a sniper herself. She asked quickly, "Have you found the other murder weapons?"

"A Beretta M9 and a Glock 17."

"Both have tactical versions that take sound suppressors. Do you have pictures of the murder weapons?"

"Not in my files. But I can request them from the police. If you don't mind my asking, how do you know so much about guns?"

Helen shrugged. "I negotiated a couple of trade deals for the US to sell weapons to foreign militaries."

Angela pursed her lips. Whether that was skepticism or something else, Helen couldn't tell. By way of distracting the lawyer from whatever she was speculating on, Helen asked quickly, "How soon will the police get back to you on what models of weapon were used in the other murders?"

Angela snorted. "These are closed cases. Unless it gets real slow down at DC Metro, it'll be weeks. I've got a contact down there, though. I might be able to hurry it along a little."

"What kinds of rounds were used in the killings?" Helen asked.

"Guess."

"Multi-trocar hollow points," she answered immediately. "Best killing rounds deliverable by handgun. If you need to drop a target with a single shot, that would be the go-to round. Am I right?"

"G2-RIPs," Angela responded.

"Ha. I was right!" she exclaimed. "Nasty round. The tip is divided into eight sharp-tipped metal petals, the trocars. They fold back on impact and rip through flesh, causing massive injury and bleeding."

"What kind of analyst *were* you?" Angela demanded.

"Foreign trade and tariffs," she answered mildly.

"Riiight."

Time for another rapid distraction. "Let's assume for now all three of the latter shootings used tactical weapons with sound suppression. If you'll give me the addresses where all four shootings occurred, I'd like to take a look at the terrain around them."

Angela threw her a skeptical look. "None of the shooting scenes are in great parts of town."

"I can handle myself."

"Interesting choice of words," the lawyer commented lightly. Too lightly.

Drat. Helen kept talking as if she was at work, when she was supposed to be Mitchell's innocent, retired mother. She never slipped up on a cover—her life routinely depended on it. She must be more rusty than she'd realized.

"Also, do you have some sort of diagram of who was standing where?"

"I do." Angela dug out black-and-white stick sketches with a victim and her client marked on each in relation to the nearest street intersections. "Let me make you copies of these." She walked over to an old-fashioned copier the size of a washing machine and ran copies of the four sketches. Helen took the drawings and noted that the streets were named on all the drawings.

"I'll take a look at these scenes and get back to you."

"You do that, Helen. And"—a pause—"thank you."

"My pleasure."

CHAPTER 9

*H*ELEN SCANNED THE STREET CORNER BELOW, REFERRING TO THE drawing beside her of where the victim had been standing and where the gunshot had come from. She matched the sketch to the physical reality below her with a practiced eye. As she'd suspected, the street was lined on both sides by two- and three-story tall buildings, most with flat roofs that would provide a perfect perch for a sniper.

Now, how to figure out how the shooter got down to the street fast enough to plant the murder weapon and flee. One city block typically was around a hundred yards long. If the murder victim was, say, one block from the person framed for the murder, a typical person might run that distance in something like thirty seconds. Give it another ten seconds to examine the victim, figure out they were dead, and think to look around for help.

That meant a shooter had about forty seconds to get down off the roof, plant the murder weapon, and get out of sight. Not enough time to run inside, run downstairs, duck outside, plant the weapon, and get back undercover.

If it were left to her, she would park near an alley and use it to flee—

Her train of thought derailed as a man started shouting on the street corner below about the deep state conspiracy to take away his life from him. Sympathy for the mentally ill man made her

turn her scope on him. Maybe she could help him get to the nearest homeless shelter where someone could point him to some
medical or psychological care.

Idly, she noted the pedestrians passing by. Most were pointedly
ignoring the ranting man. One guy was watching with some interest from across the street though.

First, to finish up here. Then, if the homeless man was still
there when she went down to the street, she'd try to help him.

Picking up her train of thought from before, she finished it this
time. If it were up to her to get off this roof fast, she would set up
a rappelling line. She glanced around at this roof and the neighboring ones she could see. All of them had something a rappelling line could be attached to—an air-conditioning unit, a
structure housing a stairwell, or a water tank. An alley to jump
down into would give more cover. . . . She looked around and saw
an alley across the street a few doors down. If the shooter had
been on that building over there, the shot would be pretty
straightforward. At least it would for a half-decent sniper.

She started a stopwatch on her cell phone. Then, as it ticked
off the seconds, she pretended to aim and take the shot down the
street, run over to the edge of the roof, clip an imaginary rappelling harness onto a pre-hung line, and step off the roof. She
counted in her head to ten. It probably wouldn't take more than
a few seconds to make the drop to the ground, but she gave it a
full ten seconds to be conservative.

Land in the alley. Unclip. Step out into the street, toss the murder weapon down that rain drain just to the right of the alley exit.
Duck back into the alley.

She looked at her watch. Twenty-nine seconds.

Totally doable.

Interesting. She went back over to her previous vantage point
and packed up her spotter's scope and drawings. She glanced
down at the street corner where the homeless man was shouting
obscenities at Uncle Sam. The observer who'd shown interest in
him before was still watching the ranter. In fact, he'd crossed the
street and was now filming the homeless man. *Odd.*

She made her way to the stairwell and raced down it, timing it for grins and giggles.

Fifty-one seconds to run down three stories of steps. No way had the shooter egressed from his sniper's nest via stairs. She was liking her rappelling theory even more.

An excellent sniper who knew how to rappel. Sounded ex-military, this killer.

She stepped outside and looked around. *Huh.* The guy shouting on the corner had disappeared. Still, she headed for the corner to look for him. There he was. Far end of the block. Just emerging from a bodega with a bottle of liquor.

She fell in behind him and hurried to catch up with him.

It only took a dozen steps for her to realize that the guy who'd been filming the homeless man was ahead of her now and was also following the homeless man. *Another Good Samaritan out to help him, maybe?*

Except the hackles tickling the back of her neck said otherwise.

Perplexed, she slowed down to trail both men from a little farther back.

The homeless man was in a hurry to get back to his tent to get drunk, apparently. She lost sight of him as he ducked into the sprawling shantytown that took up most of a vacant city block. Someone grabbed at her arm, and she snatched her wrist away, checking to make sure her watch was still on it.

A woman with a marked lack of teeth mumbled, "Got a few bucks, lady?"

"I'll be back in a minute. First I have to find someone. A guy who just passed here with a bottle of booze."

The woman shrugged, her own eyes clouded and unfocused.

Helen looked around quickly. *Darn it.* She'd lost both men. She plunged into the haphazard collection of tents, shacks, boxes, and cobbled-together shelters.

She crisscrossed the whole place and was near the far side of it when she spied a man lying on the ground—not that it was at all remarkable here, she'd learned—but another man was crouching over him. As she started toward the pair, the second man hoisted the first one up by the shoulders and commenced dragging him.

Her internal warning system fired hard, and she broke into a run toward the men.

She tripped on something, maybe a leg that someone stuck out to hinder her, and she let out a cry of surprise as she staggered and nearly went down.

The dragger looked up, dropped his unconscious companion, and took off running at high speed. If he was also a homeless man, he was in superb physical condition for one. She sprinted forward, toward where the fallen man lay in a heap. She started to hurdle over him in pursuit of the other man but caught a dark stain on the ground out of the corner of her eye.

She screeched to a halt.

That was blood soaking into dirt. She would recognize it anywhere.

She yanked out her cell phone and dialed 911 as she dropped to her knees. Setting the phone down beside the prone man, she yelled toward her phone as she searched for the source of the blood. "I need an ambulance at the homeless camp at . . ." she said, looking around frantically, "about three blocks east of . . ." she managed, rattling off the intersection she'd been checking out before. "I'm at the southeast corner of the encampment."

"What's the nature of the medical problem?" the emergency operator asked.

Helen rolled the man onto his back. That was when she spied the small, neat cut in the man's hoodie sweatshirt a little above his belly button and toward his heart. Just the spot where a knife, slipped under the ribs and angled up sharply, would pierce the bottom of the heart. It was a lethal technique that caused a quick and inevitable bleed-out.

"Stabbing," she called toward her phone. She pressed both hands over the man's chest in what she knew to be a futile effort to stem the flow of blood. It would take a swift surgeon cutting the guy open fast to get direct pressure on the punctured heart wall while a surgical team transfused a whole bunch of blood into the guy's veins to save this man. And she was neither a surgeon nor did she have a half dozen pints of blood to toss into him.

She kept up the pressure until a pair of EMTs jogged toward her and took over, but her victim was dead well before she heard the first siren.

She stood back, her hands barely bloodied. Once she'd rolled the victim off his side where the cut had been, toward the ground and able to leak, all his remaining hemorrhaging would have been inside his chest cavity. Talk about an efficient killing. Even she was impressed.

As the medics arrived at the same conclusion she had, and one of them went back to the ambulance to get a gurney to haul away the dead man, she asked around the crowd of bystanders, "Did anybody see a guy following this man just before he was stabbed?"

Nobody copped to having seen a thing.

She tried to think back to what the man watching this guy had looked like. She'd been too far away to get a clear look at him. Caucasian, brown hair, average height, average build. That was all she had. Not nearly enough to catch the guy.

She turned back to the EMTs as they got ready to wheel away the dead man. "Do you want me to contact the police? Give a statement?"

"Nah. They won't investigate this. Stuff like this happens all the time in shantytowns. Folks here'll shiv you for a few swigs of wine or because they went off their meds and think you've grown a second head. It'll be a miracle if the medical examiner can even ID this guy."

Saddened by the man's death, and the fact that he would probably get no justice for being murdered, she turned and headed back toward her car.

CHAPTER 10

*H*ELEN PICKED UP HER RINGING PHONE, STARTLED TO SEE MITCH identified as the caller. "Why, hello, darling. To what do I owe this pleasant surprise?"

"Nancy and I want to invite you over for supper tonight. Now that you're retired and will be around more, we thought we should spend more time with you."

"That, and you want to know what I found out from Angela Vincent?" she added dryly.

"That, too."

"Can I bring anything?"

"Good Lord, no," he blurted. Of all her children, he was the only one old enough to remember her disastrous attempts to become a decent home cook when he was little. Clearly, she still had work to do raising her domestic goddess game.

"When should I be there?" she asked.

"Six o'clock?"

"Perfect. See you then." *Good.* She had a few hours to get home, wash off the blood from the dead man, and make sure she had every speck of it out from under her fingernails.

She showed up at Mitch's door just as the antique hall clock inside struck six o'clock, faintly. She rang the doorbell, and her daughter-in-law, Nancy, opened the door. They hugged, and Helen held out the bottle of wine she'd agonized over for longer than she cared to admit. Not only did she have to decide between red or white, but domestic or foreign, aged or young, expensive or modest. If only every last little thing with her family wasn't so fraught with tension and judgment.

"Mitch is on the phone with the DA. Some emergency with a case that's being tried," Nancy said. "He'll join us in a bit."

Crud. She had possibly less to talk about with her daughter-in-law than with Mitch. Casting about for some topic of conversation, she glanced into the living room opening off the narrow foyer.

"Is that a new highboy? It's gorgeous!" She stepped into the living room and Nancy followed, talking enthusiastically about her latest antique find.

Honestly, she didn't understand what Mitch saw in Nancy. She was a lovely woman, a polished hostess, kind and warm. But she was so bland. She never made waves, never argued, never lost her perfect poise. Sure, she was the perfect politician's wife. But would she ever really make Mitch happy? He was so much more dynamic and fiery a personality, and surely some of that translated into his personal desires and taste in women.

While she had no desire whatsoever to know anything about her son's sex life, she had to assume he was bored out of his mind with his wife if she was the same in bed as she was outside of it.

Her own marriage might have plenty of fatal flaws, but her and Gray's sex life was not one of them. Too bad she hadn't been around when Mitch met Nancy to warn him of the importance of finding someone he was sexually compatible with. Although knowing him, he would've gone ahead and married her anyway. He was hell-bent to attain elected office.

The whole house was decorated in Federalist period antiques: the scraped hardwood floors, gas lights flickering in wall sconces, the extensive collection of plain furnishings that made the front parlor feel like a stern museum. Personally, Helen found it off-putting. She didn't like the spare, wood-dominated style of the era. Not a single chair in this room looked inviting, let alone comfortable. It was all too . . . Puritan . . . for her.

"Mother. Thank you for joining us on such short notice," Mitch said, sweeping into the room expansively. *Ugh.* He was in full politician mode.

Helen pasted on a fake smile. "Nancy was just telling me about the new highboy. It's a beautiful piece."

"Your mother brought a lovely bottle of wine, Mitchell. Maybe you'd open it for us?"

"Of course." Mitch took the bottle of wine out of Helen's hand without quite meeting her gaze. Lord, she hated this distance between herself and her kids.

She and Nancy followed Mitch into their blessedly more modern kitchen. And yet it was still dominated by wood and a huge brick fireplace in some sort of a neo-modern homage to iron pots hanging over wood fires. Frankly, she thought the notion of cooking in the 1700s sounded like miserable, back-breaking labor.

"Can I help with the meal, Nancy?" she asked.

"No, no. Everything's ready to go. I just have to plate it up and serve. Easy as pie."

She did have to admit, Nancy was an effortless and excellent party planner—a vital skill for a future politician's wife.

Helen spied the table in the dining room beyond the kitchen and counted five place settings. "Oh. Is someone joining us?"

"Why, yes—" Nancy started.

The doorbell rang just then, and Mitch hustled out of the room. Male voices and laughter came from the foyer, and Helen winced. Peter and Li had arrived. *Welp.* Wasn't this awkward?

Peter scowled fiercely as he came into the kitchen and saw her standing on the other side of the island. "Mother. I didn't know you were coming."

"I wasn't aware you and Li would be coming, either. Although, I'm delighted you're here," she added by way of conciliation.

Li came into the kitchen holding Biscuit in his arms. "We're taking him everywhere with us to socialize him," Li explained.

"My granddog!" she exclaimed, moving over to the puppy and

scooping him out of Li's grasp. "Look how big you're getting!" She nuzzled his fuzzy head and hugged his squirmy little body close. He wiggled happily and licked her chin eagerly. "Do you remember me?" she cooed. "I remember you, my brave little man."

She glanced up and caught Mitch and Peter trading rolled eyes. "What?" she demanded.

"Seriously, Mother? It took a dog to bring out your maternal instincts?" Peter grumbled.

"I have plenty of maternal instincts, thank you very much. I just had a job that forced me to travel a great deal. I did my best whenever I was home to be there for you children."

Peter snorted, Li elbowed Peter, and Mitch made a noncommittal sound. Nancy, the consummate diplomat, said smoothly, "Why don't we all sit down and I'll bring over the food."

Peter and Li fussed over unfolding and setting up a portable kennel for Biscuit while she moved over to the table and took the chair Mitch indicated beside him. Thankfully, Li took the chair on her right, undoubtedly to act as a buffer against Peter's hostility.

The food was wonderful, and the conversation turned to Washington gossip and current events.

She let the conversation wash over her while she registered that this was how normal people lived. They sat in a house without watching the windows warily for movement outside. They put their backs to doors and hallways without a second thought. They left their firearm in their purse on a counter across the room and weren't jumpy about it being out of instant reach. Strike that. They didn't have a firearm in their purse at all.

Maybe she had further to go to achieve normalcy than she'd realized.

Near the end of the meal, Liang startled Helen by saying, "Have you guys heard about the murder that's gone viral on the internet?"

Please God, let me not be involved with it—

Okay, she had a lot further to go to achieve normalcy.

Liang continued, "There are these sites on the Dark Web called thrill kill websites. Murderers film their kills and the bodies after killings and post them. My office at NSA monitors some of them."

"Do you help catch the killers?" Nancy asked, wide-eyed.

Li shrugged. "Sometimes. At any rate, this new killing was just posted. The guy re-created a famous modern art painting, except he used body parts to do it. It was actually pretty spectacular. He blew up a house with the family inside of it."

"Has anyone figured out where this explosion took place?" Helen asked.

"The video matches a house that blew up on the Eastern Shore of Maryland on New Year's morning."

"It happened so close to here?" she exclaimed in alarm. "And there were people inside the house when it blew up? That's awful!"

"Family of four. Husband, wife, and two kids. They'd lived in the house less than two months."

"And the cause of the explosion?" Helen asked.

"Unknown," Li answered. "I took a look at the police and fire investigations. They found no gas leak and no trace of any explosives. FBI came in to have a look, and they found nothing to explain the blast, either. It's a great big mystery. And in the meantime, some wacko filmed the whole thing and turned it into grisly, real-life performance art."

Interesting that the FBI hadn't found the cause of the blast. They were the best in the business at that kind of thing. While she finished her mashed potatoes, she silently commenced pondering ways to blow up a house-sized structure without using obvious explosives or a trigger. An intriguing problem.

"What painting did the wack job recreate?" Peter asked interestedly.

"A Kandinsky. It's called *Composition X*. An abstract piece. Black background, brightly colored geometric shapes arranged as if they're moving outward. The killer superimposed images of the explosion of the house, of flying parts of the house, furniture, and the bodies of the people inside on top of the painting. It even had a soundtrack. The production value was tremendous."

"Wow. Can I see the video?" Peter asked.

"It's gruesome, but I can show it to you if you'd like," Li replied. "I've got a burner laptop that I use to get on the Dark Web at the condo. I'll show you when we get home. But it's gross once you realize you just watched real people die."

"What's known about the victims?" Peter asked.

"Not much. Regular family. Moved into the house recently. Dad was a basketball coach at a local high school, mom taught English at the same school. Kids were in junior high. Nobody's found any reason why they specifically were killed. Looks like a random targeting."

Ha. Very few killings were entirely random. Something about that family had triggered the killer. Or possibly something about the house had reminded the killer of the painting he'd used in his thrill kill video. She prudently kept her thoughts to herself, however.

"Do we have to discuss the gory details at the dinner table?" Mitch complained.

Nancy laughed. "As if you haven't been talking about that murder at the National Zoo nonstop, including over meals."

"What murder?" Liang asked with interest.

"A guy got shot inside the zoo grounds yesterday. Not near the animals though. In the woods at the back of the zoo."

Helen's face felt like a plastic mask, frozen into a fake smile as she looked over at Mitchell in thinly veiled horror.

"He was shot three times. Once in the side, once in the back, and once in the back of the head, execution-style. He was a Russian tourist. Cops say it looks like some kind of professional hit."

"Was the victim armed?" Helen asked. "Was it some sort of gang-related thing, maybe?"

"Nope. He had no identification. Nothing else on him. He wasn't even wearing a coat."

Huh. The Russians had gotten to him before the police then, and stripped off his camo suit and taken his weapon. Undoubtedly they'd erased any evidence of the sniper's identity or purpose in being at the zoo in the first place.

But it did beg the question of how close that Russian cleanup crew had been when she shot the guy. Had they been dispatched to clean up after he was killed? Had any of them seen her? Did the Russians know she was responsible for knocking off their sniper? Alarm tore through her. Not good. This was not good at all.

"How do the police know he was a tourist if they don't know who he was?" she asked lightly.

"They matched him to a tourist visa. He flew into Dulles a few days ago. He was planning to sightsee for a week according to his entry documents."

Had the Russians flown the guy over to kill her, then? Cold dread congealed in her gut. That, and relief. She'd been having pangs of remorse over killing the guy without figuring out who he was first. And she really was supposed to be retired. As long as she ran around killing foreign spies, other countries wouldn't see her as being out of the game.

How many more assassins would the Russians—and anyone else she'd pissed off over the years—send after her?

"A murder inside the zoo?" Peter exclaimed. "People take their kids to that place!"

"Right!" Mitch said eagerly. "I'm trying to convince my boss to launch a big anti-crime initiative because of it. We can't have our national landmarks turning into war zones. The city relies too much on tourism to put up with crap like this. Harms the city. Harms our kids."

"That sounds like a political stump speech in the making," Helen commented, forcing herself to say something, anything, to engage with the others as if she wasn't sitting here quietly having a panic attack. Her body was alternating between hot and cold, shaky and leaden, and she didn't feel as if she could breathe properly.

She smoothed her linen napkin across her lap and realized her hands were visibly trembling. She clutched her fingers tightly under the table.

"Well," Mitch drawled with a loaded glance over at his wife, "it might be a political speech in the making."

Peter guffawed. "Are you thinking of running against your boss in the next election?"

"Let's just say I'm exploring my options," Mitch said with poorly leashed eagerness.

The kids took off instantly, discussing excitedly whether Mitch was better off running for city council or pursuing his boss's job as the district attorney, and she let the conversation wash over her without really touching her.

Her own son was investigating one of her killings. In fact, he might be planning to hang his political career on solving the case.

No way would any of them understand that the Russian sniper had shot at her first. Those were the rules of the game. *You try to kill me, I kill you. First person to succeed wins . . . and survives.* She'd had no choice.

Not only did she have to survive for herself, but for her family. She had to protect them from the repercussions of her career.

How would they be feeling tonight if she'd been the person killed in the zoo? She looked around the table, an outsider observing from afar. How different would this gathering be if they were mourning her untimely murder?

Would they mourn at all? Or would they be angry, and not even a little sad?

The one thing she did know was that they wouldn't understand. They had no idea the kind of world she lived in and the hard, split-second decisions she had to make in her work. There was so much about her, about her life, that none of them knew.

Maybe she should write it down. Leave some sort of document behind for them. Explain to them who she'd been and what she'd done—

No. She didn't dare leave any kind of incriminating evidence lying around about who and what she really was. Case in point, the National Zoo killing. None of her children must ever have the least suspicion that it had been she who killed the Russian sniper.

"Mom? You're awfully quiet over there," Mitchell said, startling her.

"Don't mind me. I'm just enjoying listening to the conversation."

"You look a little pale."

Curse Mitchell and his observational skills. "I'm just a little tired, dear." In a desperate bid to distract him, she said, "Do you have a moment for me to tell you what I found out about that thing you asked me to look into?"

"Sure. Let's head into my study while Pete and Li help Nancy clear the table."

Peter squawked about being volunteered for dish duty, and Helen patted his cheek on the way past, earning herself a black scowl. She followed Mitch into his office. He closed the door behind her.

"Drink?" he asked, pouring himself a finger of a dark amber whiskey.

"No, thank you."

He sat down at his desk and leaned back in its high leather chair, sipping at the expensive whiskey. "So, Mom. What did you think?"

"I think Angela Vincent is an astute woman."

"And?" he prompted.

"And I think it's possible her clients were framed."

"Tell me more."

"Why? So you can defeat your boss in the next general election? Do you care at all that four people have been unfairly convicted of crimes that there's more than a reasonable doubt that they committed?"

"Of course, I care about that!" he exclaimed.

If only he sounded genuinely offended. She sighed.

"Tell me what makes you think Angela's clients didn't do the murders."

She quickly went over how all four murders had identical setups—narrow streets, a single gunshot fired from a silenced weapon behind the framed person, about the same distance between shooter and victim in each killing, the possibility that the murder weapons had been planted for the police to find.

"Can you prove any of these theories?" he asked.

She shrugged. "My job was to find reasonable doubt, not proof positive that there's a serial killer loose in DC."

"A serial killer?" he exclaimed.

"Well, yes. All four killings were practically identical. What are the odds of that? I mean, I know there are a fair number of killings in the Washington metro area every year, but four that are identical?" She warmed to her topic. "For that matter, it's possible there've been even more of the same style of killings we don't know about. Only reason these four got connected was because the same attorney represented the people framed for doing the murder, and that attorney is a sharp cookie."

"Whoa. A serial killer would be a game changer in an election." Mitch leaned forward and scribbled furiously on a yellow legal pad for a few seconds.

"If you're looking for another great campaign issue," she suggested, "you should check out the homeless camp about six blocks southeast of the Capitol Building. It's a crime that so many homeless souls live so close to the center of our nation's democracy."

"And you know about that place how?" Mitch asked.

"I was checking out one of the murder scenes in person this morning. I followed a man to the homeless camp, and he was killed while I was there. It was tragic."

"Why on earth would you follow anyone, let alone into a tent city full of mentally unstable people?" Mitch demanded.

She thought fast. "I was curious. I saw him ranting on a street corner, and I wanted to see if I could help him. Maybe get him some medical care or buy him a meal."

Mitch stared at her in disbelief.

"What? I happen to have compassion for my fellow man," she said defensively.

"Just not for your kids?"

"I really wish you and Peter would let go of that tired old bone. I love you boys and your sister with all my heart, and I'm sorry I wasn't a perfect parent to all of you. I did my best with the limited time I had at home. I would like to make amends for all the time I missed in your childhoods. But you're going to have to meet me halfway if I'm to do that."

He tossed back the rest of his whiskey and set the cut crystal glass down with exaggerated care.

"It's not as if I can wave a magic wand and make it all better," she added. "I would if I could—"

"But you can't," he interrupted. "You're going to have to do this the old-fashioned way, I'm afraid."

"Meaning what?" she blurted.

"Meaning you're going to have to put in the time and the hard work, and build real relationships with your kids. And while you're at it, you might want to try doing the same with your husband."

"Mitchell, darling, I love you. But I do not need marital advice from you."

"Right." He stood up. "Thanks for the analysis of the cases."

"Are you going to ask the police to look for any more similar cases? Follow up to see if there's a serial killer out there?" she asked.

"It's not your concern, Mother—"

"I live in this town, too. And I know what to look for—"

"I've got this," he said sharply.

Right. Use her when she was useful, toss her aside when she wasn't. She might have taught him that lesson somewhere along the way. With a sigh, she stood up and followed him back to the kitchen.

Li was in the backyard, whistling at Biscuit. She slipped outside to pet the puppy, who was much more interested in exploring and sniffing the backyard than in peeing.

"How are you and Peter holding up?" she asked him.

"Okay. It's hectic trying to salvage what we can from the downstairs while we move back into the condo. We weren't expecting to have a dog in an apartment, and that's a challenge."

"You and Peter are always welcome at my house. Biscuit, too. I have a big backyard that would be perfect for him."

"That's kind of you Mrs. Warwick, but Peter still has a lot to work out where you're concerned. No offense meant."

"None taken, dear. And please call me Helen. I'm so glad he has you. You make him happier than I've ever seen him."

Liang turned to gaze in through the windows at the warmly lit kitchen where Peter, Nancy, and Mitch were laughing at something.

"Give him some time," Liang murmured. "He'll come around eventually."

"I hope so," she replied. "I truly do."

CHAPTER 11

*H*ELEN WAS BACK HOME AND IT WAS NEARLY 10:00 P.M. WHEN HER phone rang. "Hello?"

"It's me. I need to see you. Now." It was Yosef, though he sounded entirely unlike Yosef. His voice was low, nervous, and most worrying, out of breath.

"Uh, sure. Where?" she asked.

"Last place we got drinks."

The line went dead.

What on earth? He sounded as if he was being chased. It wasn't unreasonable for her to be chased, but Yossi? He'd been an analyst his entire career. He rarely set foot outside the office. He had people working for him to meet with field operatives and informants to collect information. He was the brains behind the spy network, not its hands and feet.

She raced upstairs and slipped into her secret equipment locker. She grabbed her spare Wilson EDC X9S pistol, this one a subcompact model. Unfortunately, her primary Wilson pistol was still in police custody after the New Year's Eve shooting. She grabbed a spare ammo magazine and stuffed both weapon and mag into her purse.

She was wearing sloppy jeans and an oversized sweater, and didn't have on a lick of makeup, but this was what Yosef was getting at his emergency rendezvous. She grabbed her coat and car keys, and headed out.

It had been years since they'd had a drink together, but the last time they'd done so had been downtown in a historic tavern in operation since the 1700s, close to where the White House now stood.

They'd come close to succumbing to their mutual attraction that night. He'd just gotten the diagnosis on Ruth, and he was in serious need of comfort. That was the night they'd learned the danger of mixing alcohol with the simmering, private tension between them.

She headed into DC, driving fast, grateful that the roads were uncrowded at this time of night.

Something was seriously wrong with Yosef, and she was tense as she approached the tavern on foot from her parking space a block away. Her gaze was on a swivel as she hurried down the street, gripping her pistol inside her purse. A few cars drove past, and ahead of her a couple got into a car. It wasn't exactly deserted, but it was quiet enough that anyone watching her should be apparent.

She ducked inside the tavern and paused in the tiny vestibule, watching outside from the dark, phone-booth-sized entry. Nobody hurried forward toward the bar now that she was out of sight.

If the coast was clear, why was Yosef so tense? She stepped through the inner door into the warmth and noise and bustle of an iconic DC watering hole. Even this late on a weeknight, it had a decent crowd. Most of the tables were occupied by couples and coworkers having a cold one after a late night at the office.

The low ceiling's blackened beams gave the room a welcoming intimacy. She gazed around the space, spotting Yosef immediately at a tiny table in the center of the space. A long bar stretched down one side of the room, while booths lined the other side. They were all occupied, which was probably why Yosef had settled on a more exposed table.

She pulled her chair to the side of the table and slipped into it so her back wouldn't be to the door. A file folder and a phone-sized device lay on the table in front of him.

"Thanks for coming," he muttered.

"What's up?"

"I learned something alarming just before I called you—"

A waitress come over with a menu, and he abruptly stopped speaking.

Helen ordered a hot mulled cider just to get rid of the young woman, then turned her attention back to Yosef. "How's Ruth?" she asked, as the waitress fussed over her order pad and packed up the menu, still standing beside them, well within earshot.

"Same as always. I had to stay late at the office tonight, so the nurse arranged to spend the night. She told me to get out of the house and take a mental health break, although I expect she didn't mean that I should keep working."

"Is that what this is? A mental health break?" The waitress finally moved away. Helen leaned in close to speak quietly under the general background noise. "You sounded tense on the phone. What's up?"

"First things first. I was able to arrange to have a tracking burr rubbed onto Nikolai Ibramov's coat this morning as he was leaving his hotel." He pushed the phone-like thing across the table to her. *Ah.* It was a signal tracker.

"Range of the signal?"

"About a ten-mile radius. Good for ten days, maybe two weeks. It was the best I could do without having to go up the chain of command to ask for a more expensive tracker with a bigger battery. Harder to place, those longer-life models. Can't just stick them in a pocket or under a collar. They have to be sewn in."

She was well aware of the difficulties in placing trackers. She'd done it dozens of times herself over the years. "May I take this?" She laid her hand on the signal tracker.

"Return it to me when you're done. It's checked out in my name."

"Was that wise? I'd hate to get you in trouble," she murmured.

"You mean more trouble than I'm already in?" he commented, grimly. "It's not as if I can afford to get fired and lose my medical insurance with what Ruth's care is costing these days."

Remorse speared through her. Of all people, she knew better than to put Yosef in any compromising situation that could cost him his career. And yet she'd been running around killing people left and right. She had no doubt he'd been scrambling like mad inside the agency to cover her back. It was not acceptable—at all—for retired operatives like her to continue killing after retirement.

His voice dropped to barely more than a breath of sound. "As I was saying before, I learned something disturbing at the office this evening."

Nothing ever flapped Yosef, let alone disturbed him outright. She couldn't imagine what had him so worked up. His gaze was darting all over the pub, and when he wasn't watching the other patrons, he was staring out the front window as if he expected a car full of mobsters to pull up and shoot the place to smithereens.

When he didn't speak, she nudged him a little, saying, "Talk to me, Yossi. What did you learn?"

"I pulled in a few favors over at NSA and with our own signals guys. I managed to get a bunch of government message logs for right around the time the New Year's Eve shooters came to town."

"From what agencies?"

"All of them. I was looking for traffic from a single source to each of the cities the four shooters were known to be living in in the weeks right before they came over here."

Dang. Those must've been some huge favors he called in to get the logs for multiple agencies. Even if he was a senior supervisor analyst, that still would have been a big ask.

She waited patiently while Yosef organized his thoughts and chose his words. In a public place like this, he would be circumspect in describing his findings.

"A source called Scorpius matches all my message criteria."

"Where does he or she work?"

"I can't tell. The source of the communiqués has been blocked."

"By whom?"

"No idea. Perhaps by Scorpius himself . . . or herself."

She leaned back hard in her chair to stare at Yosef. Was he intimating that an operator from inside the US government was the source of the contract to Nikolai and company to kill her?

"What did the messages say?"

"I don't know. I haven't decoded them yet." His fingers twitched on the file folder lying beneath his hand.

"Who is Scorpius?" she asked tightly.

"Unknown."

Just then the waitress approached with a tall mug of hot cider and set it in front of Helen. The scent of apples, cinnamon, and wine wafted enticingly from the drink, and she inhaled it with enjoyment.

His voice dropped until she could barely hear him murmur, "One thing I do know. This thing goes higher than I expected. There's something fishy going on here."

"Like what? A deep political game?"

"Or a conspiracy." He shrugged. "Scorpius may be a working group of some kind. Or it's possible that Scorpius is just a brilliant and manipulative lone operator."

"Yosef, I trust your guesses more than most people's cold, hard facts. Who's involved in this? Who is Scorpius?"

She heard the musical shatter of glass first, then the entire large window falling out of its frame onto the floor.

While everyone in the place turned in slow-motion shock to stare at the window, what had really happened registered to her instantly. Time slowed to a standstill as she threw herself out of her seat toward Yosef to knock him to the floor.

Many times in her career as a sniper, she'd taken a first shot, aimed high to knock out the glass of a window that might deflect her bullets. She followed that quick shot high immediately by dropping her aim and taking a second shot—the kill shot—at the heart of her target.

She hit Yosef just as the second shot slammed into him. She felt the impact of the high-velocity, high-caliber round rip into him, tearing flesh, shattering bone, shredding tissue in his chest.

Time resumed its course, and his chair crashed over backward. She and Yosef slammed hard against the floor. He hit the back of his head, and her left temple hit hard. She blinked away stars as she pressed herself up frantically to her knees, looking for where he'd been hit.

A spreading stain of red just to the right of his breastbone left no doubt as to the location of impact. She must have hit him a split second before the shot. The sniper would have been aiming to the left of his sternum for the heart, but she'd shoved Yosef about six inches to the side before the round arrived.

No. No, no, no . . .

Slapping both hands over the wound and pressing down hard, she raised her voice over the screams and cries, "Call an ambulance! Get me a first aid kit!"

She had to repeat herself several times as Yosef's hot, iron-scented blood flowed in a river of death between her fingers. His breath came in rasping, terrible gasps as he stared up at her, wide-eyed.

"Get me a freaking first aid kit!" she shouted at the top of her lungs. Panic tore through her, shredding her self-control. *Not Yosef. Not sweet, wonderful, brilliant Yosef.*

Keeping her right hand over the entry wound, she slipped her left beneath Yosef's torso to check for an exit wound. Nothing. The bullet was still inside him, which was good and bad news. The good news meant there wasn't another wound for him to bleed out from. The bad news was the bullet had either shattered inside his chest or ricocheted around enough to tear up his lungs.

A young kid dropped a big, red nylon bag beside her and fell to his knees. "I have some first aid training," he panted. "What can I do?"

Someone in the front of the restaurant took off running for the back of the place, and a stampede of panicked patrons erupted around them. Helen leaned forward protectively over Yosef as people shoved at her back and tripped over her and the kid with the first aid kit.

When the worst of the crowd had passed, she tore back Yosef's shirt to have a look at the wound. The round hole was big enough to put her thumb in. It gushed blood as soon as she lifted away her hands. Yosef took a gasping breath, and the blood in the wound bubbled ominously.

He had a bad bleeder in there, and his lung was punctured.

"Here's a gauze pad," the kid offered.

"Do you have a condom?" she asked urgently, her hands returning to Yosef's chest.

"Not in the first aid kit."

"I meant in your wallet!"

"Um, yeah."

"Get it out. Hurry!"

The kid fumbled with his back pocket, fumbled opening his worn leather wallet, fumbled for a foil condom package, and fumbled tearing it open.

"Hurry!" she snapped.

Hands shaking, he held it out to her.

"Take over putting pressure on the wound," she ordered.

The kid leaned past her and pushed down on Yosef's chest with both hands as she lifted hers away.

"Stay with me, Yosef," she said sharply, as his eyes started to glaze over. "This is going to hurt like all get-out. Yell your head off if you want to." To the kid she said, "On the count of three, lift your hands."

He nodded his understanding.

She unrolled the condom over her bloody index finger and girded herself to cause her dear friend agony. "One. Two. Three."

The kid moved aside, and she jammed her index finger as deep into the bullet hole as it would go.

Yosef roared in pain as she slipped her finger out of the hole, leaving behind the condom in the wound. She took a deep breath as she leaned down, put her mouth over the open end of the condom, and blew into it, inflating it like a balloon inside the wound.

She pinched it shut, but blood was still seeping out around the condom. She took another breath and blew again, inflating the condom balloon even more inside the wound. This time when she pinched it off, the bleeding had noticeably slowed.

Yosef had passed out, which was probably just as well. His breathing still sounded terrible and had taken on a wet, bubbly quality. He had blood in his lungs. And it sounded as if his right lung might have collapsed. That ambulance had better get here soon, or they were going to lose him, bleeding contained or not. She moved around behind his head to support his upper torso on her thighs. Being semi-upright would slow him drowning in his own blood . . . she hoped.

"Get me some tape," she told the young man. "Waterproof surgical tape if there's some in there."

"Sorry, there only rayon tape in here. We get mostly burns in the kitchen and the rayon won't stick to burned skin."

She thought fast. "Is there any thread in there?"

"There's a suture kit."

"Open that and cut a length of suture silk."

When the kid held out the piece of silk, she instructed him, "Wrap that around and around the condom under where I'm pinching it shut. We're tying off the balloon so it won't leak. We need it to keep putting pressure on whatever's bleeding in there."

The kid got to work, and in a minute or so, had the condom safely tied off and holding air. She sat back on her heels, and for the first time looked up. The tavern was a mess. The only real damage had been the broken sheet of glass, but the panicked customers had overturned tables and chairs, and food and spilled drinks were everywhere. And of course, Yosef lay in an impressive pool of his own blood.

His face was so pale. And he was so still. As if he was already gone. He couldn't die. He had to stay with her! What would she do without him? He was her rock. "Don't you die on me, Yosef Mizrah. I love you, darn it."

His eyelids fluttered a little, but he showed no other reaction to her confession.

The bartender peeked up over the top of the bar from time to time. Besides him, it was just she, Yosef, and the kid in the middle of the place.

"Pull that table over here in front of Yosef," she told the kid. He crawled on his hands and knees to a big, solid oak table and heaved it toward where Yosef lay.

"What am I doing?" the kid grunted as he pulled the table between them and the front of the tavern.

"Creating a barrier the shooter can't hit us through."

"Wha—what shooter?" The young man's voice broke on a squeak as he belatedly ducked low beside Yosef. She checked on the wound—it was seeping a little.

"Put pressure on the wound again," she ordered the young man.

She pulled out her pistol and rested the barrel on the edge of the table, scanning the street through the window opening. Storefronts with apartments above them filled her field of view. No glass was broken out of any of them, and no windows were open. She doubted the shooter had taken the time to break into a store or condo to use it for a shooting nest.

She guessed he'd stood in the recessed doorway directly across the street to take his shots. The vestibule was pitch black, so dark she couldn't see if anyone was standing in it now or not. Of course, the shooter would have fled the moment he took that second shot. He must have used a sound suppressor because she hadn't heard either shot.

Given the speed of the second shot after the first, it had to have been a professional shooter. The guy hadn't even waited for the shattered glass to clear the window frame before he'd pulled the trigger the second time. Only highly trained snipers could send off two shots at two different targets so quickly and still hit their second target.

Was Nikolai the shooter? Surely that shot hadn't been aimed at her. A professional wouldn't miss her by some three feet and hit her companion by accident.

The shot that had hit Yosef had been at exactly heart height, and had she not knocked him aside, would have penetrated right through the middle of his heart, killing him instantly.

Of course, the shot might still do so.

He couldn't die. He *couldn't*. The thought of her life stretching out for long years ahead of her without him in it was too bleak and empty to contemplate.

She said, without removing her stare from the street, "Check to make sure there's no blood in his mouth. If he starts coughing any up or blood starts to bubble out of his nose, tell me immediately."

"Um, okay." The kid was starting to sound shaky. The first functionality of panicked hyper-alertness was wearing off, and shock was setting in for the young man.

"Stay focused for me," she said. "Yosef's life is in your hands for a few more minutes. What's your name?"

"Mason. Mason Green."

"You're doing great, Mason. I can't tell you how grateful I am for your help and your courage."

"Um, why do you have a gun?"

"I work—worked—for the government. I have a permit for it. If whoever shot up this place decides to come back for more, I'll take him out."

"Good. That's good. Crap. Someone shot this guy. Crap."

"Breathe, Mason. Don't faint on me." He was panting like a dog on a hot day. "What do you do here at the tavern, Mason?"

"I wash dishes mostly. Sometimes I help cook. Or if the bar gets real busy, I come out and pull draft beers for the bartender."

"I'm going to tell the owner to give you a raise and a promotion after tonight, okay?"

"Yeah, sure." Pant. "That would be great." Pant.

"Keep breathing, son. I hear sirens. Just another minute or two."

She pocketed her pistol as the first police cars parked out front. The first cop advanced into the bar, revolver held out in front of him.

From behind the table, she called, "There are four of us in here, all victims. No hostiles in the building. Bartender is hiding behind the bar, the dishwasher and I are behind the overturned table halfway back, and my friend is lying on the floor. He's been shot and needs immediate trauma care. He's bleeding bad. Maybe a collapsed lung. Get the medics in here stat with a gurney for transport."

"Roger, ma'am," the cop called back.

She sagged in relief as she heard his radio give a burst of static and then his voice calling an all-clear for the front room before ordering EMTs inside. Quickly, she tucked her pistol back inside her purse and took over holding pressure on Yosef's wound.

A burly police officer stepped around the table, revolver still in front of him. Which was good procedure.

"Put your hands up in the air, Mason," she said pleasantly. "Forgive me, Officer, but I have to keep my hands on my friend's sucking chest wound."

"What happened here?" he demanded.

"Someone outside shot into the tavern. Two shots. First one shattered the window. Second one hit my friend in the chest. The customers panicked and fled out the back door, where they're probably milling around like scared sheep. My young friend Mason, here, brought out a first aid kit and has been helping me try to keep my friend alive."

Just then two EMTs ran in pulling a wheeled gurney and dropped beside Yosef.

"One GSW just to the right of his sternum. I inflated a condom in the wound because it has a bad bleeder in there. Sounds as if his right lung is collapsed. He lost consciousness when I inflated the condom. His vitals will be tanking hard right about now."

"Got it," one of the medics replied. "Let's move him ASAP. One. Two. Three. Lift."

The pair shifted Yosef to the gurney and raised it quickly to hip height. With Mason on one side, her on the other, and the medics at each end, they ran Yosef out the front door to the ambulance.

"Wanna ride with us?" the first medic said as he worked fast setting up an IV bag. He named the nearest hospital, where they would be taking Yosef.

"His blood type is O negative, and no. I've got something to do," Helen replied.

She climbed out of the ambulance, and as she closed the rear door she heard the medic call, "Let's roll! Drive like he's dying!"

CHAPTER 12

*H*ELEN WENT BACK INSIDE THE TAVERN QUICKLY. SHE MOVED WITH authority, praying the police wouldn't stop her. They were still busy taping off the street, and most of the cops were out back talking to patrons at the moment, so she made it inside. She hurried to the overturned table and searched around on the floor.

There. By the bar. The file folder Yosef had laid on the table. She scooped it up and tucked it inside her coat.

"What are you doing in here, lady? This is a crime scene."

"I'm getting my purse. My car keys are in it." She moved over to her abandoned purse and scooped it up, showing it to the officer.

"What's your name?"

"I already gave my contact information to that big guy who came in first," she lied. "Now, if you'll excuse me, young man, I need to get to the hospital to check on my friend who was shot and let his wife know."

His eyebrows shot up. "Oh. Right. Sure."

He obviously thought she was Yosef's mistress. Whatever worked to get her out of here without any more questions.

He was getting ready for bed when the burner phone rang. Startled and eager, he closed the door to his walk-in closet and took the call.

He skipped a greeting and bit out, "Do you have it?"

"I do. When you transfer your name and evidence to me, I will text you the name."

"Give me an IP address on the Dark Web and you'll have your mole in two minutes."

"I'll text it to you momentarily."

He rushed out of the closet in his boxer shorts and undershirt, a monumental lapse in his usual neat and orderly appearance. As he raced through the bedroom, his wife's eyebrows shot up nearly to her hairline.

The phone dinged again, and he looked down at the incoming message.

Ryan Goetz.

He quickly emailed the file he'd compiled on the Russian mole, and the burner phone dinged once more: **Pleasure doing business with you**.

He typed back, **Same**.

He typed the name Ryan Goetz into a search engine. *Capitol Heights?* That was a suburb on the southeast side of Washington, DC. The copycat lived practically in his backyard!

He spent the next hour working out the details of a plan crystallizing in his mind for young Ryan. It would definitely work. And when he was done, the whole world would know that he, the original DaVinci Killer, was the greatest of all time.

Helen made the drive home mostly on autopilot while her thoughts whirled. They'd shot Yosef. But who was *they*?

Scorpius?

Some shadowy cabal inside the US government?

An enemy of Yosef's? *But why? What had he stumbled into?* She was used to plots within plots in her line of work, but she couldn't fathom what he'd found that would get him shot within a few hours of uncovering it.

She briefly considered calling Yosef's house to let Ruth know what had happened, but the woman's health was so fragile that the shock of it could kill her. She would call the nurse in the morning and discuss with her what to tell Ruth and how to break the news to Yosef's wife. Besides, by morning, she would know if he'd lived or died.

The immediate concerns addressed and plan of action in place, her thoughts turned to what she'd whispered to Yosef just before the police arrived. Did she really love him? In *that* way?

She'd tried so blessed hard over the years not to fall in love with him. She was married, for crying out loud, and she loved her husband. *Right?*

But Yosef had always been there for her. Always had the piece of information she needed, was always the steady voice in her ear as she made dicey kills, telling her calmly that she could do it. When she lost focus, he centered her. When she was shaky, he steadied her. When an egress went bad, he was the one who found her an alternate escape route and talked her out to safety. He always brought her home. *Always.*

He'd been her lifeline, her sanity, so many times she couldn't count them. He'd taught her the ropes, turned her into one of the top assassins on the planet. It wasn't an exaggeration to say he'd made her who she was today.

And she loved him for it.

As she neared her house, she sent up a fervent prayer to whatever deity might listen that Yosef would pull through. She started to turn onto her street, but at the last second changed her mind. She heard Yosef's voice intoning, "Don't get sloppy, Helen. Stay sharp until you're back home, safe and sound."

Turning off her headlights, she slowed until her hybrid car shifted to full electric mode. Rolling in near silence, she drove another quarter mile and turned onto a dirt road that paralleled the woods behind her house. Years ago, she'd purchased a bit of land on this road and fixed up the small, decrepit barn that stood on the lot. She'd shored it up and repaired it from the inside so it was stable and safe to park in, but from the outside it still looked as if a strong wind would knock it over.

She parked inside the barn and got out of the car. It smelled faintly of hay, and she inhaled the soothing scent gratefully. She waited inside the barn until her night vision was fully adjusted.

Twenty years ago, she'd have been ready to rock and roll in just a few minutes. But her older eyes took closer to ten minutes to adapt to the dark tonight.

Finally, she eased out into the woods. The hillside above her house was densely overgrown, and it was slow going. At least it was downhill all the way to her house. No running up a steep hillside after a Russian sniper tonight, thankfully.

She approached her backyard and crouched in the brush, looking down at the house. A tiny blue light mounted on the second story corner of the house—an unobtrusive little thing a person had to know where to look for—was illuminated, which meant the house's alarm system had been turned off. And the only way to do that was from inside the house.

No interior lights were turned on, and she saw no movement. It was possible Grayson had come home without telling her, or that one of the kids had come over to the house. They were the only people besides her who knew the security codes for the alarm system.

But the children would have kept lights on while they waited for her to come home, and they would have turned the alarm back on when they left. And the odds of Gray having come home were, well, next to zero. Which meant her house had an intruder.

She eased backward, laboriously retracing her steps up the hill, and pulled out her cell phone to check for any messages from her family. They were under strict orders to let her know if they came to the house so she wouldn't freak out and try to kill them. Her kids thought it was a joke and that she wouldn't actually attack them, but Gray knew she wasn't exaggerating.

There were no messages on her phone.

Once she got access to the internet, she could pull up the security feed from her house and figure out who'd gotten in, what they did inside the house, and if they were still there—assuming they hadn't knocked out the entire system on the way in. But first she had to get out of here and find somewhere safe to go to ground. And then she had to figure what in the ever-loving *heck* was going on.

An hour later, Helen looked up and down the narrow alley. *Empty.* Working mostly by feel, she picked the back door of Angela Vincent's building. She passed through a storeroom that appeared to be shared between the pizzeria and Chinese place, and crept up a narrow rear staircase. It was dark and dingy back here, and many of the stair treads squeaked, which made for very slow going.

Eventually she reached the third floor and picked the lock on the lone door at the top of the stairs. Theoretically, this would lead to Angela's occasional crash pad. The lock turned, and she paused, taking a minute to check for contact pads or wires leading from the door. *Clear.*

Tsk, tsk. She should mention to Angela that she ought to think about installing a decent alarm system.

Helen opened the door carefully. She checked for infrared beams and pressure pads in the floor before she finally entered the space.

Whoa. She was in a chic kitchen, all quartz and sleek cabinets. *Nice crash pad.* She stepped into a small dining area with a glass-and-brushed-chrome table and leather chairs. Ms. Angela might like to remember her roots, but she also enjoyed the fruits of her labors. *Good for her.*

The living room was as elegant as the rest of the place, and Helen moved through it into the bedroom on silent feet, making sure she was alone. She stopped in the doorway, grinning. The empty bed was covered in thick fur throws, and the room had mirrors everywhere, including a big one on the ceiling over the bed.

Helen threw open a door and spun inside low. A walk-in closet. Lights came on automatically as she stepped inside. The closet was fully as nice as hers at home but less crammed with clothes. One side of the closet had a dozen women's business suits hanging in it. The other side held a half dozen men's dress shirts and a pair of expensive men's suits. Did those belong to the district attorney Angela was allegedly sleeping with? Helen did a three-sixty inside the closet and spied something that made her brow rise. What did Angela need with a wall safe nearly three feet tall? *Cash? Jewelry? A gun? Maybe sensitive files?*

She was no safe cracker. Angela's secrets inside that safe would remain secure from her. Helen backed out of the closet and crossed the room to the only remaining door.

She gave the bathroom, done in quartz and chrome, a quick once-over. *Empty.*

At last, Helen relaxed. She'd found a safe spot to hide for a few hours.

She stayed in the bathroom, closing and locking the door. Sitting on the edge of the bathtub, she pulled out her phone and called the hospital Yosef had been taken to.

"How may I direct your call?" a bored female voice said.

"Emergency room, please."

"One moment."

"How can I help you?"

"I'm calling to check on a patient who was brought in by ambulance a few hours ago. Yosef Mizrah."

"Are you family?"

"Yes. I'm his wife." *Sorry, Ruth.* It wasn't as if his actual wife could call to check on him.

"One moment."

Helen waited impatiently while the woman left the line.

"Mr. Mizrah is in surgery. When he comes out, he'll be taken to the surgical ICU."

"When will I know he's out of surgery?"

"You can leave the intensive care team your phone number and they will call you. One moment, I'll forward your call."

The line clicked as she was transferred, and she hung up quickly. The last thing she wanted to do was leave a traceable phone number with anyone. She would call again in the morning to check on him. At least he'd survived the ambulance ride to the hospital. That was something.

Was Yosef's shooting the work of the mysterious Scorpius? Had this Scorpius entity hired Nikolai to take out both Yosef and her? *Why?* Who had both of them ticked off?

She pulled out the file she'd fetched from the floor of the tavern. Inside were several sheets of plain typing paper. They were covered with rows of numbers.

Clearly, these were encoded. *Hmm.* Maybe Li could help her

find out what these communications said. And perhaps he could figure out who'd sent them and from what government agency, using the formidable resources of the NSA.

In the meantime, she pulled out the tracking device paired to the burr on Nikolai Ibramov's coat. She gave it a few minutes to calibrate and search for a signal, but the screen remained dark. He was not within ten miles of her current position. If only she'd thought to look at it immediately after the shooting. It might have told her if Nikolai was the shooter.

Mentally kicking herself, she turned the bathroom light off and headed into the bedroom. She felt weird about the idea of sleeping in her hostess's bed, so she retreated to the living room. Intending to stretch out on the sofa, she ended up curled at one end of it in the dark, hugging her knees to her chest. She might even have rocked back and forth a bit while she struggled to let go of the evening's terrors.

Who was doing this? Who'd decided she had to die, and apparently her loved ones and best friend had to die, too? It smacked of revenge. *But why?* She hadn't ever been followed this persistently in her career.

It had been a long time since she'd felt this scared and alone. A very long time. Her life had been one of total control, of calm professionalism, of never getting behind a situation. Of course, a large part of that had been Yosef speaking in her earpiece, feeding her vital information, performing remote overwatch from a satellite, or from other intelligence sources on the ground. She'd never been cast adrift quite like this.

Surely the Russian government wouldn't take out a man of Yosef's stature inside the American intelligence community. They wouldn't be willing to put their own equivalent intelligence officials in the bull's-eye. But who else could it be? Nikolai was their man.

Anatoly Tarmyenkin was as good a place as any to start exacting retribution for Yosef's shooting. For no question about it, this attack could not go unanswered.

CHAPTER 13

GOETZ'S PHONE ALARM WOKE HIM EXACTLY AT 8:00 A.M. HE BLINKED in the bright morning sun, went outside to piss in a corner of the parking garage, and climbed back into the stolen hearse. He drove to the medical examiner's office on the east side of DC, not far from the Anacostia River, arriving right at 8:30 a.m. when they opened.

A woman looked up as he approached her desk in the lobby of the medical examiner's building.

He mumbled in a thick, fake drawl, "I'm here to pick up a body, and I've never done this before. My new boss told me I would have to go to the fifth floor or something. I've got a hearse out front."

"Drive around back to the loading area. Then you will indeed go up to the fifth floor where remains are stored. They'll make sure all the paperwork is in order and then have you sign for the remains. They can show you where the freight elevator is, and you can take the remains down to your vehicle."

"Thank you, ma'am."

His homeless man collected, he headed northwest for the secluded property his parents had owned in rural Maryland, well outside the District. When they'd died, he'd never transferred the deed into his name, and it was completely off the grid. The barn on the site was perfect for what he had in mind for this art project. He pulled the hearse into the barn and got to work.

He'd picked up an old claw-foot bathtub at a flea market and had already painted it a dark gray-green to match Jacques-Louis David's painting *The Death of Marat*. His victim had been dead long enough that the rigor mortis had mostly worn off, and it was an easy, if heavy, matter to place the dead man in the tub, draping him artfully over the side to match the painting. It took him a while to use a curling iron and comb to achieve just the right unruly curls in the man's shoulder-length dark hair. A few more props—a simple, wooden writing desk across the top of the tub, a handwritten letter with a list of names of Jacobite rebels on it, and he was nearly ready to film.

He fiddled with the lighting until he was satisfied with how it shone off the corpse's alabaster pale skin, and then he filmed the body, moving around it in a semicircle that would create a 3D effect and bring David's painting to mind-blowing life.

Helen woke with a start. She realized with horror that a sound from downstairs had awoken her. She glanced at her watch, appalled to see it was nearly 9:00 a.m. Last night's stress had taken more of a toll on her than she'd realized. *Lord, getting old is the pits.*

Feeling guilty, she snuck out the back way without her hostess being any the wiser. Her first errand was to stop at a mega-store and buy new clothes, a wig, makeup, and a scarf. Her second task was to ask Liang about the encrypted sheets of numbers she'd retrieved from the pub last night. She sat in her car in the parking lot of the store to make that call.

He sounded surprised when he answered his cell phone.

"Hi, Li. I'm sorry to bother you at work, but I need your help with something. It's urgent. Can we meet?"

"Is this about Peter?"

"No. It's something else. I'd rather not talk about it on the phone."

"I can meet you for lunch, I suppose." He sounded both skeptical and curious. Both of which were reasonable reactions to a cold call from one's not quite mother-in-law when one worked at a highly classified government security agency.

"Lunch would be perfect," she said warmly. "You pick the place since I'm the one putting you to the inconvenience."

He suggested an Asian restaurant in Fort Meade, Maryland, which she assumed was near the NSA headquarters, at noon.

"I'll see you then. And thanks," she said gratefully.

Next up on her morning agenda, a visit to Yosef. But that would require a disguise. Hence her earlier purchases. She transformed herself using the mirror behind her visor. It took a while, but eventually she stared back at a dark-haired, olive-complexioned woman with a tired demeanor, the kind most people wouldn't look twice at.

She drove across DC to the big hospital Yosef had been taken to and parked in the garage beside it. She tied a scarf over the wig. Since she didn't have access to her collection of tinted contact lenses, which were at home, she slipped on a tinted pair of reading glasses that would somewhat disguise her light-blue eyes.

All the while she thought about Ruth and her mannerisms, speech patterns, and way of moving. A quick and effective method of developing a disguise was to pretend to be someone else she knew fairly well.

It wasn't hard to channel her own frantic worry for Yosef into her Ruth character as she entered the hospital and went to the front information counter.

"My husband was shot last night. They told me he's in the surgical ICU. Where can I find that?" she asked nervously.

"Down that hall, up the elevator to the second floor, and then follow the signs when you get out."

The surgical ICU was a busy place with a dozen ICU rooms arranged in a circle around a central nurse's station. She repeated her story at the counter, identifying herself as Ruth Mizrah. A nurse stood up to escort her into Yosef's room.

She'd seen people pale and still in hospital beds before, and hooked up to lots of machines, but this was her Yosef. An urge to sob and fling herself on top of him startled her.

"He's in and out of consciousness, Mrs. Mizrah. You can sit with him for a bit if you'd like, but don't expect any response from him."

"What can you tell me about his injuries? I was told he was shot in the chest."

"You'll have to speak with the doctor, ma'am."

"When can I speak with him?"

"I'll ask the doctor on call to swing by to chat with you as soon as he can. He's with another patient right now."

Crap. She couldn't afford to stay here for long. Odds were excellent that whoever had shot Yosef was lurking nearby, waiting to see if Yosef died, and waiting to see who stopped by to visit him. She would have to call the ICU later and try to get the doctor on the phone.

"Is my husband going to make a full recovery?" she asked anxiously.

"He's stable now, ma'am. But he was very seriously wounded."

Which was medical speak for maybe he would pull through.

She swore silently, but nodded meekly as Ruth would have.

"Will he hear me if I pray for him?" she asked.

"Can't hurt," the nurse said with a kind smile.

She nodded again, her focus fully on Yosef. She perched on a high stool the nurse pulled over for her and reached out carefully to slip her hand underneath Yosef's, which lay still and limp on top of the blanket, and began murmuring in Hebrew. She only knew a simple children's prayer in that language but hoped the nurse would buy it.

The nurse left the glass-walled room, and Helen fell silent. The quiet beeping of several monitors created an electronic cacophony.

Surreptitiously, she pulled out the signal locator married to the tracking burr on Nikolai Ibramov's clothing. She turned it on and it scanned for several seconds. The screen remained blank, which meant he wasn't nearby. Good to know. She relaxed fractionally and turned her attention to Yosef.

"Oh, Yossi. I'm so sorry I wasn't faster. A decade ago, I'd have knocked you out of the way a tiny bit sooner."

His hand twitched slightly beneath hers.

"Can you hear me?" she asked quickly.

Another twitch.

"Do you have any idea who did this to you?"

Nothing. His hand lay still and cool beneath hers.

"Can you still hear me?" she tried.

Nothing.

She sighed. No answers would be forthcoming from him for a while, apparently. "Get better, my sweet Yossi. I miss you . . ." she added in a rush, ". . . and I need you."

She left the room quietly, the pained rasp of Yosef's breath a grim reminder of how close he'd come to dying.

Oh, yes. Somebody was definitely going to pay for this.

He used a lock pick gun to let himself into the impostor's apartment. The blast of color from dozens of posters of paintings thumbtacked to the walls of the living/dining room was a shock to his senses. No surprise, every image was of a great painting depicting death. He recognized most of them.

Temptation to tear the posters down and burn them to ash nearly overcame him, but he gritted his teeth and moved beyond them. He walked past a filthy kitchen piled high with dirty dishes and trash.

The fact that such a . . . *pig* . . . dared pretend to be him was infuriating. He was supremely neat. Orderly. Controlled at all times. Disgust and rage churned in his gut, threatening to disrupt his concentration once more.

He walked into the single bedroom. One entire wall was covered with monitors and computer towers. Bingo. There was the computer nerd he expected. An unmade single bed took up the remaining sliver of the bedroom.

He didn't bother trying to tap into the computers. Anyone who used the Dark Web on a regular basis not only had excellent firewalls and security but was probably more than a little paranoid. Besides, he could see the impostor's work on the Dark Web for himself. No, he wanted to know the man behind the travesty.

And once he knew his target, he would plan and execute an appropriately disastrous end for him. Before he died, this impostor would know the full measure of his folly in daring to copy the greatest killer of all time.

He opened his equipment bag and went to work installing tiny, military-grade surveillance cameras all over the apartment. Given the general level of neglect and disarray, the odds of the copycat discovering any of the hidden cameras was close to zero.

He finished up, made sure he'd left no footprints in the worn shag carpet, and backed out of the apartment, carefully locking the door behind himself. He stripped off his latex gloves, stuffed them into his pocket, and headed downstairs.

A man, about the same height as him and athletic in build, wearing a baseball cap that hid his features, and bearing an ID badge from a funeral home, passed him on the way up the stairs. He instinctively ducked his chin and turned his face away from the funeral home worker. Without looking back, he lengthened his stride and moved away from the impostor's home.

Soon, you presumptuous moron. Soon, we will meet, Ryan Goetz, and you will die. Slowly. Excruciatingly painfully.

Helen used wet wipes in the car to strip off the heavy Ruth makeup. She stuffed the wig into a shopping bag and stowed it behind her seat. She used the makeup again, judiciously this time, to make herself *not* look like she'd been awake most of last night trying to figure out how to force Anatoly Tarmyenkin to tell her what the hell was going on.

There was only so much makeup could do though, and she feared she was looking fully her age today as she pulled up in front of the restaurant a few minutes early to meet Liang. *So be it.*

She went inside and spotted Li across the dining room, seated in a booth. She slid in across from him. "Thanks for agreeing to meet me on such short notice. How are you, Peter, and Biscuit faring in the condo?"

"It's survivable. And at least this time around we don't have to make a million decisions about the construction. We're using the materials and finishes we chose last time. And, we got to fix a few minor annoyances we discovered from living in the short time we were there."

She winced at the reminder that their house had been brand-new. "Did that pretty little Renoir pastel in the kitchen survive the carnage?"

"It did. The only piece in our collection that was destroyed beyond repair was the Louis XV credenza in the front hallway. It was shot all to hell."

"I'm so sorry about that. Can I buy you a replacement for it?"

He smiled gently. "It was one of a kind."

She smiled sadly. "Which is your ever-so-polite way of saying I couldn't afford to replace it even if another one could be found."

He shrugged, not disagreeing with her statement.

A waitress came over and greeted him by name in Mandarin, and he answered back fluently. Glancing over at her, he asked in English, "Do you know what you'd like to eat?"

"What do you recommend?"

He smiled and turned to the waitress, speaking quickly. Given that she nodded and left, Helen assumed he had ordered for both of them.

"So, Mrs. Warwick. What is this urgent problem you need my help with?"

She was never going to win the war to get him to call her Helen in the more casual American way. Reluctantly accepting being called Mrs. Warwick, which made her feel a hundred years old, she pulled the folder out of her purse and laid it on the table in front of him.

Li opened the file, glanced at the sheet of numbers, and looked up at her quickly. "Where did you get this?"

"From a very old friend."

"Do you know what it is?"

"No, dear. That's why I brought it to you."

"It's an encrypted file."

"Ah. And what are the odds you can decrypt it?"

"None without some serious computing power."

"But you have access to decryption computers at your office, do you not?" she asked.

Li pulled out his cell phone, turned on the flashlight function, laid down the phone, and placed the top sheet of paper on it. Even from where she sat, she could see the CIA watermark on the paper, beneath the dense rows of numbers.

Li yanked his phone clear and slammed the file shut. "Where

did you really get this? Do you have any idea where this is from? This is classified material," he hissed.

"I told you. A very old friend gave it to me. He told me the information contained in it is very important for me to know."

"Does this friend work at the . . ." He broke off, glanced around the crowded restaurant, and lowered his voice before finishing, "agency?"

"Do you really want me to answer that?" she asked back quietly.

He stared hard at her. "No. I don't."

"Can you decrypt it and tell me what it says?"

"Absolutely not. You don't have the security clearances to know what it says."

"My dear boy. I spent the past three decades with nearly the same security clearance as the president of the United States."

"As a trade analyst at State?" he challenged.

She didn't rise to the bait. She stood by her statement. He could do with it what he wished.

"I should have you arrested for being in possession of this material," he muttered.

"You could. But I'd be released within the hour. I've worked in this town for a long time. I'm not without a friend or two in high places."

He sighed. "What's so important about whatever this message says?"

"It may help identify the person behind the attack on your house."

"You mean the robbery?" he shot back ironically.

She shot him a withering look that told him in no uncertain terms not to be obtuse. They both knew it had been no robbery, particularly since none of their art or valuables had been taken.

"Were you the target that night?" he asked quietly.

"What do you think?" she tossed back at him.

He shrugged. "What I can't figure out is why some retired, mid-level trade analyst would rate such a spectacular attack."

She studied him intently. "Then let me ask you the same. Were *you* the target of the attack?"

Definite alarm entered his dark eyes. But whether it was at the notion of being the target of the attack or at the fact that she'd figured it out, she couldn't tell. "Why would anyone attack me like that?" he answered.

Which, of course, was no answer at all. She knew the technique well. She leaned forward, looking him directly in the eye. "Liang, I like you. A lot. And I love how happy you make Peter. I'm secretly hoping the two of you get married, have children, and live a long and blissfully happy life together.

"However, I would not take kindly to you endangering my son's life. If there's any chance that attack was aimed at you, rather than being a simple robbery gone wrong, I expect you to take every security measure at your disposal to protect my son. Is that clear?"

"Yes, ma'am. Crystal clear."

Satisfied that he fully understood her unspoken demand to invoke NSA security protocols, she relaxed and sat back. "That's why you and I both need to know what those papers say. If they can tell us why the attack happened, perhaps they can also tell us what or who the target was." She added with quiet determination, "I will keep my family safe, at all costs. And for the record, I will continue to consider you part of my family unless or until you give me cause to do otherwise."

"Fair enough."

They nodded in mutual understanding, one professional to another. Just how much did he know about her real career anyway? Sudden suspicion that he knew more than he was letting on coursed through her. But then, she knew more about his job than she was letting on as well.

He gathered up the papers and put them back in the file. "I'll see what I can do. But if there's classified information in this, I can't share it with you."

"It's not as if I'm a security risk. I've kept classified information to myself throughout my entire career."

He frowned. "The first rule of communications security is never to share classified information unless the other person has a need to know, in addition to the proper security clearance."

"If those sheets say what I think they do, I will most definitely have a need to know."

"If I can crack this message, I'll be the judge of that."

She didn't like it. But she also didn't have any choice, she supposed. It wasn't as if she could waltz into CIA headquarters and demand to have it decrypted. Not to mention that the subject of the message undoubtedly had a network of loyalists and spies throughout the agency.

"Do me a favor, Li. Don't say anything to Peter about this."

He leaned back, obviously not pleased at that. "You do realize this is exactly the kind of secretive behavior that drives your son nuts, right?"

She leaned back herself to stare at him. "So you're telling me you share every single detail of your job with Peter?"

"Of course not. I work with classified information all day long."

She shrugged. "Then you probably shouldn't be lobbing stones at me while we're both living in the same glass house."

"Exactly what sorts of trade deals did you work on over at State?"

"The kind that I didn't come home and talk with my kids about," she snapped.

Thankfully, the food arrived, and she was able to drown her irritation at his refusal to just help her and not ask any questions in a delicious dish he called *changfen*. It was paper thin sheets of rice starch wrapped around various fillings of meat and vegetables. It reminded her of a spring roll but more delicate and sophisticated.

Li insisted on paying for the meal, even though she argued that she was the one who'd asked for the meeting. He played the respect-for-his-elders card, and there wasn't anything she could say to that without coming off as petty and childish. The unspoken argument, of course, was that he was a wealthy man and could certainly afford to feed his boyfriend's mother a decent meal.

He walked her outside, and she kissed him briefly on the cheek. "Thank you for your help. Give Peter my love, and give Biscuit a belly rub for me."

"Will do."

She noted as he turned to head for his high-end electric car that he didn't respond to her comment about helping her. Granted, she respected his insistence on properly securing classified material. But he was young, naïve even, if he thought the world was so clearly black-and-white.

Ah, well. He would learn.

CHAPTER 14

*H*ELEN'S CELL PHONE RANG JUST AS SHE TURNED OUT OF THE restaurant parking lot, and she sent it to her car's Bluetooth system. "Hello," she said.

"Helen, it's Angela. My contact down at DC Metro just called, and he's pulled the evidence from all four of the murders. I was wondering if you could meet me down there. He can't take the evidence out of the building, but he can let us have a little time with it."

"When do you want to meet?"

"Now, if you're not busy."

Tracking down Anatoly would have to wait a few hours. "Now's fine."

Angela gave her the address of police headquarters, and Helen headed into downtown DC. There was some sort of demonstration taking place on the Mall today, and traffic was more snarled than usual. It took her nearly a half hour to finally park in a public garage near the police station.

She paused on the front steps, hinky about strolling into a police station. Her last experience in one had been far from pleasant. She suspected the only reason she'd gotten out of there without being charged with manslaughter was because she had such a fabulous attorney. She also suspected she was still fairly high on the department's radar after the incident on New Year's Eve.

She walked into the lobby of the large municipal building, and Angela came forward to meet her. "Thanks for coming on such short notice."

Angela texted someone, and in a minute, a handsome Black police officer came into the lobby. He kissed Angela's cheek and murmured, "Hi, Mom."

Mom? Angela's son was a cop? That must be handy in Angela's line of work.

"This is my son, George Vincent."

Helen held out her hand. "Nice to meet you, Officer Vincent."

He shook her hand firmly and said to his mother as he escorted them to an elevator, "I've pulled the case files and evidence boxes from the cases you asked about. They're in a conference room upstairs. I'll have to stay with you while you examine the evidence, since I signed for everything."

As they walked down a long hall, several cops passed them, and Helen noted that the glances they sent in Angela's direction were none too warm. It was nice to know that someone was less popular than she was with the local men and women in blue. Moreover, the focus on Angela diverted attention away from her.

George led them to a conference room, where a long table dominated the tight space. A half dozen cardboard boxes stood on the table. He waved a hand. "Have at it, ladies. I hope you find what you're looking for."

They dug into the folders, and it didn't take long to verify that every killing precisely fit Helen's hypothesis of how the actual killer had pulled off the crime and managed to frame someone else for it.

George piped up. "I can ask the homicide guys in neighboring police departments to take a look at their cases for the past few years."

Angela asked him, "Can you poke around a little in the DC homicide division? Find out if any other murders here fit this profile?"

"Sure. I'll ask around. I do know there haven't been any recent shootings like these. After my mom got suspicious, I've been keeping an eye out for matches."

Helen leaned back in her chair. "I wonder why the killer stopped."

Angela shrugged. "Maybe he got arrested for something else. Maybe he moved away. If we're lucky, he died."

"He was on a roll, killing about every four weeks. Why stop unless he got spooked?" Helen asked.

Nobody had an answer for that one.

Helen followed up with, "Do we know if the police department looked for any recently retired military snipers who moved into the area about the time the murders began?"

George reached for the first murder file. "I saw something about that in this case . . . there was something about the round used in the shooting being military grade that led the detectives to consider a military killer. . . ." He thumbed through it. "Here. They interviewed a guy named Ryan Goetz in conjunction with this case. He was discharged from the military and moved to DC shortly before the first murder. Flunked out of sniper training and was released from active duty."

Helen frowned. "Which was he? A lousy shot or a nutcase?"

"I beg your pardon?" Angela asked.

"Those are the two main reasons people fail sniper training. They're not a good enough shot, or they're deemed not mentally stable enough to continue with the training. Prospective snipers undergo extensive psychological testing before they're selected for the training, and they're retested during it, once they're under the stress of the training environment." She shrugged. "Given that he left the military altogether, I'd guess he failed the psych evals."

George nodded. "There's a note in here that the detectives thought Goetz was deceptive during the interview. He was tailed for several weeks, but they found no evidence to pin anything on him."

"Did they search his house?" Helen asked.

"No."

"So. They lean on the guy for a while and the shootings stop . . .

and they didn't think that was cause enough to get a warrant and look at his home?"

George shrugged. "Civilians have rights." He added, "If they leaned on him and he quit killing people, that's something."

Helen snorted. "Serial killers don't stop killing. They just change their modus operandi. Whoever the killer is, he'll have found a bigger, better way to murder people by now. We just haven't caught him yet."

"That's grim," George muttered.

Helen looked over at Angela. "I think you've got a decent case for getting your clients acquitted."

"Yeah. Now I just have to get a judge to listen to me."

"That's why you're a top-notch defense attorney," Helen reminded her.

They headed back downstairs, escorted by George, and Angela murmured, "Thanks for pulling that evidence, son."

"I would say anytime, but you know I have to be careful about doing favors for my lawyer mother."

Angela shrugged. "These are closed cases. They're not a threat to anyone around here."

"Not until you overturn them," he bit out.

"We're on the same team, the police and me," Angela retorted. "We all want to see justice done. You tell your critics around here that if they do their job correctly, I won't jump down their shorts."

George merely rolled his eyes as he showed them outside. He dropped an affectionate kiss on Angela's cheek. "Keep doing you, Mom."

"And you do you, Boo."

Helen looked on a little jealously. Angela was lucky her son didn't hold her job against her the way her kids did.

As she walked back toward her car, Helen was actually relieved to know she wasn't the only mother on the planet whose work drove her kids crazy. Maybe when things calmed down a little in her life, she would sit down with Angela and ask her how she navigated working against her son. Of course, Angela had the advantage of being able to tell her son what she did for a living.

With a sigh, Helen slid behind the wheel of her car. It was time for her to gear up and go hunting. Without telling her kids about it, and without sharing the reasons why. She owed answers to Yosef to find out why he'd nearly died, and she owed answers to Peter and Liang.

Tired all the way to her bones, she pulled her car out of its parking spot into traffic.

Once more unto the breach.

CHAPTER 15

*H*ELEN WIPED SWEAT OFF HER BROW AND PUSHED A STRAY HAIR OFF her face. She'd been digging for a half hour and still hadn't reached the box she'd buried here a few years ago. What had she been thinking back then to bury it so bleeding deep?

It didn't help that it had rained for the past two days, delaying her trek out here, and she was now covered in mud.

She was a half hour or so southeast of Washington, in Cedarville State Forest. It was 3,500 acres of wooded land with all the recreational amenities of most state forests. More to the point, it was secluded, and not the kind of place that was ever going to change its topography or cut down all the trees. Which made it the perfect place to hide a cache of emergency supplies.

She'd followed the paper map she drew three years ago and came straight to this ancient, contorted Virginia pine tree. The trunk bent over at a ninety-degree angle about six feet off the ground, and a new trunk grew vertically from the horizontal piece. The Piscataway tribe of Native Americans who used to winter over in this area had likely tied down the sapling two hundred years ago when it was young, to use it as a marker tree, pointing toward a campsite or perhaps a good fishing area. The swamp, forming the headwaters of the Charles River, was close by and was still considered an excellent fishing area.

She'd chosen this spot because it was one of the highest elevation points in the park and the least likely to flood. Even though the trunk she'd buried was watertight, there was no sense risking her gear being ruined by water seeping into it.

Her shovel finally clanged against metal. *Praise the Lord and pass the potatoes.*

She cleared off the top of the box and lugged it out of the hole. She wiped away the muck covering the locking mechanism and dialed the six-digit combination into the lock built into the box. Holding her breath, she lifted the lid.

Everything inside was dry. *Thank goodness.*

She pulled out the big canvas duffel bag stashed in the trunk and loaded up all of the surveillance equipment, weapons, ammo, clothing, cash, and other necessities for the well-equipped assassin.

She put the trunk back down into the hole, which was easier and less conspicuous than carrying it out, and began the work of filling in the hole. It didn't take long, since it didn't have to be hidden this time. She shouldered the heavy duffel and began the hike back to the parking lot.

The drive to the northwest side of DC and Embassy Row took a full hour, and it was late afternoon before she finally managed to find a parking spot down the street from the Russian embassy.

It was a Friday, and many of the high-level Russian diplomats would head out of town for the weekend to cabins and lake houses. It was a Russian thing—the tradition of owning a dacha. The country estates away from the noise and pollution of big cities had been status symbols of the elite nobility for centuries.

A big Mercedes with blacked-out windows rolled out of the embassy compound, but Helen didn't follow it. None of the flunkies would dare to leave work early on a Friday. Not until the ambassador himself left the building.

She did, however, follow the second Mercedes that left the embassy. The station intelligence chief would likely be the next to leave, since the other flunkies would know he had access to all the surveillance cameras in the building and could watch who bolted out of the embassy the second the ambassador left.

The big Mercedes was easy to follow, standing out as it did among the smaller and more brightly colored American vehicles. No surprise, it drove northwest out of the district and headed for a small, private lake a little over an hour away. The country was hilly and heavily wooded. *Very secluded.*

She drove around to the other side of the lake on a narrow tar and gravel road, searching for a driveway that didn't have a security gate across it. She finally found one and turned down the driveway, praying the owners were not home.

At the end of the gravel driveway was a rather decrepit cabin that looked out of an earlier era. She risked going onto the covered porch and peering in through the windows. The interior of the building was coated in a thick layer of dust.

She headed for the detached garage. After she picked the lock, the door rolled up with some protest. It was less dusty in here, likely because of the wind blowing through the plentiful cracks between the vertical strips of old wood siding. She pulled her car inside and closed the door behind her as she headed down the hill to the lake.

Sticking to the forest at the edge of the water, she used binoculars to peer at the big, modern house across the lake that she hoped was Anatoly Tarmyenkin's dacha.

It was a two-story brick home, and the entire back of the house consisted of floor-to-ceiling windows that would take advantage of the lake view. They also afforded her a terrific view of the interior. She memorized the layout.

The house was decorated in traditional Russian style with lots of dark, jewel-toned colors, plenty of gold gilt, and extravagant art. It was the samovar, though, that made her sure a Russian owned it. The giant copper and brass contraption, used for boiling water and brewing tea, took up an entire wall.

While she was examining the place, she noted that the power line coming in from the road led to the attached garage. That was where she would find the master electrical panel and, if she was lucky, the controls for the alarm system.

The temperature dropped precipitously as the sun went down,

and she shivered as she hid in the bushes, peering at the house. *Finally, movement.* Three men came out of a hallway and entered the living room.

She zoomed in on the closest face. Didn't recognize him. Zoomed in on the second one. *Bingo.* That was Anatoly. She checked the third man and didn't recognize him either. He was built powerfully enough that he was bursting out of his suit. *Definite bodyguard type.* A fourth man came out of the kitchen, and Anatoly and his guards moved toward the dining room.

She waited until they were all seated eating to see if anyone else showed up. Unless there were more bodyguards sleeping right now in preparation for pulling the night shift, she was only looking at a three-man security team. *Not bad.* She'd dealt with worse before. Of course, she'd been a lot younger before, too.

Satisfied that she'd seen everything she needed to for now, she retreated up the hill. Half-frozen, she cracked open the garage door and climbed into her car to turn on the engine and, more importantly, the heater. While she sat in the driver's seat, shivering and rubbing her hands together, she turned on the radio to catch a weather forecast.

". . . snow moving in later this evening along with frigid temperatures. Wind chills below zero are possible, and the high tomorrow could remain in the single digits. . . ."

Great. Her emergency gear stash had everything she needed to execute an assassination, but it didn't have arctic survival gear in it. Her heater was already starting to lose the battle against the bitter cold. She had no choice. She was going to have to go into the cabin and search for a source of heat to get her through the night.

The lock on the front door was laughable, and she stepped inside gingerly. As she'd feared, even the floor was covered with a thick layer of dust. This place hadn't been occupied for months, if not years. Resigned to dusting it from top to bottom, she went hunting for some sign of a furnace.

Nada.

The cabin had only a cast-iron wood-burning stove for heat.

Which explained the lack of visitors to this place in the dead of winter. She was relieved to find a large stack of wood inside a lean-to attached to the kitchen by a door. Quickly, she hauled in an armload of wood and started a fire in the stove. It would take a while to heat up the heavy cast iron, but once it got hot, it should radiate plenty of heat into the modest space.

While the wind howled outside, she cleaned the cabin, wiping it down from top to bottom. She was glad for the exercise, as the inside of the cabin was frigid and her breath hung in thick clouds as she worked. It took a full hour to wipe away all the dust that would give away her presence. Hopefully, this place would have time to get dusty again before its owners showed up to stay sometime next spring.

She fed more wood into the fire and huddled next to the stove, which was giving off enough heat now to beat back the vicious cold within about a six-foot radius. Smoke would be visible from the mouth of the chimney, but there was no help for it. She would freeze to death if she tried to tough it out in her car.

Over the course of the evening, she made a mental map of the house across the lake, adding to it every likely security feature the place might have and considering possible methods to infiltrate it.

Killing Anatoly would be a breeze from here. With her long-range sniper rifle, she would have no trouble taking him out from across the lake. But that wasn't her goal. She needed to talk to him first. Find out why his government kept trying to kill her . . . and now Yosef.

She could always just walk up to the front door, knock on it, and ask to speak to him. Although she doubted his security team would let her in. A boat across the lake would be fastest, but far too visible. Not to mention the lake was frozen at the moment. Like it or not, she was going to have to go cross-country and approach the house through the woods.

She ate from her emergency rations, melting snow on the top of the stove in a pot she borrowed from a kitchen cabinet to rehydrate the freeze-dried food.

The stove continued to pour out heat, and by midnight the

main room was warm enough for her to take off her coat. She pulled the cushions off the sofa to lay them close to the stove, and borrowed blankets and a pillow from the bedroom. She loaded the stove with a big pile of wood, stacked more pieces by the fire so she wouldn't have to go outside in the middle of the night, and settled in rather more comfortably than she'd expected a few hours ago.

Morning brought cold so intense it made her teeth hurt when she stepped outside. She took a wool blanket with her, wrapping it around herself as she huddled in the lee of a tree, hiding from the bitter wind.

Fine, dustlike particles of snow that had fallen overnight whisked around her in the gusting breeze, stinging her cheeks like tiny needles. She pulled the blanket over her head and across her face until only her eyes and mittened hands clutched around the binoculars were exposed.

This was exactly why she'd always specialized in urban assassinations. Give her a nice hotel room and a perch inside an empty office building any time over this back-to-nature crap.

When she'd been younger, much younger, she'd taken a few assignments that involved outdoor surveillances like this one. But she didn't ever recall one being quite so cold. Maybe her aging bones were becoming more sensitive to misery.

It was around noon when someone opened the curtains in one of the bedrooms to let light pour through the wall of glass. What were the odds that glass was bullet resistant? Could she cut out a piece of the glass, maybe? Unfortunately, she didn't have a glass cutter on hand, and she hated to leave the site and potentially lose contact with Anatoly.

She watched the room carefully for several minutes, and her patience was rewarded. Anatoly came over to stand in front of the window. He absently scratched his belly as he gazed out at the lake. She caught herself cringing back into the shadows and ordered herself to be still. The human eye was much better at spotting movement than at making out the still shape of a woman huddled next to a tree several hundred yards away. If she were to bolt up the hill, for example, Anatoly would easily see her. He turned away from the window and disappeared from view.

Tonight she would head over to his house and run whatever security gauntlet his men had set up around him. And then she would have her answers from him.

Helen's phone vibrated shortly after she returned to the cabin and huddled in front of the stove, warming her hands. She didn't recognize the number, and picked it up cautiously. "Hello?"

"This is Doctor Bronheim. I'm the attending physician for your husband. I'm sorry I wasn't able to speak with you this morning. Do you have a moment to talk?"

She sat up straight. "I do. What can you tell me about Yosef's injuries and condition?"

"As you know, he was shot once in the chest. The bullet struck his sternum, which is the big bone running down the middle of your chest that the ribs attach to."

She knew what a sternum was—all assassins had a good grasp of human anatomy and where the kill zones were on the body—but she made an interested sound and let the doctor continue.

"Your husband's sternum was cracked but didn't shatter, which is good news."

No kidding. Most people died from a bone fragment off the shattered sternum puncturing a vital artery or the heart, or they died of shock. But either way, they ended up dead.

"The bullet ricocheted into his right lung, which collapsed. The round hit a few ribs, then lodged in the back of his right scapula. That's his shoulder blade."

"Were you able to remove the bullet and repair the damage?" she asked.

"The trauma surgeon recovered the bullet. Your husband's lung is more or less reinflated but will take some weeks to recover. The sternum was stabilized with surgical glue, and it will take several months to heal. The cracked ribs will heal on their own. The worst risk to your husband's recovery will be infection. Bullets are dirty things with plenty of bacteria and substances like gun oil on them. We're administering high-dose antibiotics to your husband intravenously and monitoring his vitals as he recovers from shock."

"Has he regained consciousness? He only mumbled a few words when I visited him."

"We have him sedated to keep him resting quietly. He will need to be very careful until his sternum heals, Mrs. Mizrah. In the next day or two, as we wean him off the most powerful painkillers and make him understand that he must be still, he should become more alert and responsive."

"Where's the bullet?" she asked.

"I beg your pardon?"

"Where's the bullet?"

"It's standard procedure to hand such things over to the police. It's evidence in the investigation of how your husband was shot."

"Thank you," she murmured. "Perhaps it will lead to the terrible person who shot my poor Yossi."

"Don't hold your breath. The bullet will have been badly damaged by bouncing off all those bones—" He broke off. "Sorry. I didn't mean to be graphic."

"When will he wake up again?" she asked.

"I would think within forty-eight hours or so we'll be able to wean him off the sedation."

"Thank you so much for calling me, Doctor."

So. She had until the end of the weekend to get some answers from the man across the lake and, if they weren't the right answers, to make Anatoly Tarmyenkin pay for hurting Yosef.

CHAPTER 16

GOETZ SHIVERED IN THE RECESSED DOORWAY OF A STORE, BUNDLED up in a fluffy down coat, a knit cap, a scarf wrapped around every bit of exposed skin except his eyes, and a thin pair of leather gloves. Which meant his hands were jammed deep into his coat pockets at the moment.

He needed the gloves to keep a good grip on his knife. It took a surprising amount of force to jam even a really sharp knife into human meat. Of course, if he got it just right, he would slip the blade between his victim's ribs from the front and into the lung, which was soft as warm butter. A blade slipped into lung tissue nice and easy. Then, all he had to do was tip the blade up, nick the bottom of the heart, and wait for the poor sod to bleed out. *Easy peasy.*

It was becoming almost routine to pick off his victims these days. Tonight he'd moved to the south side of the homeless encampment in search of his next art subject. The next painting he'd chosen only required a skull, so he didn't have to be choosy out here. Man or woman, young or old, it didn't matter. As long as the person had decent teeth.

Of course, that ruled out the meth heads in the camp. That stuff rotted a person's teeth like nobody's business.

He'd set up shop between a liquor store and the camp, certain that someone would come along eventually, looking for a little liquid warmth for their belly on this wicked cold night.

He was not wrong. A small woman with wild gray hair walked past him toward the liquor store. *Go inside. Buy a bottle of gin. And freaking hurry.*

He stomped his feet both with cold and impatience. Surely she knew what brand of gin she preferred. *Just grab a bottle and get back out here—*

Here she came. The woman clutched a brown paper bag to her chest, walking back his way fast. He timed his exit from the doorway so he was far enough in front of her not to startle her.

"Cold night, huh?" he said loudly as she approached him.

Her head jerked up. She eyed him suspiciously. *Shoot.* He needed to make her smile. "Can I buy you a cup of coffee, ma'am? It's awful cold for you to be outside." He reached into his back pocket and pulled out his wallet, flashing the cash inside.

He pulled out a twenty-dollar bill and held it toward her with his left hand.

That made her smile all right. Showing two complete rows of strong, healthy teeth, she moved closer to take the bill.

Jamming the wallet into his coat pocket, he gripped the knife inside and whipped it out fast. He jabbed hard, calculating that he would have to go through several layers of coat to kill her.

She yelled and jumped back. The blow hadn't killed her.

He leaped forward, slamming into her and knocking her to the ground, cursing his head off. He had to work fast to kill her and get her off the street before anybody else came along, otherwise everything would be ruined. He slashed the knife across her throat, and hot blood spurted all over him. He swore even more violently as he slapped his hand across her mouth to keep her from making any more noise.

She grabbed at his wrist and managed to get her fingernails under the end of his glove. She scratched the heck out of his wrist in her effort to pull his hand off her mouth. All the while, blood went everywhere. She was supposed to bleed out internally. He hadn't taken into account just how many layers of clothing she would be wearing.

Stupid, stupid, stupid.

If a bunch of sweaters derailed him, the greatest murderer ever, he was going to be mad at himself until the end of time.

Thankfully, the woman started to lose strength beneath him. He planted his knee in the middle of her chest to hold her down as her last, thrashing death throes waned and stopped altogether.

He jumped to his feet, overcome by the smell of blood, thick in the air. Bending down, he grabbed the woman under the armpits and dragged her toward the alley where his car was stashed. He couldn't afford to go back and grab the booze she'd dropped nor to make an attempt to clean up the blood. He would have to throw away his boots when he got home, darn it. And they were his favorites. But he'd undoubtedly left footprints all over the sidewalk, thanks to her refusal to die.

He reached his car, a junker he'd picked up a few days ago, and stuffed her into the trunk. She was going to bleed all over it, but if he was lucky, the blood would freeze and not stink up his workshop. He backed out of the alley, exiting onto the street the next block over.

He lurched hard when he heard a faint thumping noise from the back of the car. The old broad wasn't dead? *Sonofa—*

He pulled over a few blocks away from where he'd attacked her, went around to the trunk, and opened it up. Sure enough, the woman stared up fearfully at him. She had almost succeeded at kicking out one of the taillights.

He pulled out his knife and slashed her throat one last time, this time cutting her head halfway off. Which was no big deal. He would finish the job when he got home anyway. Sure that she was dead this time, he closed the trunk on her. Pissed at how stubbornly she'd clung to life, he pushed the taillight back into place, got back in the car, and continued his journey.

Leaving his face completely covered, he drove out of downtown Washington and headed for the barn at his parents' old place. *Time to get to work.*

Helen drove around to the other side of the lake, creeping along the icy road at only a few miles per hour, headlights off.

Thankfully, the layer of new snow on the ground reflected even the faint starlight brightly. She passed the driveway leading to Anatoly's estate and went perhaps a quarter mile on down the road before she found a driveway that wasn't blocked right at the road with a big gate.

She turned in and drove perhaps a hundred feet up the drive where she encountered a tall security gate. But she had the cover she needed to hide her vehicle. She turned the car around—a dicey Y-turning maneuver that took a while on the tight, slippery driveway. When she finally had her car faced out toward the road, she pulled off to one side of the drive as far as she dared and then spent a good half hour dragging over dead branches, brush, and leaves to cover her car from view from the road.

Man, she hated working in these conditions. Everything took twice as long as it normally did, since she had to move slowly and be careful not to sweat. Any dampness in her clothing or against her skin on a night like this would be a recipe for a deadly case of hypothermia.

Finally, she started the long hike through the woods toward Anatoly's estate. At least she was approaching the house from the same end his bedroom was on. She walked past a sprawling log cabin that looked as if it had been here a hundred years, and then past an ultramodern house made of concrete half domes that looked as if it had been dropped here from a twenty-second-century moon base.

The next property should be Anatoly's.

She slowed, creeping through the trees one step at a time. The snow crunched under her feet, and she lost all feeling in the tip of her nose, despite it being covered with a scarf. The short-barreled urban assault weapon clutched in her hands was so cold through her gloves it felt as if she were carrying a block of dried ice. She didn't even know if her index finger would move to pull the trigger if she needed to fire it.

It was a good thing she loved Yosef more than life, or she wouldn't be out here in these conditions to avenge his near death. She wanted her life back. She wanted to spend time with her family, learn how to live like a normal person, and not spend every waking minute looking over her shoulder for the next person trying to take her out.

She stopped short, faced with the eight-foot-tall hurricane fence around the Tarmyenkin property. *Here goes nothing.*

She connected a bunch of electrical leads—six-foot-long wires with metal clips at each end—to the fence wires on each side of a square about two feet wide and tall down by the ground. Then she clipped out the section in between with wire cutters—which was damned hard work with her hands half-frozen. Finally, she slithered through the hole on her belly. Of course, she caught a face full of snow in the process and had to stop, crouching just inside the fence to warm her face with her hands. She seriously didn't need to get frostbite out here.

Finally, with feeling in her face somewhat restored, she crept on. For lack of a good arctic camo suit, which would have been white, she was stuck blending into the black shadows of the trees. These woods were clear of brush, which was good security practice, so she was forced to move slowly and plan a path from tree to tree.

While she was at it, she kept an eye out for trip wires. There was no way to spot pressure pads under the layer of snow, so she stuck to the ground at the bases of trees where she hoped thick root systems would make it impossible to bury pressure-sensitive plates . . . or anything more exciting like landmines.

The end of the house nearest to her was dark, but the other end, where lay the kitchen and living room, was lit up. The security guards probably took turns staying up all night.

She approached the side door to the garage and mentally groaned at the pair of high-quality German dead bolts. Nobody made locks like the Germans. She stripped off her mittens and went to work with her lock picks. It took upward of a half hour to finally open both locks in between breaks to stuff her hands back into her mittens and tuck them under her armpits to regain feeling.

The good news was none of the security men had run an exterior patrol around the house on this viciously cold night.

She slipped into the four-car garage and headed for the electrical panel on the wall and the smaller circuit panel beside it. Ideally, the smaller panel would control the alarm system. It had a small padlock on it, so simple she could've opened it with a bobby pin. Her lock pick popped it within a few seconds.

She examined the panel by flashlight. The system was probably a year old, but she was familiar with it. The big problem with this model was the battery backup supply to keep the system operational for up to two hours. She would have to flip all the circuit breakers and then wait it out until the system failed.

She noted the labels on the various circuits: heat sensors, motion detectors, pressure detectors, infrared grid, laser grid. She had to give Anatoly credit. He hadn't left out a bell or a whistle. He just hadn't defended the electricity that ran the system very well.

Rather than merely flip off all the circuit breakers, which would allow one of Anatoly's men to reactivate the system as soon as someone thought to check the circuit box, she carefully removed the metal pipe at the top of the box, sliding it up to reveal the wires into and out of the device. She snipped all of those, one by one. Then she slid the tube up another six inches or so and cut off lengths of each wire as long as her finger. That way the ends of the cut wires couldn't easily be spliced back together to restore the alarm. The whole thing would require an electrician to repair it.

Carefully, she slid the metal tubing back into place, hiding the gap in the wires, and screwed it back onto the circuit box.

Now the battery was carrying the load of the entire security system. And when someone came out here to check the power, everything would appear perfectly normal.

Using a towel she pulled out of her small backpack, she wiped the garage floor on her way back to the door, erasing all of her wet, snowy footprints. She closed the door behind her, and shivered as the bitter wind seeped through her clothing. Although it was an almighty pain in the tuchus, she laboriously relocked the two dead bolts behind her as well.

She backed off into the woods on the lakefront side of the

house, where she could watch events unfold inside. She found a little hollow to lie down in. Carefully, she brushed away the snow and filled it with handfuls of the driest dead leaves she could find. Then she laid a crisscrossing grid of dead branches across the narrow gully. Finally, she covered the branches with a thin sheet of heat-reflecting mylar, which in turn she covered with the thick wool blanket she'd stolen from the cabin.

At last she lay down on the wool blanket, pulled the loose end of it over herself, and pulled the sheet of black, plastic mylar over that. She tucked in the blanket and mylar around her and fully over her head, effectively making her a burrito. Now the trick would be to stay awake and not freeze to death out here while she waited for the battery on the alarm system to fail.

Goetz had trouble getting the corpse out of his trunk. Either rigor mortis or the freezing cold—or both—had stiffened her body into an awkward jumble of limbs, clothing, and frozen blood.

Jiminy Christmas. What a mess. He was going to have to dump this car and get a new one after the mess she'd made in it.

He finally managed to haul her out of the trunk and dump her on the dirt floor of the barn. It was colder than a witch's tits tonight, but he had quite a bit of work to do to prepare his next art installation. He'd decided to take on a still life this time, a Picasso titled *Still Life with Skull.*

Which, obviously, required a skull. He'd decided to incorporate the making of this installation into the video, including acquiring his skull. To that end, he filmed the dead woman curled on the ground from several angles. Then he set the camera on a tripod, and from a distance of about a foot, filmed the reciprocating saw slicing through the woman's neck.

He was careful to wear gloves and make sure his hands didn't show up in the video at all. Only the blade cutting through the flesh of her neck, then the chewing through the bones of her cervical vertebrae.

Bits of flesh and bone flew outward from the twin blades. He reveled in how cinematic it was. The sound was equally gruesome, and he hoped it had picked up clearly on the feed. His fans were going to love it.

Once the head was detached from the body, he carried it by the hair in one hand while pointing the video camera at it with the other. Blood and fluids dripped from the severed neck, and he made sure to capture those as well.

He carried it across the barn to a crude wooden table he'd built of scrap lumber. A tall plastic bucket sat on it, and a heat lamp pointed down at the white bucket, illuminating it in red light.

He lifted the plastic lid off the bucket, filming it all. A few flies flew out, but he didn't care. There were plenty of maggots already living in the paste of beer and mashed potato powder in the bottom of the bucket. He was using a combination of fly maggots and dermestid beetle maggots to clean the skull. The flies would clean away the majority of the major tissues, and the beetles would delicately clean the remaining bits of tissue off the bones.

He gently set the skull into the bucket and closed the lid. In a few days, he would have a nice, clean skull to use for his art installation.

The Picasso was all wild angles and white, intersecting planes, with a contorted pitcher standing on the table beside the skull.

He'd invested in a modest welding setup and had watched a bunch of videos on how to use it. *Might as well get to work a little while the maggots did theirs.* He wasn't tired after the adrenaline rush of murdering the woman, so he got started, cutting some of the half dozen steel sheets he'd purchased with the torch. He filmed enough of it to capture the sparks flying against the blackness of the night, and the steel glowing white-orange as he cut it.

As the night grew even colder, he finally knocked off, driving his regular car away from the barn toward home and his nice, warm bed.

It had taken upward of a half hour to prepare her little nest, but it was time well spent. By creating an air pocket between herself and the ground, she not only stayed dry, but gradually built up a modicum of warmth inside her mylar shell.

From time to time, she folded back the top of the burrito to peer out at the house through her binoculars. Even though she was less than a hundred feet from the house, she was able to set the binoculars at low magnification and use their light amplification feature to make out details inside the house. Two men sat at the kitchen table, and on a couple of her visual checks, one of them was moving around the house, going from door to door and window to window, running a routine security check.

When Helen's watch said it had been two hours since she'd sabotaged the alarm system, she lifted the end of the blankets to peer at the house once more. This time she didn't tuck her head back into her shell but kept watching.

It took about fifteen minutes for the battery to finally fail. The house didn't look any different, but all of a sudden both men jumped up from the kitchen table and raced through the home and down the hallway toward the bedrooms.

Good bodyguards. Their first thought was to secure their principal and likely to wake up the third bodyguard. Lights went on around the house, and two of the bodyguards swept the place, handguns drawn. The weapons were overkill in her opinion, but if they made the men feel better, more power to them.

One of the men put on a coat and disappeared from view. No doubt he was going to check the circuit breakers. She would lay odds the guy probably would make an exterior sweep of the house, too. She briefly debated taking him out now. Unfortunately, as easy as it would be to pick him off, his absence would alarm the other two guards. They might just have a protocol in place to whisk Anatoly away from here rather than come outside to check on their missing comrade.

Better to wait and take out all three men inside the house.

She spied the outdoor man coming around the end of the garage. He checked all of the sliding glass doors at the back of the house from the outside. Then he did an odd thing. He pulled out his cell phone and appeared to pull up some sort of app. He stared at it for perhaps a minute.

Then he pulled out his sidearm, pointed it and the phone directly at her, and strode aggressively toward her hiding place. As if he knew *exactly* where she was hiding.

How? she screamed silently.

Not that it mattered right now. He was coming fast, and she only had a few seconds to get ready for a confrontation only one of them was walking away from.

CHAPTER 17

*H*ELEN THOUGHT FAST. IF SHE JUMPED UP OR IN ANY WAY SURPRISED the guy, he would shoot first and ask questions later. She could pull her weapon up to her face and shoot him, but the noise would freak out Anatoly and his men, and they would either rush out here, guns blazing, or worse, flee with Anatoly.

Her only options were to lie here and pretend not to see the guard coming, to let him find her and apprehend her, and to stick to her original plan. It went against every ounce of training she'd ever had, and it was all she could do to lie there and let that guard storm toward her.

She cut a quick hole in the blanket and mylar below it, and shoved her backpack and weapons under the grid of branches and hopefully out of sight. The gear and weapons were expensive and hard to obtain discreetly. It was the best she could do before the Russian security man stopped practically on top of her and ripped away the blanket.

She rolled onto her back, hands held above her head, smiling guiltily. "Hi, there," she said meekly.

"Who are you?" he demanded in accented English. "Get up!"

She sat up and very slowly rolled to her hands and knees.

"I said, get up!"

"I am getting up, sonny. I'm an old lady, and it's very cold out here tonight. My joints are creaky and I'm half-frozen. This is as fast as I can move."

She pushed her rear end up in the air in a downward dog pose her yoga instructor would be proud of. She stopped there, rear still upward. She hoped she looked as absurd as she felt. She made a halfhearted effort at pushing herself upright but failed. She peddled with her feet a couple of times, making sure to slip in the snow and gain no traction from that direction either. She grunted a little, as if straining to hold her ridiculous position.

She heard what she was waiting for, a sound of disgust from the guard. There it was. He'd dismissed her as a crazy old lady.

She moaned, "Oh, no. I think I'm stuck. And my arms are about to give out. Can you give me a boost, young man?"

Making a sound of irritation in the back of his throat, he pocketed his phone and reached out with his free hand to grab her nearest arm. He gave her a yank, and she popped upright, staggering to gain her balance. She reached for his shoulders, and as her right hand approached his face, she made a quick fist and squeezed the spritzer attached to the tube threaded up her sleeve.

She was careful to hold her breath as the puff of nerve gas enveloped the Russian's face. It was windy out here, and the last thing she needed to do was knock herself out. A person could die of hypothermia fast out here on a night like this.

The Russian had long enough to register surprise as he stared at her, wide-eyed. Then his legs collapsed and he fell forward, slamming into her.

She might be in decent shape, but she was not strong enough to absorb a two-hundred-plus-pound man's dead weight. She toppled over with him on top of her.

The air whooshed out of her as he smashed her flat.

"Good Lord, you're heavy," she complained as she shoved at him, laboriously rolling him off her and into the little hollow.

She bent down, watching him breathe. When he was about to inhale, she squirted another puff of the gas into his face. He was a big boy after all, and she needed him to stay unconscious for at least an hour. She pulled the wool blanket and mylar cover over him and tucked it all in over his head. Not only would it conceal him, but she wasn't here to kill anyone she didn't have to.

Except for Anatoly, potentially.

She picked up his cell phone off the ground where he'd dropped it and tucked it into her coat pocket, then she headed for the house. She'd hoped to wait until everyone had settled back down before entering, but the guy behind her and however he'd found her so unerringly had moved up her timetable.

One thing she knew from her many years in this business: No plan went exactly the way it was supposed to, no matter how perfect or foolproof it might be.

She sprinted for the garage in hope that he'd left the door unlocked when he'd come out to make his rounds. He had. She slipped into the dark space and stopped to unwrap the scarf from around her face and head. She stripped off her bulky down coat and mittens as well. Her jeans, turtleneck, and wool ski sweater were not nearly enough to hold off the chill that instantly penetrated them, but she needed to do everything in her power not to look like a threat to the men inside. She pulled out a pair of wire-rimmed reading glasses with lenses that didn't affect her excellent eyesight, donning them tactfully. She took down her hair, which she'd sprayed with gray hair paint earlier, and let it hang around her face. She'd expected that the dry, cold air outside had accentuated the wrinkles around her eyes and between her eyebrows as well as the ones starting on her upper lip.

She hurried to the house door and threw it open, making sure to hold her hands away from her body in plain sight. The hallway was empty. As far as she could tell, she would have to follow this hall into the foyer and go up the main stairs to reach Anatoly's bedroom. But first she had a couple of security men to take out.

She made it all the way to the foyer without encountering the man she knew to be moving around the first floor. Rather than go looking for him, she unlocked the front door, opened it, and then closed it again, not bothering to be quiet about it.

She stood meekly, hands resting on top of her head, waiting for the Russian to race to the noise. Which he did.

He tore around the corner, gun in front of him in both hands. He skidded to a stop on the slippery marble floor, staring at her,

perplexed. An old lady posing no threat was clearly the exact opposite of what he'd expected.

"Who are you?" he demanded in Russian.

She was fluent in the language, but chose to tilt her head, staring at him as if she didn't understand.

He tried again in English. "Who are you?"

"I'm an old friend of Comrade Tarmyenkin's mother. I need to
speak with him."

Again, not what the guy had expected.

"May I lower my hands?" she asked. "My arms are getting tired."

When he didn't immediately refuse, she lowered her hands to
waist height. "I would like to speak to your superior . . . or are you
the head security guard?"

The guy looked over his shoulder at the staircase briefly. *Got it.*
The head of the detail was upstairs with Anatoly.

He moved toward her, and she let him come. His pistol lowered to his side as he approached.

Mistake, junior.

He reached for her upper left arm, and she let him grab it. He
gave her a little shove toward the hallway leading to the kitchen,
and she stumbled, exaggerating the movement until she nearly
fell down.

The guard lunged for her, catching her shoulder and dragging
her back upright with his considerably superior strength.

As she came up, she reached for his chest, held her breath, and
squeezed her right hand. In the still air of the house's interior,
she saw the little vapor cloud in front of his face. He inhaled, and
the cloud disappeared.

"I'm sorry," she mumbled. "I'm so clumsy—"

She threw her arms around the man's waist as he went down,
falling with him but managing to break his fall so that it was more
of a controlled slump than a loud crash. She gave him a second
puff of her magic gas as well. She hooked her hands in his
armpits and leaned back, pulling for all she was worth. It took a
half dozen heaves, but she managed to drag the guy's body down
the hall and around the corner into the kitchen. She grabbed his
legs and turned him so he wasn't visible from the foyer.

Feeling for his ear, she pulled out the earpiece. Then she crouched beside the guy, groping the collar of his sports coat.

There it was. The thin wire sewn into a seam on the underside of the lapel. There would be a microphone built in somewhere by his throat.

Casting her voice as low and scratchy as she could, she whispered in Russian, "Can you come down here to the kitchen? There's movement outside that's not our man."

A male voice swore in her ear.

A few moments later, she heard rapid footsteps on the stairs. Straddling the downed man, she waited just inside the kitchen door, arm held out shoulder-high. The head of the security detail rushed into the room, and she sprayed her knockout gas at him.

But he was moving too fast to get a full dose of it, and he spun around to face her. Assessing the situation with impressive speed, he charged forward. She ducked, barely evading his fist as it slammed into the stove behind her, cracking the glass.

She came up right fist first, aiming at his face with another spritz. As he turned his face away from the attack, she snapped her left fist forward, smashing the butt of her hand up into the base of his nose.

Blood spurted from his broken nose. Most attackers would have staggered back from the explosion of pain in their face but not this guy. He jabbed up hard with his left fist, catching her in the solar plexus. Not only did he knock the wind out of her, but he temporarily paralyzed her diaphragm, which meant she had only about fifteen seconds of hard exertion left before she passed out.

She threw herself forward at the Russian as he leaped back. She stepped on the unconscious man between them, which gave her just the six inches or so she needed to reach her attacker's face. She sprayed her bottle one last time, praying she wasn't out of the knockout juice.

This time he inhaled a big, full breath of the stuff and staggered backward as she slammed into him. They went down together, with her landing on top of him. They made such a loud noise as they went down that Anatoly couldn't have failed to hear.

Sure enough, a man's voice shouted from upstairs, "Sergei! What was that? Are you all right?"

There was no help for it. Sergei wasn't going to answer, and she wasn't going to be able to fake his voice.

Quickly, she gave the last Russian bodyguard a second shot of the spray, but she was about out of the stuff and gave only a half-hearted mist. She pumped the spritzer a few more times, but nothing came out. She hoped this last guy had gotten enough gas to stay down long enough for her to have a heart-to-heart with her target.

She pulled out her own handgun and retraced her steps to the foyer. Anatoly Tarmyenkin stood on the landing, pointing a handgun of his own in her direction.

"Good evening, Comrade Tarmyenkin," she said calmly. "You're a difficult man to have a conversation with."

"A conversation?" he echoed, looking over her shoulder for his security team. Did he think they were outside or something? That if he delayed her with small talk they would come to the rescue?

"Would you like to come down here, or shall I come up there to join you?" she asked. "Or I suppose we could just shout back and forth at each other."

"I'll come down, I think."

Right. To be closer to his security team, whom he wrongly thought might still come to the rescue.

He walked along the hall with its balcony railing and turned the corner to come down the stairs. That was when he saw one of his men slumped at the bottom of the stairs.

"What have you done to Timofey?" he demanded.

"He's taking a little nap. He's not injured in any way. I'm not here to kill your men."

"Are you here to kill me?"

She looked up at him over the barrel of her weapon. "Obviously not, or you would already be dead. I'm very good at my job, Anatoly."

"The way I hear it, you've retired from your job. So what is this?"

"This is a conversation. I have a few questions for you, and your answers will determine what happens next."

"I could shoot you, you know," he said, truculently.

"You could try. I'm willing to bet my life on my reflexes—and my aim—being better than yours. You shoot at me, maybe you hit me, maybe you don't. Odds are very low you pull off a lethal shot from that angle or direction. But when I shoot back, I will, without a doubt, kill you. Personally, I like those odds."

Anatoly was silent for a long time, mulling over his options. She waited him out, letting him stew.

"If I agree to come down there, will you put down your weapon? Swear not to kill me?"

"No. I will not. I would never make such a promise to anyone." She stared up at him. "How stupid do you think I am?"

He shrugged. "It was worth a try."

"Please don't insult my intelligence. I've been in this game as long as you have. Old spies like us, we don't get to be old by being idiots."

He smiled a little at that.

"I just want to talk," she said evenly. "As an act of good faith, I've gone to a lot of trouble not to kill your men. If you refuse to talk with me, I'll kill them all on my way out the door." She left it hanging, unspoken, whether or not she would kill him, too.

He sighed. "You leave me no choice. I will come down and speak with you. But you will regret this stunt, Mrs. Warwick."

"Maybe. Maybe not."

She backed away from the foot of the stairs as he came down toward her. When he reached the foyer, she backed through the opening that she knew led to the big living room with its panoramic view of the lake. She backed around the furniture as Anatoly slowly stalked her. They both kept their pistols trained on each other.

"If you would like to sit in that chair," she said, indicating an armchair on the far side of a round poker table, "I will sit in this one."

"Very well." Anatoly sat in the chair, and she did the same.

She laid her pistol on the table, maintaining her grip on it as it lay on its side. Anatoly did the same. Of course, he might not be aware that she could hit a bull's-eye at twenty-five feet holding her pistol in this particular grip.

"All right, Mrs. Warwick. We are seated and appear to have a truce. What is so urgent that you felt a need to invade my home and attack my men?"

"Yosef Mizrah was shot several days ago."

She wished the room was more brightly lit so she could gauge Anatoly's reaction, but he seemed sincere when he asked sharply, "Is he dead?"

"No. He survived." She waited a moment. "Did you order the hit?"

"Absolutely not."

His voice was firm, he didn't hesitate, and he didn't look away from her when he made his declaration. That was good news. The last thing she wanted to do was start a war between his intelligence agency and hers, knocking off top officials in a spiraling cycle of tit for tat.

"What do you know about who did order the hit?"

"Nothing, Mrs. Warwick. I would never order my counterpart murdered. You know the rules as well as I do. Had I ordered dear Yosef shot, he would be well within his rights to do the same to me. I happen to value my life. I have a wife. Grown children. Grandchildren. I would like to see them grow up."

He fell silent.

"What do you know about the attack aimed at me on New Year's Eve?"

"Nothing."

This time, his body language didn't scream of honesty.

"Try again, Anatoly. And if you value your ability to play with your grandchildren without a limp, perhaps tell me the truth this time."

He huffed. "I swear to you. I had nothing to do with it."

"But you know who did."

"I heard a rumor. No more."

"Which was?"

"That an asset of ours might have picked up a side job."

"From whom?"

He shrugged. "I do not know."

"How could your asset pick up a job without you knowing what it was or who ordered it?"

"Because the asset is a contractor. He freelances now and then when we don't have work for him. These aren't the good old days when target lists were longer than our assassins could possibly get to."

She knew what he was talking about. For a few years there, after the alleged end of the Cold War, when the United States and Russia were fighting all their battles by proxy through third parties, she'd gone from assignment to assignment without hardly getting a moment to breathe, let alone getting enough time to decompress, go home, and see her family. But in the past few years, the work had slowed down considerably. Too late for her to raise her children and get to know her family though.

"Let me guess. This contract killer who might have taken a freelance job to off me is Nikolai Ibramov?" she said lightly.

Anatoly looked startled for an instant before nodding slowly, smiling a little. "Very good, Mrs. Warwick. I always was impressed by your skill at your work."

She shrugged modestly. "Did Ibramov hire his own crew, or did his employer choose his kill team for him?"

"This, I do not know."

She leaned forward, staring intently at Anatoly. "Who did your rumor name as Ibramov's employer for the hit on me?"

"No actual identity. Just a code name." His expression turned sly. A little smug. He uttered a single word. "Scorpius."

CHAPTER 18

SHE SWORE UNDER HER BREATH. AN AMERICAN HAD HIRED IBRAMOV to take her out? Or was Anatoly lying? Maybe he hoped to finger a high-level US government official as a gambit to get her to kill him for the Russians? It was the sort of ploy Yosef would pull.

Always with these guys, it was a game within a game.

Anatoly purred. "I gather from your surprise that you've heard of him or her? Perhaps you know the identity of Scorpius?" It was an obvious attempt to take control of the conversation. "My government would be eternally grateful if you find this person and eliminate him or her. We would be happy to make a sizable contribution to your retirement account, should you do this. Enough to see you safe and comfortable throughout your old age. It's the least we could do—"

She waved the pistol at him in a gesture to silence him. "Where is Ibramov now?" she bit out.

"I'm sure I don't know. I don't keep track of part-time contractors like him when they are not working on my clock."

Which was a lie. The Russians, and the Americans for that matter, kept extremely short leashes on their wet-work operators. People like Ibramov and her could not be allowed to run around randomly killing anyone who pissed them off or someone they were paid to off. They had to keep their noses clean enough so they could do their government's work successfully.

"Who usually hires Ibramov when he's off your clock?"

"The Chechnyans," Anatoly said promptly.

Another lie. Yosef had mentioned that Ibramov was shacked up with the Bratva in New York, not Chechnyans.

She let the lie slide. Let Anatoly think he was pulling the wool over her eyes.

"Tell me something, Mrs. Warwick. Why did you kill my man in the zoo?"

Interesting. Did he already know she'd killed the sniper, or was he fishing to find out if she'd done it? Not that she particularly cared either way. She shrugged. "He tried to kill me. And speaking of which, did you order him to take me out after you left the meeting with Yosef?"

Anatoly frowned. "I did not."

"Did someone in your government order the hit on me?"

His frown deepened. "Definitely not. He worked directly for me and would have informed me of such an order from anyone else."

"Well then, you had a rogue agent on your hands. As I was leaving the zoo, he took a shot at me that would have killed me if not for a gust of wind and a bit of luck."

Anatoly stared at her hard. "So you're saying he shot first?"

"I am. If your people examine the northwest corner of the bear house, you'll find a chip taken out of the stucco from the bullet that barely missed my head. After he took that shot, he fled into the woods on the gravely mistaken assumption that he could get away from me after trying to kill me."

"Foolish boy," Anatoly commented dryly.

"Indeed."

"You are in luck, Mrs. Warwick. Because I happened to have a backup man in the zoo who witnessed the exchange between you and my . . . overzealous . . . sniper, I know you are telling me the truth."

There had been another man in the park? Why didn't he stop her from killing his buddy, then? Was it because the first shooter had truly gone rogue, or was Anatoly lying about there being a second man? But for what Mitch had said about the murder, she was inclined to believe Anatoly.

"Normally I would put out a sanction on an American assassin who killed one of my people," Anatoly continued. "But I find myself in the unusual position of owing you a debt." He raised his hands from the tabletop. "I'm going to reach into my pocket and pull out my wallet."

Her fingers tightened around the trigger of her weapon, and she nodded.

Very slowly, Anatoly reached into his back pocket and pulled out his wallet, which he opened with care, and pulled out a one-dollar bill. He laid it on the table and pushed it across to her. "Consider this . . . how do you say it in English? *Retroakteevnuiye?*"

"Same word in English. Retroactive," she supplied.

"Retroactive payment on a contract between you and me to dispose of a disloyal and unreliable asset."

"Keep your dollar. What I want in payment is the name of whoever paid him to try to kill me."

"I insist you take payment. That way, I can claim to my government that there is no need to sanction you since you were merely fulfilling a contract assassination for me. Please, Mrs. Warwick. Take the money and help me save your life."

She stared hard at him. "Why do you want to help me?"

"Call it professional respect. Or perhaps nostalgia for a time you and I both remember when there was respect between our intelligence services."

Or perhaps it was no more than enlightened self-protection. Case in point, her presence in his house right now with all of his security guards unconscious. She was a very dangerous person to pick a fight with, after all. Personally, she hoped it was the nostalgia.

"I miss the old days, too," she said wistfully. "At least back then I knew who the enemy was. Nowadays, it's hard to tell."

"If you will forgive my observation, your country has lost its way. You have far too many enemies from within. My own country did the same after the fall of the Soviet regime. Jackals ate away at Mother Russia from inside her womb. Mark my words. The only cure is to cut them out and crush them."

"We've got this little document called the Constitution . . . it has protected us for hundreds of years against jackals. I would like to think it will continue to do so." Even as the words came out of her mouth, they had a prophetic ring to them.

"I hope you are right. I do not know if your fellow Americans have the courage to cut the jackals out of their own belly if it comes to that."

"That's what people like me are for," she replied lightly, disturbed at the imagery Anatoly's words called to mind.

He replied heavily, "We shall see."

She fell silent, and so did the Russian spymaster.

"What can you tell me about the identity of Scorpius?" she asked.

"Not much. We think he may be killing people to move aside those who stand in the way of his advance—" He broke off.

Without warning, a man staggered out of the kitchen from behind Anatoly and to his left.

Crap. The burly head guard had woken up. And he was pointing a pistol at her.

She dove out of her chair as the Russian raised a pistol and fired a half dozen times in quick succession. The tempered-glass windows behind her shattered and fell in slow motion to the ground outside.

She rolled to her feet and sent one shot in the general direction of the guard and, crouching low, bolted out through the window opening. The back of the house had several terraced concrete patios, and she raced down those at high speed. No one had been out here to pack the snow, so it wasn't slippery. She took the path of least resistance, opting for speed over stealth, and sprinted down the hill toward the lake, zigzagging as she went.

Four more shots rang out behind her, and they all missed. The guard must still be only half-conscious to have missed her wildly with every round. If she wasn't mistaken, his weapon should be empty now. She heard running footsteps behind her though, and heavy breathing. He was conscious enough to give chase.

The lawn leveled out beneath her feet, and then all of a sudden she was skidding sideways, flailing her arms to stay upright. The dirt beneath the snow had turned to ice. She'd run out onto the surface of the lake.

She turned left and ran gingerly toward the property her car was parked in front of. She heard cracking noises, felt the ice giving way beneath her feet. This wasn't a part of the country that got cold and stayed cold enough for lakes to freeze over heavily in the winter. As it was, the middle of this little lake was covered with only a thin layer of black ice with wisps of snow blowing across it.

She hoped that moving fast and being the first person to cross this ice would keep it from collapsing beneath her. And she desperately prayed it gave way under her pursuer who, drugged though he might be, was gaining on her fast.

She looked over her shoulder, appalled to see how close he'd drawn to her, and ran for all she was worth. Every few steps, one of her feet slid out, and she had to stumble, right herself, and press on. It was exhausting, and she wasn't going to be able to keep up this pace all the way to the house down the lakefront.

A hand brushed at the back of her coat, and she jolted. A burst of adrenaline renewed her flagging steps for perhaps another hundred feet, but then she felt a hand close on the neck of her coat.

Frantically, she ripped down the zipper and let both of her arms go back as he yanked violently at it.

The Russian tore the coat off her back, but the movement must've thrown him off balance, for she heard a crash behind her. He grunted hard, and a sheet of ice beneath her feet tilted up and back toward the man.

She scrambled forward, throwing herself off the sheet of failing ice. She sprawled on her belly and scrabbled forward, desperately seeking purchase on the slippery surface with her hands and feet. She pulled herself a few yards ahead, then pushed up to her hands and knees.

She looked over her shoulder and spied the Russian, waist-deep in dark, thrashing water, pulling at the edge of the ice in a futile effort to drag himself out of the water. He would eventually break through the ice and make it to shore, and she needed to be well away from here before that happened.

She climbed carefully to her feet and took off running again, angling toward shore, where she hoped the ice was thicker.

The yard of the property she'd parked at loomed ahead. She made her way to the bank of the lake and shoved through the underbrush frantically. She skirted the tall, iron fence around the estate and broke into relatively clear forest.

Breathing painfully, the air so cold it burned her lungs with every breath, she forced herself onward. As she spotted the taillights of her car ahead of her, it dawned on her that her car keys were in the pocket of the coat she'd abandoned on the lake.

She sprinted to the rear tire of the car and dropped to her knees beside it, fumbling frantically for the spare key in its magnetic holder. She spied a flash of movement through the trees. *Crap.* The Russian had almost caught up with her again.

She felt the bump of the magnetic holder, jerked it free of its mooring, and jumped up, fumbling to open it while she headed for the driver's side door.

A shot rang out. She instinctively ducked, even though the bullet would have hit her about the same time she heard its sound if it were going to hit her. Another shot, and a piece of bark flew off a tree just over the car's hood.

The magnetic box opened, the key fell out, and she bent down, scooped it up, and jammed it in the door lock. Her fingers were half-frozen and clumsy. She dived into the car, reaching for the ignition as she simultaneously stomped on the brake pedal and pulled her door shut. A huge shape loomed just outside. She slammed the car lock and threw the car into drive as the Russian flung himself at her window. She hit the gas, and her little car jumped forward. The Russian hung onto the door frame for a few seconds before falling away. She reached the end of the driveway and shot out into the road. She hit the brakes, threw the car into a left turn, and skidded dangerously close to the ditch along the far side of the road before her tires finally caught enough traction to make the turn and right the vehicle.

She accelerated away from the man behind her with reckless speed, shooting down the icy road until she'd passed the entrance to Anatoly's estate and left it well behind, too.

She took her foot off the gas and proceeded at a slightly more moderate pace as the narrow road twisted and turned out of the valley. Finally, she came to the main road, which had at least been plowed, and bumped over a pile of snow and onto the salted pavement.

More relieved than she'd been in a long time, she accelerated away from the lake and headed back toward Washington.

CHAPTER 19

*H*ELEN CHECKED OUT OF THE HOTEL ROOM SHE'D SPENT THE RE-
mainder of the night in. Despite a long soak in a hot bath, she was
stiff and sore this morning. She moved slowly and carefully, which
lent even more credence to her disguise as Yosef's timid wife as
she donned the Ruth disguise and went to the hospital to visit her
husband.

She was relieved to find out he'd been moved out of the ICU
and into a regular room. She wound through the maze-like hospital to his room and pushed open the door quietly. He was
asleep. She sat down beside the bed, relishing the peacefulness of
the moment.

He still had a lot of monitors and tubes hooked up to him, but
she gathered his condition was much improved and he was out of
the woods. The relief that swept over her was shocking in its intensity. She had no idea what she would do if she lost this man.
He was her rock. Her touchstone on everything decent and good
in the world.

Once upon a time, Grayson had been that person in her life.
But he'd drifted away a little more with every trip overseas she
took. She couldn't put her finger on the exact date when they'd
become strangers to each other, but it had been a long time ago.

He raised the kids and held down the fort. She traveled the
world doing her country's work abroad. She didn't think he'd felt

emasculated by his role as primary parent to the kids, but he did resent her lack of participation. She hadn't been there for the injuries and illnesses, the school plays and sports, the celebrations of excellent report cards. Nor had she been there for the first heartbreaks, the insecurities, the failures and dashed dreams.

She'd missed all the important events in her kids' lives, and she'd left Gray to make excuses for her absence. He had a right to resent her.

He'd asked her more than a few times over the years to quit her job. To find something else to do that would keep her home in Washington full-time.

But she'd been addicted to the work. To the adrenaline rush, the danger, the satisfaction of a kill well made. And through it all, she'd been addicted to working with Yosef.

She'd told herself that her feelings for him were merely part and parcel of her job. But now she was retired and he was lying in a hospital bed. There was no way to avoid the truth. Her addiction to this man had everything to do with her feelings for him and little to do with their working relationship.

He was married. She was married.

They would probably drive each other crazy within two weeks if they tried to make a go of an actual romantic relationship. Goodness knew, she had no desire to jeopardize their deep friendship by trying to make it more than it was.

But what if they did work well together as a couple? What would it be like to live with a man who knew everything about her? From whom she had no secrets at all? With whom she could completely and totally be herself?

It was tantalizing to imagine.

Yosef moved slightly in his sleep and groaned under his breath. His hand moved vaguely toward his chest as if to massage away the pain there.

She reached for his hand, intercepting it before he could disturb the heavy bandages wrapping his torso and right shoulder.

As her fingers wrapped around his, guiding his hand back down to the bed, his eyes opened. Their brown depths were sleepy, but aware. He frowned for a moment. Then recognition flared in his gaze. "Helen?" he rasped.

"Call me Ruth in here. I told them I'm your wife. It was the only way they'd let me in to see you."

"How is Ruth?"

"The same. I spoke with her nurse the morning after you were shot, and the company that provides care for her has had nurses with her around the clock. I told them to tell her that you'd been called out of town on business. I didn't want to worry her until—" She took a deep breath. "Until we knew you were going to pull through."

He nodded a little. "Thank you."

"I thought I might go over to your place to visit her once I knew you were okay to tell her there'd been an accident, but you're fine."

"I'd rather you let her believe I'm out of town. She likes it when I travel. I bring home stories to tell her about the exotic places I've seen."

"Of course." She paused. "How do you feel?"

"Like I took a high-caliber slug in the chest and nearly died."

"Fair. Are you in a lot of pain?"

He shrugged then winced, silently answering the question. "I'll live. How did Helen Keller put it? All the world is full of suffering. It is also full of overcoming."

She didn't doubt he had the quote exactly right. The man had a nearly eidetic memory for everything he'd ever read.

With a glance at the door to make sure it was closed, she said quietly, "I had a little visit with Anatoly last night. He's adamant that neither he nor his government had anything to do with your shooting."

Yosef's eyes opened wide, and he studied her alertly. "Do you believe him?"

"He lied about a couple of things in our conversation, and his tells were fairly obvious. He gave me no signs of lying when he said they had nothing to do with shooting you. That's why I let him live."

One corner of Yosef's mouth turned up slightly. "My fierce Amazon protector."

"Darn tootin'. Somebody shot my Yossi, and when I find out who it is, he or she is going to pay."

He shook his head a little. "Before you embark upon a journey of revenge, first dig two graves."

"Confucius?" she grumbled. "Really?"

"He knew wherefore he spoke."

"Aren't you the guy who told me we have to draw lines in the sand from time to time and not back away from them, not one inch?"

"Yes, but I also am the guy who tells you over and over not to take action until we are certain we have the right person. It's worth taking the extra time to be sure we have the right target in your sights before you pull the trigger."

"You're no fun."

He smiled a little and placed his hand over hers, where it rested on the edge of his bed. "I appreciate your righteous anger on my behalf. We will find out who shot me and why. And when we do, we'll take whatever action is necessary to send a message to the shooter . . . and whoever hired that bastard."

"You don't think the shooter was the originator of the hit?" she asked quickly.

"Professional assassins rarely choose their own targets. And surely the person who shot me was a professional. You saw the attack. What do you think?"

"It was one hundred percent a professional job. The speed of the two shots, the accuracy of the shot at your chest, the way absolutely no sign of the shooter was left behind to identify him or her—no question, it was a pro."

"There you have it. Someone hired the shooter to kill me."

"Any guess who put the hit out on you?"

He fell silent. "I've had a lot of time to think about that."

"And?"

"I hesitate to say anything because you might go off half-cocked."

"If I promise not to kill anyone until you give me the green light, will you at least share your suspicions with me?" When he continued not to speak, she added, "It would be a tragedy if something happened to you and your suspicions died with you."

Yosef's gaze shot to the door in alarm. "Do you have reason to believe the shooter is trying to come back to finish off the job?"

"No. Security at the hospital is good enough to give an assassin pause. And speaking as a professional, why would I attempt to kill someone at the one place that can stop almost anyone from dying? Better to wait until you're back home and well away from emergency trauma care."

He grimaced at her pithy observation.

"Well?" she prompted. "Who do you suspect?"

He sighed. "Scorpius."

"Interesting. That was who Anatoly speculated was behind the attacks on me and you."

"Did he say anything more about Scorpius?" Yosef asked quickly.

"He said it's a person in the US government who may be killing people to get them out of the way of his or her advancement. He also told me he heard a rumor that Scorpius hired Nikolai Imbramov to make the New Year's Eve hit."

Yosef speared her with a gaze that betrayed just how brilliant a mind worked behind his mild-mannered façade. "Did you believe him?"

"He appeared to be telling the truth. He did seem rather smug when he dropped the name. As if he counted it a win for his team that the Russians were aware of Scorpius's existence."

"If Scorpius is embedded as deeply and as high in the government as I believe him or her to be, Anatoly has reason to be smug. It means the Russians may also have a source highly placed inside the government. How else would they be aware of Scorpius's existence? To my knowledge, I'm one of a handful of people who has even seen the word Scorpius."

She frowned. "Is Scorpius a Russian mole?"

"Anything is possible."

"I hate it when you say things like that. I like to deal in absolutes. Good guys, bad guys. Evil bad guys in need of killing by good guys like me."

"The world is not made up of absolutes, Helen. We've had this conversation before. The world is painted in shades of gray."

"Screw gray. I hate gray." She leaned down closer to him and asked under her breath, "What was in the encoded messages you brought to the pub with you the night you were shot?"

"I don't know. But I believe they were generated by Scorpius. I was hoping you might ask your son's companion if he would be willing to run them through the NSA's decryption protocols. If Scorpius is burrowed in as deeply as I think he is, I can't risk decoding the documents at Langley."

"Great minds think alike," she replied lightly. "I already passed them to Liang. And he was none too happy I had them. He threatened to arrest me for having classified material." She added quickly, "And don't worry. I didn't tell him my security clearance was higher than his."

"Past tense, my dear."

"I know. I know."

He smiled gently. "When I'm back on my feet, I'll continue my search for the identity of Scorpius. And I may even ask you to eliminate him or her. If Scorpius is as highly placed as I suspect, I probably won't be able to use an internal agency asset to eliminate the threat. But you have to wait for me to make the call. Okay?"

"I'm not Rambo. I am perfectly capable of being patient and disciplined. I don't barge around shooting everything that moves."

"Your recent activities notwithstanding," he commented dryly.

She rolled her eyes at him. "I didn't go looking for trouble. It came looking for me." She added peevishly, "I'm retired."

"Right." He closed his eyes for a long moment, as if he was growing tired.

"I should let you rest."

She started to extricate her hand from beneath his, but his fingers tightened over hers and he murmured, "I've been thinking about something else."

"What's that?"

"I'm not convinced the attack on New Year's Eve was directed at you."

She stared at him, stunned. "I beg your pardon? Are you telling me that hit was aimed at Peter? Or Li?"

"Possibly. I'm just saying that we should not make assumptions before we explore all the alternatives."

"I should warn them then. They need to be careful. Take security precautions—"

"Helen. You can't tell them anything. If they suddenly start acting paranoid, whoever's out to harm them would spot it immediately."

"He's my son! And he loves Liang!"

"I'm sorry. You can't tell them." His voice, though weak and raspy, was implacable.

"Dang it, Yosef. I can't sit by and let one of my children be harmed. I *won't* sit by. Nobody messes with my family—"

He cut her off gently. "I debated a long time whether to say anything at all to you or not. I knew you would feel this way. But I have a compromise to offer you."

"Which is?" she snapped.

"I'll request a security team to keep an eye on your son and Liang. Quietly. From a distance. Nothing that would catch the attention of anyone following them or plotting to harm them. If someone actively tries to hurt them, you can claim motherhood and that you were only protecting your child. No jury would convict you."

"Gee. Thanks. I'm so glad I have your permission to be a parent."

"A careful, low-key parent who keeps her distance from her family until absolutely necessary."

"You're asking me to stay away from my family? Are you nuts?" Every bone in her body was screaming at her to gather her family close and hover over them like a protective mama bear until this whole mess was resolved. Which was to say, until she killed Nikolai and whoever hired him to go after her, or Liang, or all of her loved ones.

"Helen—"

"Ruth," she interrupted in an urgent whisper.

"Right. Ruth, if we spook Scorpius, we'll never figure out who he is, what he wants, and why he's coming after us."

"All right, already. I get it. I'll lay low." She added, "But you promise the agency will protect Peter and Li?"

"Li mostly, I should think," Yosef said tiredly. "And I promise. I'll call in whatever favors it takes."

"Okay. That's good. Thanks." She breathed a sigh of relief. Then what Yosef had just said struck her. "Why do you think Li was the target?" She felt bad for badgering Yosef with all these questions when he was clearly flagging, but she had to know.

"Your son is an art dealer. His boyfriend is a high-ranking NSA analyst specializing in counterterrorism, both foreign and domestic. Which one makes more sense for a hit squad to go after?"

"Counterterrorism, huh? Li has never said a word about what he does over at NSA."

"Then forget you heard it from me."

"It's forgotten."

She stood up and brushed the hair back from Yosef's unnaturally pale brow. "Rest. Get better. I need you back at full strength to help me sort out all this craziness."

"Be careful, Helen. Keep your head down."

"Are you kidding? I haven't even slept in my own bed in days."

His eyes popped back open in concern. "What about the security team on your house?"

"Someone got in anyway."

Yosef swore under his breath. "I'll make a call. Have the detail increased in size. And I'll kick some butts while I'm at it."

"Don't worry about me. I know how to stay out of sight. You taught me well."

His eyelids drifted closed as she turned away from him and headed for the door.

She stopped for a moment, resumed the persona of Ruth Mizrah, and slipped out of the room, clutching her purse protectively against her chest.

* * *

It felt weird to take off the disguise of being Ruth minutes before tiptoeing into the sickroom of the actual Ruth. She hadn't seen Yosef's wife in several months, and the deterioration was dramatic. She lolled to one side in her hospital-style bed, hands clawed against her chest, her facial features distorted by loss of muscle control. She looked emaciated and at least twenty years older than Helen knew her to be. It broke her heart to see how ALS had ravaged this brilliant, lovely woman.

She sat down by Ruth's bed and touched her elbow. Ruth's eyes opened groggily.

"Hi, Ruth." She couldn't tell if Ruth even heard her, let alone understood her. But Ruth seemed to be making an effort to hold her gaze on her, so she continued. "Yosef mentioned that he was going to be out of town for a bit on a business trip, so I thought you might like a little company while he's gone. I wonder where he went. Maybe to one of his precious archaeological digs in the Middle East. You know how much he enjoyed the idea of finding a pharaoh's tomb." She babbled on about the heat and dust and hidden Egyptian treasure, anything to fill the empty space in the room.

Thankfully, after only a few minutes, Ruth began to droop and her eyelids began to drift shut.

Helen stood up, and on impulse, leaned down and kissed Ruth's paper-dry cheek. "When I look at you, I still see the beautiful young woman with flowing brunette hair and a smile that lights up a room. And I know Yosef does, too."

She straightened, and a premonition flowed over her that this was the last time she would see Ruth alive. She whispered past the constriction in her throat, "He loves you very much."

As she turned away to leave, she paused in the doorway to glance back. A single tear track glistened on Ruth's averted cheek.

She couldn't leave like this. She hurried back to Ruth's side and wrapped her fingers around Ruth's deformed hand. "Ruth. I promise you. When you're gone, I'll look after Yosef. All his friends will. We'll make sure he keeps living life, reading and traveling, and sharing his brilliance with the world. And we won't forget you. Not me. Not Yosef. Not anyone who knew you. Your life mattered. You made the world a better place."

Ruth's chin dipped slowly, wobbling, a painfully difficult gesture of acknowledgment.

Helen felt the tears spilling over onto her cheeks as well. She was abjectly grateful that Ruth didn't open her eyes and look at her, for she thought the moment might have broken her.

She fled the room and raced down the stairs, not stopping until she was resting her forehead on the front door.

She dealt in death every day. But the kind she dealt out was sharp and quick, painless. Or at least if not entirely painless, nearly instantaneous. This death by slow degrees that Ruth was facing, and Yosef with her, was almost too much to bear thinking about, let alone living through.

How they did it, she couldn't fathom. She supposed they didn't have any choice but to find a way forward. They both woke up every day and got through it somehow. Their courage was humbling.

She had to find out who'd tried to kill Yosef. She *had* to.

This morning, when she stepped outside of Yosef's house, she didn't feel any eyes upon her. Still, she moved quickly to her car and drove around the Virginia suburbs long enough to be certain she hadn't been followed. In this, at least, she was at home. She knew how to operate in urban environments and how to spot other operators as well.

She was contemplating turning her car toward home to see if her house was safe yet, when her cell phone rang. The caller ID almost made her swerve off the road, she was so startled.

She turned into a random parking lot and took the call. "Why hello, Grayson. To what do I owe this surprise?"

"Not a pleasant surprise? Just a surprise, huh?" he retorted. "Hello to you, too."

She sighed. *Typical.* She couldn't even say hello to her husband without it turning into a fight. "How are you, Gray? And where are you?"

"I'm still in Brazil. One of the graduate students working with my team got sick, and we brought her out to a village so she can be transported to a hospital. There's a cell phone tower here, so I have service. I got quite a collection of texts and emails from the children, I might add. What on earth's going on around there?"

"If you were home, you'd know," she snapped.

He accused angrily, "You promised things would be different when you retired."

"Things *were* different. And then someone shot up Peter and Li's house, and things have been kind of crazy ever since."

"You swore to me you would never bring your work home to us, Helen. You *swore*."

"I don't control what other people do. I've kept my promise and kept my work away from you and our children for all these years. But I can't help it if someone else decided to randomly attack me for no apparent reason. I've been retired for months, thank you very much."

"Peter is livid. And worse, he's scared. That's your fault."

She sighed. "I know. And I'm doing everything in my power to fix the situation. I've called in favors from everyone I can think of to find out who shot up Peter's house and to figure out why."

"In the meantime, your children are freaked out and don't understand why you're behaving strangely. They're worried about you. Why can't you just act like a normal parent for once? You said you would work on being a better mother now that you're retired."

Silence crackled across the connection. It was an old fight they'd fought hundreds of times over the years. She was tired and distracted and had other problems to deal with right now besides her husband's petulance. Furthermore, she had no desire to rehash old conflicts and hurts that had no solutions.

Grayson was a good man, but sometimes he had the emotional range of a spoon. If she asked him to see the current situation boiling around her from her point of view, he would only grow more defensive and say something else to draw emotional blood.

She sighed. "How have you been? Are you eating enough?"

"I'm fine."

Silence fell again. He was pissed off and not prepared to play the polite charade of civilized marriage today, obviously. None-theless, she tried. "How's your work going?"

"Excellent. We reached the valley we were hoping to explore. I've discovered three new species of frog, one of them completely unique. The botanist with the team has discovered over a dozen new species of plants and collected samples. The ornithologist thinks she's identified a couple of new bird species as well."

"So you'll be able to apply for protected status for the valley like you hoped?" she asked.

"Definitely."

"How much longer do you plan to be down there?" Which was to say, how much longer did she have to sort out the mess here in Washington before he came home?

"I don't know. The locals are telling us we should take a look at another river basin near here if we want to find unique species. We've filed paperwork with the Brazilian government to do a sur-vey and explore it. If that comes through, I may be here several more months."

"I'm so glad you feel free to attack me about letting down the family while you gallivant around jungles thousands of miles from home for months on end."

"I was home the whole time the children were growing up. Where were you?"

She retorted, "I was serving my country and making enough money to keep you living a comfortable lifestyle and the children in the best private schools." This, too, was an old and tired argu-ment with no solutions and no prisoners taken.

"We could've lived off my salary—"

She cut him off. "And yet I heard no complaints out of you or the children when I brought home my paychecks. Let it go, Gray. It's water under the bridge. The children are grown and living their own lives. It's only you and me now."

It hung unspoken between them that the children had, for a long time, been the main glue holding the two of them together. She loved her husband. She loved his curiosity, his intellect, his wry humor. She'd always found him insanely attractive and they'd always had a smoking-hot love life . . . when they were in the same place at the same time. Their problem had always been the travel that both of their careers required of them.

He'd resented not getting to travel when the children were little and she'd been running all over the world. Once Jaynie left for college, he felt as if he had decades' worth of field research to make up for missing out on. And now the shoe was on the other foot. She was stuck at home with the family, resenting his absence, while he ran hither and yon chasing down the next new species of frogs. It was ironic. But mostly it just sucked.

She said lightly, "When you do decide to come home, I would appreciate it if you gave me a call before you get on the plane. That way I'll be able to make sure all the gunmen are out of our house before you get back."

"That's not funny."

"Who says it's a joke?" she bit out.

"Are you in danger?" he blurted.

"Oh, now you figure that out? Thanks so much for expressing concern that four armed gunmen burst into Peter's house and tried to murder me. It was super exciting barely escaping with my life, and it was delightful hiding in a locked bathroom with Peter and Li's puppy until the SWAT team arrived. It's how I hope to spend every New Year's Eve going forward."

"Helen—"

She cut him off. "I'm having a grand time living each day not knowing if whoever shot up Peter's house is going to jump out from behind a bush and mow me down in the street. It's fantastic living in hiding, couch surfing at other people's homes because I'm too scared to go back to my own bed, and waiting for someone, anyone, to tell me what the heck is going on and why I seem to be the target of it all."

Whew. She hadn't realized she was holding that much pent-up stress until it all came tumbling out like that.

"I'm sorry, Gray. I shouldn't have dumped all of that on you—"

"Helen. I didn't realize you were afraid. I just . . ." He hesitated. "I don't associate you with being scared of anything. You're so strong. Always have everything under control. You never need help." He added, "Is there anything I can do for you?"

And there it was. The basic decency of the man. The thing that kept her hanging on to the tattered threads of their marriage in hopes that one day they might be able to weave it all back together into some semblance of a loving relationship.

"Thanks for asking, but there's nothing anyone can do right now."

"What about Yosef? Your old boss knows things, right? Has people he can call in, I don't know, the intelligence community or something?"

"He was shot in a restaurant a few nights ago and nearly died. He's in the hospital but should make a full recovery, assuming nobody tries to kill him again."

"Holy crap. What's going on up there? I should come home—"

"No. You shouldn't," she cut him off forcefully. "You would just be one more person for me to worry about. Stay where you are. But I'm not kidding. When you do come home, give me warning before you just show up. Things are . . . unpredictable . . . right now."

He swore under his breath. "Helen. I can't just leave all that to you."

"Yes. You can. I have the contacts to deal with it, and you don't. But do me a favor."

"Name it."

"When you talk with the kids, tell them I'm not crazy. Tell them . . . tell them I'm more shaken up by the shooting at Peter's house than I'm letting on and to cut me a little slack. I need a little space to deal with it on my own."

"In other words, you want them to stay away from you until you've single-handedly identified and taken down whoever attacked you?"

They'd never talked about her work. Ever. She was pretty sure he'd figured out what she did, but they'd always had a silent deal that if he asked no questions, she would volunteer no lies as answers. This was as close as he'd ever come to actually acknowledging that she had the skill set to literally take down her attackers.

Was she ready to admit to him what she'd done for all those

years? Was she ready to see the horror in his eyes that his wife, the mother of his children, was a murderer? Surely that was how he would see her job.

She replied lamely, "I'm working with a lawyer Mitchell introduced me to. If I can figure out who attacked me at Peter's, she'll do the takedown. A legal takedown."

Grayson made a noncommittal sound, and she didn't press the issue. As yet another awkward silence fell between them, she resorted to the old standby, "Well, I'll let you go." It sounded like a cold brush-off, so she quickly added, "I'm sure you have a bunch of calls to return and stuff to do before you head back out into the jungle. Thanks for calling. It's good to hear your voice. I love you."

"Right, then," he replied briskly. "Love you, too. Stay safe."

"You too."

The line went dead in her ear. She stared at the blank face of her phone for a long time. As interactions with him went, that hadn't been disastrous. But she was startled by the vehemence of her outburst to him. She *was* tired, and she was more stressed out than she'd been aware of. Maybe she was more ready to retire than she'd realized.

Or maybe she just needed a few weeks on a lonely beach somewhere to soak up the sun and stare at her toes. She was only fifty-five, for crying out loud. That was a long way from dead. At least it was if she had anything to say about it.

Biscuit had taught her one thing for sure—she wanted to be a grandma and spoil her grandchildren rotten. She wanted to do all the things with them that she'd missed out on doing with her own children. It was probably too late to make it up to her own children, but maybe she could make it up at least a little with their children.

It wasn't much, but it was something to hang on to. And in her experience, a little hope was a whole lot better than no hope at all.

CHAPTER 20

*H*ELEN GOT IN LINE TO ORDER A COFFEE AND LOOKED AROUND THE shop surreptitiously, sizing up everyone in the place, as she always did. There. In the corner. She spotted Angela Vincent, who'd asked her to meet at this café. Angela wasn't alone. Helen didn't recognize the man seated beside Angela. He was dressed in a military fatigue coat that had seen better days, and he could use a shave.

Something about him triggered alarm bells in Helen's head. Maybe it was the way he held himself, coiled as if he could explode into violent action at any moment. Or maybe it was the way his sharp poise contrasted so oddly with his attire. If it was a disguise, it was a terrible one.

For a disguise to work, a person had to become their clothing. Present exactly the image the clothing brought to people's minds when they glanced at it. Exploit the tendency of most people to make snap judgments based entirely on physical appearance.

She picked up her drink and followed her instinct, blending into the crowd clustered around tables, easing toward Angela and her companion surreptitiously. She parked with her back to them around the corner, as if she were waiting to get into one of the restrooms in the back of the store, and shamelessly eavesdropped on them.

Angela was speaking. "... and you didn't have any trouble getting your prescriptions?"

"No. Thanks for helping out with that."

"I love nothing better than using my legal letterhead to scare jerks into doing their jobs." A pause. "How's the new place working out?"

"Fine."

"Promise me you're sleeping in it."

Helen couldn't see him, but she sensed a shrug in his silence.

Angela's response was sharp, if quiet. "I got that place so you'd have somewhere safe to sleep, Clint. There have been a bunch of murders not getting properly investigated recently, and I need to know you're okay."

"I can take care of myself." He sounded amused, maybe a little insulted at the inference that he couldn't.

"I don't worry about you when you're on your meds, Clint. But when you go off them . . . you could end up in trouble."

"Meaning I'd become a victim? Or that when I go off my meds I might actually be the serial killer who's running around DC right now?" he snapped.

Angela made a pained sound. "What would I do without you? Promise me you'll take care of yourself and that you'll sleep in the apartment I got you."

Helen didn't hear a response, and she couldn't see Angela's companion from here.

Silence fell between the pair, and she obviously wasn't going to hear anything else. She stepped around the corner, and said brightly, "There you are, Angela. I hope I haven't kept you waiting."

Angela slid off her high stool and gave Helen a quick hug. It startled Helen, but she rather liked having a friend who felt comfortable hugging her. She hugged Angela back and smiled at the lawyer as they both slid onto barstools.

"Helen, this is Clint Tucker. Clint, this is the woman I was telling you about. Helen Warwick."

"Ma'am," he said briefly.

Ex-military, for sure. Only they said the word "sir" or "ma'am" with that complete familiarity. Shaggy hair and unshaven cheeks aside, he looked like a Special Forces type. His gaze was never still, ranging around the coffee shop much as hers did. And he seemed to be sizing up people much the way she did. *Yep.* He, too, was a trained killer. She could spot a kindred soul from a mile away.

Angela said, "Clint is my eyes and ears on the street. He investigates stuff for me, and he's the person who first spotted the similarities in the cases I showed to you."

Helen's gaze snapped to him. He was studying her intently, a tiny frown between his brows, as if he was struggling to reconcile her appearance with his gut feeling that she was more than met the eye. His gaze slid away immediately, and his expressions smoothed out to one of bland boredom.

She bit back a smile. He was so totally a Spec Ops type.

"How long have you been out of the service?" she asked him.

His gaze, when it turned back to her, was completely unreadable. "A while."

Angela interjected, seemingly oblivious to the silent sizing up going on between them, "I asked you here to talk with Clint because he's seen a couple of interesting incidents recently that might be connected to my cases."

Helen looked at him expectantly, and he exhaled a little harder than necessary. "I doubt they're connected," he commented.

"Do tell," she said mildly.

He leaned in a little, his shoulders hunched as he planted his elbows on the table. The true size of him beneath the baggy coat became obvious. His shoulders were broad and thick. Muscular. Not a man to mess with in a dark alley.

"I . . . spend time . . . in a homeless camp in east central DC from time to time. I look out for the folks there when I'm around." He spoke slowly, choosing his words carefully. Didn't want to reveal too much about himself to her, huh? *Fair.* She wasn't in the business of laying all her cards on the table either.

He continued, "In the past week, a couple of the regulars have gone missing. Killed. Both of them."

He had her full attention now.

"You saw the first one. You're the lady who showed up right after Jimmy J. was killed, aren't you?"

"Jimmy J.?"

"Schizophrenic guy. About thirty years old. He was knifed in broad daylight in the camp. And right after it happened, a well-dressed woman ran up to him and chased off the killer. Called the police. Tried to stop Jim from bleeding out. That was you, wasn't it?"

She shrugged. "I did try to help a man who'd been stabbed last week."

"What were you doing there?" he blurted. "Not exactly your stomping grounds, is it?"

"I was investigating one of Angela's murders. Taking a look at the murder site for myself."

"What did you see?" he asked.

She sensed the quiz in the question. Was she credible or not? She answered with a gentle smile, "The murder site was a box canyon a sniper would have a hard time missing a target in. Egress route from the roof of any one of several buildings would be a breeze. Multiple alleys to use as escape routes, multiple hiding places to dump the murder weapon. If I were trying to frame somebody for a kill, that's the spot I'd do it."

He leaned back hard, arms crossed, staring at her. "Who are you?" he demanded.

"I'm a retired analyst for the State Department. I negotiated trade deals."

"Right," he bit out. "And where did you learn to shoot?"

She had to smile a little. There was no conning a con artist. One shooter knew another when he heard her talk about a field of fire. "I did a little competition shooting in my youth. Before I got married and had kids."

Make of that what you will, Clint Tucker, retired Special Forces operative.

For her part, Angela was looking back and forth between the two of them, as if sensing the currents flowing between them. Helen couldn't tell from the lawyer's expression if she understood the unspoken sparring between her and Clint or not.

Eventually, Angela murmured, "Tell her about the second murder."

"A couple of nights ago, a longtime member of the homeless community went missing. A woman calling herself Gilda. She drinks a bit. If she can scrape together some cash from panhandling, she buys herself a bottle of vodka and drinks herself into a stupor for a couple of days. Night before last, she was seen leaving her hooch—that's a hut built of whatever materials a person can find and bang together into a shelter—"

Helen nodded, and he continued, "She told the guy in the hooch next door to watch her stuff until she got back. Except she never came back."

"What makes you think she was killed?" Helen asked.

"When I went down to the liquor store to see if she'd been in to buy herself a bottle of vodka—which she had—I found a huge bloodstain on the pavement. I called the police, but they said a puddle of what might look like dried blood wasn't enough to send someone out to investigate. They said to call back when I had a body or a crime in progress."

Helen winced. In the part of town she lived in, a puddle of blood would have gotten a full crime scene team response. But here, it didn't even rate a cop stopping by to check it out. "I gather nobody's seen Gilda since?"

"No, ma'am."

"What do you think happened?" she asked.

He shrugged. "There's been a guy hanging around the camp recently. Doesn't live there. Just skulks around the edges of it watching people come and go."

"What does he look like?" she asked.

"White guy. Thirtyish. He had light brown hair the first few times I saw him. A week or so back, though, he dyed his hair dark brown. That's what caught my attention."

"Height and weight?"

"Average height. Looks like an athlete gone to fat. Like a guy who sits all day doing his job."

Unlike Clint, who looked as if he worked out constantly under that deceptive jacket and baggy clothing.

"Would you recognize him if you saw him again?" she asked.

"Yeah."

"Could you call me if you see him?"

"I suppose."

She fished a pen out of her purse and wrote her phone number on a napkin, which she pushed across the table at him. He took a hard look at the number then wadded the napkin and shoved it in his coat pocket. Obviously, he'd memorized it.

On a hunch, she asked him, "Have you scoped out any other streets in the metro area that are set up for murder the same way Angela's murders were?"

Clint glanced over at Angela quickly. Which told Helen he had, indeed, reconnoitered other possible murder sites and given a list to Angela.

She, too, looked over at Angela expectantly.

The lawyer shrugged. "I gave the list to my son. He's keeping an eye out for murders at any of those locations."

Helen frowned. "Why wait until another person dies? Why not stake out the sites now? You could stop a needless murder and catch the real killer."

Clint cut in. "Besides the fact that Angela and I aren't exactly a government agency and don't have the resources to stake out a dozen potential murder sites, as far as I can tell the canyon-style killings stopped a while ago. They happened fairly regularly, but then they stopped."

"How regularly?" she asked curiously.

"Every four weeks or so."

"How can you be sure they've stopped altogether?" Helen challenged.

"I've got my sources."

"And your sources are aware there's a serial killer on the loose for the past year?"

"Yes, ma'am. Word's been out on the street for a while. The

homeless community is well aware of it. They've been staying off the streets at night for months."

"Why aren't the police doing something about this? And for that matter, why isn't the district attorney all over this?" She aimed the second question squarely at Angela.

She shrugged. "He's got no proof. I've got Georgie looking for other killings that match my four cases. When we've compiled a complete list of killings, I plan to take it all to the DA." She added, "In an official capacity."

"Have you at least mentioned it to him?" Helen asked.

Angela threw her a withering look. She couldn't tell if Angela was silently communicating *Of course I have*, or *Are you kidding? And wreck not only my career but my hot affair?*

Helen commented, "My son hasn't said anything about it, and the subject of murders in the District of Columbia came up over a supper several nights ago. He'd have mentioned it then if he knew anything about a serial killer."

Angela replied, "It's not as if the police and DA want to scare the populace by announcing there's a serial killer on the loose. People panic, the phone lines go crazy, and everyone breathes fire down their necks until the killer is caught. Better that they investigate it quietly and catch the guy before they announce how many people he's killed."

Clint added in, sourly, "As long as he's killing poor folks and homeless people, it's not as if anybody in law enforcement or the media is going to get too riled up over it."

"That's a cynical view," Helen responded. "I'd like to think our police and prosecutors care about the lives of every citizen equally."

Angela smiled at her as if she was achingly naïve, and Clint rolled his eyes. *Fine.* Call her a starry-eyed optimist. She clung firmly to the belief that the universe bent toward justice. She had to. It was how she'd rationalized her work through the years. She was the pointy end of the spear of justice.

Her phone vibrated. Frowning, she pulled it out of her pocket to glance at it.

Holy crap. The program tracking the burr on Nikolai Ibramov's coat had just sensed him nearby. He was back in town.

She gulped the rest of her coffee and said to Clint, "Call me if any more residents of the camp go missing."

He nodded in the affirmative. She stood up, said a quick farewell to Angela, and hurried out of the coffee shop.

Time to go hunting. And to find out what the hell was going on.

CHAPTER 21

*H*ER FIRST PROBLEM WAS TO FIGURE OUT EXACTLY WHERE NIKOLAI was. Her second, and possibly more pressing, problem was that she really needed to get into her house and get her full surveillance kit out of her storage room.

She was relieved that Yosef had promised to up the number of men around her house. But they would surely recognize the kind of gear she needed to haul out of the house. She would have to pull into the garage, load everything in her car's tiny trunk, and hope it all fit.

She'd compiled her equipment over many years and had tweaked every piece of it to her exact specifications. Hundreds of thousands of dollars were invested in her collection of weapons, gadgets, and gear.

She put her phone on the dashboard of her car and followed the homing beacon across Washington toward Nikolai. It was a bit of a game to find streets that led toward the signal, which was moving and changed direction several times.

The good news was the signal shifted slowly. Nikolai was probably on foot. The bad news was that, when she got close, she was going to have to park her car and continue her pursuit on foot. She had no desire to close in on him yet. Her only goal right now was to find where he was making his home base. He wasn't anywhere near the hotel from New Year's Eve, which meant he'd found someplace else to shack up.

She drove within a block of the signal. It was a mixed residential and commercial area. Which meant it was crowded and busy, and Washington, DC's chronic parking shortage was at its worst.

It took her close to an hour to park her car, close in on the signal on foot, and finally make visual contact with Nikolai. The only disguise she had with her at the moment was her Ruth getup, so that was what she used.

The problem with portraying a timid, middle-aged woman was she couldn't sprint down a street or aggressively cut across a street in the middle of traffic without drawing a lot of attention. Middle-aged women in skirts and cardigan sweaters didn't race around like maniacs.

Not to mention, she didn't particularly want to run around like a maniac if she could avoid doing so. She was already stiff and sore from the exertions of the past several days. She needed a massage in the worst way as well as several days of complete rest to recuperate fully.

It took all of her patience, honed over decades of surveillance work, to pace herself to trail along behind Nikolai in her Ruth disguise.

It struck her forcefully that today was nothing like the work she'd done over the years. The man she was tracking today had tried to kill her. He'd attacked her in her son's home. He'd probably tried to kill Yosef. This was *personal.* She was out here as a mother, a wife, a friend, and she was pissed.

Sure, she was scared for her family, but mostly she was angry. *Furious.* It was all she could do to keep her steps steady and unhurried to remind herself she could not pull out her pistol and wax this jerk the moment she caught up with him. She owed her family and Yosef her best work, her patience, her meticulous planning and thoroughness in hunting down Nikolai Ibramov. Of all hunts, she had to get this one right.

She followed him for a dozen blocks, closing in bit by bit. Finally, his signal stopped moving, and she was able to catch up with the red dot on the face of the tracking device. She moved across the street from his current, stationary location. He'd gone into an internet café, as it turned out.

She stared doubtfully at the computer café. Did she dare go inside and get eyes on her target? It would be extremely risky. After all, he surely knew what she looked like. He had to have tracked her before attacking her on New Year's Eve. He no doubt had studied her face in detail and would recognize her through any but the most extreme disguise.

Her Ruth outfit would protect her from a casual glance by Nikolai but not an up-close-and-personal encounter. *Nope.* She needed to hold her ground out here. If he left from a back door, the tracking device would let her know.

She parked inside a drugstore across the street from the internet café. Nikolai stayed inside long enough that a drugstore clerk came over to her to ask her if she needed help finding something . . . and broadly hinted that she appeared to be loitering and should move along.

She bought a bottle of water and a protein bar, which she consumed while still standing inside the store, ignoring the glares of the clerk.

At long last, Nikolai emerged from the café. She slipped out of the drugstore and eased into the foot traffic behind him. He seemed to have picked up a bodyguard. A huge dude with a suspicious bulge under his left armpit had joined Nikolai and walked along beside him.

He wasn't exactly a great bodyguard. His gaze didn't move around much, and he didn't seem aware enough of his surroundings. Maybe he figured he could overpower any threat that presented itself with his gigantic body. Still, his presence did force her to keep well back from the pair and not engage Guardzilla.

Nikolai and his babysitter turned into a convenience store, which forced her to turn into a bookstore next door. She was blind in here, but she had the tracking burr to let her know when he moved again.

It didn't take long. The burr moved around the shop, stood at what was probably the checkout counter for a minute, then moved rapidly toward the back of the shop. She paralleled him, heading quickly toward the back of the small bookstore.

"Hey, you can't go in there! It's employees only back there—"

Whatever. Ignoring the kid behind the cash register, she hustled through the storeroom. She paused in front of the delivery door until the dot was solidly moving away from her.

"You've got to get out of here," the kid tried again.

"Fine," she snapped. She pushed open the door and stepped outside into the alley. She glanced quickly to her left, prepared to duck back into the store if Nikolai spotted her. She saw a pair of dark-clad male backs retreating quickly, and they never looked back at her. She hustled after her quarry.

Nikolai and his escort slipped out of sight around the corner, and she took off running. Being no amateur, she stopped shy of the corner. She crossed to the other side of the alley and peered out into the street. No pedestrians were acting startled, as if Nikolai had taken off running or had paused just around the corner, obviously waiting to pounce on someone.

She stepped out, staring straight ahead, not looking obviously for Nikolai off to her right. In fact, she turned left and walked away from Nikolai and his bodyguard for a dozen steps. The dot on her phone continued to move away from her, and only then did she reverse course. There they were. About a hundred feet in front of her.

She slowed her steps to let them pull ahead of her a bit more. Nikolai's escort carried a pair of grocery bags now, which appeared to be full of food. Bad tradecraft, that. Bodyguards needed to keep their hands free at all times to grab for a weapon or grapple with a hostile.

Nikolai had to be getting close to home. No self-respecting assassin weighed himself down with bulky, awkward props like groceries before commencing a lengthy evasion protocol.

Nikolai and his giant buddy turned into a doorway ahead of her, and she immediately turned left. She ducked into the lobby of a small walk-up building just behind a resident, stopping inside the entrance, hiding in the shadow of a large potted plant.

Nikolai had disappeared inside a similar building across the street. She didn't see him, but she did spot the big guy hanging around in the lobby.

Another resident entered the lobby she was lurking in, and she followed the man into the elevator. He pushed the button for the third floor, then she pushed the button for the fifth, which was the top floor.

Moving out into a narrow hallway, she headed for the fire escape door at the end of the hall. The door was wired with a simple contact alarm. She fished a pair of plastic gift cards out of her wallet. Slipping one into the doorway and holding it in place, she leaned on the crossbar and opened the door. Then, placing the second card across the tongue of the door to keep it from locking behind her, she eased it shut again.

The building across the street was one story shorter than this one, and she moved within a dozen feet of the edge of the roof before falling to her knees and crawling to the edge to look down. What she wouldn't give for her binoculars right now.

Over the next half hour, she spotted several people coming and going from the building. Of interest was the fact that every person she saw was a man with short hair and a dark suit. Most of them were built like brick houses. For all the world, it looked like a mob crash site. Nikolai's red dot hadn't moved more than a couple dozen feet in the past hour. She was satisfied this was his home base.

Backing off the roof, she retraced her steps to the ground floor. She waited in her lobby until she saw a man with the first woman she'd seen exit Nikolai's building. She paralleled them to the next corner before crossing the street to fall in behind them. It was dinnertime, and the streets were crowded.

She was able to move right up behind the couple. They were silent for the most part, but then the man muttered something under his breath and the woman turned her head and snapped back at him in Russian.

He pulled the scarf from around his neck and handed it to the woman. Helen got a good look at the back of his neck, covered with tattoos. She didn't need to see any more. Nikolai was shacking up with a Bratva crew.

She peeled away from the Russians and headed back toward her car.

* * *

Her house was dark when she drove past it. She headed around the block to park in the barn behind her property. Cautiously, she approached the house from the woods, crouching to watch for movement. All was quiet. Was the security team entirely out front? Or was at least one of them lurking out here in the woods?

She debated walking right up to the front door and letting herself in. Thing was, not only would the security team see her, but it would expose her to any hostiles out here, too. *Better to make the stealthy approach.* If Yosef's security team spotted her, they would understand her creeping up to her house in this manner.

She moved off to one side and approached the house at an oblique angle from the garage side. She darted into the shadow of the house, then sidled around to the back door leading into the garage. Once inside, she worked fast, turning off all the master circuit breakers.

Then she eased into the mudroom and immediately placed her hand on the biometrically activated alarm system. Its battery would last for hours. It had to be deactivated. All was silent and still around her. The house was cold. In her absence, the thermostat was programmed to drop to sixty-two energy-saving degrees.

She pulled out her handgun, left her purse on the kitchen counter, and commenced clearing the entire house. It was strange spinning into bathrooms, yanking open closet doors, scanning rooms with the infrared scanning app on her cell phone, performing electronic scans for bugs or cameras, and checking in every single nook or cranny a human could hide in. Thankfully, she'd played enough hide-and-seek with the children over the years to know where all those spots were.

After a tense half hour, she stood in her master closet—the last space in the house she'd examined. The house was clear. Whoever had broken in had not left behind any gadgets or surprises for her. Which meant they'd probably only been here with the intent to kill her. Which pointed at Nikolai. One more outrage to hang upon his head. One more reason to kill him at her earliest convenience.

She shone her flashlight at her purse rack. It didn't appear to have been disturbed. Nervously, she opened the hidden door and flashed her light at the walls. She breathed a sigh of relief at the sight of all her gear, undisturbed.

She pulled out a large duffel bag holding all the electronic gadgets required to engage in proper surveillance. She added in a long-range sniper rifle and her favorite medium-range sniper rifle. For good measure, she threw in a short-barreled urban assault rifle that was built for close quarters. She added sights, spotting scopes, and extra ammunition before zipping up the bag and carrying it into the closet.

She plucked a couple of hairs from her head and tucked them in the gap as she closed the hidden door. It was a simple hack to tell if an object had been moved, but sometimes simple was best.

Carrying the bag out into her dark bedroom, she froze as she heard a movement downstairs. Had she missed some device that had let Nikolai know she was here? She'd hoped that, by cutting off the power to the house, she'd disabled any bugs.

Swearing under her breath, she yanked out the urban assault weapon, eased home an ammo mag, and crept out into the hallway.

Whoever was in the house was fumbling around downstairs in the dark.

How had they gotten past the alleged security outside?

Rage at having her sanctuary invaded—the family home—soared through her. Channeling the rage into cold precision and total focus, she eased down the stairs on quick, silent feet. She spun into the living room, easing through it into the dining room. She plastered herself to the wall beside the swinging door and waited, listening. The intruder bumped one of the counter stools.

She tensed, readying herself for action. Very slowly, she slid down the wall until she was curled up in a tiny ball low to the ground.

The door swung open beside her, and a dark shape advanced into the dining room. She surged up behind him, jamming the barrel of her rifle hard against his kidneys. "Don't move or you're dead," she snarled.

The intruder's hands went up in the air, head-high, and she noted with surprise that they were empty. *No weapon?*

"Mrs. Warwick?" a wobbly voice squeaked.

Shocked to her core, she yanked her finger away from the trigger of her weapon. "Liang?" she blurted. "What are you doing here?"

"Is that a gun against my back?"

She swung the weapon down and tucked it inside her coat fast. "No, darling. It was my fingers. I wanted to make you think I had a gun, of course. I thought you were a robber. Speaking of which, how did you get in here?"

"Peter has a spare key, and the security guard outside said it was okay for me to come in. Since when do you have a security guard?"

"Since your house was blown to bits."

He absorbed that in silence, and she declined to offer any further explanation. Eventually, he asked, "Why is the power out?"

"I don't know. I was just heading for the garage to check that out. It's why I put my coat on. Just a second . . . let me run out and check the circuit breakers."

Without sticking around to see if he bought her lies, she rushed through the kitchen to the garage. She quickly hid her rifle behind the front tire of Grayson's SUV, then turned on the master circuit breakers.

Li showed up in the doorway. "That's got it. Whatever you did. The lights are on now, and the refrigerator's humming."

She jogged up the steps into the house and smiled brightly at him. "Sometimes when it gets cold and the furnace has to work too hard, it overloads the system and the master breaker trips. I've been meaning to have somebody come out and look at it. Can I make you a cup of tea, dear?"

"Um, sure."

She filled the electric kettle and turned it on. While it heated, she pulled out a wood chest holding various teas. "What's your pleasure?"

"Do you have something mild? Maybe a jasmine tea or a chamomile?"

"I have a lovely white jasmine tea. Very delicate. Not much caffeine."

"Perfect."

She bustled around getting out teacups and spoons. "What brings you to the house? Have you figured out what was in those documents I gave you?"

He frowned. "I've got a partial transcript. It appears to involve someone giving authorization to a subordinate for a mission of some kind. The decryption key changes when the message gets to the part of passing on specific instructions."

"Can you read enough to know if it was an order to attack or kill me . . . or you?" she asked, reluctantly.

"Sorry, no."

Li's expression abruptly closed up, tighter than a drum. He knew something about the instructions the operative had been given, but he wasn't sharing what he knew with her.

Frustrated, she probed as gently as she could, asking, "Can you tell who sent the message?"

"It partially decrypts to something like Scorn or SCOTUS. The computer didn't have enough information to extrapolate the word. It was probably a name of some kind. Which means it could have been anything."

Yeah. Like Scorpius. Had she not heard the name from Yosef and then from Anatoly, she might not have been so certain about it. But Yosef had been shot moments after uttering the code name. "Do you think it's the name of a person? Or maybe an operation? Don't they name their missions and stuff at the FBI and CIA?"

Liang shrugged. "Could be either a person or a project. No way to tell."

"Huh. Well, thanks, anyway. Will you keep trying to decode the rest of the message, then?"

A stubborn look entered his gaze. *Rats.* No question about it, she was bumping up against something classified, and he was going to dig in his heels and refuse to tell her about it.

"You wouldn't have any idea that message even existed if I hadn't brought it to you," she reminded him. "And I had high-level security clearances for decades in my work at State. I know how to keep a secret."

He snorted. "That, I can believe."

"Why? Does Peter accuse me of keeping secrets from him or something?"

"Or something," he answered dryly.

She rolled her eyes. She loved her middle child to death, but he had a streak of drama a mile wide in him. Li's wry smile faded, and she stared at him expectantly.

It took a few seconds, but finally he sighed and lowered his voice. "We got a request from the CIA to fully decrypt the message."

"Who made the request?" she asked, startled.

"Let's just say it came from the top. The very top."

Not helpful. It was entirely possible that this Scorpius person was at the very top of the agency, given what Yosef had said before he'd been shot. She poured the boiling water over the tea bags and carried the cups over to the island. She set a cup in front of Li and slid onto the stool perpendicular to him.

Li played with his tea bag, studying her intently as he dunked it. "Who gave you the encoded message, again?"

"An old friend who didn't know who else to turn to."

"And he or she thought the message had to do with who shot up our house and nearly killed you?"

"Possibly," she answered cautiously.

"Interesting."

She pounced on that. "Why?"

"No reason. It's just interesting."

"C'mon, Li. You and I both know what we're dancing around here. Shall we be frank with each other?"

"You go first."

She sighed. How much was she willing to give up to him in order to gain a modicum of trust, or at least information, in return? "I was more than a simple trade analyst at State, and my

travels abroad involved somewhat more than simple negotia-
tions."

He nodded, actually looking relieved at her confession.

She continued, "I have some idea of what you folks over at the
NSA do on a daily basis. I'm not naïve. You may not be a spy, but
you're not far from it."

"In the same way that you, too, weren't exactly a spy but weren't
far from it?" he echoed.

"Exactly."

"Why didn't you hand the message over to the CIA when you
got it?" he asked curiously.

She peered at him from under her brows. "You know perfectly
well why not. It *came* from the CIA. I couldn't very well give it
back."

"Why not?"

"Because my friend indicated that there's a problem inside the
agency that this message might make reference to."

It was his turn to pounce. "What kind of problem?"

"I'm sure I have no idea. I worked over at State. I'm not privy to
the internal workings of the CIA."

Thankfully, she'd told the lie so many times over so many years
that it came to her as naturally as the truth would have. She didn't
worry that Liang would sense dishonesty from her.

He took a sip of his tea and made an appreciative sound. She
did the same, savoring the delicate floral tones of the tea.

Without warning, he asked, "If I request your personnel records from State, what will I find?"

"You'll find exactly what you expect. A record of thirty years of
service, moving up through various positions dealing with the foreign trade sector."

He pursed his lips skeptically and took another sip of tea. Then
he said, rather innocuously, "Your furnace doesn't seem to be working properly. Are you sure you'll be warm enough if you stay here
tonight?"

"Don't worry about me. I can always pile a couple of extra blankets on the bed. And now that the power's back on, it'll warm the
place up soon enough."

He finished his cup of tea and stood up.

"What brought you over here tonight, Liang? Did you come to tell me about what you decrypted, or was it something else?"

"Peter was worried about you. He's been trying to call you for a couple of days, but you've been ignoring his texts and not returning his calls. He got so worried that I told him I'd drive over here after work and check on you. To make sure you're not dead."

"That's sweet of you. And as you can see, I'm alive and kicking. Please give Peter my love."

"Mm," he said noncommittally.

"Peter and I have had our problems over the years, and I know he thinks I chose my work over him. But I swear, I didn't. Things were complicated between me and Peter's father, and to be blunt, we needed the money. I love all my children desperately, and I hated being gone so much when they were young." She added soberly, "Now that I'm retired, I hope to repair my relationship with Peter. I wouldn't presume to ask him to meet me halfway, but I do hope he'll at least give me a chance to make it up to him and try to build a new relationship."

Li smiled a little, and if she wasn't mistaken, seemed to be silently encouraging her to hang in there.

"Peter is the most stubborn of all my children, which is saying something. But since he got that from me, I can't very well blame him. I'm patient. I have faith he'll come around eventually."

Peter nodded, hugged her quickly, and took his leave.

It was only after he'd left that she had to wonder why he hadn't called her to tell her what the partial decryption had revealed. Nothing he'd told her tonight was even remotely sensitive, let alone classified.

And now that she thought about it, the notion of Peter being so worried he sent Li over here to check on her struck a faint discord in her belly. She recognized a lot of herself in Liang. There was more to him than met the eye. Much more. He was a secret keeper, too.

Did Peter know his secrets, or did Li keep them even from his lover? She couldn't imagine that Peter would ultimately tolerate Liang keeping secrets from him, given how much he hated the

same trait in his mother. But didn't shrinks say that people had a
tendency to marry their parents? She hoped Li's relationship
with Peter was never as contentious as hers was.

She carried her gear bag downstairs, fetched her Tavor assault
weapon from under Gray's car, loaded it all in Gray's SUV, and
buttoned up the house. She turned on all the alarms again, and
headed out.

Goetz was exhausted, but exhilarated. He'd been welding
and sanding and painting for three days nonstop. He'd even taken
a day off work to finish the setup of the Picasso still life. Meanwhile,
the maggots had worked diligently, too.

At the end of day two, he'd opened the bucket long enough to
film the bloated head, covered in a thick layer of maggots feasting
away. It was disgusting, but utterly fascinating as he zoomed in on
the writhing mass of wriggling white maggots. His viewers were going to be grossed out, but they also wouldn't be able to look away
from the video once it was all spliced and edited together.

Wagner's *Ride of the Valkyries* would be perfect for this video. Its
dark crescendos would build as he chronicled the building of the
still life, culminating with the final piece.

It had taken five days, all told, but the skull was polished clean,
and he'd hosed off the maggots and placed his trophy in position
to complete the recreation of Picasso's still life. It wasn't half-bad,
if he said so himself. He'd taken his time filming it, playing with
various lighting arrangements until he'd gotten it just right.

He hummed along with the music as he worked at his computer, producing the video. The first time he added the music
track and played it through, he couldn't resist singing along, "Kill
the wabbit. Kill the WABBIT! KILL THE WABBIT!"

Chortling, he continued making final adjustments to the mix
of still images and video. As the crashing chords of the final movement of Wagner's piece pounded through the speakers, the video
panned around the still life, viewing it in a 3D format Picasso
could only have dreamed of.

Not only had he completely eclipsed the original DaVinci

Killer, but now he'd also eclipsed Picasso himself. Dang, he was good.

It was nearly dawn when he finally posted his video to the Dark Web and sat back in satisfaction to receive the adulation that was his due.

He didn't have long to wait. Many of his ardent fans had undoubtedly set up notifications for whenever he posted a new video. Within minutes of it going live, the likes were pouring in by the thousands.

Comments came in from all over the world in dozens of languages, many of which he didn't understand. But he didn't need to. They loved him. They bowed before his creative genius. And he was the undisputed king of the Dark Web.

He was just pushing back his chair to go to bed and get some well-earned sleep when a comment caught his attention among the fast-scrolling stream rolling in. Or more accurately, the name of the commenter caught his attention.

He pulled his chair back in and scrolled back up through the comment section in search of it.

There it was.

OriginalDaVinciKiller.

The comment merely contained a link to a private message.

His jaw dropped and he whooped in delight. He'd caught the eye of his inspiration? The master was here to acknowledge the transcendence of his student?

He clicked on the link.

You putrid little pissant. How dare you copy my genius, you halfwit knockoff. I'm coming for you. I'm going to make you suffer like no human being has ever suffered before. And when I'm done, I'm turning you into an art installation that's going to make every one of these amateur, crap videos you've posted look like the crayon scribblings of the mental toddler you are—

He grabbed the entire monitor and threw it across his bedroom.

It crashed against the wall. He followed after it, kicking and stomping on it until it was a twisted ruin of plastic and wires. His rage not spent, he punched the wall, burying his fist in the drywall, leaving behind a hole all the way through to his living room. He turned back toward his computer array and barely managed to stop himself from wrecking it all. Instead he let out a primal scream at the top of his lungs.

He would find the original DaVinci Killer first, and he would make an art installation of *him* long before the guy could do it back.

Still seeing red, he turned to his wall of worship. Somewhere in here, there was a clue to the original DaVinci Killer's identity. And when he found it, the bastard was toast.

CHAPTER 22

*H*E LOOKED UP FROM HIS DESK AS HIS EXECUTIVE ASSISTANT AP-
peared in the open doorway.

"You asked me to let you know when the team found something on Nikolai Ibramov?"

"Enter," he ordered, relaxing in his high-backed leather chair.

"He appears to be in the Washington, DC, metro area."

"Where?"

"Um, the team doesn't have visual confirmation of his location,
but we suspect he's in hiding in a known Bratva crash pad on the
north side of town."

"How do you know he's there if you've got no visual on him?"

"Because of this, sir." The assistant held out a grainy eight-by-
eleven photograph in black-and-white. Which meant it had probably come from a satellite.

The image showed a short section of street with flat-roofed
buildings on either side. From this angle, he couldn't make out
the faces of any of the several pedestrians on the sidewalk nor
could he read any license plates from the cars in the street. "What
am I supposed to be looking at?"

"The roof on the west side of the street—that would be the one
at the bottom of the picture—appears to have a surveillance hide
built on it."

He brought the picture closer and studied it intently. Indeed, a small rectangle a slightly lighter shade than the roof came into focus. It was placed right at the edge of the roof, overlooking the street.

"Who's in the hide? Do we know it's not the FBI or some other law enforcement operation?"

"We sent a guy over there a couple of hours ago to attempt to make an identification. He says it's a middle-aged woman."

His gut clenched with foreboding. "Indeed? And who is she?"

"You're not going to believe this, sir, but she's a federal employee. Or she was until a few months ago. Helen Warwick."

Of course it was her.

He drummed his fingers on his desk as he thought fast. If she was only out to kill Ibramov, she would actually be doing him a favor. But if she tried to talk to the guy, that could be a problem. "I want twenty-four-hour surveillance on Mrs. Warwick. When she moves on Ibramov, I want to know immediately, no matter the time, day or night."

"We don't know why she's watching him—"

He cut off his assistant sharply. "She's going to kill him. And as soon as she moves on him, I want to know. Understood?"

"Yes, sir."

His eyes narrowed. He didn't tolerate anything but complete obedience and subservience from his direct employees. His assistant hastily lowered his gaze to the floor. *Better.* Why was he still standing there in the doorway? "Is there something else?" he snapped.

"Um, possibly. You asked us to watch your message traffic, incoming and outgoing, a few days ago. . . ."

"And?"

"It's possible that a message was copied, or possibly rerouted. We can't be sure. There's no direct trace of an incursion into your email, but we got a warning flag that something might have happened."

"Which message?"

"We can't tell. We're not sure anyone even got into your account. Our tech guy is tracing it through the servers now."

His fingers drummed faster. He relied heavily on his communications being completely and securely encoded. "I've been assured that my encryption protections are the best there are. Was I misinformed?"

"No, sir. Your encryption is the best available, anywhere."

"Then assure me my communications have not been compromised."

"We're sure everything is fine. We're just being careful and verifying it," the assistant said hastily.

"It's your neck if you're wrong," he said silkily.

The assistant visibly swallowed. *Good.* He liked his employees scared. The edge that fear gave people made them sharp.

"Keep me informed." He nodded his dismissal, and the assistant backed out of the doorway with alacrity. *Yes, indeed.* He liked to keep everyone around him afraid.

Helen sat back from the window of the empty office, the lawn chair beneath her squeaking in protest at her abrupt movement. What was going on over there?

A tight cluster of big, thuggish men piled into the auto shop every morning. They were probably bodyguards for a higher-ranking principal. She'd spotted Ibramov in the crowd each of the past two days.

Of interest was the fact that no cars ever came in for repairs, and no cars emerged from the shop. Everybody wore suits as well, which wasn't exactly ideal clothing for working on greasy cars. It was obviously a front. Or maybe a money laundering outfit.

This auto shop would be no easier to infiltrate than the Bratva-occupied building Nikolai was living in. He rarely went out of the building, and when he did go out for groceries or the occasional bottle of booze, he was always with an armed escort.

She could, however, draw him outside. And she liked this place on an isolated highway outside of DC for that more than the urban setting of the apartment building.

The trick would be to draw all the men out of the auto shop and then convince them they needed to flee for safety. Under the cover of that kind of chaos, she would get her best shot at Nikolai.

She waited until dark, and crept across the street. Keeping well back from the building, she walked around it, familiarizing herself with the woods beyond the junkyard. The terrain rose and fell gently, just enough to hide a person standing down in one of the shallow gullies. In the low spots, the snow was knee-deep, but on the ridges, it was mostly blown down to the wet leaves.

Directly behind the junkyard, a packed dirt path mostly free of snow trailed straight away from it. Frozen tracks in the mud indicated that it was used frequently. She paralleled the track, interested to see where it led.

She eventually emerged onto the edge of a narrow, snow-covered road cutting through the woods. She scrubbed at the snow with her hiking boot and found a gravel road bed underneath. Directly across the road was a long driveway meandering back through the trees toward the vague shape of a log cabin in the dark. She didn't see any lights on inside the structure.

She spotted a fresh set of tire tracks on the snowy road and tracked them to her left. Well past the cabin was an open field with a one-story white farmhouse set back a little from the road.

An inordinately large metal barn stood behind it. It looked more like an airplane hangar than a barn. She crept into the woods beside the field, and when she reached the end of the trees, she'd also reached the back of the building.

Sure enough, a very long, narrow strip of paving stretched away in both directions, and the entire back side of the metal structure was taken up by doors as tall as the building. They were closed right now.

She eased up to the side of the hangar and peered in through a small window. Inside was an office, but the far wall of the room was glassed in, and through that she spied a helicopter, a two-person Cessna with high wings, and a sleek business jet. Looked like a Learjet, although the angle was bad to make out its silhouette, and the hangar was quite dark.

Blue, flickering light came from what was probably a bedroom in the rear of the house. Someone was watching television, but no other lights were on. Curious, she retraced her steps through the woods until she was even with the house. She peeked in the window in the garage wall and spotted one of the big, black SUVs the Bratva used. She'd seen enough. She slipped back into the woods.

It was a longer hike back to the auto shop than she'd realized, and she was cold, tired, and wet when she finally got back to her car. Now that she had the layout of her attack site and had a decent idea of her target's daily routine, it was time to head home and plan her attack.

When she got back to her car, she checked her cell phone, and was startled to see a text from Liang. It said merely, **I have more information.**

Interesting. She texted back, **I'd love to hear what you have. Can we meet now?**

We're at an auction. Can you meet me here? Text me when you arrive and I'll come out.

By "we," he obviously meant himself and Peter. **Where?** she typed.

He texted her the address, and she texted back that she would be there in under an hour.

She drove all the way across Washington to Kalorama, a prestigious zip code just east of Massachusetts Avenue and Embassy Row in Northwest DC, and parked behind the large, unmarked building bearing the address Li had sent her.

I'm here, she texted him.

I'll meet you in the parking lot out back.

Doesn't want Peter to know he's talking to the monster-mom, huh? she thought. She rolled her eyes and leaned on the hood of her car, gazing around at the Bentleys, Bugattis, and plentiful Italian sports cars cramming the parking lot. How on earth did the boys run in these financial circles?

It was surprisingly dark out here. If she were the proprietor of an establishment like this, she would light up the whole exterior like a sports stadium. Sure, people might prefer their privacy and anonymity in a place like this, but it was hazardous to keep a parking lot like this wreathed in the kind of shadows criminals loved to work in.

"Mrs. Warwick?"

She spotted Liang moving toward her hesitantly. His eyesight must not be adjusted to the dark like hers was. "I'm over here, Li." He joined her quickly once he had her voice to zero in on. When he joined her, she pushed away from her car and said, sincerely, "Thanks for texting me. What have you got?"

"We decrypted the rest of the message."

"And?" Why was he hesitating to tell her what it said?

He glanced around to make sure they were alone, then lowered his voice until she could barely hear him, standing two feet from him. "It appears to be a sanction on someone here in Washington. By a government official."

"That's illegal!" she blurted.

"I'm aware of that," he replied dryly.

"Who sent the message?" she demanded.

"An entity called Scorpius."

"An entity?"

She made out his shoulder lifting and falling. "It could be a person," he murmured. "Could be some sort of operating group. Or it could be a mission name."

"Who's the target?" she asked reluctantly, mentally girding herself to have to explain why she'd been sanctioned.

"We couldn't tell from the message, but it appears to be an employ—"

She saw movement out of the corner of her eye. She didn't have time to identify who or what it was, but her instincts screamed a warning and her training took over. She lunged forward, slamming into Liang. She grabbed him around the waist and twisted her entire body, throwing herself into a ninety-degree turn and flinging both of them toward the ground as a quiet spit of sound was followed by a metallic ping.

"Crawl for the loading dock," she whispered urgently. "Stay down and go fast." She rolled off him, pulling her pistol as she moved. She rose to a crouch behind a Rolls-Royce sedan and peered around its bulk. The shooter wasn't showing himself at the moment.

She backed up a few yards, covering Li's retreat. She heard him breathing hard in panic. Not used to getting shot at, was he? *Good to know.*

Her gaze roved across the cars, not exactly unfocused, but taking in everything as she sought the slightest movement. *There.* A shadow shifted. She aimed quickly and sent a shot in that direction. She was more interested in suppressing the shooter than in killing him. She had to get Li inside in one piece. Peter would *kill* her if anything happened to his boyfriend.

She sent two more shots into the shadows in the next thirty seconds. Finally, Li reached the base of the concrete steps at one end of the loading dock.

He started to reach for them, but she put a hand on his back and held him down. She risked leaning down to whisper quietly, "Are any of the doors unlocked?"

"They're all unlocked. Staff will be in the back wrapping the sold items right now, prepping them for pickup."

"Security guards?" she bit out.

"Several."

She nodded. "I'll go first. I'll throw up the first garage door partway and call for you to move. Run to me as fast as you can, but stay low. When you get to me, throw yourself down onto your stomach and roll underneath the door. I'll cover you."

"You have a gun?" he demanded.

"Yes." She raised her right hand to show it to him.

"Do you know how to use that?"

"Yes, I do," she answered impatiently. "You know what you have to do?"

"I heard you."

"Okay. Here we go." She rose to a half crouch and took a hard look around the parking lot. No movement. But he was out there. She could feel him.

Using herself to draw fire away from Li, she darted up the steps and ran the dozen feet to the first big garage door. She followed her own instructions and dived for the concrete. Landing on her side, she spotted a muzzle flash and shot toward it, three shots in quick succession.

She rolled onto her other side and shoved the door up about eighteen inches. "Now, Li," she called out low.

She rolled back over and scanned the parking lot, pistol held out in front of her. She ejected her empty magazine and slammed home her spare, shooting at anything that moved, not caring if it was the shooter or the wind blowing. The fact that she was steadily peppering the lot with lead would keep the guy's head down for the precious seconds she needed.

Li grunted as he landed behind her and rolled under the door. She shot her last two rounds and followed him, rolling inside fast. She slammed up against him and yanked the door down.

She looked up into the barrels of a pair of revolvers. Above them, two grim-faced security guards glared down at her. She laid her pistol down slowly. "It's not loaded," she said meekly.

Liang sat up.

"Mr. Chong! Does Pete know you're back here?"

"He's out front. He's bidding tonight, not selling. I went to the parking lot to find his mother and escort her in, but we ran into a bit of a problem."

"You're Mrs. Warwick?" the second guard asked her.

"I'm Peter's mother, yes."

The first guard asked Li, "What kind of problem?"

"We thought there might be someone in the parking lot stalking us. Mrs. Warwick pulled out that toy gun of hers and waved it around to scare him off."

"Are you okay, Mr. Chong?" the guard asked, helping Li to his feet.

Leaving her weapon on the floor, she let the other guard help her up. She went into her helpless, hand-wringing act. "I'm really sorry if we startled you gentlemen," she said breathlessly. "I've been so scared since someone tried to rob the boys a few weeks ago. That's when I got this."

She bent down and picked up her pistol by the barrel, which was still hot, and dropped it into her purse. She didn't acknowledge the existence of the sound suppressor screwed onto the end of it, and hoped the guards either didn't notice or wouldn't ask about it.

"I'll see Peter's mother into the auction, gentlemen," Li said. "Sorry for startling you." He took her by the elbow and steered her over to an interior door.

As the guards disappeared outside to take a lap around the parking lot, she glanced up at him. Liang was staring at her as if she'd grown a second head. *Well, fudge.* It was pretty hard to disguise the fact that she'd known exactly what to do out there, and that she'd had a silenced weapon in her purse and obviously knew how to use it.

His stern gaze demanded answers, but she stared back at him implacably. No way was she explaining any of it to him. He scowled at her, and she lifted her chin stubbornly. Finally, at an impasse, he looked away from her. She let out the breath she'd been holding.

Li put a hand lightly in the middle of her back as he reached around her to open the door for her, and two things happened simultaneously: He gasped, and she noticed a sharp burning sensation starting in the middle of her back, traveling up across her right shoulder blade.

"There's blood on my hand," he muttered. "You've been shot."

"Trust me. I have not been shot. I might have been winged, but I didn't take a round."

"How can you be sure of that?" he demanded. "People often don't know they've been shot for several minutes after the fact. The adrenaline blocks their pain receptors."

"I know what taking a bullet feels li—" She broke off, horrified.

"Nonetheless, you're bleeding. I'm taking you to a hospital."

"No!"

"I'm not arguing with you about this. Peter would kill me if you died because you refused to acknowledge you were hurt and I let you walk away."

There was steel in Liang's voice that gave her pause. Who knew he could be so assertive? She'd never seen any hint of this side of him before. "Fine," she sighed.

They retraced their steps to the loading dock, and she saw flashlight beams bobbing across the parking lot. "Where's your car?" she asked, eager to get out of here before the guards figured out that a half dozen or more car windows were broken and possibly that multiple bullet holes had appeared in the customers' high-end cars.

"Over here." He led her quickly to a conservative Mercedes and opened the passenger door for her.

"Do you have a towel so I don't bleed on your car?"

He opened the trunk and fetched a towel, which he passed to her. She bunched it behind her back while he pulled out into the street.

"An urgent care place will be fine. I don't need an emergency room," she tried.

He glared at her and kept on driving.

"Please don't make a huge fuss out of this. They're going to swab my back with some alcohol and put a bandage across it. It'll be fine in a few days."

"You haven't seen your wound—"

"I can feel it."

He huffed. "You're still going to an emergency room." He added ominously, "And I'm telling Peter."

"C'mon, Liang. Don't freak him out. I'm fine."

"What about me? It so happens I'm rather freaked out, too."

"Why?"

"My boyfriend's nice, pie-baking mother just ran around like a commando shooting up a parking lot with a military-grade sidearm."

She squeezed her eyes shut in dismay. Leave it to the NSA guy to know a military-style weapon when he saw one. She should've known he wouldn't miss her competence in a gunfight, either.

They drove in silence for several minutes, and Liang surprised her by asking out of the blue, "Do you happen to know anything about police cars parking outside our building at all hours of the day and night?"

"I might have called in a favor to make sure you boys are safe until we can figure out who was behind New Year's Eve."

"Thank you," he replied simply.

"You're welcome."

Li parked the car in front of a hospital emergency entrance and opened her passenger door for her.

She got out and stood in front of him, not moving. "I'll make you a deal. I'll go in there and let them look at my back, and they can do whatever they want to it, if you'll promise not to tell Peter anything about tonight. Tell him I fell in the parking lot and scraped up my back. You thought it should be looked at."

"I don't make a practice of lying to my partner."

"You also don't tell him everything. Not with your job." He glared at her, but when she glared back, his gaze slid away. *Uh-huh.* She was right, and they both knew it. She added pleadingly, "I'm not asking you to lie. I'm only asking you to omit telling him something."

"An omission is still technically a lie."

She huffed. "Do you have to split that ethical hair with me right this second?"

He shrugged, looking unmoved.

"Fine. I'm not going inside."

He rolled his eyes. "You're as stubborn as Peter."

"Oh, no, Liang. I'm a great deal more stubborn than Peter. It's one of the reasons why he resents me so much. He never could outlast me in a contest of wills."

"God save me from you Warwicks."

She heard the surrender in his exasperated outburst. She replied with as much grace as she could. "Thank you, dear. There are a few things about me that I'd rather not have my children know."

"Like the fact that you handle a pistol like a Navy SEAL?"

She laughed a little. "I'm a retired woman of a certain age. I couldn't be further from a Navy SEAL." She added lightly, "And besides. What Navy SEAL knows how to bake an apple pie?"

"I'm sure some of them do," he retorted. He rolled his eyes and turned stiffly to walk her into the emergency room. He clearly didn't like their deal, but her secret was safe with him. For now.

The nurse who looked at her back was sympathetic. "Anything

you'd like to tell me about how you got that burn, ma'am? Or that scratch on your arm?"

What scratch on her arm? *Oh.* The spot she'd gotten creased by a bullet at Peter and Li's house. It was mostly healed, and the scab was starting to fall off, in fact. It didn't look as if it was going to leave much of a scar, either.

Of course, two bullets in two weeks wasn't a great track record. Funny how she'd gotten both injuries when Liang was involved—

The nurse was staring at her expectantly.

She sighed. "I didn't want to come here at all, but my son's boyfriend insisted."

"If you'd like to report any abuse, we've got a terrific support network—"

"I slipped on some wet water in the kitchen." If the nurse had mistaken it for a burn, she was happy to lean into that story. She added, "I hit my back on a hot oven door as I went down. I promise you, nobody has ever lifted a hand to me." She said it in a tone that made clear she would kick anyone's butt who tried it.

"All right, then. Let's get some salve on your burn and get it bandaged up."

A doctor poked his head in briefly to look at the stripe across her back. He declared it nothing serious and left the nurse to finish up dressing the wound. It was less than an hour from the time she walked into the ER until she walked out. Luckily, they'd hit it on a quiet night.

She stepped out into the waiting room and swore under her breath. Peter was there with Liang, and he looked ready to explode.

"Did you have to call him?" she complained to Li. "It took them two minutes to put a bandage on my boo-boo."

"How is it you always manage to get into trouble, Mother?" Peter bit out. She knew that white ring around his tight mouth. He was furious. At her. Again. *Oh, joy.*

She threw up her hands. "Don't blame me. I didn't start it."

Li jumped in. "She's telling the truth, Peter. Someone was trying to boost a car in the parking lot, and we startled him. Your mom only tried to protect me. For which I am grateful, I might add. She took a bullet for me."

Looking over her shoulder in alarm that one of the nurses might hear the word "bullet" and want to call her back inside to question her in detail about exactly how she got hurt, she hustled the two men out the door toward the parking lot. They stopped beside Li's car.

Peter scowled back and forth between them, obviously suspicious that they weren't telling him everything. Finally, he muttered, "Fine. Thanks for protecting Li." Then he asked, quite angrily, "Why were you even at the auction house, Mom?"

"I just wanted to invite you and Li to dinner. I was in the area, so I stopped by when Li mentioned you two were at an auction tonight. I find the whole art and antiquities world fascinating, but I know very little about it. I thought maybe we could . . ." She searched for a plausible word. "Bond over it."

Peter snorted, making clear his opinion of the two of them bonding over anything.

"If one of you could give me a ride back to my car, I'd appreciate it. Or I can just call a cab—"

"I'll take you," Li volunteered.

She air-kissed Peter, who tolerated it stiffly. "Despite what you think of me, I love you, dear, and I'm very proud of the man you've become."

He opened his mouth, undoubtedly to say something snarky, but she laid her fingers on his lips. "Let it be, just this once."

Feeling a prickle of tears in her eyes, she turned quickly and reached for her door handle.

The ride back to the auction house was quiet.

"Thank you for bringing me back here, Liang," she said formally.

"Do you always lie so easily?" he blurted.

"All parents lie to protect their children, and yes, that comes as naturally as breathing. You'll be able to do it when you have children one day." She didn't want to fight with him any more than she wanted to fight with Peter, and she climbed out of the vehicle quickly.

There were police all over the parking lot, and people were having to show their driver's licenses to be allowed to leave the crime scene. On the assumption that the guards had told the police that Liang Chong and a Mrs. Warwick were involved in the shooting, she whipped out an alternate driver's license to show the police officer guarding the exit, grateful that Yosef hadn't confiscated her fake identification documents when she retired.

She drove away from the auction house thoughtfully, circling back to the realization that the one thing both shootings aimed at her had in common was Liang. And Yosef had indicated that it was possible the New Year's Eve shooting hadn't been aimed at her.

Would Li have told her if the decrypted message from Yosef indicated that Liang himself was the target of the assassination contract? Somehow she doubted he would confess such a thing to her.

The one sure way to find out was going to be catching up with Nikolai Ibramov and asking him directly who his target was. And the sooner the better.

CHAPTER 23

*H*E WASN'T FOND OF BEING OUTSIDE ON A COLD, WINDY NIGHT LIKE this, but it felt good to go hunting again, old-school. His blood ran a little faster, his body felt a little lighter, his senses were sharper. He stared down at the street below, idly watching the occasional pedestrian hustle past, huddled deep inside a coat. His target wasn't due for another few minutes, and the patsy he was setting up should arrive any minute.

He checked to make sure the postcard of Kandinsky's *Composition X* was tightly wedged under a piece of loose tar paper where the wind wouldn't blow it away. He'd already hidden a postcard of *The Death of Marat* under the leg of a steel water tank he'd used to anchor his line.

The main challenge with this kill had been convincing his victim to show up at this place, at this time, and doing so without leaving behind any trace of his contact with him. He'd used a burner phone and carefully crafted a message dangling the possibility of breaking open a huge criminal case. One constant of all elected officials was their ambition.

The patsy had been a different kind of challenge, but dangling the prospect of an easy payday had taken care of that. In fact, as his gaze roamed up and down the narrow street, flanked by a row of brick buildings, he spotted his patsy coming around a corner from behind him. *Right on time.*

He went very still. The guy stopped exactly where he'd been told to, and looked around expectantly for the person who was allegedly going to meet him here and hand off a package to him to deliver.

He turned his attention to the street corner in front of him, perhaps a hundred feet away. It was a short, easy shot. But, to be safe, his pistol barrel rested on a bipod stand that steadied it even more. He'd screwed a cheap sound suppressor onto his weapon. It would quiet the shot enough to make sure every window on the street didn't open, but it would be loud enough for the patsy to hear and react to it. That was important. He needed the patsy to notice the victim getting shot and run for him.

He settled into a state of total relaxation. As he waited for the victim to appear, he reviewed the plan one last time.

Shoot. Bipod inside his coat. Pistol in thigh holster. Run for the side of the roof—

There. His victim had just stepped around the corner.

Showtime.

The man in the expensive wool coat looked around the intersection for several seconds, then turned and walked quickly toward the address he'd been texted. He was moving too quickly. The shot had to be adjusted.

He repositioned the bipod fast, dipped the tip of the barrel down, sighting beyond the sound suppressor. Aiming at the target's face, he squeezed the trigger.

The spit of sound was loud in his ear. He waited only long enough to watch his target fall backward, then moved by rote. Stand stowed, pistol holstered, brass casing picked up. Push upright. Sprint to the side of the roof.

Quick check of his harness clip, lean back, then the sickening step over the edge. Two big jumps down the wall and his feet hit the ground. Release the harness. Drop a postcard of the Picasso *Still Life with Skull.* Quickly, he kicked some gravel over it to hold it down. Dart to the end of the alley, peek around the edge of the building.

Perfect. The patsy was racing toward the fallen man.

He darted out into the street and dropped the pistol into the letter slot of a mailbox.

Now for the pièce de résistance. He laid a postcard behind the mailbox, weighed down with a rock so it wouldn't blow away. The glossy picture on the front of it was Salvador Dalí's *Christ of Saint John on the Cross*, which depicted Jesus hanging limp on a cross suspended in a black night sky above the brightly illuminated earth far below. *Let them chew on that for a few days.*

The patsy had just reached the victim. *Time to go.* He ducked back into the alley.

He yanked the second rope that released the knots on the two ropes and gave both a big pull. They slithered to the ground around him. He gathered them messily and shoved them into the backpack he wore for the purpose.

A sprint to the far end of the alley, then he stepped out calmly into the street, walking away from the murder behind him. He'd almost reached the car, parked two blocks away on a street with no security cameras, when he heard the first, distant siren.

Sedately, he drove to where he'd parked his own car, climbed into it, and drove home well satisfied with the night's work. Take that, Goetz. *You're toast now, my little copycat. And you don't even know it.*

Helen jolted awake to the sound of her cell phone ringing. Its face said the time was a little after 1:00 a.m. Alarm that something had happened to Yosef had her reaching for the phone before the second ring.

"Hello?" she said tensely.

"Mrs. Warwick? This is Clint Tucker. I'm sorry to call you so late, but something's happened. I need you to come down here."

She sat up. "Where are you?"

"Southeast DC. The canyon killer has struck again. But this time he didn't kill a nobody."

"Who did he kill?" she demanded as she climbed out of bed and headed for her closet.

"Just get down here. Angela needs you. I'll text you the address."

What on earth? Was Angela already representing the person who was going to be framed for this kill? Was she having trouble getting the police to check out the nearby rooftops? It wasn't as if the police would listen to her if they wouldn't listen to a prominent attorney whose son was in the police department. Nonetheless, she pulled on clothes, grabbed a warm coat, and headed out.

When she arrived at the murder scene, it was lit up bright as day with the spotlights mounted on police cruisers. An entire city block was taped off with crime scene tape, and a crowd of bystanders and journalists milled around at one end of the crime scene. She pushed into the crowd, asking nobody in particular, "What happened?"

A woman close to her said, "A guy got shot."

"Who did it?"

"They didn't catch anyone."

With the judicious application of a few well-placed elbows, she reached the front of the crowd. She spied her son, Mitchell, on the other side of the police tape, talking to a man in a civilian suit with a police badge hanging from a chain around his neck.

"Mitch!" she called.

Her son looked up sharply, scowling when he spotted her in the line of journalists. He strode over to her, the set of his shoulders defensive. The journalists around her shouted questions at him, but he ignored them all.

He lifted the police tape and grabbed her elbow, pulling her under the flimsy yellow barrier. He didn't let go of her as he led her well away from the reporters.

"What are you doing here?" he demanded.

"A friend of Angela Vincent's called me. Apparently her serial killer has struck again?"

"Looks that way." He huffed. "You might as well go talk with Angela. She's pretty upset."

"Why? Is she representing whoever got framed for this killing like the other ones?"

"No. The murder victim is the district attorney."

Helen stopped in her tracks and stared at her son. "As in your boss?"

"Correct."

"Oh. I'm so sorry, Mitchell. You must be in shock—"

"I'm pissed. I want to know who did this, so I can put the perpetrator away for the rest of his miserable life."

"Should you even be here? Isn't this a conflict of interest to be at the crime scene if you might end up prosecuting this case?"

Again he scowled. "Rules get bent when one of our own is murdered."

She spied Angela ahead of them, and she did indeed look devastated. "Excuse me, Mitchell. I'm going to go talk with Angela."

She walked up to her friend and spoke her name quietly. Angela turned around, and Helen opened her arms. Angela walked into her hug and clung to her so tightly it was hard for Helen to breathe. Sobs wracked Angela's body.

Angela cried hard for about two minutes before Helen felt her gather herself. The sobs stopped, and in a few moments, Angela's head lifted from her shoulder. The attorney stepped back from her, nodding once, cloaked in resolute grief with a stoicism that shouted of Angela having endured something this terrible before.

"What can I do?" Helen asked simply.

"Tell the police what we know about the serial killer who's doing this. They were more interested in securing the probable murder weapon—which one of them found in a mailbox down the street—than they were in listening to me. I might not have been exactly rational when I first got here and saw—" She choked up. "Oh, God."

She wrapped Angela in one more quick, fierce hug. "I've got this."

Helen marched over to the largest cluster of police, the one that included multiple men in civilian suits. They would be the homicide detectives. "Excuse me, gentlemen. Has anyone been up on any of the roofs along the street yet to find out where the killer shot from?"

They turned her way as one, looking at her like she had a third eye in the middle of her forehead. "Who are you?" one of them bit out.

"Helen Warwick. Mitchell Warwick's mother. I've been analyzing a series of killings in the district over the past year for Angela Vincent. We've found four other killings identical to this one, and in every case, it appears a silenced weapon was shot from a rooftop to kill the victim. The murderer then rappelled down from the roof—"

"We already have a suspect in custody . . . ma'am." The derisive delay before the guy called her "ma'am" was unmistakable.

Screw him.

"Let me guess. Your suspect is saying he was just walking down the street when he heard a shot ring out and saw the victim drop to the ground in front of him. He ran to the guy to see if he could help, called 911, and then you guys showed up and arrested him."

"I don't see journalist credentials around your neck, lady. I'm not answering any questions."

The anger in his voice made it clear she had it exactly right. This was one time when she wished she was wrong. Clearly, the cops weren't going to listen to her. She shrugged and walked away from them. Instead she headed back to Mitch.

"Do you want to catch the real killer?" she asked him tersely.

"Of course."

"Then come with me. I'll need your clout to get the police's attention."

"Huh?"

"Come with me," she ordered him.

He fell in beside her as she started walking slowly down the street, gazing up at the roof lines. "What are we doing?" he demanded.

"Pacing off a hundred feet or so from the victim. The shooter would've had to have been at least this far away to have made the shot and have enough time to plant the murder weapon before making his escape."

"What are you talking about?"

"I told you before. Angela and I believe the real shooter is going on rooftops to make his kills." She stopped in the middle of the street. "This building has an alley beside it. And that building across the street and down two doors has an alley. The shooter will have used one of these buildings. Come on. We have to get up on the roofs and check them out."

The first roof was pristine. A layer of several-day-old snow coated it, and not a single footstep marred it. "Nope. Not this one," she announced from the doorway.

Mitch followed her back downstairs and into the street. "This is ridiculous, Mother—"

"Humor me."

He huffed and followed her into the apartment building across the street. They walked up an interior staircase and emerged onto the roof. This one was not as well insulated as the other one, and no snow covered it. She walked gingerly across the loose tar paper, making sure not to trip on the flapping edges of the black sheets.

She went over to the edge of the roof and gazed down. "Perfect angle to kill the DA as he rounded the corner down there."

Mitch stared down at the crowd of people around the tarp-covered corpse of his boss.

"Look at this!" She crouched down, spotting a postcard wedged partially under some tar paper.

"Don't touch it!" Mitch barked.

"I wasn't going to." She rolled her eyes at him as he knelt beside her, shining his cell-phone flashlight at the glossy picture.

He jolted. "That's one of the paintings re-created by that thrill killer Liang told us about."

"Whoa," she breathed.

Mitch made a quick phone call and asked a detective to join them on the roof to collect possible evidence. While he did that, she wandered over to the rainwater cistern that would be the likeliest spot to anchor a rappelling line.

"Mitch!" she called. "I've found another postcard." This one was wedged beneath one of the galvanized metal legs bolted down to the roof.

"Sonofagun," he breathed. "That's another painting the DaVinci Killer re-created. Do you suppose the same guy who committed those murders did this one, too?"

"That would seem to be the logical inference," she replied. "Although, why would the killer finger himself?"

On the other hand, they were talking about a psychopath who was bragging all over the Dark Web about his kills. Maybe he wanted to take credit for this string of murders as well.

Shrugging to herself, she walked over to the edge of the roof. "Look here, Mitch. The edge of the roof shows some fresh wear, as if a couple of ropes bit into the edge of these old bricks."

Mitch took pictures of the marks with his phone while they waited for a detective to join them. Helen leaned over the edge of the roof and looked down at the alley below. "It's only about twenty-five feet to the ground. A person who knew how to rappel could get down there in just a few seconds. C'mon. I think I see another postcard down there."

"Mom. You can't go into the alley. You might ruin any footprints or other evidence down there."

"Fine. But what do you want to bet there's another postcard of a painting down there?"

The detective kicked them off the roof with orders not to contaminate his crime scene, and they retreated to the street.

While Mitch showed the detectives his pictures of the postcards and rope marks, explaining his mother's theory of how the shooting had happened—thankfully leaving her name out of it and taking credit for the theory on his own—she looked around for Angela. She didn't spot her friend, but she did look back at the detectives as one of them pulled out his own cell phone to show Mitch a picture of another postcard that had been found behind the mailbox containing the murder weapon.

"What's that painting?" Mitch asked.

"The back of the postcard says it's a Salvador Dalí painting. *Christ on a Cross* or something."

"*Christ of Saint John on the Cross,*" Helen corrected him. "It's in the Kelvingrove Museum in Glasgow, Scotland."

Mitch threw her a quelling glance. She held up her hands and turned away from him. She found Angela overseeing the transfer of the district attorney's body into an ambulance. Angela looked numb. Shock must have set in. Clint Tucker stood beside her with his arm around her shoulders.

Helen said quietly, "It's another murder just like the ones you spotted, Angela."

Clint bit out, "Yeah, except this time someone high-profile died. The police will turn themselves inside out to catch the killer now."

Why would the district attorney be roaming around in this part of town at this time of night? This was an old, humble corner of the downtown area. There weren't any snazzy restaurants or watering holes around here of the kind the DA would frequent.

Her antennae wiggled that something was off about this murder. Had the DA been set up? Drawn to that street corner for the express purpose of being killed? Why would the serial killer draw out the kind of victim that would bring the entire police department out looking for him?

Was the killer trying to get caught? Or upping the thrill of killing by doing it under the nose of the entire police department?

How was she to know the mind of a killer . . . or at least *that* killer? She wasn't a psychopath.

Clint was speaking again. "Dude messed up this time."

She shrugged. "He left behind some clues this time. Maybe he wants us to catch him. Stop him."

"What kind of clues?" Clint asked quickly.

"Postcards of some paintings that have been re-created recently on a thrill kill website. The killer posed dead bodies to look like famous paintings."

Clint's brow shot up. "Sounds creepy."

"It's sick," she replied. "My son's boyfriend showed me one of the videos. In it I saw he blew up a house with a family of four inside. Killed them all instantly. Then he superimposed video of the explosion on a Kandinsky painting."

"And you think that's who did this murder?" Clint asked. "Does that mean this thrill killer did all the canyon murders?"

"Possibly. Angela and I were talking with her son the other day about how the canyon killings seemed to stop a few months back, and I made the observation that he could have moved on to a new and improved method of killing."

"Seems strange that he'd leave a calling card after having never done it before," Clint commented.

"Who knows?" Helen replied. "One thing I do know, though. The police are all-hands-on-deck to solve this one."

The ambulance doors closed, and Clint led Angela toward a beat-up pickup truck that he helped her into. They drove off, following the ambulance on its sad journey to the medical examiner's office.

Helen stared after the retreating red lights. She would be wrecked if someone she loved were killed.

A little voice in the back of her head reminded her that she'd done exactly this to dozens of people in her career. She'd left behind a long trail of devastated loved ones with unspeakable grief and unanswered questions.

It was her job. Just her job. If she hadn't made the kills, someone else would have.

But she felt sick to her stomach.

CHAPTER 24

*T*HE NEXT FEW DAYS PASSED WITH HER TRYING AND FAILING TO FIND a way to draw Nikolai outside of his apartment or the auto shop. She took a break from her surveillance though to attend a memorial event for the district attorney.

Out of long habit, Helen blended in with a group of people entering the gathering being held at the Congressional Country Club in Potomac, Maryland. She was no fan of crowds. They made her feel hemmed in. Claustrophobic. This was being held in lieu of a funeral, out of respect for the man's atheist beliefs.

A crowd of lawyers and staff from the DA's office huddled at the bar, drinking hard. The city council was clustered in front of a fireplace across the room. A group of what looked like family members sat in chairs off to her right, wearing black and looking heavily medicated. Which was probably for the best. Journalists and miscellaneous attendees like herself floated from group to group awkwardly.

She spotted Angela Vincent at one end of the bar and headed for her. "I'm so sorry for your loss," she murmured to her friend.

Angela's eyes were red, whether from crying or drinking—or both—Helen couldn't tell. "His ex-wife had the gall to show up. She's probably angling to overturn the will and get her hot little hands on his bank accounts."

Helen glanced over at the black-clad crowd of mourners. "Is the ex still in the will?"

"Oh, hell no," Angela said fervently under her breath. "He left everything to his kids. A son and a daughter. They're both adults, so the ex-wife doesn't have a chance at a dime."

"And you're sure the will is airtight?"

Angela rolled her eyes. "I wrote it."

Helen laughed. "Then I have no worries for his children."

Angela turned to the bar and gestured for a refill. Helen glanced past her to Clint Tucker, standing on the other side of her. He nodded slightly. *Good.* Angela wasn't overindulging. At least not here.

"Mother," a male voice said from behind them.

Helen looked over her shoulder at George Vincent, looking handsome wearing a suit. He hugged his mother and then whispered politely, "Mrs. Warwick. Nice to see you again."

Angela asked, "Any progress finding more killings like—" Her voice broke.

George glanced around before lowering his voice to answer. "We've identified another dozen or so homicides from suburbs around the area. Now that this high-profile case has called attention to my inquiries, we're getting all the resources we need."

Angela turned back to the bar to accept her drink and toss it back. Helen smiled at her son. "If there's anything else I can do to help, let me know."

"Our homicide guys are in agreement with your analysis of the crime scenes."

She smiled a little. "Well, that's nice."

"If there's ever anything I can do for you, let me know. I owe you one. It looks like I'm finally going to get my shot at the homicide division because of this."

She glanced back and forth between him and Clint. "Actually, I could use a small favor. From each of you. Nothing major."

"Name it," George replied.

"I'm trying to flush a guy out of hiding. I need to ask him a few questions. I know where he's living and working, but they're not places I can just march into and ask him my questions."

Clint studied her intently. "What do you need from us?"

"I need to make my guy nervous. From you, I need a homeless person to park outside the apartment building he's living in and watch it. Nothing aggressive. Just sit there and watch it for a day or two. I'll pay whoever takes the gig."

"That's easy enough to arrange," he replied.

"Oh, and if anyone comes out of the building to confront your guy," she added, "tell your person not to engage with them. Leave the area. Under no circumstances challenge them."

That sent both Clint's and George's eyebrows up. "Who's coming out of the building?" Clint asked.

"Bratva muscle. It'll be a low-level guy, but they tend to swing their fists first and ask questions later."

"Bratva?" both men exclaimed under their breath.

She ignored them and turned to George. "I know it's outside of your jurisdiction, but northwest of DC, up by Great Falls, there's an auto shop that appears to be a Bratva front."

"You want the joint raided?" George asked.

"No, no," she answered quickly. "I'd like you to walk into the place in uniform and ask around about a guy named Nikolai Ibramov. They'll lie and say they've never heard of him, and then you should leave."

"Then what?" George asked suspiciously.

"I'll take care of the rest. I'll flush him out on my own. I just need to put him on edge so I spook him—he'll bolt in panic. I can catch up with him once he runs away from his protection."

"What if his guys run with him?" George asked reasonably.

"It won't go down like that. They'll all bolt. Only the top guy's bodyguards will stick to him. The rest will jump ship in every direction and scatter."

Clint frowned. "How do you know they won't come at you in force?"

"Because they won't know I'm there, my dear sir."

Both men opened their mouths to respond to that, but she was saved by a familiar voice. "Mother? What are you doing here?"

She turned with a smile to face Mitchell. "I came to offer moral support to my friend, of course. And now that I've done so, I'll be leaving. After all, I'm not a close friend of the deceased, or a family member." She gave Angela a quick hug, told her to call if she needed anything, and stepped away from the bar.

"Walk me to the door, Mitchell?"

As her son offered his arm to her she asked, "Any progress on catching the killer?"

"The serial killer theory is looking better and better. I'm the golden child of the department for going right to Angela's old cases and pulling them out as examples of identical killings. They all think I'm a genius to have remembered such obscure cases."

"What they don't know won't hurt them, eh?"

He shrugged and grinned at her as they reached the door. "I got lucky. That's not a crime, is it?"

"Not at all, darling. I'm delighted to have had even a small part in advancing your career." She patted his cheek. "I'll see myself out to my car. You go back there and impress all the power players in the room with your charm and wit."

He'd turned away before she barely got the last word out of her mouth. So single-minded, her boy. Once he had a goal in mind, nothing could stop him. He was like her in that. A lot like her.

Sunrise the next morning found Helen back at her surveillance hide on the roof across from the Bratva apartment building. True to Clint's word, a homeless man in an assortment of mismatched clothing shuffled down the street and set up shop only a dozen yards or so away from her position. Helen jolted. That was Clint. He must not have wanted to put anyone he knew at risk from the thugs across the street. *What a good man.*

Clint pulled out a piece of cardboard, and she craned to read it: HOMELESS VETERAN. WILL WORK FOR FOOD.

Ugh. To think that many homeless people were veterans made her both sad and angry. She watched as Clint set out a baseball cap upside down for donations and appeared to doze off. She would bet he was wide awake and watching everything that went on around him though.

It only took until midmorning for one of the thugs to sally

forth from the apartment building and tell Clint gruffly to move along. Clint picked up his capful of change and dollar bills and shuffled off, presumably to get some lunch.

Yet, in under an hour, Clint was back in his spot.

This time it took only a few minutes for someone to come out and chase him away. Interestingly, Clint didn't go so quietly this time. When the thug reached for his arm, presumably to throw him, Clint neatly broke the Russian's grip, and for just a second, dropped into a defensive fighting stance. But as quickly as he did it, Clint relaxed his body, slumped his shoulders, and shuffled away.

The Bratva man stared after Clint until he turned a corner a block away and disappeared from view.

Oh, nicely done! She made a mental note to compliment Clint on his acting skill. He'd telegraphed loud and clear that he wasn't just some random homeless dude. That slick move to break the thug's grip shouted of military or police training. Which meant he was possibly an undercover law enforcement type watching the building.

That should make the Bratva crew inside jumpy as heck.

Perfect.

Helen crawled along in the ditch, cursing the deep snow that kept getting inside her coat and melting down her neck. Unfortunately, this was the only decent approach to the auto shop where she wouldn't be seen. She crawled within about fifty yards of the building and stopped.

She shrugged out of her slim profile backpack and pulled out a specialized low-velocity rifle. She laid it on top of her pack and checked it over to make sure it was dry and ready to go, then she loaded the first of the specialized rounds she would be using today. The first round was a simple slug designed to poke a hole and not much more.

The Bratva crew usually left the auto shop around 5:30 p.m. Sunset was shortly before that. She would wait until the last possible minute to take her shots, so darkness would fall soon after she commenced hunting Nikolai.

She waited perfectly still in the snow, doing her best to ignore the cold gradually seeping through her white-and-gray arctic camo suit. Five o'clock came and passed. She climbed the side of the ditch so she could peer out above the berm at the front of the shop. She had to shoot before the daily caravan of SUVs pulled up out front to take the crew back to DC.

Five fifteen. She dared not wait any longer.

She lifted her low-velocity weapon, disliking how the sound suppressor made the barrel tip inordinately heavy. To compensate for it, she propped the barrel on a small, folding stand she set up in front of her, and waited for a car to come along the road. In general, firearms were incredibly loud beasts, and even with a suppressor to muffle the muzzle blast, the sound of a gunshot was hard to hide. Especially from people who knew the sound of gunfire intimately, as the Bratva men inside the shop would be.

Here came a truck. *Excellent.*

She took aim at her target, a barrel marked as holding gasoline that sat along the side of the shop wall. The last time she'd surveilled the shop, she'd seen a guy bump into the barrel, and it had rocked as if full of a sloshing liquid.

The truck drove past the auto shop, and she squeezed the trigger. She waited for several tense seconds for a reaction. Although the shot had sounded loud to her, nobody rushed out of the shop.

One shot down.

Through her sight, she spied a finger-sized hole about ten inches from the bottom of the barrel with clear liquid pouring from it.

She loaded the second round carefully. This one was an incendiary round loaded with chemicals designed to ignite on impact. Perfect for setting a puddle of gasoline on fire.

She waited several more minutes so the gasoline leak could grow and spread. And then she set her weapon on the tripod once more and took aim. No truck came along, but a heavy-duty pickup approached as she was beginning to despair of any vehicle passing by to cover the noise of her shot.

She would take it. She held her breath and squeezed the trigger smoothly.

The round flared as it hit the pavement a foot in front of the barrel and ricocheted up into the barrel itself. The puddle of gasoline flared up immediately in waist-high flames. The barrel's top exploded as the container split and the fuel inside ignited, sending flaming gasoline flying about thirty feet in all directions. More barrels standing beside the building caught fire, and a gout of black smoke billowed up into the sky immediately.

Whether it was the smoke or the sound of the barrel bursting that caught their attention, it had the desired effect. Men streamed out the front of the auto shop, handguns drawn, anticipating an attack. They looked around in confusion, and several headed back inside, no doubt to lead out the rest of the crew.

The edge of the roof had caught fire now, and flames were licking up the slanted roof hungrily. Someone came out with a fire extinguisher, but he aimed the foam at the flames and not at the base of the fire and did little good.

The wooden fence at the back corner of the building had also started to burn, and something on the other side of the fence was starting to send up gouts of black smoke. Maybe a pile of tires, given the foul smell.

She kept a sharp eye on who all came out the front of the shop, milling around, waiting for the SUVs to get there to haul them away. She wondered if they'd bothered to call the local fire department.

Out the back of the shop, she saw a group of men carry out a half dozen big metal boxes. They looked like cash chests. They loaded the boxes on a pair of all-terrain vehicles that took off down the path behind the shop into the woods.

Still no sign of Nikolai. He must still be inside helping to rescue whatever loot they planned to haul out of the shop before it burned down or the authorities came.

The convoy of SUVs screeched up to the shop, and a man surrounded by four others—none of them Nikolai—hustled into the first vehicle and peeled away. There went the big boss. More boxes came out the front door and were shoved into the backs of the vehicles. Still no sign of her quarry.

She heard a siren in the distance—someone must have spotted the giant cloud of black smoke rising into the sky and called it in.

C'mon, Nikolai. Run.

CHAPTER 25

*T*HERE.

A man, alone, had just come out of the rear of the shop. He sprinted across the junkyard and headed into the woods on foot. He looked back over his shoulder as he slipped out the rear gate, and she got a good look at him.

Nikolai.

She crawled to the edge of the ditch, rolled over the edge, and pushed to her feet. Counting on the chaos behind her to hide her movement, she headed for the trees, running low.

As she hit the woods behind the junkyard, the snow deepened precipitously, and she found herself slogging through knee-deep snow on the ridges and thigh-deep snow in the gullies. She stopped to unstrap her pack and pull out the pair of snow shoes stashed inside. She stepped into their bindings and took off once more. *Much better.*

It was still grueling going, but at least all her energy was going into forward speed now and not climbing out of the snow with each step. She angled to her right, searching for the path. Nikolai would no doubt run along that, as it would be clear of snow. Catching a glimpse of something moving right to left across her field of vision, she swung her urban assault weapon out of its holster along the side of her pack. Stopping at the top of the next ridge, she pulled a knife out of her ankle sheath and jammed it into the trunk of the nearest tree. Propping the barrel of her weapon on the knife to steady it, she lined up her shot for slightly behind where Nikolai should be now.

She needed to keep him panicked, keep him running. What she didn't need was for him to turn around and decide to shoot it out with her. While she had complete confidence in her skills, he was still a formidable threat.

She took the shot, letting it ring out loud in the silence of the forest. Grabbing her knife, jamming it back into its sheath, and shouldering her rifle, she took off through the trees again.

This time she angled left, toward the cabin in the woods. Nikolai wouldn't have taken off back here without any destination at all in mind. He was too well trained for that. On the off chance that there were high-quality weapons stashed in the cabin, she moved at maximum speed to try to head him off.

If her shot had had its desired effect, he would have veered off the trail by now, realizing the openness of it made him a sitting duck for the sniper out here. And if he'd done that, she now had a significant speed advantage on him with her snow shoes only sinking a few inches into the snow with every step. She might be an old lady, but she could outrace him now.

Concentrating on breathing deeply and evenly, she swung her arms in rhythm with her feet, mimicking the stride of cross-country ski racers. The sun had set and dusk was falling around her, turning the snowy forest into a thousand shades of silver and gray.

She peered ahead of her for movement, for any sign of the narrow road.

A shot rang out ahead of her. She froze, panting hard. Sounded like a small caliber handgun fired a few hundred feet from her position. She hadn't heard the round hit anything near her. Nikolai had probably made a wild shot over his shoulder in hope of slowing her down.

It had the opposite effect. She was close to her target now. With an extra burst of effort she sprinted forward. She heard a branch crack in front of her and began to slow, creeping forward now, using tree trunks for cover.

Dusk was thickening into twilight. She peered around cautiously. Nikolai was no amateur. He would go perfectly still if she got close to him. She would have to discern his shape among the shadows and not rely on seeing him move.

Very quietly, she unshouldered her weapon and brought it into firing position. Scanning the forest over the tip of her barrel, she sought her target. He was close. She could feel him.

She took a step forward.

Another step.

Another careful scan.

It was almost dark enough to don her night optical devices, and when she did that, she would have Nikolai dead to rights. Her NODs had an infrared feature, and the Russian's body heat would light up like a beacon out here in this cold. Unless, of course, he'd taken time to don heat-suppressing camouflage clothing before he'd fled out here.

She eased forward a few more steps.

All of a sudden there was an explosion of movement about fifty feet ahead of her, on the other side of a stand of thick underbrush. Even denuded of leaves, the tangle of vines and brambles obscured her view.

She raced right, veering around the obstacle. Nikolai had sprinted off to the left and was making no attempt at silence or stealth. Which meant the cabin must be very close.

Without warning, she burst out of the forest and into the edge of a clearing, where the cabin now stood in front of her. There was no sign of Nikolai, and a fresh set of footsteps went up the stairs onto the covered porch. *Hell's bells.*

She backed into the woods and hunkered down to see what he did next. She had no interest in barging into the cabin and getting into a close-quarters fight in an unfamiliar structure. Not against a trained operative like Nikolai.

He was undoubtedly peering out the windows, searching for her. By now it was entirely possible he had a sniper weapon and his own heat-seeking vision enhancement. Either way, she was wearing heat-suppressing clothing and would be nearly invisible to him. To that end, she pulled the face flap up over her cheeks to the bottom of her NODs, which covered her upper face.

She backed up behind a big tree and leaned against it, resting as she opened her pack and pulled out the low-velocity weapon again. She had plenty more incendiary rounds inside. She opened the metal box they were stored in and pulled one out. She loaded it and peered out around the tree. She took aim at the nearest window and fired the round into the cabin.

Moving fast, she circled behind the cabin, loaded another incendiary round, and shot it in through another window. By the time she moved around to the third side of the building, she saw flickering light from inside. At least one of the rounds had found a flammable material. She shot one more round inside, then packed away the weapon and prepared to move out again.

Her legs felt heavy, and her lungs ached from breathing in the cold air under so much exertion. But she was determined to catch Nikolai and get some answers from him. Who had hired him? Who was he supposed to kill? What did he know about why she and Yosef had been targeted, if they were in fact his targets?

She was parked to one side of the cabin with a clear view of both the front and back doors. He would have to come out soon. Smoke was starting to wisp through the broken windows. She flipped up her NODs as she started to see flames. Through the sensitive optical equipment, the firelight would be blindingly bright.

She spotted movement off to her left. Nikolai must've climbed out the window on the other side of the cabin. He was running for the rearward shed, weaving randomly as he went, making him a nearly impossible target to hit.

She lurched forward, rifle at the ready in front of her, closing fast on the shed. What was he up to?

The front door of the shed swung open all at once, and she heard the roar of an engine. A snowmobile burst out of the structure and careened toward her. She pulled off a quick shot that shattered the windshield but didn't hit Nikolai—or at least it didn't incapacitate him. He steered hard to the side, throwing up a rooster tail of snow that deluged her as he picked up speed and tore around the side of the house.

Swearing, swiping madly at the snow on her goggles, she ran for the shed. God willing, there would be another snowmobile inside.

There was.

But it had no key.

Swearing up a blue storm, she tore the fiberglass cover off the steering column and bit the tips of her gloves with her teeth as she yanked her hands free and went to work hot-wiring the engine.

She had the thing running in under a minute, which was nothing short of a miracle. She leaped aboard the vehicle and lurched out of the shed into the gathering darkness. As she cleared the cabin, which was burning merrily now, she flipped her NODs over her eyes and headed down the driveway. Fortunately, Nikolai's snowmobile left clear-as-a-bell tracks on the snow-packed road, and she followed them grimly as they turned to the right. She opened up the throttle all the way and tore after him.

She had two advantages over her quarry: She was lighter than he was, and her snowmobile had his tracks to follow, which meant her vehicle wasn't plowing its way through the deep, new-fallen snow. She spied him on the road well ahead of her. The gap between them narrowed steadily. Another minute or two, and she would catch up to him.

But as she crouched over her speeding snowmobile, she spotted a pair of headlights in the distance. *Crud.* This road was barely wide enough for one car. It certainly didn't have room for a car and a snowmobile.

As she watched in dismay, the car closed rapidly on Nikolai's snowmobile. Neither vehicle slowed. But at the last second in the game of chicken, Nikolai swerved off the road and into the drainage ditch to the right of it.

Man and machine went flying, tumbling over and over as the snowmobile rolled down the steep incline. God only knew if Nikolai had even survived that. Appalled, she leaned down even lower on her machine. She had to get to him before he died. She *had* to know who hired him and why.

The car roared forward, unconcerned.

Coming straight on toward her.

It was closing on her fast. Really fast.

Frantic, she started looking for a spot to get off the road. But this section of the road passed through what looked like a flood plain, and was raised about six feet above the forest floor on both sides. There was no help for it. She was going to have to drive into a ditch like Nikolai had.

Rather than wait for the car to be right on top of her, she let go of the throttle. The snowmobile slowed rapidly. Carefully, she eased as far left on the road as she could, eyeing the big black sedan bearing down on her fast. Then, at the last second before the vehicle hit her, she turned hard to the right so she could go straight down the steep slope, nose first.

Just as her tail end cleared the road, the vehicle raced past. She caught a glimpse over her shoulder of a high-end European model car with blacked-out windows. And then all her attention was on the plunging fall of her snowmobile as she tried to keep it pointed straight down the hill.

She succeeded, maybe a little too well. The nose of the snow-mobile plowed into the deep snow at the bottom of the hill and dug in. The back end flipped up in the air and cartwheeled. She flung herself off to the side as hard as she could, narrowly avoiding being crushed by the heavy machine. She landed hard on her back. *Who ever said snow made for a soft landing?*

She lay there for a moment, making faint choking noises as she tried to breathe, her diaphragm momentarily paralyzed. She hated having the breath knocked out of her like this. She knew from experience that all she could do was try to relax and wait for her body to restart respiration.

All at once, she gasped on a hard inhalation. *Better.* She took a few more grateful breaths, then rolled onto her side and pushed up to her hands and knees. Where were her NODs? They'd obviously been knocked off in the crash.

She looked around frantically, but there was no sign of them. They were undoubtedly buried in the thigh-deep snow somewhere nearby. But there was no way to find them quickly. And time was the one thing she didn't have right now. At least she still had her backpack and rifle slung over her shoulders.

She slogged back up the embankment to the road and took off running as best she could. The tire tracks of the recent car passing were reasonably solid, and she followed them the hundred yards down the road to where Nikolai had crashed. She started down the embankment toward the snowmobile lying on its side, but her feet went out from under her. She slid the rest of the way down the slope on her rear end.

Slogging through nearly waist-deep snow, she made her way around the vehicle. Nikolai was not under it. A trail of broken snow led away from the vehicle into the woods. She paused long enough to don her snowshoes once more, then followed the trail, deeply grateful that he'd once more broken a path for her.

The bright snow reflected the starlight enough that she wasn't blind out here, but she sorely missed her NODs and their infrared function. She hated having to rely on good old-fashioned eyesight to find Nikolai.

About a hundred feet into the woods, his path veered left and paralleled the road. Which meant he was heading toward the house with the airstrip behind it. She swore under her breath. If he got to a vehicle and took off, she would never catch up with him. And knowing him, he would go to ground for months or years to come, taking all his answers with him.

Following his GPS, he turned his Mercedes into the narrow driveway—and swore luridly at the sight that greeted him. The cabin in front of him was on fire. Flames burst out every window in such ample measure that surely nobody was alive inside.

This was where his team had told him he would find Nikolai Ibramov and the infuriating woman chasing him. No way could he let Helen Warwick talk to his hired killer. Ibramov knew too much, enough to potentially lead the Warwick woman to uncover his identity. And that would not do at all. He'd worked too hard for too many years to get to where he was now. His grand goals were almost within reach—only a few more rungs of the ladder to climb—a year, maybe two away.

He backed his car out of the driveway and headed back down the road. What were the odds those two snowmobilers hadn't been out for a joy ride but had been Ibramov and Warwick in the middle of a grim chase?

He stomped on the gas pedal, and his car fishtailed ominously. Swearing, he took his foot off the gas and let the car settle. Driving more temperately, he headed down the narrow road in search of his prey.

He would kill them both if it was the last thing he did. Nobody got in his way. *Nobody. Not Goetz, not these two.*

The snowshoes must've given her more of an advantage than she realized, for in a few minutes, she heard noise in front of her. Crunching snow. Another minute brought her close enough to hear frantic panting. She slowed down a little to catch her breath lest she give away her presence so loudly.

Keeping pace behind him now, she followed along, trying to rest. The way her heart was pounding and her breath was laboring, she couldn't take an accurate shot right now if she tried. Best to slow down her bodily functions a bit before closing in on Nikolai.

Finally, when she was breathing more smoothly, taking deep, controlled breaths, she lengthened her strides a bit. Not so much as to wind her again, but enough to slowly close the final gap.

Off to her left, she heard the faint noise of a car. Then it stopped. Must be that cursed car going back the way it came. She guessed it was one of the Bratva men checking up on the cabin, or maybe looking for Nikolai. The cabin must be fully engulfed in flames by now. She would bet the driver had given up Nikolai for either dead or fled. Why else would the car leave the area?

She couldn't tell where they were in the woods, but she and Nikolai had to be getting close to the house and hangar.

It was time to end this.

Moving forward quickly, she closed in on Nikolai as stealthily as she could. Ahead of her, the forest brightened significantly . . . as if a clearing lay in front of her. *No!*

Unshouldering her rifle, she used the low-light feature of her telescopic sight to scan the woods in front of her. *There.* A movement.

Her gunshot was loud in the silence of the woods, and the impact of the round on the tree made a distinctive thud. Bark and bits of wood flew in all directions.

More importantly, Nikolai ducked and veered away sharply from the tree, fleeing to his right, deeper into the woods. She followed him grimly. Every time he tried to turn back to the left toward the house and hangar, she sent a gunshot between him and the open field.

After the fourth shot, he startled her by stopping in his tracks. He turned around slowly to face her, hands held well away from his sides. Why wasn't he shooting back at her? He would be an excellent marksman. All hitmen were.

She stared warily at him, the crosshairs of her sight on his face.

They stood that way for many seconds, him frozen in place, her waiting for him to twitch.

Finally, she called out, "Where's your weapon?"

He called back, "I lost it when I crashed the snowmobile."

Whether or not she believed him, she wasn't about to let down her guard.

"Why won't you let me go left?" he asked.

"I know there's a house in that clearing," she replied.

"What do you want?" he called. "You could've killed me by now."

She considered for a moment before shouting, "I want answers to some questions."

"What questions?"

"Who hired you to kill me?"

"I was never hired to kill you!"

"Why did you and a team of men attack me at my son's house, then?"

"We weren't after you. Believe me, if we'd known *you* were inside, we'd have left well enough alone!"

"You know who I am?"

"Your reputation precedes you, Mrs. Warwick."

"Did you try to kill Yosef Mizrah?"

A long pause. Then, "Yes."

"Who sanctioned the hit? Was it your employer?"

"No. Not the Russians. An American."

An *American*? *Holy cow.* An American had ordered the hit of Yosef and the attack on Peter and Li's home? Was Scorpius real, then? "Government?" was all she could manage to call back without choking.

His reply was short. "Yes."

"Who?" she called, holding her breath in anticipation of finally knowing the answer. "I want a name."

Cursing, he parked his car beside the house that Ibramov and Warwick would surely be heading toward. A house had all manner of weapons and useful resources for people like them. Especially since he'd put both of them on foot in the woods.

He went around to the trunk of his car and opened it, pulling out the custom-made sniper rig he preferred for most of his kills.

He looked up as the front door of the house opened and a man stepped out onto the porch. "*Kto eta?*" the guy called out in Russian. *Who is that?*

"*Smyert*," he called back. *Death.* He chambered a round and lifted the weapon quickly. He shot the guy in the middle of the chest, watching alertly as the Russian staggered down the front steps, fumbling at his chest. Whether he was reaching for a holstered weapon or trying to stem the flow of blood, he couldn't tell and didn't much care.

Keeping his weapon trained on the man until he fell to the ground, he waited for the last twitches to stop. The snow under the man's body turned black as blood seeped from the fatal wound.

* * *

The resonant report of a rifle firing made Helen's head jerk up, away from her sight. Where had *that* come from? It sounded off to her left, some distance away. She scanned the woods quickly, looking for a new threat, but spotted no movement in the trees.

She looked back at Nikolai, or at least where he'd been standing. But he was gone. In her moment of inattention, he'd fled. Cursing, she started after him grimly.

What American inside the government had gone after Yosef? Yossi was a very senior intelligence official. Highly respected. Deeply apolitical. Known for being an honest and ethical man. Why would anyone go after him?

There. Movement off to her left. It was Nikolai floundering through the snow, disappearing behind a large tree surrounded by thick underbrush.

She raced after him, annoyed to see he'd reached the edge of the woods.

The snow was shallower in the open field, where wind could blow it away and scour the ground, and Nikolai was moving quickly now. Worse, he was zigzagging randomly, which would make him nigh impossible to shoot, particularly if she wanted to stop him without killing him.

Frustrated, she shouldered her weapon and cleared the margin of the trees.

Nikolai was headed toward the big airplane hangar. In another second or two, he would disappear behind it. Was there something in there that he knew about and she didn't? Like a weapon stash?

It made sense. Normally, given the choice of a thin-skinned metal building or a solidly built house, anyone with a lick of sense would head for the shelter of the house.

Bang!

A gunshot rang out deafeningly loud. She dived instinctively for the ground, expecting the shot to be followed up quickly by another one.

Except what she saw as she rolled onto her belly, lying uncomfortably on top of her weapon, was a man standing behind the open trunk of a big black sedan—*the* big black sedan. The muzzle flash had come from the rifle, which he was pointing at the man now staggering drunkenly toward the airplane hangar.

She rolled off her rifle, grabbed it in both hands, and rolled back to her belly just as a second shot rang out.

This one sent Nikolai flying. He landed on his back and didn't move again.

He'd just killed the guy who was going to name the American who'd hired him! Swearing up another blue storm, she turned her weapon on the man by the car.

But he'd pivoted quickly after the killing shot and was taking aim at her now.

She pulled off two fast rounds, not particularly caring about aiming so much as suppressing his fire. He ducked behind the car and stayed behind its cover, making no move to break for the cover of the nearby house.

As for her, she jumped to her feet and headed back toward the trees, zigzagging as she went, which was bloody awkward in a pair of snowshoes, as it turned out.

She fell, and as she rolled onto her side, she tucked and half turned to see if the man was still trying to kill her. He was just stepping out from behind the car. She sent another two shots very generally in his direction. She probably hadn't even hit the house, but the noise and muzzle flashes sent him back behind the car.

She clambered to her feet, summoning an extra burst of adrenaline-induced speed and diving for the cover of the first bush. She crawled on her hands and knees for perhaps a dozen feet, receiving a face full of wet, freezing cold snow.

She turned, flopped to her belly, and scanned the field quickly. The man hadn't followed her into the open.

As she watched and waited, the car engine started. Furious that he'd killed Nikolai, she shot out both tires on the near side of his car. Yet he threw the vehicle into reverse anyway. She lined up the passenger window this time and shot it out. She made out the shadowed silhouette of a man, ducking low over the steering wheel. The vehicle backed up quickly, skidding in the snow.

He threw it sideways into a Y-turn, then started forward. As he initiated the aggressive maneuver, she reached into her pack fast and found the metal box with the last incendiary round in it. She manually chambered it and took aim. She had one shot at this before he reached the end of the driveway and got away.

She lined up her sight on the side of his car, aiming at the engine. She squeezed the trigger, willing the round to its target.

A flash of light came from under the front end of the vehicle, and then immediately flames and smoke began to rise from around the edges of the front hood. The car rolled perhaps another hundred feet before coming to a stop.

Unlike in the movies, the car didn't explode, but it was definitely on fire. Flames rose a couple of feet from the radiator and around the seams of the hood.

She saw the far passenger door open. The driver tumbled out and, crouching low, ran for the front porch. He made it to the front door and ducked inside the house without ever giving her a clear sight line to shoot him.

Cursing, she lowered her weapon and pulled out regular ammunition. What she really wanted to do was get close to this dude and demand to know why he'd killed Nikolai. What did *this* guy know about who hired Nikolai and why?

She waited in the snow perhaps five minutes. No doubt the man inside was searching the place for useful equipment, maybe making a phone call to bring in reinforcements. She doubted he was Bratva. They tended to travel in packs, and if he was important enough to drive that snazzy sedan, he would have a team of bodyguards and a driver. So who was he?

She contemplated making a run at getting up close to the house, or maybe heading down to the car to see if anything inside could identify the driver. But it was entirely possible the man was waiting inside, back far enough from one of those windows to shoot her if she showed herself. It was what she would do.

No, she was going to sit tight and let him make the first move.

While she waited, she replayed the events of the past few minutes in her head. She registered that the man inside the house had been wearing an expensive wool coat. It was knee-length. And he'd been wearing dress shoes. He wasn't planning to run around in the woods shooting at people, then.

She also noticed a lump lying on the far side of the porch steps. The more she looked at it, the more certain she became that she was looking at the feet of a dead man. Wool Coat Man hadn't headed for the detached garage, and the SUV that was probably still inside. Surely by now, he'd found the car keys. Was he so certain she would blow up that car, too?

All of a sudden the man burst out the back door of the house, running from her left to right. He apparently had a good idea of where she was hunkered down—instead of zigzagging left and right, he was speeding up and slowing down randomly.

He was headed for the hangar.

Why there? It made no sense.

She pushed to her feet and paralleled him, staying inside the tree line at the edge of the property. He disappeared inside the hangar. Stillness and silence fell again around her. What was he doing in there? What was so important about that building that had sent both Nikolai and now this man to it?

She jolted when she heard a loud screeching noise of metal on metal. *What on earth?*

It belatedly dawned on her that she was hearing the hangar doors open. Being even with the front of the building, she took off running toward the back, where it opened out onto the airstrip.

She was just in time to see a helicopter swoop out of the enclosure. It stayed low as it cleared the hangar, then tilted forward sharply and accelerated hard. A blast of snow and ice crystals pelted her. She threw a hand up over her face as it turned slightly to place the hangar between her and it.

She ran forward, swearing, into the rotor wash as it lifted away rapidly into the night.

She rounded the corner into the hangar and spied the small

Cessna sitting there. She had taken some flying lessons . . . something like thirty years ago. Did she dare chase after the helicopter?

She would have a speed advantage. The Cessna would top out at about 180 knots, and that tiny helicopter probably couldn't do more than about 130. But it would have a severe maneuverability edge.

Her shoulders slumped. Whoever he was, he'd gotten away.

Speaking of which, she ran back outside, over to where Nikolai lay in the snow, eyes staring vacantly up at the night sky. She checked for a pulse, but he was definitely dead. She reached for his arm and heaved him over onto his side. The back of his coat had a ragged tear in it, and underneath the fabric, his back showed a black, gory hole.

She searched in the packed, bloody snow where he'd lain and found what she was looking for. She picked up the deformed, flattened round and pocketed it.

Glancing toward the car, she was disappointed to see the whole thing was now on fire. The passenger compartment was engulfed in flames, and any evidence that might lead her to the identity of the driver had already been consumed or would be soon.

She trudged back toward the house as exhaustion suddenly caught up with her. She felt every one of her fifty-five years as she headed inside. A quick look around didn't reveal anything of great interest. Clearly, whoever guarded the hangar stayed here, eating frozen dinners, watching television, and sleeping in the messy bedroom.

Last, she headed out front to check out the dead man. Bratva tattoos covered his neck and the backs of his hands. She should probably get out of here before any of his buddies came to check on him or the glow in the horizon of the cabin she'd torched.

She reached into the dead man's pants pockets and found what she was looking for—a key ring. She opened the garage door and climbed into the SUV inside. It reeked of cigarette smoke. But, it ran, and the heater worked. She backed it out of the garage and drove around the burning sedan. She had no idea where the dirt road went, but the sedan had come from the north, so that was the direction she headed.

She drove for perhaps ten minutes on the narrow, one-lane road before it joined a paved, two-laned road. Since Washington was southeast of her location, she turned east.

Eventually she ran into a major highway and recognized where she was. It would take about a half hour to drive back to Washington, another half hour to ditch the SUV and catch a ride, and another half hour to be home. She had no idea what came next. Her only lead on who'd attacked her and Yosef was dead.

CHAPTER 26

*H*E FLEW BACK TO WASHINGTON IN SUCH A RAGE THAT HE COULD hardly see the helicopter's instrument panel through the haze of red obscuring his vision. He'd barely killed Ibramov in time to stop the idiot from blurting his name. To Helen Warwick no less.

He couldn't believe she'd slipped away from him. Of course, he knew her reputation for getting the job done, but she was a middle-aged, washed-up assassin. He should've taken her down without breaking a sweat. As it was, he'd barely gotten away, and she blew up his car.

Where to land? Any airport he landed at would ask questions. There were various helipads all over Washington, DC, but he couldn't exactly abandon this bird on one of those without drawing a lot of attention. Irritated, he pushed the collective, forcing the aircraft down until he was high enough above the trees not to attract too much attention, but low enough to slide under the radar covering this area. It had been years since he'd flown, but as he recalled, all of DC's skies were restricted airspace of one kind or another.

He needed to find an open field. Something big enough to land in, isolated enough that this helicopter wouldn't be spotted for a few days. But not so isolated that he couldn't hike out to someplace where he could catch a ride. *What a mess.* And it was all the Warwick woman's fault.

He spied a clearing in a stretch of woods that might work. He slowed down and circled back to the spot. It had been forever since he tried to hover, and he couldn't hold the light little bird still. But he got enough of a look to know the rotor blade would fit with perhaps twenty feet to spare on each side. It was tight for a very rusty aviator, but as good as he was going to get.

Holding his breath, he eased the bird down.

He landed hard enough to clack his teeth and snap his chin down. But any landing he could walk away from was a good one, right? He cut the engine and spent several minutes wiping down every surface he could possibly have touched during his flight.

Finally, he walked away from the helicopter. He considered burning it, but the smoke and flames would draw too much attention.

With a sigh, he headed into the woods toward the nearest road. The forest floor was wet and slushy. His shoes were ruined and his feet, freezing. Irritated to no end, he pondered the myriad ways he was going to make Helen Warwick suffer for this moment someday.

But not tonight. His first order of business was to capture the copycat DaVinci Killer and teach the whole world a lesson about messing with the Original DaVinci Killer. There would be time enough for Helen Warwick another day. After all, he was an exceedingly patient man. Especially when it came to serving revenge to those who got in his way.

He knocked on the apartment door quietly. Given that Goetz had been online only a few minutes ago, shooting off his mouth about anyone who thought he wasn't the real DaVinci Killer saying that to his face, he didn't have to knock loudly.

The door opened.

Goetz stared at him for a moment. All of a sudden, recognition flared in his eyes and he started to slam the door shut. As if that wasn't an entirely predictable response.

Almost casually, he pulled the trigger of the dart gun he held hidden in the folds of his long neck scarf. He took a quick step forward, jamming his shoe in the sill, preventing Goetz from shutting the door all the way.

Goetz staggered back, staring down at the small, fluffy-tailed dart sticking out of his chest. "What did you do, man?"

He pushed his way into the apartment and closed the door quietly. "I ensured your cooperation with my little plan for you, Mr. Goetz."

"Who are you?"

"You know who I am."

"I know you're Scorpius—"

"Don't call me that!" he snapped. "To you, I'm the DaVinci Killer. The *only* DaVinci Killer." He poked a finger into Goetz's chest, a few inches to the left of the dart. "You are a fake. A pale shadow of me. And your reckoning has come."

"My kills were a hundred times better than yours, old man. You're obsolete. I blew you away. People don't even remember you anymore."

"Ah. But they're about to. You're going to put me in the history books, my boy."

Goetz staggered, caught himself, blinked hard a few times.

"That's the tranquilizer you're feeling."

"Not . . . going to . . . kill me?"

He laughed richly. "As I recall, I made my intentions perfectly clear. No, Ryan. I'm not going to kill you. At least, not yet. First, I'm going to make you suffer."

He took a step forward, and Goetz reached out to hang on to his shoulders. He let the kid hang on. And he leaned in close to whisper in his ear, "I'm going to make you scream. And scream. And scream. Until you can't make another sound."

Goetz's knees buckled, and he wrapped his arms around the younger man, catching him before he could thud loudly to the floor.

He left swiftly. He had only about two hours to execute the next part of his plan, which involved fetching the van he had stashed down the street and transferring Goetz into it.

And then . . . oh, and then he got to play.

Over the years, he'd rarely allowed himself to turn his sadistic impulses completely loose. He dared not. But tonight he would. In all their vicious glory.

Helen pulled into her driveway very late, profoundly relieved that Nikolai Ibramov wouldn't be trying to kill her or her loved ones again.

She threw her muddy camo suit into the washing machine and went up to her secret room to clean her rifle. As she hung it back on the wall, she remembered the slug she'd stuck in her pants pocket. Pulling it out, she turned it over in the light.

The round looked more like a half-dollar than a bullet. It obviously had been some sort of hollow point or trocar-tipped round to have deformed this severely. Nothing else would tear a fist-sized hole through Nikolai's chest except a very large-caliber round, and Wool Coat Man hadn't been wielding a big enough weapon for that.

Padding down the hallway in her socks, she headed for Jaynie's room. She pulled her daughter's microscope down off the shelves over her desk and plugged the device in. Placing the slug under the lens, she peered through the eyepiece at it. There was a bit of striation around the pencil-eraser-sized bit of the round that hadn't flattened out like a pancake.

As she recalled, there was a way to take pictures with this gadget. She found a USB port and rummaged around in Jaynie's desk drawers until she found the right kind of cord. She plugged in her phone and took a series of pictures of the markings on the surviving shaft of the bullet. These rifling marks were as distinctive and individual to a single weapon as a human fingerprint.

Maybe Yosef could have someone run these images through the federal law enforcement database of rifle marks.

She stared down into the microscope. *Who are you, Wool Coat Man? Why were you out there in the middle of nowhere? And why did you silence Nikolai before he could name whoever had hired him?*

Was Wool Coat Man the person inside the US government who'd hired Nikolai in the first place? Was he Scorpius? Or a member of whatever Scorpius was? What did Scorpius have against Liang? Had Scorpius hired Nikolai to kill Yosef because Yossi was getting too close to Scorpius's identity?

She went to sleep chewing on her questions and woke no closer to any answers.

He waited until Goetz had fully regained consciousness before he got started. He wanted the boy to fully experience the horrors in store for him. Goetz stood on a wooden platform about two feet tall, lashed hand, foot, chest, and neck to a full-sized Christian-style cross. The base of the cross sat on the floor of the barn behind the platform, which arrayed Goetz's spread-eagled arms across the horizontal beam.

When Goetz was awake enough to shout and thrash against his ropes, he stepped up behind him and removed the blindfold. The kid went silent. *As well he should.* The installation he was about to become the star of was spectacular.

He'd spent days stretching a massive piece of sail canvas over the floor of this barn and painting it with a satellite's eye view of the world. He'd mimicked Salvador Dalí's mostly gold and yellow tones in the rendering, and they shone brightly under the spotlights he'd installed to light the interior of the barn.

The walls were draped from floor to ceiling with black tarps that admirably mimicked the inky void of space.

"What is this?" Goetz demanded.

"It's your final art installation. But this time, you get to be the man in the painting. Fitting, don't you think?"

"You crazy sonofabitch! I'll kill you! I'll put you in a painting—"

He laughed shortly. "And how exactly do you plan to do that when I'm done crucifying you?"

"Crucify—" Goetz panicked then, and struggled in earnest. Which only earned him a few nasty rope burns.

"Are you done?" he asked dryly, when Goetz finally stopped thrashing, either from exhaustion or futility.

Goetz spit out a curse at him.

"Shall we begin?" He turned on the video camera mounted on

a tripod in front of the platform so as to capture everything he did to Goetz. Then he picked up the tools of his trade, and moved back to his victim.

Goetz's eyes went wild, terrified, as he lifted a small sledge-hammer and a large railroad spike. He placed the tip of the steel pike against Goetz's left wrist, where it would pierce between the bones of his forearm and bear his weight when Goetz was finally suspended from the cross.

He drew the hammer back and gave it a satisfying blow. Goetz screamed. He relished the sound mightily. Another blow, and Goetz passed out. It was probably more the shock of having a spike driven through his arm than the actual pain that had over-whelmed the guy. He finished driving the spike deep into the wooden cross he'd built for this project, then stepped off the plat-form to wait for Goetz to revive.

He repeated the process with Goetz's right wrist. He used a long spike for Goetz's feet, driving through both feet just below the ankle joints so the weight of his shin bones would rest on the spike and help support him.

Then he carefully pulled the platform out from under Goetz's unconscious body. He'd never crucified a person before, and his-torical accounts of how to do it properly were surprisingly sparse. Goetz sagged as his arms stretched to take his weight, but he stayed in place on the cross. Concerned that the angle the cross was supposed to hang at might cause Goetz to tear off of it, he lashed a thin but strong nylon rope under Goetz's armpits and around the intersection of the vertical and crosspieces. He tied it off in back.

Meticulously, he applied flesh-colored paint to the rope so it would blend in with Goetz's skin and not ruin the aesthetic of the crucifixion. He stood back a few yards, satisfied that the rope was basically invisible.

He took his time draping the white loincloth that Dalí had painted on his Christ, and he pinned it carefully in place to the sides of the cross.

Oh, that is lovely. He made sure to film the finished crucifixion in loving detail, capturing it from every angle.

Then he began the laborious process of hoisting Goetz up to the ceiling. In Dalí's painting of *Christ of Saint John on the Cross*, Jesus had hung from a cross far above planet Earth, looking down at it as if it were no more than an atom in the infinite expanse of the universe.

He was huffing from exertion when he finally got Goetz all the way up near the thirty-foot-tall ceiling, which was also painted black. He climbed the ladder he'd brought for the purpose and attached the thin steel wires he'd installed yesterday to the eye-bolts on the back of the cross. Then he untied the hoisting rope, climbed down the ladder, and stowed all his tools in the van.

He went back inside the barn to check on his Christ.

Goetz was groaning as he slowly regained consciousness.

"Can you hear me, Ryan?" he called up.

A groan. He would take that as a yes. "I thought you might like to know how you're going to die. As it turns out, the weight of your body hanging like this is going to cause hyperexpansion of your chest muscles and lungs. The only way you'll be able to breathe before long is going to be by pulling yourself up by your arms. Eventually, you're going to become too exhausted to do that anymore. Then, you'll slowly die by asphyxiation. As your lungs fail, they will begin to fill with fluid and possibly blood. You'll very slowly, painfully drown. Oh, and the slightest movement will cause you excruciating agony. You can scream all you'd like. I've taken you someplace where nobody will hear you."

"You bastard," Goetz gasped.

"Oh, I'm significantly worse than a mere bastard. You see, I'm enjoying this. At any rate, in a few days, I'll send someone here to find you. And that is when the world will learn of my true mastery of the art of murder. You will be forgotten. I will retake my position as the one and only DaVinci Killer upon the world stage."

Goetz swore at him, then devolved into coughing. He screamed in pain and passed out again.

Sadly, he feared the boy was neither physically nor mentally strong enough to last very long. Goetz had no grit. But then, most serial killers turned out to be pathetic losers. Unlike himself, of course. He was an artist. *A connoisseur of death.*

Speaking of which, it was time to record the completed art installation for posterity. Maybe he would post it on the thrill kill site Goetz had used. Maybe he would keep it for his private enjoyment. He hadn't decided yet.

He filmed the interior of the barn and its contents from every angle, appreciating the lighting he'd set up. One spotlight shone up at Goetz, illuminating him in a heavenly nimbus of light. The space was actually brilliantly lit with several spotlights pointing down, but the black walls and ceiling absorbed all the reflected light, which gave the space an otherworldly quality. It really did feel as if the whole room hovered several thousand miles above the earth.

Deeply satisfied with his work, Goetz's screams still echoing like sweet music in his ears, he drove away from his greatest creation ever.

When Helen woke up in the morning, she went through the now familiar routine of soaking away her copious aches and pains in a very hot bath, and then stretching slowly and carefully. When she could sort of move like a normal human being, she went downstairs to make herself a cup of coffee. As she contemplated how many aspirin she could safely take at once, her cell phone rang.

It was the hospital Yosef was in. She picked it up quickly, alarmed. "Is everything all right with my husband?"

"There you are, Mrs. Mizrah. We've been trying to get a hold of you since last evening. Your husband is being released today."

Her phone had been turned off the whole time she was running around in the woods chasing Nikolai and shooting at Wool Coat Man. "That's wonderful news!" she exclaimed. "When can I come get him?"

"He'll be ready to go in about an hour."

"Perfect. Thank you for letting me know."

She gulped down her coffee, microwaved and ate a frozen breakfast sandwich, threw on her Ruth disguise, and headed out.

*   *   *

When she entered his room, Yosef was sitting on the edge of his bed while an orderly tied his shoes. He looked up and smiled at her. As always, the gentleness and wisdom in his eyes melted her heart. He opened his mouth to greet her, but she cut him off, worried he might not remember that she was pretending to be his wife.

"Hello, darling," she gushed. "I can't wait to get you back to our house and put some color back in your cheeks with some good home cooking."

"I can't wait to watch you make me matzo balls," he replied dryly.

She made a face at him. Her cooking was famously wretched, and she wouldn't know a matzo ball from a meatball.

A nurse came in and thrust a pile of paperwork at her. "These are his discharge papers. All of his post-care instructions are in there. Here are his prescriptions for pain meds and anti-inflammatories. And here's the number to call if he develops any of the symptoms on this list. If you'll bring your car around to the underground exit, I'll meet you there with Mr. Mizrah."

Yosef rolled his eyes at the wheelchair the orderly pushed in, and Helen took the plastic bag with his meds and personal items in it. She found the discharge exit about the same time Yosef arrived, and waited in her car while the orderly helped him into the passenger seat.

She headed toward Alexandria and his home.

"So, Helen. I hesitate to ask what you've been up to while I was out of action."

"Well, I crocheted a doily and made a nice wreath for the front door."

He snorted at the idea of her doing anything remotely crafty or domestic.

She filled him in quickly on everything, finishing with Nikolai's death last night.

"And you have no idea who the man in the wool coat was?" Yosef asked.

"None. He wore a hat with a brim that cast his face in shadow and covered his profile. His coat was long and bulky enough that I couldn't even tell you what his build was like. I'd guess he was around six feet tall. But that's it. Oh, I did recover the slug that killed Nikolai, though. It's got some markings on it."

"Now what?" he asked.

"Now you tell me who you think Scorpius is," she replied.

He frowned. "Scorpius?"

"Yes. When we met at the pub where you were shot, you started to tell me about a mole or a secret group inside the agency called Scorpius. You thought maybe he or it was behind the attack on me at my son's house."

"I'm sorry. I don't remember anything from the last hour or so before I was shot."

"Liang decoded the messages you had me give him. They did originate with Scorpius, but Li couldn't tell me what agency he works in or who, specifically, the message traffic was ordering killed."

"He couldn't tell you, or wouldn't tell you?"

"I don't know, honestly. You should ask him . . . in your official capacity. Maybe he'll talk more freely with you."

"Worst case, we can take them to someone else to decode. You do have a copy of them, don't you?"

"Of course I do. This isn't my first rodeo. I'll bring them over to you."

"Tell me about our meeting in the pub."

"Well. We agreed to ditch our spouses and elope to Bali, where we're going to start a resort for international fugitives modeled after the bar in the movie *Casablanca*. You get to be Rick, and I'll be Ilsa."

He threw her a disapproving look.

"Fine. You were nervous when you asked me to meet you at that pub. Really nervous. Whatever you learned from those messages had you shook. We talked a bit about Scorpius, and then you were shot."

"Interesting."

He sounded tired, so she didn't push him to see if he could remember more about what he'd been thinking that night. She parked in front of his house and helped him inside. The nurse who'd been caring for Ruth hurried downstairs to greet them. She took one look at Yosef and ordered him upstairs to his bed. She helped Helen walk him to the elevator at the back of the house and tuck him into bed.

As much as she loved Yosef, she was grateful to hand off the bag of pills and care instructions to the nurse, who nodded efficiently as she looked through them.

Helen murmured to the woman, "Feel free to bring in another nurse if Yosef and Ruth are too much for you to handle alone—"

"I've got this. Ms. Ruth sleeps around the clock. I'm bored to tears most of the time. Having Mr. Mizrah here to look after will give me something to do."

"You're sure?"

"Honey, I was a trauma nurse for twenty years. I can manage an entire emergency room staff and a dozen patients requiring critical care at the same time."

Helen smiled in relief. "Then I'll leave you to it."

Her cell phone rang as she was heading back out to her car. "Hello, Mitchell. To what do I owe this lovely surprise?"

"Are you busy this afternoon?"

"No. Why?"

"I'm calling a family meeting."

"Indeed?" Traditionally, they'd only had such powwows when something serious occurred.

"Can you be here at, say, one o'clock?"

"Yes. Can you give me a hint what this is about?"

"No, Mother. I'll see you then."

She set her hair in hot rollers, donned makeup and clothes formal enough for Mitchell's tastes, and drove over to his house, arriving exactly on time. Peter's sports car was already parked in the driveway.

She was pleased to see a police cruiser sitting down the street. *Thank you, Yosef.*

She sat in her car for a moment, breathing slowly and reciting to herself, "I'm a mother. A wife. A normal woman living a normal life. Nobody is trying to kill me anymore, and I can relax."

But no matter how many times she repeated the mantra, it didn't seem to want to stick. She was going to have to fake her way through this meeting.

"I'm pretending to be a mother, a wife, a normal woman . . ."

To that end, she made a conscious decision to leave her purse, and the handgun inside it, in the car today.

Feeling naked and hating every second of not being armed, she climbed out of her car and walked resolutely up the sidewalk to the house. She could do this. She still had her hands and knew some unarmed combat. And there would be all kinds of knick-knacks inside the house that would make for decent improvised weapons.

The front door opened before she could ring the doorbell, and a fast-moving blond shape bolted out of the house. Arms wrapped around her neck and all but choked the life out of her.

"Jaynie? Is that you? Oh, how I've missed you!" She hugged her youngest fiercely, delighted to see her.

Jayne released her and stepped back, and Helen looked her daughter over from head to toe. "What a delightful surprise. It's wonderful to see you, darling. I love this look on you."

Jayne, the rebel of the family, had been going through a truly unfortunate hippie stage the last time she'd been home but finally appeared to be coming out of it. The dreadlocks were gone, and her blond hair was straight and silky over her shoulders now. Although Jayne was wearing jeans, these were nice ones with no tears, and they fit her. Jayne's simple turtleneck sweater was tasteful. Classy, even. Why, if Helen wasn't mistaken, she had a bit of makeup on, too. Would wonders never cease?

She linked arms with Jayne, and they walked into the house together. "When did you get back to town?"

"About a half hour ago. Mitch picked me up at the train station. I made him promise not to tell you I was coming, so I could surprise you."

"To what do we owe the pleasure?"

"It's a three-day weekend at the university, and Mitch called a family meeting. I had the time off, so I decided to jump on a train and see what all the fuss is about."

"Do you have any idea why Mitchell called this meeting?"

"No. You?"

"No idea." Jayne steered her left into the colonial antique-filled living room.

"How's Columbia, darling?"

Jayne shrugged. "Rife with academic politics. They think they're all so sly and clever about it, but they haven't seen the way this town does dirty dealing."

Helen laughed a little. "Your father always complains about office politics. Jockeying for grant money was the worst."

Jayne laughed. "I'm lucky. I got a government grant so my colleagues can't touch it. They're jealous though, and take every opportunity to snipe at me."

"Ignore them. Once you're done with your dissertation, you'll never see them again. Speaking of which, how's the beast coming along?"

"I'm in my third revision of it. If I never see another study of social media and authoritarian regimes, I won't shed a tear."

"I'm so proud of you, sweetheart."

"I don't have the PhD yet."

"I'm so proud of who you've become. I don't care about your degree." She winced. "I mean, I'm proud of your academic accomplishments, of course—"

She broke off as Jayne stared at her. "Who are you and what have you done with my mother?"

Peter strolled into Mitch and Nancy's ugly, stilted parlor just then. "Didn't you hear, sis? Mom turned over a new leaf when she retired. She's trying out what it's like to be a human being."

Helen smiled sweetly at him. "Maybe you should give it a try sometime, dear."

Jayne laughed. "Ouch! Nicely done, Mom."

Liang came into the room. "Did your mother tell you she bakes now? She made Peter and me an apple pie a few weeks ago."

Jayne stared at her, looking truly aghast. "You bake?"

Helen shrugged modestly.

Peter muttered, bitterly, "Not that anyone got to eat it after she got our house shot to hell—"

Nancy bustled in just then, interrupting him. Helen was amused at the chilly look Nancy shot Peter before coming over to air-kiss Helen's cheek and give her a light, patently insincere hug.

"Where's Mitchell, Nancy?" Helen asked.

"He ran out to do a last-minute errand. He'll be back any minute, I imagine. Can I get you something to drink? I have snacks in the kitchen. Tea sandwiches, some fruits and cheeses. I'll serve lunch in a bit."

Of course she would. Nancy was nothing if not the consummate hostess. Rather than stick around to take barbs from Peter, Helen wandered into the kitchen and nibbled at a miniature cucumber and watercress sandwich while Nancy brewed her a cup of tea.

The front door opened, and she heard Jayne scream.

Helen tensed, ready for battle, and lunged over to one side of the kitchen door. Why, oh why, had she left her purse—and pistol—in the car? She spun into the hallway fast and low, her hands held out in front of her defensively.

What on earth?

She straightened and stared in shock.

"Grayson?"

"Hello, wife of mine."

"Well, hello." Belatedly, she hurried forward and hugged her husband.

He released her and she stepped back, looking over at Mitch. "You weren't messing around when you called a family meeting. What is this all about?"

Mitchell gestured toward the living room. "Everybody, if you'd go into there, we can get started."

Helen couldn't help it. The open curtains made her too nervous to stand. She walked over to the big picture window and pulled them shut before she perched on the hard, uncomfortable sofa between Jayne and Liang. The silk cushions were stuffed with horsehair, packed to the consistency of concrete.

Mitchell struck a dramatic pose in front of the fireplace. "I gathered you all here today to make an announcement and ask for your help."

"With what?" Jayne demanded.

"I've decided to run for office."

A general outburst accompanied that. Helen sat back, studying her eldest closely. He was flushed and excited. Ambition clung to him like his spray tan—attractive, but with a certain fake quality.

Gray responded, "What office, son?"

"District attorney of Washington, DC."

Gray nodded gravely. "That sounds like a fine plan." Then he broke into a big smile. "How can I help you win?"

Mitchell laughed. "You may regret saying that, Dad. I'll put you to work."

Mitch turned to her. "Mom? What do you think of my plan?"

"I'm surprised you didn't invite my mother to this meeting. She knows every power broker inside the Beltway and most of the ones outside it. If you want to win, she's the person you want in your corner."

"I know that," he said impatiently. "But I need all of you to be on board before I mention it to her. She'll take the bit in her teeth and run with it the moment I tell her I'm even thinking of going into politics."

"True," Helen conceded.

"Besides, Gran's in Palm Beach doing the snowbird thing right now."

Helen barely managed to bite back a snarky comment about that being no loss.

Mitch looked at her intently.

"What, dear? You look like you want to say something."

"I'm going to need you to behave, Mother."

She folded her arms across her chest. Stared at him steadily. "Just what do you think I'm going to do to *mis*behave?"

"I have no idea. But I need you to be home consistently, look like a mother on camera, and do *motherly* things."

"Like bake apple pies?" she asked, dry as a desert.

"Exactly."

"And not get shot at by robbers?"

"Yes. That, too."

"Well then, by all means, I'll tell all the robbers in Washington, DC, to be sure not to break into any homes I happen to be visiting."

He rolled his eyes at her, and she rolled hers back. It was not her fault Nikolai and his team had hit Peter and Li's house when she was inside. By his own admission, Nikolai said he would never have done it if he'd known she was there.

"And while I'm at it, I'll be sure to tell all the art thieves in the metro area to leave Peter and Liang's art collection alone so I don't get caught in the crossfire."

She felt Liang's uncomfortable weight shift beside her. He'd caught her subtle reference that he and Peter had been the target of that attack and not her, had he? *Good.*

Peter piped up hotly. "You always attract trouble, Mother. Don't blame us. You're the one who shot back at those men in our house. If you hadn't done that our house wouldn't have been destroyed—"

"Peter. Enough," Liang bit out.

Shockingly, Peter stopped.

Which was just as well. She would've hated to have to point out that if she hadn't shot back, she would be dead and their house would still be destroyed. Not to mention, they might be without millions of dollars' worth of art as well.

Everyone was staring at Liang now.

He, in turn, looked intently at Peter. "If your mother hadn't defended herself, it's entirely possible she would have died. She protected Biscuit and defended her son's house. You keep accusing her of not having maternal instincts, but she protected what was important to you. It's what mothers do. They protect their young."

She stared at Li along with everyone else, stunned that he, of all people, would come out swinging on her behalf.

"That's crap—" Peter retorted.

Liang talked over him, not raising his voice, but with unmistakable authority. "When that carjacker shot at us in the parking lot, your mother protected me. She put herself in the line of fire to cover me so I could get to safety. She got shot, for crying out loud. And when I asked her why she did it, she said because you'd kill her if something bad happened to me. She did that for you, Peter. She protected what you love. It doesn't get more maternal than that."

Peter's jaw hung open for a moment, then snapped shut. He remained silent this time.

Liang looked around at everyone in the room. "It's none of my business, but in the time I've known all of you, you've been hard on her. I don't know what she's done in the past, and it's not my place to comment on that or forgive any of it. But since she's retired, she's been trying to be a good parent. From where I sit, she's met you halfway. But none of you have bothered to meet her in the middle. It's only fair you give her a second shot."

She laid a hand on his knee. "It's all right, Liang. I've failed them in the past."

Liang shot her a frustrated look. "Your son has no right to tell you to behave. That's not the place of a son toward his mother."

She smiled gently at him. "You're very Asian at your core, aren't you?" She hesitated, then added, "Thank you for the support. It means a great deal to me."

Gray leaned forward, surveying everyone. "What just happened? I'm lost."

She replied lightly, "Nothing, dear. But it seems time for a vote. All in favor of Mitch running for district attorney?"

A chorus of ayes rang out.

"Opposed?" she said.

Silence.

"There you have it, darling. We're all behind you." She stood up quickly, not the slightest bit interested in dragging out the drama with Peter and Li any further. Thankfully, Liang and Nancy caught the hint and stood as well. Jayne wasn't far behind.

Helen followed her daughter-in-law quickly to the kitchen. "What can I do to help with lunch?"

Nancy made up jobs for her until the meal was served, for which Helen was abjectly grateful. They made it almost to the end of lunch without an incident. Gray regaled them with tales of his latest trip to the Amazon, Jaynie talked about her work in New York, Liang talked about how the re-renovation of their house was coming along, and Mitch filled them in on the details of when and where he would announce his candidacy for district attorney. Peter was sullen and silent, but he could get over himself.

Just as the meal was ending, Helen's cell phone buzzed in her pocket. She fished it out. Almost all of the people in the world who had her personal phone number were sitting at this table. Had something happened with Yosef? She'd left the nurse her number.

The caller ID said it was Angela Vincent. She also wouldn't call for no important reason.

"Excuse me," Helen said politely, pushing her chair back. "I need to take this call."

She went into the front room to take the call in private.

"Helen, it's me. I need you to get down to my office right now. It's an emergency."

"Can you tell me what it is? I'm with my family."

"I'm sorry. But you've got to come. Trust me."

She sighed. "Okay. I'll be there as soon as I can."

"Hurry."

She pocketed her phone and went back into the dining room. "I'm sorry, but a friend has an emergency. I'll come back here as soon as I can."

"See?" Mitchell exclaimed, throwing up his hands. "This is what I'm talking about!"

"It's your colleague who called me," Helen snapped. "So get over it."

Mitchell's eyebrows sailed up. "Angela? What does she want?

What emergency? Does this have to do with her clients who were wrongly convicted? I'd like to go public with that when I announce my run for DA."

"I'll let you know when I get back."

Mitch seemed mollified that whatever crisis called her away probably had something to do with him. Lord, that boy could be self-centered sometimes. Did he really get that from her?

With a sigh, she turned and left the house.

CHAPTER 27

*T*HE POLICE CARS IN FRONT OF ANGELA'S OFFICE WERE HELEN'S FIRST clue that something big was up. Her second clue was the crowd of people filling the second-floor office from wall to wall.

"Ma'am, you're going to have to leave," some guy in a suit, standing close to the door, told her.

"Angela just called and asked me to come down here—"

"Are you Helen?" he blurted. She nodded and he raised his voice. "She's here! Make a hole, people."

What on earth? The man took her by the elbow and practically shoved her through the crowd until she reached Angela's desk.

Her friend was sitting at her usual place behind it. The old rotary phone that usually sat on one corner of the desk was hooked up to a machine about the size of a bread box by enough wires that it looked like it was in an intensive care ward. Helen commented dryly, "Is your phone critically ill?"

Angela glanced at it, startled, and broke out in a smile. "Nope. Just bugged and set up for call tracing."

"Does that have to do with why you asked me to come down here?"

Angela held out a clear plastic protector sleeve with a sheet of paper in it. "This came in the mail a few hours ago."

It was a plain sheet of white paper with mismatched letters of various fonts and sizes glued together to form a message. Although it might be as cliché as all get out, it still sent a chill down her spine. She read the text.

If you want to know who killed your lover, have Helen answer my call.

She looked up, alarmed to see every pair of eyes in the room staring at her accusingly. "What? You think I know who killed the district attorney?"

"You did know exactly how the murderer was executing his kills," Angela said grimly.

Helen shrugged. "Anyone who's ever shot a weapon could have figured that out."

Angela gestured around her. "This is a room full of cops and FBI agents, and none of them figured it out."

She wasn't about to admit to being a contract killer for the CIA. She shrugged again. "I was just lucky, I guess. My mother always says I have a vivid imagination."

"Do you know anyone who might be a serial killer, ma'am?" asked a stern-looking guy standing just behind Angela's chair.

"And you are . . ." Helen replied.

"Special Agent Waltrip. FBI. Washington, DC Field Office."

"No, I do not know anyone who might be a serial killer, Agent Waltrip."

"Any idea how this one knows you?"

Probably from my work. The community of government contract killers was pretty tiny, after all. "No. No idea," she answered.

"Any idea why this one picked you to communicate with?"

"No. I'm as clueless as to why I'm here as you are. What do you people want me to do, anyway?"

When the agent merely pressed his lips together and refused to answer, Angela piped up. "The killer called that phone about an hour ago. The FBI had me pick it up. As soon as I said hello, the killer said, 'You're not Helen,' and hung up. Next time he calls, they want you to answer the phone. Try to keep him on the line. Get him talking. Figure out what he wants and why he contacted you."

She frowned. "Why me?"

Waltrip shrugged. "Because the killer says so. We need a break in this case. And if he's willing to talk to you, so be it."

She frowned. What was going on around here? Had the killer spotted her scoping out his old kill zones? Was he impressed—or angry—that she'd figured out his method of murdering folks and framing others? How did he know who she was?

So many law enforcement types crammed in the same room made her nervous. She'd left a trail of dead bodies behind her in the past several weeks, some of which were prosecutable murders, even if a jury would likely acquit her for acting in self-defense.

Her cell phone vibrated with an incoming text. No doubt it was Mitch wanting an update. She pulled it out and stared at the message, startled.

New plan. Go outside. Alone.

Was this the killer? How on earth had he gotten her private cell phone number? She didn't give it out to anyone she didn't know intimately. Was this a ploy to get her outside, away from the protection of the crowd of cops, so the killer could shoot her? She thought fast about the layout of the building. The killer's use of the word "alone" indicated that he had visual contact with Angela's office or somehow knew it was crammed with law enforcement officials. She eased out of the crowded office and headed upstairs toward Angela's crash pad.

"Where are you going, Mrs. Warwick?" an alert FBI agent challenged her.

"I need to use the restroom. There's one up here, and I'm hoping it's not occupied."

The guy shrugged—not that she was waiting for his permission—and she continued up the flight of stairs. The door at the top was unlocked, and she let herself into Angela's place. It was disheveled. Papers were scattered on the dining table, a coat lay over a chair, and she spied the bed unmade through the doorway to the bedroom. *Poor Angela.* She was having a rough time.

Helen moved swiftly through the kitchen to the fire escape and let herself out onto the metal stairs. She hurried down them, careful not to make any noise. When she reached the bottom, she hugged the wall of the building and looked around. Only one building, directly behind her, had any sight lines from a window to her. She crouched down, squatting on her ankles, which put her below a fence and out of sight from the other building.

She texted back **What now?**

She only waited a few seconds for the reply. It was a string of numbers separated by spaces: **1907 50 1492 3.**

She waited for upwards of a minute and finally texted **Is that all?**

Several minutes passed, and the murderer didn't seem inclined to text her any further. She swore under her breath. She sucked with codes, particularly numeric ones. But she knew someone who didn't suck at them. Given that the killer had started his earlier text with the phrase "New plan," she gathered he was done communicating everything he'd planned to tell her.

Since nobody seemed to be looking for her yet, she decided to bail out while the going was good. She took off her navy blazer, revealing her white blouse and pulled her hair up into a short ponytail. Anything to change her profile just enough to throw off a casual observer. She slipped around the building and hustled down the street to her car.

The drive to Alexandria was quick on a Saturday, and she pulled up in front of the Mizrah house in record time.

She jogged up the front steps and rang the doorbell. The nurse answered. "Hello, Mrs. Warwick. Are you back to check up on us? Both my patients are resting comfortably."

"I need to speak with Yosef. Is he awake?"

"I am now," he called from the living room.

"Why aren't you upstairs in bed?"

"I've been in a bed for a week. I was sick of it."

"I'm sorry," Helen murmured to the nurse as she swept past the woman. "I should've warned you he would be a terrible patient."

"What's up?" Yosef asked.

"I have a puzzle to solve, and you're the best in the business at such things."

"You came all the way over here to have me solve a puzzle?" he asked, looking perplexed.

She glanced significantly at the nurse before he murmured, "Perhaps you could go look in on Ruth, Louise?"

The nurse caught the hint and headed upstairs. When Helen heard the bedroom door close, she filled in Yosef on the letter to Angela and her friend's call to come to her office. She finished by pulling out her phone and showing Yosef the string of numbers. "What do they mean?"

He stared at them for a few seconds. "Paper and a pencil," he muttered. "In the top drawer of my desk."

Helen rummaged in the old desk until she found a pad of paper and a couple of pencils.

Yosef noodled with the numbers for a while before looking up. "It's not a cypher. There's no mathematical connection between these numbers. Which means they have some other specific meaning. Hand me my laptop."

"The obvious assumption seems to be that 1907 could be a date."

Yosef frowned. "What of significance happened in 1907?"

She shrugged. "I'm no historian." Then she added thoughtfully, "But if that's supposed to hint at a place I'm to meet the killer at, would the date have something to do with the local area?"

"That's a good thought. Let me see what things of significance happened in the Washington area in 1907."

She sat and waited while he typed on his computer, seeming to browse aimlessly. But of all people, she knew how entirely *not* aimlessly this man's mind worked. It took about a half hour, but finally he sat up straighter.

He typed quickly, nodding as he did so.

"What have you got?" she asked.

"The main train station, Washington Union Station, was completed in 1907, and its address is Fifty Massachusetts Avenue."

That explained the 1907 and fifty. "What about the other two numbers? 1492 and three?"

"I'm working on it . . ." A flurry of typing erupted. "Aha! I've got it! At least I think so."

"What?" she demanded

"The fountain in front of the train station is called the Christopher Columbus Fountain. Hence 1492. The year Columbus is traditionally believed to have first landed in North America."

"Columbus *didn't* land here in 1492?" she asked.

"He landed in the Bahamas in October of 1492. He also explored the coast of Cuba on that voyage around Christmas of 1492. But he never landed on the actual continent of North America."

"Any idea what the three refers to?" she asked.

"No idea. I suspect we'll have to go to the Columbus Fountain and have a look around. I'm sure it's a reference to some specific location."

"Are you strong enough to make a trip to Union Station with me?" Helen asked, doubtfully.

"Nothing energizes me more than a good puzzle," he declared.

"Let's make a break for it before Louise comes back downstairs, then. She'll try to stop you from going out, and I'd hate to have to kill Ruth's nurse."

Yosef snorted, and she jumped forward to help him sit up. It broke her heart to see him this weak and debilitated. They slipped out the front door, and she helped settle him in the passenger seat of her car.

Once they were safely away from his house she asked, "How long until you're fully recovered from your injury?"

He shrugged. "Docs say four to six months until my sternum is fully healed."

"Wow. That's a long time."

"It's a big, thick bone. Takes a while to heal from being split in half."

"Your sternum split in half?" she squeaked.

"They told me it's cracked almost all the way through." He added, quietly, "They also told me I'm lucky to be alive. Thanks for knocking me out of the way of that bullet."

"I'm sorry I didn't knock you completely out of the line of fire. I wasn't quite fast enough—"

"You saved my life. That's plenty fast for me." He placed his hand on top of hers, where it rested on the shift stick. He squeezed her fingers briefly.

They drove back to Union Station, where she parked in a handicapped parking space. Even though she didn't have a placard to do it legally, Yosef was clearly handicapped. She would gladly pay the fine if she got a ticket. It was worth every penny to save dear Yossi any unnecessary exertion.

They walked slowly to Columbus Fountain in front of the station. Yosef sat on the edge of the raised knee wall that arced around the front of the fountain while Helen crawled all over the fountain in search of whatever the number three referred to. She explored every nook and cranny of the huge fountain and found absolutely nothing that could be construed as a clue. No message, no marking, no carving or date, nothing.

A police officer eventually came over and told her to quit climbing on the fountain. She joined Yosef, sitting on the low wall in front of it. "We struck out," she murmured.

Yosef frowned. He was looking down at his cell phone. "Did you know there's a private event space inside the station? It's called the Columbus Club. Maybe that's what the 1492 referred to."

"It's worth a look. We're already here." She helped Yosef to his feet and walked slowly beside him as he shuffled into the cavernous marble edifice. They found the Columbus Club, or at least the door to it, but it was locked.

"Block me from view," she muttered. "I'll pick the lock."

"Has anyone ever told you you're a scary lady?" he muttered back.

"Several people. Including you, as I recall." She rummaged in her purse and pulled out her picks. The locks were old and, although well made, relatively easy to pick. She bent one of her picks in the process, but it was a worthy sacrifice. "Got it," she murmured.

"Wait for it . . . wait . . . wait . . ." Yosef murmured under his breath. "Now. Coast is clear."

They slipped into the dim room and closed the big door behind them. It was a large space that would easily hold several hundred people. "Now to find the three our killer was referring to."

She parked Yosef in a chair and started to search the room. She found it under the third window on the far wall of the room. Lying up on the high sill, tucked in a dusty corner, was a piece of printed card stock free of any dust. It had been put there recently.

She took it over to Yosef. He read the name on it. "Amtrak. It appears to be a luggage claim tag. Baggage claim is over by Gate A. Not far from the Amtrak ticketing counter."

"Where's Gate A?" she asked.

"Not a train person, are you?" he asked wryly.

"Not when it's faster to fly."

"Ah, Helen. You go through life in too much of a rush. You should slow down a little. Savor the small things from time to time."

"I thought I was going to do just that when I retired," she retorted. "But you can see where that got me."

"I made a few phone calls earlier. Asked around about Scorpius."

"Any luck making an identification?"

"If it's a person, he or she has gone completely to ground. Erased all trace of himself—or herself—in the government computer network. It's as if Scorpius never existed."

"Why do you suggest Scorpius is a she?" Helen asked.

Yosef shrugged. "I'm an equal opportunity analyst."

They reached the baggage claim area for Amtrak and handed over the claim ticket. The attendant brought them a nondescript black suitcase, smallish, with wheels and an extendable handle.

Helen reached for the zipper, and Yosef mumbled, "Not here."

"Of course. Sorry. I'm interested to see what's inside."

"As am I," he replied evenly.

They made their way back to her car. It was a bit of a hike, and Yosef was clearly winded when they got back to the vehicle. He sat in the front passenger seat while she climbed in the back seat with the suitcase.

She asked, warily, "Should we call in the bomb squad or have this thing X-rayed?"

"This serial killer's preferred method of killing is a firearm. He's precise. Surgical. Only kills the person he wants to kill. Only frames the person he chooses to frame. He won't blow up his victims with something as messy as a bomb that has high potential for innocent victims."

"Sometimes you scare me, Yosef."

He shrugged. "It's a simple profile to arrive at."

She would hate to hear what his profile of her sounded like. Carefully, she unzipped the suitcase and lifted the top.

The inside was stuffed messily with men's clothing. Jeans, a T-shirt, a flannel work shirt, muddy tennis shoes. Even socks and underwear were inside.

"Don't touch anything," Yosef told her. "Don't contaminate it with your DNA. Use a tool . . . a pen or something like that to lift the clothing. See if you can find blood on any of it."

"You think the killer sent us the clothes of a victim? *Ee-yew.*" She pulled her slim ankle knife out of its sheath and lifted the shirt with the blade.

Yosef snorted. "Leave it to you. I say to use a pen, you use a knife."

"It's metal and was handy," she snapped, examining the shirt. "I don't see any blood." She examined every piece of clothing, finally concluding, "Nor are there any tears or stains to indicate someone was killed wearing any of this."

"Look in the pockets."

She did so and frowned. "There's a sheet of paper with what looks like a latitude and longitude position written on it."

"Where is the location?" Yosef asked.

"I don't know. Close, though." She climbed out of the back of the car and into the driver's seat. She turned to her navigation system but jumped violently as someone knocked on her window. It was the police officer from the fountain. She rolled down the window, suppressing her irritation. "Can I help you, Officer?"

"You can't park here."

"No problem. We're just leaving. Have a good day!" She rolled up the window before he could ask for her driver's license or try to issue her a ticket. She backed out of the spot quickly and drove away from the train station. She stopped a block or so away in a parking lot next to a bar. She programmed in the latitude and longitude numbers, and her navigation system quickly calculated a route.

"It's partway between here and Baltimore," she announced. "Maybe a private home. Looks like a rural area. But there's a road to it. Wanna go check it out with me?"

Yosef grinned. "Absolutely. You get to have all the fun out in the field while I'm stuck at my desk all the time."

"I may declare it not safe for you and back out of wherever it is if I don't like what I see," she warned. "I'm not driving you into a death trap. I almost lost you once, and I won't risk you again."

He smiled over at her. Their gazes met for a microsecond before they both looked away. *Nope.* They couldn't go there. Gray had just come home, for heaven's sake, and Ruth was still alive, if not kicking.

"Why don't you rest while I drive? It'll take about forty minutes to get there according to my navigation system."

He smiled gratefully and reclined his seat. Lord, he was weak. He'd never been the athletic type in the past, but she'd never seen him this quick to tire. Deep alarm at the thought of losing him speared through her. Weird that she didn't have the same reaction when she thought about Gray.

She loved him, and he was the father of her children. But she'd always made a point of living independently from him. She could survive on her own without Grayson. But Yosef? He was another story. How would she carry on if something happened to him?

With that cautionary note in the forefront of her mind, she stopped about a quarter mile short of the destination the serial killer had sent them to.

Yosef woke with a start. He put his seat upright. "Is this it?"

"No, it's a little bit farther down the road. I thought I would go in on foot and reconnoiter on my own."

He threw her a damning look. "Who is it that always says two guns are better than one?"

"That's me. But you're in no shape to be crawling around in the woods in the middle of a gunfight."

"I'm not dead," he declared. "And I'm not about to see you get yourself dead."

She weighed the stubborn set of his chin and decided against arguing with him. "Have you got a gun on you?" she asked, doubtful.

"No. But you always have a spare."

She sighed. He wasn't wrong. "In the glove compartment. There's a latch on the ceiling and a hidden compartment that drops down."

He reached into the glove compartment, fumbled around, and pulled out a Glock 22 pistol and spare ammo magazine.

She sighed. "If you're coming along, I'll drive in closer to the target. I don't want to give you a heart attack."

"Helen . . ." he said warningly.

"Don't you Helen me. You were in the ICU only a few days ago, fighting for your life."

He rolled his eyes at her, and she rolled hers back. Which was why they were both grinning as she parked her car a second time, pulling off the narrow road and tucking her car behind a bushy pine tree. She spent a few minutes pulling branches and brush over the hood and wheels, while Yosef looked on. Satisfied that it was both hidden and ready to roll quickly, she nodded at him.

"How do you want to do this?" he asked low.

"We'll separate and come in from different directions."

"Ah, yes. Make separate targets of ourselves. If one gets fired at, the other can crossfire at the shooter," he said eagerly.

"You're having too much fun out here," she grumbled. "This is serious."

He shrugged, and his smile widened.

"You'll approach whatever structure is in front of us from this side," she told him. "I'll circle around behind it and approach from the rear." With another sniper, she would go all the way around to the far side, but Yosef wasn't an expert at controlling his field of fire and she didn't want him to accidentally shoot her. "When you've found a good spot with solid cover and a clear shot at the building, you sit tight. I'll go in from your left and have a look at the building. You cover me. Nothing more. Got that?"

He threw her a terrible salute.

"Do you have earphones for your cell phone?" she asked him.

"In my pocket," he declared. "I was listening to music when you came to the house."

"Perfect. Put those on." She inserted her wireless earbuds as she talked. "I'll call you, and we can communicate over the phones if we need to."

He poked in his wireless earbuds.

"Ready?" she murmured.

"Ready."

She heard him loud and clear in her earpieces. "Move slow. Take your time. There's no rush on this."

He nodded and followed her into the trees. When she judged them to be parallel to the structure her Google Earth map depicted in a clearing somewhere to their right, she paused, pointed to the right, and waited for Yosef to peel off and head in that direction. She continued on straight for another thirty yards or so before she made the turn. Now that they were apart, she moved more quickly. She wanted to be in position before he approached the structure in case someone tried to take him out.

She ran for perhaps a minute, then slowed as the trees thinned ahead of her and to her right. She continued forward more slowly until she stood at the edge of a small open area with a large barnlike structure in front of her. The siding was rusty galvanized aluminum. The old, wavy kind that tended to peel back at the corners.

The barn stood a good thirty to forty feet tall. She estimated it was eighty feet long and about half that wide. And it had definitely seen better days.

She scanned the woods around the clearing and saw nothing. No movement. No signs of life. She caught the slightest shift of a leaf where there shouldn't be a breeze off to her right. That would be Yosef.

"Are you in position?" she whispered.

"Yes."

"What do you see? Is there a vehicle parked in front of the barn?"

"No. I see some tracks in a muddy spot. Someone was here not too long ago."

"Any movement?"

"No."

"We'll sit for a few minutes. Wait to see if anything happens."

"Yes, ma'am."

She scowled over her rifle sight. She happened to have a short-barreled urban assault weapon in the trunk of her car, and it was that she'd brought out here. Ten minutes passed with not a hint of anyone else being here. The birds went back to singing and bickering over territory. A few spring peeper frogs took up a tentative chorus. It was the warm day that had brought them out.

"I'm going to circle around to the front," she breathed to Yosef. "You stay put."

"Roger."

She backed up and moved off to her left. She approached the side of the barn opposite Yosef and studied the open yard in front of the structure. Yosef was right. Someone had driven in, then back out. The two sets of tracks were distinctive. They could be a few hours old, or a few days. There'd been no rain or snow in the past forty-eight hours to mar the prints. Using the telescopic feature of her sight, she searched for footprints but found none. The dirt and gravel directly in front of the barn were too hard-packed for that. A large sliding door on the front of the building was shut. A hasp was closed over a metal loop, but there was no lock on the latch.

Through cracks in the siding, she caught a few glimpses of what looked like some kind of fabric or maybe tarps hanging down. What did the killer have waiting for them inside anyway?

"Do you stand by your hunch that our killer isn't a bomber?" she muttered into her coat collar.

"I do."

"All right, then. I'm moving in. Cover me."

She eased out of the woods into the edge of the clearing. Nobody reacted. "I think it's safe for you to join me, Yosef." She would breach the big space first with Yosef covering her from the doorway.

He moved out of the woods with admirable stealth and joined her at the door. She whispered for him to cover her as she opened the door. If nobody reacted, she would slip inside with him taking her place in the doorway. He nodded, holding her pistol in both of his fists in front of him. The way she heard it, he was a reasonably good shot. But firing at a paper target in a shooting range was a whole different thing from shooting at a living person. Lots of excellent shots didn't have what it took to pull the trigger at a living target.

She eased back the barn door a few inches, squeaking it loudly. She ducked low and swung back along the wall, her entire side pressed up against Yosef's.

She heard a low moan from inside. Yosef lurched against her, and she frowned. *That sounded human.*

Lying on her belly, she pulled herself forward with her elbows and peeked around the doorjamb. Her eyes took a few seconds to adjust to the dark interior after the bright outdoors. The walls were draped in some sort of black cloth that reflected no light whatsoever. The entire floor of the barn was covered with some sort of smooth flooring. Floodlights shone down on it and up toward the ceiling, which also seemed painted black, or maybe covered in more of the black draping.

Ignoring whatever the lights pointed at, she scanned the entire space at chest level. There appeared to be nobody inside.

Another moan, louder this time, made her look toward the far end of the structure.

She pushed to her feet and stared in complete and utter shock. "Oh. My. God."

CHAPTER 28

"**W**HAT?" YOSEF SAID SHARPLY FROM BEHIND HER.
"The building is clear. Sort of," she mumbled over her shoulder as she stepped forward into the weirdly black space. She cleared the space again from inside, and stood on a smooth painted surface that felt like tent canvas.

Spotlights from above lit the floor, which was painted in varying shades of gold, brown, and sea green. Just in front of her on the floor was a rowboat that appeared to be painted, maybe tied off at the edge of a lake or a sea. She took a few more steps and spied a line of what looked like distant mountains painted from left to right across the entire width of the barn.

Yosef gasped behind her. She looked over her shoulder at him. He stared up at something beyond her in utter horror. And then he started praying aloud in Hebrew.

Reluctantly, she looked up at what had made him gasp, up toward the ceiling at the far end of the cavernous space.

A man—an actual man—hung from a cross suspended from the ceiling. The cross was mounted at an angle, tilted forward enough that the tragic figure seemed to float over the landscape painted on the floor below. A brilliant spotlight illuminated the man, whose loins were loosely draped with some sort of white linen-ish cloth.

As she stared up at the apparition, her mind refusing to believe it was real, something dripped from the crucified man's bound feet. It splatted against the canvas loudly in the silence.

Yosef rushed past her. "We've got to get him down. If he's still bleeding, he's still alive."

Her brain locked up for a moment. That was really a living man up there, nailed to that cross. She lurched into motion behind Yosef. "Call 911," he bit out as he moved toward the far wall, no doubt to examine how the poor man was suspended up there.

Dialing the police, she had to resort to giving the operator the lat-long coordinates, since she had no idea what the address of this place was—or if it even had one. Then she called Angela.

"Helen?" answered the voice on the other end. "Where did you go? You just disappeared! The FBI guys are furious."

"I got a text from the killer. He gave me a math puzzle to solve, and I took it to a friend who's the smartest puzzler I know. He figured it out, and it took us to, um . . . a barn. You should probably bring everybody. And hurry." She rattled off the coordinates again.

"I can't find a way to get him down," Yosef called from the far end of the big barn.

She hurried to join him, circling wide of the three pools of blood, one under his feet and two collecting under each of his outspread wrists. The cross hung some ten feet away from the end wall, and no ropes or another means of hoisting him up there were apparent. She made out black wires suspending the cross from the ceiling, but they disappeared behind the black draping, and she had no way of telling where they went. She started working her way around the barn, lifting the black tarps hanging down to cover the walls.

Meanwhile Yosef called up to the man, "Can you hear me? We're here to rescue you! Wake up! Talk to me!"

She'd made it most of the way around the barn when the man on the cross moaned again.

She rushed to stand beside Yosef, joining him in shouting for the man to wake up.

Very slowly, his eyes opened. They were glazed over, as if he were drugged, or more likely, in unbearable pain.

"Who are you?" she shouted up at him.

"Da. Vin. Ci," he gasped. Between each syllable, he took a rattling, wet-sounding breath.

"He's got blood in his lungs," she told Yosef under her breath. "We've got to get him down soon or he'll die."

"Blood collects in the lungs of crucifixion victims," Yosef murmured back. "It's how they usually die. By slow asphyxiation. They drown in their own blood."

"He sounds close to death. But there's no way to get up there. No ladder. No ropes. I have no idea how he got up there. It's as if whoever did this to him hoisted him up there in a cherry picker or something."

Yosef murmured back, "We have more pressing issues to ask him about than how he got up there." He called out to the crucified man, "Who did this to you? Do you know him?"

"No," the man gasped.

Helen called up, "Did you kill the district attorney? The person who led us here says you did."

The man's eyes opened all the way at that. "No!"

"But you did kill other people on the street, yes?" Yosef asked gently.

She looked over at him in surprise.

The man stared down at Yosef and said nothing. Even though he was some thirty feet above them, Helen could swear she saw a stubborn look enter his eyes.

Yosef spoke even more gently. "Son, you're dying. I don't think help is going to get here in time to save you. Wouldn't you rather meet your maker with a clean conscience? We're not law enforcement. We're just two people trying to help ease your last moments. If you have anything on your mind, now is the time to tell it to me."

"Swear," the man gasped. A little blood bubbled from between his lips. "Won't tell."

"I swear upon the Holy Torah, the Bible, and my mother's grave I will not repeat anything you say to me while you live."

The man sagged . . . if it was possible to sag while spread-eagled and nailed to a giant cross. Helen could see the ends of what looked like metal railroad spikes protruding from his wrists and feet.

"I'm. New. DaVinci. Killer."

Helen stared. The dude who'd been creating art installations of great paintings depicting death using the bodies of—

She looked around. "Is this one of your works of art?" she blurted. Was the guy committing a spectacular suicide with one last display?

"No," he ground out, coughing. A gout of blood fell to the floor below him, hitting with a wet splat. His bloody spittle made a scarlet smear across the depiction of a sun-drenched planet Earth far below the heavenly, floating Christ he depicted.

"What's your name, son?" Yosef asked, so kindly it almost made her want to weep.

"Ry. An."

"Ryan What? I'd like the world to know the identity of the DaVinci Killer one day. You will be famous for centuries to come, son."

Had Yosef heard of the DaVinci killings, or was he just going with the flow and assuming that, if the guy had a moniker like that, he was likely a serial killer?

"Goetz."

Ryan Goetz. She knew that name. The police had questioned him after the last canyon killing. And the killings had stopped. Had he moved on from those and taken up doing these DaVinci killings?

"Did you shoot a bunch of people from rooftops and frame other people for your killings?" she blurted.

It took a moment for his gaze to shift to her and focus. "Yeah," he sighed, before coughing again and spraying more blood below. His eyes drifted shut.

"Ryan," Yosef said loudly. "Open your eyes. Who did this to you? What can you tell me about your killer?"

Ryan's eyelids fluttered open. He coughed violently, all blood this time. A lot of it.

"Ryan!" Yosef shouted. "Who is your killer?"

"My. House." A long sigh. "It's there."

What did that mean? It was there. The identity of his killer?

Without warning, a long shadow fell across the painting, as if someone had stepped into the open barn door. Helen spun around but not fast enough.

Ryan's head jerked up, and he shouted hoarsely, "Scorpius! No!"

Bang!

A deafening gunshot rang out. She dropped instinctively, reaching into her purse as she rolled into the fall. She sent one quick shot in the general direction of the doorway, not with the intent to hit the shooter but to suppress any more fire from him until she could gather her wits.

The person in the doorway, backlit by the sunlight so she couldn't make out anything but a black shape, spun out of sight. She heard footsteps running on the gravel outside the barn.

She jumped to her feet and glanced up at Goetz on his cross. His head had fallen forward, his chin landing awkwardly on his chest. Blood streamed from a wound in his chest, exactly over his heart. He was clearly dead now.

She looked down at Yosef lying on his side, gasping in pain.

"Are you hit?" she asked urgently.

"No. Hurt my chest when I hit the deck. Go after him."

"I'm not leaving you!"

"Have to. Catch Scorpius."

Her gaze whipped up to the door. Scorpius was just outside? The man who'd ordered Nikolai to kill her? The traitor spy?

"Go, Helen."

"Get to the car if you can. I'll meet you there." And with that, she sprinted for the door, fumbling to free her pistol from her purse and grabbing the spare ammo magazine. She dropped the purse and spun outside.

She didn't spy any movement from the direction of the driveway nor did she hear a car. He was still on foot then, out here, somewhere.

She peered around the end of the barn. *Clear.*

Racing to the back side of the structure, she repeated the maneuver. This time when she peered around the corner, she saw distant movement in the woods. The bastard was running away.

She followed grimly, determined not to let Scorpius slip away from her. She was positive this was the one and only shot she would get at him before he disappeared for good.

He must've heard her, as a shot rang out from ahead of her, and a big hunk of bark flew off a tree to her left. It was a wild shot, undoubtedly meant to slow her down. She put on an extra burst of speed.

The brush grew thicker as they plunged deeper into the woods. Brambles caught at her pants and vines tangled around her feet. Where was he? She'd lost sight of him. She stopped, listening hard. *There.* Off to her right. It sounded as if he'd veered in that direction.

She moved out, more slowly now. As it turned out, her progress was nearly as good when she walked more carefully as it was when she tried to run. She stopped again to listen, but this time heard only silence.

Her gut shouted at her that he was ahead, lying in wait for her. It was what she would do if she were being pursued by an assassin. She would turn and fight.

She eased even farther off to the right in hope of circling around his ambush.

A twig snapped and she lurched, spinning left toward the sound just as a gunshot rang out.

Thank you, little bunny or squirrel. Now she knew where Scorpius was. Half crouching, she eased toward the source of that shot. As she went, she plucked leaves and picked up twigs, stuffing them in her hair and in the collar of her coat. She stuffed them in her coat and pants pockets, too. When she stepped through a low spot she paused, lifting away the leaves silently to expose a pocket of muddy dirt. Using her fingers, she smeared it on her face, as well as in long stripes on her coat.

She continued forward slowly. *Come out, come out wherever you are, Scorpius.*

Bang!

She sprinted a dozen yards to her right as quietly as she could, and crouched behind a tree.

Bang!

She felt the impact of the bullet in the tree at her back.

Crap. Scorpius had visual on her. It was only a matter of seconds until he closed the gap and killed her.

She ran straight forward, using the trees for cover as best she could. She pitched forward and fell as a small gully dropped away beneath her feet. Praying Scorpius wasn't close enough to have heard her grunt when she fell, she scrambled frantically on her hands and knees, crawling along the path of the ravine. A nasty tangle of brambles and bushes extended across it. She crawled up to its base. Which was when she realized the undergrowth didn't actually grow out of the gully floor. It just hung over it.

Using her pistol and thick sleeve, she lifted the mess of branches, vines, and thorns and crawled under it. She emerged out the back side of it and pressed up to her feet. She took off running in a crouch.

Her legs were killing her. She was tired and out of breath. She wasn't strong or fit enough to run around out here all day. She had to bring this thing to a close—and soon—or she would die.

Bang!

She barely managed to force herself not to flinch or drop to her belly. The shot sounded well over her head. Maybe it had been a random shot to get her to bolt from her hiding place.

Quickly, she assessed her situation. She was no commando trained to skulk around in the woods in complete silence. But Scorpius obviously was. He had her at a huge disadvantage. He also had a rifle, and she only had her trusty pistol. While she was an excellent shot with it, he had range on her. He could afford to sit off at a distance and pick her off as soon as she tried to move.

She had to do something drastic, something out of the box to change the odds, or she was going to die. Moving only her gaze, she looked around frantically for an option.

Over there.

From this angle, low to the ground, she could see under the hanging boughs of a pine tree. It had long needles as thick and lush as a Christmas tree. Although narrow, this pine was easily thirty feet tall.

It could work.

Pulling herself forward on her belly by digging her toes into the dirt and dragging her body forward with her elbows, she low-crawled the dozen yards over to the tree. There was no leaf cover around the base of the tree, so she held her breath as she dragged herself the last several body lengths across the needle-covered snow.

Once she was underneath the tree, the network of branches close to the trunk were bare and brown. They weren't very thick, but they would have to do. She put her foot on the lowest branch, about knee-high, and stepped up onto it.

Working as fast as she could, she climbed the tree. She couldn't help shaking the branches some, particularly as she got higher and they thinned to less than the thickness of her wrist.

She felt the two branches she was standing on bend beneath the weight of her feet. She could go no higher. She partially sat down on the branch behind her hips to distribute her weight even more, while wrapping her left arm around the trunk to help support herself.

She was a good twenty feet up in the air, staring down at the clear area around the tree. She gripped her pistol tightly in her right hand. Now it was a waiting game.

That, and a desperate hope that Scorpius didn't think in three dimensions as a killer.

Because of all her years doing urban kills, she was extremely proficient in the art of hiding high inside a building, or on a rooftop, and shooting down at her targets. She thought in three dimensions all the time. It was the only thing she could think of that might give her a tiny edge against the assassin stalking her out here.

It took a while for Scorpius to close in on her last position in the gully. She heard a single scuff of leaves from that direction, but it was enough to tell her where he was. She shifted carefully to more fully face in that direction. Her perch was beyond precarious up here, and she hoped fervently that the branches wouldn't collapse out from under her.

She concentrated on slowing her breaths, but it was hard to do when she was also busy wondering if they were her last.

She spied a hint of movement in the woods. And then she saw him. *Scorpius.* He glided stealthily from the cover of a big oak tree to the cover of one a few feet away. But in that moment, she got a good look at him.

It was Scorpius, all right. She could recognize that long wool coat and old-fashioned fedora anywhere. It was the same man who'd shot Nikolai, the man she'd chased through the woods, the very same who'd made his escape in that helicopter.

Once more he eased out from behind a tree and into the shadow of another. She had to give him credit. He moved as if he were a part of the forest. His feet didn't make a sound. Only her vantage point up here, with a clear view down below, allowed her to see him at all.

It was tempting to shoot at him now. But she dared not miss. She would get one shot at him before he spotted her up here and killed her. The downside of this perch was that she had no means whatsoever of moving out of it quickly. She was a fish in a barrel up here as soon as Scorpius saw her.

Patience, Helen. Let him come closer. All the way into her guaranteed kill zone.

Bit by bit, he made his way toward the edge of the clear area, perhaps ten yards from her pine tree. The next time he stepped out, she would take her shot.

Except the next time he moved, he didn't come toward her as she'd expected. He moved off to his left.

She swore silently. He was going to skirt around this open area. Or maybe he sensed a trap. Either way, she had to shift her hold on the tree trunk and turn her body to the right to get any kind of a shot at him. It was a huge risk. But she had no choice.

The next time he moved, she timed her own move for just as he stepped behind the tree trunk. She winced as the fabric of her coat made the faintest of swishing noises as it rubbed the tree trunk.

Scorpius spun out from behind the tree, eye to his rifle, scanning the clearing.

Thirty-five years of marksmanship and countless life-or-death shots taken came together in that instant. She exhaled, held her breath, and raised the pistol in a single, coordinated instant.

In that same moment, Scorpius spotted her. His rifle swung up toward her, aiming high in the tree.

There. Her front and rear sights formed a perfect line across his chin, and she squeezed the trigger.

Bang!

BANG!

They fired at nearly the same time.

Her bullet flew a tiny bit faster, by a fraction of a second. It was *just* enough to throw Scorpius backward, *just* enough to make his rifle pull up, *just* enough to send his bullet over her head by a few inches, thudding into the trunk of the pine tree and pelting her with pine needles and splinters of wood.

Below her, Scorpius's face exploded and his body launched back, a cloud of red mist hanging in the air where his head used to be.

She continued to train the pistol on her target as he lay still on the forest floor. She counted to sixty in her head before beginning the laborious process of climbing down the tree. She stopped after every step to stare at Scorpius intently, to make sure he hadn't moved a muscle.

She jumped down the last four feet or so and crouched where she landed, peering out from under the branches. From this angle, Scorpius's body was a pair of combat boots and some gray wool.

That was a weird clothing combination. Usually snipers who ran around in the woods wore full combat gear to go with those boots. *Why the dress coat and hat?* Maybe he'd expected merely to drive up to the barn, kill Goetz, and drive away. She shrugged.

Pistol at the ready in a two-fisted grip before her, she crept out from under the pine tree. She eased forward, one careful step at a time, prepared to shoot again at the slightest twitch he made.

Finally, she came within view of his face. Or where his face should have been. It was gone, and in its place, bone, blood, and brain coalesced into a disgusting goo. He was very dead.

All of a sudden, she felt light-headed. Her knees went weak, and her legs were actually trembling.

She'd done it. She'd killed Scorpius.

It took her a good thirty seconds of leaning against a tree to catch her breath and begin to feel steady again.

She knelt beside the corpse. A quick search of his pockets revealed no personal items. No wallet, no cell phone, not even a set of keys. His clothing didn't have any labels in it, either. Classic assassin behavior. She didn't wear anything that could identify her when she'd gone on her missions, either.

She did take his hat, which had fallen off his head when he hit the ground. It had some blood and brain matter on it, but was otherwise intact. She stuffed it inside her coat, mashing it flat.

In the absence of a face to photograph for confirmation of kill, she screwed up her resolve and reached into the gore of his face to pluck out a bit of jaw that still had a molar embedded in it. She dropped the bone and tooth in her pocket.

Grossed out, she backed away from the body and pulled out her cell phone. She snapped a series of pictures of the corpse for posterity.

Then she looked around the woods. Trees and more trees were all she could see. *Which way back to the barn?*

She pulled out her cell phone and prayed she got a signal. It was weak, but it was enough for her to plug in the barn's coordinates to her navigation app, and for it to point the way back.

Following the blue line on her phone, she hiked back to the barn significantly more quickly than she'd gone into the woods.

Once she spotted the clearing and the big barn in front of her, she circled to the right, sticking to the cover of the trees. She approached her car cautiously. The branches that hid it were still in place.

Alarm flared in her chest. *Yosef had better be all right.*

She crept up to the passenger door and peered inside.

Thank God. Yosef was seated in the car, head back, eyes closed. But he was breathing. She slipped around to the driver's door and opened it.

Yosef murmured, "Did you get him?"

"I did. Unfortunately, I destroyed his face, so I couldn't tell you who he was or show you a picture of him. I got a tooth, so perhaps an identification can be made from that."

Yosef frowned. "Any self-respecting Russian mole doesn't leave his actual dental records lying around."

He was not wrong. "At least we know he's dead, whoever he may be," she said stoutly.

"Thank God."

"Amen," she agreed.

Yosef sat up straighter in his seat. "We need to go. I expect the cavalry will arrive shortly, and I'd just as soon not be here when they do. I'm tired, and they'll have far too many questions for us."

"Ha! You want to find out where Ryan Goetz lived and go visit his house," she accused him. "You think there's a clue to Scorpius's identity there."

Yosef smiled a little and shrugged. "Ryan did say, 'My house. It's there,' when I asked him who his killer was."

"Do we tell the police about Scorpius's body in the woods?" she asked soberly.

Yosef was silent for a moment. "I think not. We have enough to identify him ourselves, and it would cause the police to ask you the kind of questions the agency would rather not have you answer. I'll let my superiors know. Later."

"I would rather not have to answer police questions, either," she said fervently.

"Then we're in agreement. And we should get going."

"Sit tight while I uncover the car," she told him.

It didn't take long for her to uncover the vehicle and get back in the car. She drove as fast as she dared to the first intersection, a large, two-lane road. She turned onto it and had driven perhaps a quarter mile when she saw police sirens behind her. They slowed and turned, disappearing from sight.

She and Yosef had made it out just in time.

CHAPTER 29

SHE GLANCED OVER AT YOSEF, WHO WAS BUSY ON HIS PHONE. "ANY luck finding out where Goetz lives . . . lived?"

"East side of Washington. Capitol Heights." He reached forward to program the address into her car's GPS system. They reached the Beltway, which went all the way around the District of Columbia, and she turned south.

"I think you had better call that lawyer friend of yours first and ask her to join us. If we're going to engage in breaking and entering, we should probably have legal counsel present."

"You were okay with me opening up the Columbus Room."

"We were just there to retrieve something. And it was a public space. This is a private home, and I don't fancy going to jail for breaking and entering while also interfering with a murder investigation."

It was a strange time for Yosef to stand on his moral high ground, but she knew better than to argue with him. He never, ever changed his mind once he dug in his heels on a moral issue.

She dialed Angela.

"My God, Helen," answered her voice. "Did you see it?"

"The crucifixion?" Helen asked grimly.

"Yes. I think I'm going to be sick."

"Angela, is there any chance you can get out of there? I really, really need you to meet me someplace alone. Like, right now."

"Why?"

"I'll explain when you get here."

"But this could be the guy who killed—"

She cut her off. "He's not. But he may know who is. Please, please come meet us."

"Us who?"

"Are you coming or not?" Helen demanded.

A huff. "Fine. I'll borrow my son's car."

"Come alone. Call me when you're on the road, and I'll tell you where to meet us."

"Why all this secrecy?" Angela demanded.

"I'll explain when—"

Angela cut her off. "I know. I know. When I get there."

"Exactly."

Since they had a head start on Angela, they took a few minutes to pull off the highway and park outside a coffee shop with good Wi-Fi. Yosef connected his phone to that and did a quick internet search.

"Aha! I found it!" he exclaimed, startling Helen.

"Found what?"

"The painting. It's called *Christ of Saint*—"

She finished the name of the painting in unison with him. "—*John on the Cross.*"

"By Salvador Dalí," Yosef said lamely. "Are you familiar with it?"

She replied, "A postcard of it was found at the crime scene where the district attorney was murdered. The police believed the DaVinci Killer was taking credit for killing the DA by dropping postcards of the paintings associated with his previous killings all over that crime scene."

Yosef frowned. "Ryan told us he didn't kill the DA."

"Do you believe him?"

"I suspect most men hanging on a cross don't tend to lie with their dying breaths," Yosef answered dryly.

She shrugged. "He did take credit for being the DaVinci Killer and for doing the other canyon killings."

"Like I said. If he readily admitted to being a serial killer but didn't take credit for the DA's murder, I'm inclined to believe him."

"Then who did kill the DA?" she asked. "Whoever did it had to be familiar with Ryan's work, and furthermore, knew Ryan was the DaVinci Killer. A friend? Family member?"

"I'm hoping we'll find the answer to that at his home," Yosef answered soberly.

She pulled back out onto the Beltway.

Angela joined Helen and Yosef at the top of the stairs on the third floor of the apartment building.

"What in the Sam Hill are you doing?" Angela demanded as Helen bent over the doorknob, working on the lock with her picks.

Yosef said quietly, "The young man crucified in that barn wasn't dead when we found him. We were able to speak with him briefly before he died. He denied killing your friend but did admit to committing the other canyon killings . . . and to being the DaVinci Killer."

"The guy who makes his victims into paintings?" Angela blurted.

"The very same," Yosef answered. "He also told us his name. Which is how we found this place, which we believe to be where he lived."

Angela's jaw dropped. "Why didn't you stick around the crime scene and tell the police that?" She started to reach for her purse, but Yosef put a hand on her arm. "It's a matter of national security."

"How's that?" Angela asked suspiciously.

The lock popped open under Helen's hands, and she straightened. "Perhaps we should take this conversation inside?"

Helen opened the door and called in. "Anyone home?"

Silence. She pushed the door fully open and stepped in. She felt for a light switch beside the door, flipping it on.

Angela gasped behind her. It was obvious why. The entire living room was plastered with colored posters of paintings. And every single one depicted something having to do with death. Skulls and religious killings. Battlefields, deathbeds . . . it was gruesome and overwhelming,

The three of them stood in the center of the room, turning slowly, taking it all in.

"I'm going to go ahead and say I think our guy was telling the truth when he claimed to be the DaVinci Killer," Helen commented.

"What does all of this have to do with national security?" Angela demanded.

Yosef answered, choosing his words carefully. "Before he died, Ryan indicated that his murderer was a person of interest to the Central Intelligence Agency, for which I happen to work."

Angela stared at Yosef for a moment, then pivoted to Helen. "You're a spy, too, aren't you? It's how you knew all that stuff about guns and sound suppressors!"

"Angela, on my word of honor, I'm not a spy nor am I an employee of the CIA." And that was about as much as she could say on the subject without breaking her word of honor.

Thankfully, Angela seemed to accept the statement. "And how do you know the dead man was killed by this . . . person of interest?"

Yosef said quietly, "Just before he was—" Yosef broke off. "Before he died, Ryan used a code name known to me. It's not a common word, not the sort of thing a man would say randomly with his last breath."

Angela frowned. "So the district attorney was murdered by the CIA? Why?"

"Hopefully, not someone in the CIA. But that's why we're here," Helen answered. "To get some answers before the various alphabet agencies swoop in on this place and lock it all down so you—and Yosef and I—never get any answers."

Angela nodded slowly. Then she said, "So the owner of this place is the crucified guy. Did he by any chance give you permission to enter the premises before he expired?"

"Yes. Yes he did," Yosef answered firmly.

Ryan had mentioned evidence in his house, but did that really constitute permission to enter? Even if he was dying when he said it? But who was she to question Yosef's interpretation? Helen nodded in agreement with Yosef's answer.

Angela nodded once more. "Then you do have legal standing to be here. And given the unusual nature of his demise, it makes a certain sense to want to verify his story of being a famous serial killer, does it not?" Angela asked.

"Indeed it does," Helen replied.

"Well then, what are you waiting for?" Angela demanded. "Search the place. You don't have long before the cops get here. They were cutting the dead guy down as I left. First thing they'll do is fingerprint him. And as soon as they know his name, they'll find this place, too.

Swearing under her breath, Helen headed for what had to be the bedroom door. As she reached for the doorknob, she heard a faint beep behind the panel. "Both of you stand back," she said sharply. She turned to Yosef. "Are you really, really sure this guy wasn't a bomber?"

Yosef nodded. "I would stake my reputation on it."

"You're about to stake your life on it," she retorted. She didn't have a single tool with her to even begin dismantling a trap. They really should wait for specialists to get here. But the identity of Scorpius was tantalizingly close. How did Scorpius know the man hanging dead in that barn, and why had Scorpius shot Goetz?

She eased open the bedroom door a fraction of an inch.

Nothing exploded.

She heard another beep and realized she was hearing a computer. She opened the door all the way and saw an impressive array of computers and monitors taking up the entire far wall.

She moved into the room quickly, cleared the bathroom, stepped back out into the bedroom . . . and stopped in her tracks. "Yosef. Come look at this."

He came into the bedroom, where she gestured at the wall to the right of the doorway. It was covered with photographs, newspaper articles, drawings, maps, and pictures of people with big red X's drawn over the faces. Strands of red yarn were pinned in a veritable spider web across the whole thing.

"Wow. Is that some sort of spy operation or something?" Angela exclaimed.

Yosef and Helen didn't answer. Instead they pulled out their cell phones and started taking pictures.

Once they both had a record of the entire mess, they took a look at it in more detail. Angela was the first to point out a sketch of what looked like a street on graph paper. Stick figures were drawn at an intersection, standing down the street, and up on a rooftop. Angles and math calculations lined the paper beside the sketch.

At once Helen recognized them as a sniper's sight line angles being worked out. Ryan also had done the math on how much a bullet would sink in the time it took to fly from the stick figure on the roof to the stick figure at the corner. "Angela, I think that sketch will be plenty to get your clients cleared of the murder charges, or at least get them new trials."

"These are the victims my clients were accused of killing," Angela declared, pointing at four of over a dozen pictures of faces X-ed out on the wall.

"Look at this up here," Yosef murmured to Helen.

She looked at where he pointed. "It looks like he was trying to work out the identity of someone," she commented.

Yosef pointed at an index card with the words *First Da Vinci Killer* printed in sloppy letters.

"Whoa," Helen breathed. "Didn't Ryan say something about being the new DaVinci Killer?"

Yosef looked up at her, eyes wide. "He did. Which suggests an *old* DaVinci Killer." He glanced at the bulletin board and gestured at a half dozen images of dead people posed as paintings, with more pinned beneath them. "I'll bet these were the original one's kills. Ryan must have emulated the first DaVinci Killer. He was a copycat."

Yosef bent down to examine the pictures more closely. "Look at the dates on these pictures. Some of them are nearly twenty years old. Ryan would have been a child if those are the dates the people in the pictures died."

"There are . . . what . . . a dozen of them up there?" Helen gasped.

Yosef thumbed through the overlapping, colored photos. "Closer to twenty." He took the pictures down, laid them on the bedspread, and photographed them all.

While he did that, Helen followed the red yarn farther down the wall. "Yosef. Look."

About halfway down the wall was a word scrawled across the top of a newspaper article. *Scorpius.*

Below it there were spaces for three pictures. The man on the far left, she recognized as Andrew Mizuki, the deputy director of the CIA, the number two man in the entire agency. Beside him was a picture of Lester Reinhold, the director of operations for the agency. And to the right of that was a blank space.

She leaned down and looked closely. As she feared, there was a pinhole in the wall. At some point, a third photograph had hung beside the other two.

Her nose nearly touching the wall, she caught a glimpse of something barely hanging out from the bottom of the newspaper article above her. The one with Scorpius's name on it. Something was tacked up behind it.

Curious, she unpinned the article and peered at what looked like a grainy photographic enlargement of two men talking on a street corner. She studied it for a moment and then gasped.

"Yosef! This is Nikolai Ibramov!"

"Who's he talking to in the photo?"

"I can't tell. The man's back is turned. But that's Scorpius's hat and coat." She reached into her coat and pulled out the fedora she'd taken from the assassin's corpse.

Yosef looked back and forth between the hat in her hand and the one in the picture. "They look identical."

She turned the picture over. In ballpoint pen, Ryan had scrawled a note: *Scorpius meets Russian hitman.*

She stared again at the picture. Scorpius had been behind it all. The attack by Nikolai and his men on New Year's Eve. Framing Ryan Goetz for killing the district attorney. And Ryan's murder, apparently. Which meant . . .

"Yosef. Scorpius has to be the original DaVinci Killer."

He nodded gravely. "I believe you are right. And Goetz believed he was a senior official inside the CIA."

"Do you suppose Goetz figured out that Scorpius was whoever was pictured in the missing photo?"

"It would certainly explain why Scorpius felt obliged to crucify him. Eliminate a copycat *and* protect his identity."

Yosef stood well back from the wall, staring at it as a whole. He swore quietly. "That third picture is not the only thing missing from the wall." He moved forward and reached out. "Look here. And here. The yarn ends are just dangling. They don't lead to anything. But all the rest of the yarn ends are carefully tucked behind something and pinned in place. Someone has been here and pulled several items off this wall . . . hastily, if I had to guess."

"Sounds to me like your Scorpius beat us here," said Angela. "It would make sense that he came here to cover his tracks before—or maybe shortly after—he crucified Goetz."

Gratitude flooded Helen. She was thankful Scorpius would never have another chance to betray the United States, nor would he ever kill again. She didn't often have an opinion about her kills, but today's had been a good one. *A really good one.*

"Well, kids, I hear sirens," Angela declared. "We can stay in here and face the music, or we can go back outside and pretend we were never here. Your call. I'm good either way."

Helen glanced over at Yosef. He looked gray with stress and fatigue. "Let's go," she said. "We got our man."

"Now we just have to give Scorpius a name," Yosef replied.

She smiled in relief. "Sounds like a project for a quiet, retired person with nothing much else to do."

"Unless," Yosef said ominously, "Scorpius wasn't working alone."

CHAPTER 30

*H*ELEN TUGGED AT HER NUBBLED PINK-AND-CREAM WOOL SUIT AS her mother whispered from her left, "Don't fidget."

"My pearls are choking me," she muttered back. Not to mention her pantyhose were digging painfully into her waist.

"The pearls are lovely. And so are you."

She shot a sidelong scowl at her mother. Between Constance and Nancy, the two of them had made sure Helen's hair was shellacked into an old lady helmet head that aged her by at least a decade. A makeup artist had done her face with Constance looking on, pouring out a steady stream of criticisms. When Helen finally got a look at herself in a mirror, she thought she looked like a clown, frankly.

Nancy swore the heavy makeup was necessary to not look pale and anemic on television, but Nancy and Mitch could have this fake, plastic existence, thank you very much. She had more important things to do. Like find out the identity of Scorpius and help Yosef uncover just how much damage he'd done while burrowed deep inside the CIA.

The bank of lights flashed on overhead, and she jumped, startled. Mitch stepped forward and took his place at the podium. He looked charming and at ease, and a moment of maternal pride passed through her.

From her right, Grayson reached out and linked his fingers

through hers. Without moving his lips, he murmured, "Smile, Helen."

Right. Happy family. All-American. Pure as the driven snow.

Mitch launched into his speech about the problems confronting the District of Columbia, and the need for a strong partnership between law enforcement and the district attorney's office to stem the recent tide of violence and right unfortunate wrongs.

While he droned on about reversing wrongful convictions and endorsed prison reform, she scanned out across the crowd. Was Yosef right? Did Scorpius have help betraying the United States? How deep did the rot go inside the agency?

Mitch finished his prepared remarks, and the press conference shifted into questions and answers. Off to one side of the room, slightly behind the podium, Helen spotted a movement. Someone was waving at the stage. Subtly, but waving.

She turned her head casually, pretending to look around the room, and spotted a man so nondescript her eyes would have passed right over him had he not lifted the hand now crossed over his chest and raised his index finger at her. *Aw, hell.* She knew the type all too well.

A moment of premonition swept over her, and a spot on her back, between her shoulder blades, itched for a moment, as if an invisible target was pinned there.

Who was coming for her?

Her rational mind said it was all over.

Despite Ryan Goetz's dying confession to her and Yosef swearing that he had not killed the district attorney, the police chief and acting district attorney had decided to declare Goetz the killer and close the case. Which didn't change anything. The district attorney's actual killer was dead as well. She and Yosef had agreed not to make a fuss about Goetz posthumously taking the fall for that one murder he didn't commit.

Nikolai was dead. Goetz was dead. Scorpius was dead.

It *was* all over, she insisted to herself.

Her family was safe.

No, a little voice in the back of her mind whispered. *It's not.*

She frowned.

The man in the corner frowned slightly. Looking directly at her, he crooked his finger, indicating that she should join him.

What on earth?

She murmured an excuse to her mother and backed out of the line of family members behind Mitch. She stepped down off the raised dais, picked her way through the jumbled electrical wires, and slipped behind the curtain hanging at the corner of the stage. She made her way over to the man.

"What do you want?" she murmured tersely.

"My boss needs to speak with you. Now."

"Your boss had better be pretty damned important to pull me out of my son's big announcement."

"Come with me, Mrs. Warwick."

Feeling the reassuring weight of her pistol in her purse, she spared the man a terse nod. He moved smoothly, with deceptive speed, to the exit behind him. He was definitely a trained special operator. Secret Service maybe? Or was he private security?

She stepped out into an alley behind the convention center. A black town car with blacked out windows sat there, idling quietly.

"Ominous, much?" she muttered.

She hung back as her escort opened the rear passenger door and gestured for her to enter.

Just then a man leaned forward from inside, looking up at her. "Get in, Helen. We have to talk."

Shock rattled through her. James Wagner. The director of Central Intelligence. Head of the CIA, in the flesh. "James. What are you doing here?"

"Please. Join me."

She stepped into the vehicle. It rolled forward ponderously, heavier than a regular car. Armored, of course.

"I need your help, Helen."

"With what?"

"I have reason to believe the man you killed in Maryland last week was not Scorpius."

"What?" she squawked. "Why do you think that?"

"I can't brief you in until you agree to take the job."

"What job?"

"The one I'm about to offer you."

"I'm retired. . . . My family . . ." she sputtered.

"But are you? Do people like you ever really retire?"

"I'd like to think so."

He sighed and said heavily, "Your nation needs you, Helen."

"Get someone else," she snapped.

"There is no one else. Say yes. Hear me out and you'll know why I came to you. Why you'll accept this job."

He was too sure of himself. He had something. Something he thought he could hold over her to force her to come back into the fold. Warily, she asked, "What will you do if I say no?"

He leaned back and smiled a little. As if he took pleasure in horse trading with her. A sentiment she emphatically did not share. She was out, damn it. Done with all this cloak-and-dagger nonsense.

Wagner practically purred as he said, "I understand your son has just thrown his hat into the ring to run for district attorney of DC."

He didn't phrase it as a question, so she didn't provide an answer. She merely waited, mentally bracing herself for the other shoe to drop.

"It would be a shame if certain damaging information about your son came to light."

"What information?" she demanded, angry in spite of herself.

"Take the job. Do it for your family."

Damn it. He knew her kryptonite, and he wasn't afraid to use it against her. "If I do this job for you, I get all existing copies of whatever it is you've got on my son?"

"You have my word on it."

She closed her eyes and sent out a silent apology to Grayson and her children.

Then she opened her eyes and stared coldly at the DCI. "I'm in."

Helen Warwick will return.

Keep reading for a special preview . . .

CHAPTER 1

*H*ELEN WARWICK, UNCOMFORTABLE IN THE LOCKED AND ARMORED confines of the black town car, stared intently at the man across the back seat from her. "Let me make this perfectly clear, James. I'm not coming back to help you. I'm protecting my family. That's all."

The director of Central Intelligence, James Wagner, shrugged. "That's enough."

"So. What dirt have you got on my son?" she demanded. "It had better be good. In this day and age, aspiring politicians can get away with practically anything and not be ruined by scandal."

Another shrug.

Not going to tell her what he was using to coerce her into going back to work at the agency, was he? *Jerk.* The problem with playing poker against other spies was they didn't give away their cards. At all.

She tried another angle. "What makes you think the man I killed last week—in self-defense, I might add—wasn't Scorpius?"

Wagner pursed his lips. Not planning to tell her that either, was he?

Anger exploded in her gut. A few months ago, she would have dutifully let him drive her back to Langley or to a safe house somewhere to brief her in on her next mission. She would have left her family behind, dutifully flown halfway around the world, and quietly killed whomever her country needed her to eliminate.

But no more. She'd turned fifty-five, and the CIA—this man specifically—had terminated her employment and summarily kicked her to the curb.

Her gaze narrowed. "Darling, I'm afraid you've made a small miscalculation."

"What's that?"

"You need me. But I don't need you."

"What about the file on your son? If he wants to become the next district attorney of Washington, DC, you do need me to keep it buried."

It was her turn to shrug. "For all I know, you don't have anything on Mitch. He's planned to go into politics ever since he was a child. He's kept his nose clean—or at least knew not to get caught—for a very long time. And here's the thing, my dear boy."

James Wagner was only a few years younger than her, but he'd never worked in the field. He'd never been shot at. Never been alone in a hostile country on his own and on the run. He might know how to play politics, but he didn't know how to play chicken with people like her. He was a child—an *infant*—in her world.

"What?" he finally blurted when she didn't continue.

"I can hunt Scorpius without you. And I'm confident that with my . . . unique skill set . . . I can clean up any mess my son might have made in the past."

"Scorpius is bigger than you know."

Indeed? She absorbed that with interest. Scorpius was more than one person, then? Not that it changed her target. Cut the head off the beast, and the body still died. She didn't need to take down the whole Scorpius team, just the shadowy figure of a man she'd glimpsed once on a cold winter's night, wearing a wool coat and an old-fashioned fedora. Moments before he'd killed the one man who could identify him.

It had been Scorpius who sent a hit team to kill her in her middle child Peter's home and Scorpius who almost killed her longtime handler and dear friend, Yosef Mizrah. Scorpius was a dead man walking. She would find him, and she *would* kill him before he harmed anyone else she loved.

"Look, Helen. We have a mutual interest in seeing Scorpius eliminated. Let me help you help your family."

Oh, and now he was taking a conciliatory tone with her? After he'd threatened Mitch? The problem was, James knew where to find her entire family, and he'd just unsubtly reminded her of that fact.

Worse, he knew her loved ones were her Achilles' heel. If she didn't play ball with Wagner now, he would undoubtedly ruin the lives of her younger children, Peter and Jayne, too, maybe even that of her husband. No matter how estranged she and Grayson might be, she was still fiercely protective of the father of her children.

And if going after her immediate family didn't make her toe the line, the bastard wouldn't hesitate to turn on her mother or Yosef. One by one, he would dismantle the lives of everyone close to her.

"I have no reason to trust you," she bit out.

"You have no reason to distrust me."

She answered lightly, sweetly even. "Other than getting unceremoniously tossed out of the agency because a day on a calendar came and went? Other than getting no support whatsoever from the agency after I retired and an old enemy tried to kill me? Other than the agency throwing me to Russian wolves without a second thought? Why no, James. I have no reason at all to distrust you."

"It's policy for field operators to retire at—" he started.

She made a sharp slashing gesture with her hand, cutting him off. "A policy that obviously can be overlooked given that we're sitting here right now and you're trying to bring me back into the fold."

He sighed. "I made a mistake by sidelining you. Is that what you want to hear me say?"

"I want to hear you say you'll leave me and my family alone and never darken my doorstep again."

"I can't do that. You're the only person who can help me now."

She leaned back against the leather upholstery, assessing him. That was quite an admission from him. He had the entire CIA to draw from and she was the *only* one he could turn to? "My, my. You must be in quite a pickle if I'm the only person who can help you. Do tell."

He hit the button on his armrest to raise the soundproof, bullet-proof partition between them and the driver. Given that it was al-ready fully raised, she judged his jabbing at the button to be a nervous tic. James Wagner was scared, huh? *Fascinating.*

He lowered his voice. "I can't give you the details here. But Scorpius is inside the agency and highly placed enough to cover his tracks. I need someone from outside the agency, someone I know not to be Scorpius, to find him and take his ass out."

"Is it because I'm retired or because Scorpius tried to kill me that you're convinced I'm not him?" she asked dryly.

"Both." He added in a rush, "Helen, there is no one else I can ask this of. Everyone—literally *everyone*—at the agency is a suspect."

"Why not bring in the FBI or the NSA to hunt your guy?"

"Because I don't know how wide Scorpius's reach is. How deeply he has infiltrated other branches of government."

Okay. That was alarming. "You think Scorpius is running a spy ring? Or a conspiracy of some kind?"

"You tell me."

Studying him closely, she asked bluntly, "How bad is what you've got on Mitch?"

James answered equally bluntly, "There's no statute of limita-tions on murder."

Murder? *Mitch?* Not a chance.

Sure, she could kill without batting an eyelash. But Mitch? Was he that ruthlessly ambitious? Had someone gotten in his way? Pushed the wrong button? Did her elder son have the same abil-ity to kill that she did?

Oh, God. Had she passed on some sort of fatal genetic flaw to him? Had she unconsciously taught him to be just like her? Was this her fault?

She had to talk to Mitch. Find out what had happened. Fix it for him before it derailed everything he'd worked so long and hard to achieve.

"Take me back to my son's press conference," she told Wagner. One of his men had whisked her out of Mitch's public announcement of his candidacy for district attorney. She'd only gone along with Wagner's man in the first place because she didn't want to make a fuss on Mitch's big day.

"Will you do it, Helen? Will you come back to the CIA and hunt Scorpius for me?"